D1565390

ALSO BY HOPE JAHREN

The Story of More

Lab Girl

ADVENTURES of MARY JANE

HOPE JAHREN

DELACORTE PRESS

Text copyright © 2024 by Hope Jahren
Jacket art copyright © 2024 by Jill De Haan
Map art copyright © 2024 by Virginia Norey

All rights reserved. Published in the United States by Delacorte Press, an imprint of Random House Children's Books, a division of Penguin Random House LLC, New York.

Delacorte Press is a registered trademark and the colophon is a trademark of Penguin Random House LLC.

Visit us on the Web! GetUnderlined.com

Educators and librarians, for a variety of teaching tools, visit us at RHTeachersLibrarians.com

Library of Congress Cataloging-in-Publication Data is available upon request.
ISBN 978-0-593-48411-1 (hardcover) — ISBN 978-0-593-48412-8 (lib. bdg.) — ISBN 978-0-593-48413-5 (ebook)

The text of this book is set in 11-point Warnock Pro Light.
Interior design by Cathy Bobak
Family tree art by kafian/stock.adobe.com

Printed in the United States of America
10 9 8 7 6 5 4 3 2 1
First Edition

CONTENTS

INTRODUCTION

On my bookshelf, I have a stack of what I call *comfort books*. When it's too sweltering or frigid to go outside, when it's too late or early to write, when I'm too self-satisfied or full of self-pity to be tolerable company, I take one of them down and read it for the second, or tenth, time. *Adventures of Huckleberry Finn* is one of those books.

Thirty-odd years ago, I was that student who annoyed everyone by asking, over and over again, "Why don't the female characters in this book *say* anything?" or "Why don't the female characters in this book *do* anything?" or, just as often, "Why aren't there any female characters in this book?" Neither *The Old Man and the Sea*, nor *Billy Budd*, nor *Lord of the Flies* escaped this multilayered critique. I never got a satisfying answer, either, unless you consider "It's time to let someone else talk now" somehow illuminating.

Years later, someone handed me a copy of the novel *Wide Sargasso Sea* by Jean Rhys, and I wish I could remember who it was. I do remember how spellbound I was by the story of Bertha, Rochester's "intemperate" ex, who serves as a one-dimensional bogeywoman in the timeless classic *Jane Eyre*. From *Wide Sargasso Sea* I learned that Bertha's real name was Antoinette, and that the attic of Thornfield Hall was merely her final stop on what had been an astonishing journey across the world. I don't know why Charlotte Brontë didn't think to tell us about it, but thank goodness Jean Rhys did.

We can fix this! is what immediately occurred to me after I learned Bertha's real story, and I believe it now, more than ever. We can reveal to ourselves all that the classics never did. We can tell the story of these side characters as a favor to the great authors who are a little too dead to do it themselves.

One rainy day in 2014, I was contentedly rereading my favorite comfort book and chafing at the ineptitude of Mark Twain. You see, the character of Mary Jane never sat right with me. I just couldn't square her gullibility ("Take this six thousand dollars . . . and don't give us no receipt for it") with her deft execution of good-cop-bad-cop in chapter 26. Neither could I reconcile her passivity ("You tell me what to do, and whatever you say, I'll do it") with the fact that a boy as intrepid as Huck falls so deeply in love with her ("I reckon I've thought of her a many and a many a million times"). *That girl is up to something,* part of me kept insisting.

Bereft of a teacher to harangue, I heard my own words come back to me: *I can fix this!* Thus began my decade-long expedition through the parks and forts, to the museums and libraries, on the riverboats and canoes that led me to the real "red-headed one."

So here you have it: the true story of Mary Jane, offered without apologies to Samuel Clemens, who I dare to think might have liked it anyway.

You may say what you want to, but in my opinion she had more sand in her than any girl I ever see; in my opinion she was just full of sand. It sounds like flattery, but it ain't no flattery. And when it comes to beauty—and goodness too—she lays over them all. I hain't ever seen her since that time that I see her go out of that door; no, I hain't ever seen her since, but I reckon I've thought of her a many and a many a million times.

—Huck Finn speaking about Mary Jane
in *Adventures of Huckleberry Finn*
by Mark Twain

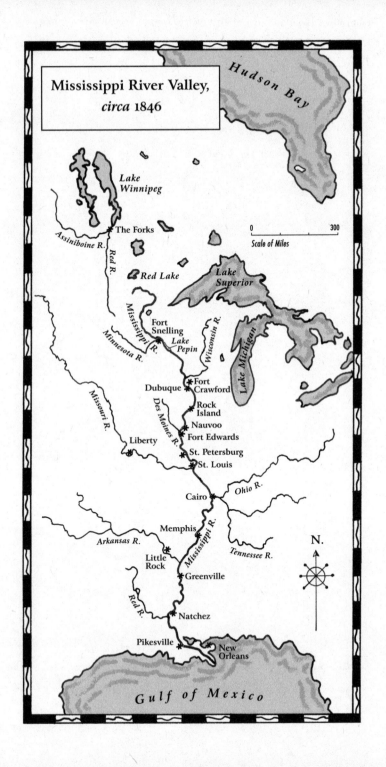

Mississippi River Valley,
circa 1846

THORVALDSEN and WILKS Family Tree

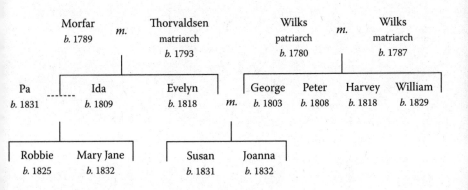

Morfar *b.* 1789 — *m.* — Thorvaldsen matriarch *b.* 1793

Wilks patriarch *b.* 1780 — *m.* — Wilks matriarch *b.* 1787

Pa *b.* 1831 ------ Ida *b.* 1809   Evelyn *b.* 1818 — *m.*

George *b.* 1803   Peter *b.* 1808   Harvey *b.* 1818   William *b.* 1829

Robbie *b.* 1825   Mary Jane *b.* 1832

Susan *b.* 1831   Joanna *b.* 1832

PROLOGUE

You don't know about me unless you have read a book by the name of *Adventures of Huckleberry Finn*, but it doesn't matter. That book was made by Mr. Mark Twain, and he told the truth about me, as far as he knew. In his defense, he didn't have much to go on, and he did mainly get right what he put down. In the end, I made it into twenty-eight pages of his three hundred and sixty-six page book. I'm not mad, though. It happens. There's a lot more story to every single one of us, beyond what gets put down.

For what it's worth, here's my side of things.

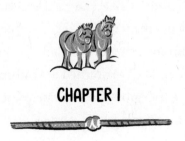

CHAPTER 1

-The Fire-

We smelled the fire before we saw it.

It didn't smell like a fireplace. It didn't smell like a campfire, either. Do you know what a musket smells like after the bullet's been fired? Or singed hair on a branding iron? Or a shirt forgotten under the iron? Or a wet saddle too near the campfire? Or maple syrup boiled over onto coals? The fire didn't smell like any of those things. It smelled like all of them mixed together.

It wasn't the smell of something burning. It was the smell of *everything* burning.

It smelled like the end of the world.

When we got closer to the fire, I recognized Ma by her outline. A small black figure with all Hell coming undone behind her.

When we got closer still, I saw that it was her back to us. I don't know how she stood the heat: I had to squint my eyes against the hot blast, and she was a good ten feet closer to the fire than I was.

Then again, Ma is extraordinary. She's more than tough. Her softest parts are made of steel and hard leather. And smart, too. She can tell exactly what I'm thinking, just from one look at my face. And I can from hers, too. We don't get along overly well.

I walked closer, until Ma turned around and saw me, and I saw her, against a background of heaving flame.

And the look on her face said, *Not again.*

-Starting Over-

We dug. We dug until we couldn't dig anymore. And then we dug some more.

Hansel tried to help, but the ground was too frozen for him to do much besides bust up his paws, and finally, Morfar made him back off. He didn't like not pitching in, and made sure we knew it by barking now and then.

Bam! Ka-POW!

We heard a terrific noise behind us. The sky lit up, then splinters rained down. It came from at least a mile away, so it didn't rattle us much. It just meant that the fire had burned its way into the gunpowder shed, was all.

Morfar paused and leaned against the shovel. "*Ja* then, we go down to Fort Snelling a little early this year."

Ma gave me a look that told me it was my turn to dig. While I did, I felt snow splattering onto the top of my head. It was coming down in big wet clumps and that was a lucky thing. Fire can't jump across snow, and it sure can't jump over slush. To-night we'd sleep in the barn, less than a hundred yards from the inferno, but just as safe as if we were off on Mackinac Island.

I stopped digging when a metal box showed itself out of the dirt. It wasn't filled with diamonds, but it still counted as trea-sure to us. Four times a year, Morfar buries the last quarter's record books near the creek where the ground doesn't freeze as hard, so he can answer to the Company in case of raids or thieving or fire.

Under the records-box was blankets and medicine that Ma had put in, wrapped in waxed leather. We'd have that, and the clothes on our backs, until we heard the ice break up on Lake Winnipeg. That's what means the Red River's flowing, so you can travel south on it.

It's five hundred miles down to Fort Snelling. We know the way because we go down every year to spend the summer and get me at least some schoolroom education. We usually go in May, but this year it'd be March.

"Same as in otten-tirty-tree after the last full burn-down."

"You were a baby, Mary Jane," Ma added, "you probably don't remember." She said it as if I hadn't paid enough attention at the time.

"Each an' every trading post is built on the cinders of the last," sighed Morfar, and he should know, as he's been head clerk for the Company since 1821.

There's a difference between being disappointed and sur-prised, and he was the first but not the second. Really, there's so much gunpowder stored in the Northwest Territory that a person ought to be surprised every time a trading post *doesn't* burn down, given the oil lamps, the candles, the tobacco pipes, and the rum-soaked characters lighting them.

Ka-POW!

Far behind us, we heard another keg go off like a cannon. We wouldn't be getting any sleep that night, or maybe even the next.

Ma and Morfar hoisted what we'd dug up onto their backs while I filled the hole. They turned and walked towards the barn and I followed them, dragging the shovels behind me.

I could have walked beside them, but I didn't. I followed instead.

It was second nature, as I've been following Ma and Morfar since I was born. They go down south in the spring, and up north in the fall, and I've followed, year after year, for my whole life.

Well, of course I do. That's what you do when you're a little kid. But now that I'm fourteen, it feels different. There are times when I don't want to follow, but I don't know where it is that I want to go, either.

-Next-Best Everything-

We slept in the barn that night, and every night until we left. We didn't have our goose-down comforters, but we had the next-best thing as wool blankets. We didn't have our flannel pajamas, but we had the next-best thing as long underwear. We didn't get any peace and quiet, but we had the first-best thing of a carnival going on all around us.

To voyageurs, a fire at the trading post means three things, all of them good: sleeping inside, finishing off the rum, and heading south early. I should have mentioned tobacco as well, as there's no way to trace inventory after a burn-down—same goes for spirits. The sleeping inside part is just to make the counting of who got out in time that much easier.

Row on, row on, another day,
Ply, ply the oar and haul away!

After the whaling songs started up, we knew the voyageurs would be up all night long and so would we. I, myself, love to hear them, but Ma won't let me join in for fear I might have some actual fun for once in my life.

Instead, I sat on a smoked-up buffalo skin, sipping snow-melt and freezing my insides. We didn't have our copper tea-kettle, but we had the next-best thing as a pewter one that Ma wouldn't let me drink out of because the lead in it would make me grow up stupid.

"It's too late for me," said Morfar as he gulped down his tea.

When we'd come back in October, there'd be a brand-new trading post built from the ground up and we'd get our old tea-kettle back because metal doesn't burn. That one's made of iron so if I do turn out an idiot we'll know it wasn't from that.

"*Ja,* soon as the snow's melted, the Company, you betcha, they'll send a big crew to clean up and start building." Morfar had cheered up.

"They'll also send a tally-man to sift the ashes for teeth and start replacing." Ma had cheered down.

Anyway, she's right: a voyageur's life isn't easy or long, and however they got to us, there's more where they came from.

Morfar slapped both thighs and stood himself up. "*Mariyane*, let's me and you go for our walk. There's a fine full moon tonight, the kind you should use for some-ting."

Hansel ran to the door and barked, wanting to go with. Him and me and Morfar headed to the pines for our loop through the woods. It was the same route we'd taken since I could walk, and before that Morfar carried me, which I even sort-of remember.

Sure enough, the moonlight reflecting off the snow was bright enough to make us squint. It made the birch trees glow like great bleached bones, like the ribs of the dead whale Morfar found as a boy back in the *hjemmeland*. He said they were so hungry they ate the rotten blubber . . . but not as hungry as the next year, when they boiled and ate their shoes.

"One, two, tree, fjour, five . . ." I counted trees, copying Morfar's *hjemmeland* accent. "*Six, sept, huit, neuf, dix!*" I switched to the numbers we used with the voyageurs.

Morfar gave me a sum, inventing the numbers as he went.

"Tirty-five and seventy-six and fjorty-one less sixty-two and eleven less tventy less sixteen and fifty-tree less tventy-one and sixty-six and tventy-five less tirty-seven less fifty and seventy-two anna tventy-otta makes . . ."

"Two hundred and one!" I completed his thought.

He switched to money: "A dollar and a qvarter plus six nickels and tree dimes less fifteen cents anna half dollar less a dime and two nickels less a dollar and otta cents makes . . ."

"One dollar twenty-eight cents!" I said, more or less automatic.

I have a gift for numbers, and I got it from my morfar. He can't read, but he sure can cipher, which is what has kept him indoors as a clerk instead of outdoors as a trapper, freezing his toes off one by one.

Hansel was stopped up ahead, waiting, having cleared a path for us through the snow. Standing there in the twilight, he looked just like a doe—same color, too.

"*Mari-yane*, do you remember the year we got Hansel?" asked Morfar.

"Eighteen thirty-seven. Nine years ago. I had just turned five," I answered. "He was the best puppy in the whole world!"

"*Ja, ja* . . . Hansel an' Gretel you two were always since the day he come to us."

Hansel doesn't care one way or the other about me, but he loves Morfar beyond anything. Except Morfar has told Hansel to love me, so he goes ahead and does it. It sounds convoluted, but it all makes sense to a dog.

"The Company president, he wrote me a letter, said in it I could have any-ting I wanted 'in recognition of twenty-five years of fate-ful clerkship.'"

"And you asked for Hansel!"

"*Ja*, you betcha! I always did want one of them Great Danish hounds, big like a horse but gentle anna sweet. It took them some years, but *ja*, they did find us a whelp."

Hansel came running back to us. I flopped his ears back the right way, and he dog-kissed my hand as a *Thank you.*

"Promise me, *Mari-yane*, whenev'r you get the chance to make friends with a dog, you will. It's never a mistake to do so," he said, and I promised I would.

We'd come to the end of our loop. I sang out as we opened the barn door:

Home again, home again, jiggety jig . . .

It's a ditty the soldiers down at Fort Snelling bawl out on Saturday night and it makes Morfar laugh when I sing it. I'm careful to do it where Ma can't hear.

Ma had got a little fire going somehow, and Morfar sat happily down beside it. I didn't because there wouldn't be any pudding that night so what's the point? It almost made me cry to imagine the shelves of candied fruit all burned-up, and to know we wouldn't have anything good to eat before we got to Fort Snelling. Even worse, there'd be less and less of what we *did* have to eat until we got there.

The voyageurs hadn't imagined it yet: they were caterwauling to beat the band. Ma had her mean face on, but like I said, I don't mind the noise. Then I recognized a snoring that all the singing in the world couldn't have drowned out. I knew right away who was doing it, too.

I investigated up and down, until I found Peter Pond, dead asleep behind a bale of hay with a bottle in his hand. He was drunk, he stunk, and his face was redder than a beet, as usual.

I was mighty glad to see him, even if nobody else was.

CHAPTER II

—Who I Am, Anyway—

Peter Pond—what a character! I'll tell you all about him, but not just yet because maybe by now you're curious who I am. I'll keep it short, I promise.

The most important thing about me is that I'm Ma's daughter and Morfar's granddaughter, but I guess you already gathered that much. Technically I am also Pa's daughter only I never met him. He set off to help with the Removal just as Ma was getting heavy with carrying me, and none of us ever heard from him again.

Pa died down in the Arkansas Territory in 1831, but Ma didn't find out until 1832 when she wrote to his Lieutenant and heard back about how the death gratuity would go to his lawful wife, who wasn't her, by the way. Turned out he had married a Sauk woman in Fort Shelby two years before he married Ma. So there she was, saddled with two bastard children, one of which was me.

You might be wondering who the other bastard is, so I'll tell you. It's my brother who had hair so ugly he ran away from home trying to find a hat. He told the minister he was pre-destined to bat first for a New York baseball club, and the next day he was gone. That was six years ago, and we haven't heard from him since. His name was—*is*—Robbie.

My own name is Mary Jane and I am named after two headless queens. I was born in 1832, which makes me all of fourteen years old.

What else?

I am tall and thin, but not too thin, and I am strong enough to pick up Hansel clear off the ground, and he's not exactly light. I tan in the summer and don't burn, the way Ma says my pa did because of the Scot in him. Still though, my skin never gets too far from its winter pale. My hair is red but actually *auburn*, which is a French word meaning *towards brown,* and not like my brother's whose was—*is*—bristly orange. At least, I think it so. It's getting so I don't remember him too well.

We're by no means rich, but we're better off than some, and I try to be grateful. I have some nice things, all my own—including an ivory comb with only two teeth missing—but I keep them down at Fort Snelling because it's cleaner there and doesn't burn down nearly as often.

My first-best thing is my *A Child's History of England* book by Charles Dickens with a red velvet cover. If you haven't read it, you really should. It covers eighteen hundred and ninety-six years, starting with Julius Caesar and going all the way up to Queen Victoria, who is sitting on the throne at this very minute.

Now, every king's story has the same old plot: take power, use power, lose power. It's the queens' stories that are all different and interesting. Like Queen Edburga, who poisoned her husband, and Queen Elfrida, who was secretly married to two kings at once. Further on there's Queen Anne who ruined the Church, and Queen Mary who saved it. Every single one of the queens in that book had herself an exciting life—it might have ended early, or in a bad way, but it was never less than an incredible adventure.

I could recite you whole pages from *A Child's History*, I've read it so many times. There's only one thing wrong with it, in my eyes: it doesn't always tell you the year when something happened. It should, because if you know *when* something happened, you can figure out what came before and after, and from that you might piece together *how* it happened, or even *why*.

When you know the numbers, then you know some-ting, as Morfar would say.

So I put the dates in myself—in ink, right on the very pages—and it made what Mr. Dickens wrote even better. Trust me on this: when you find something lacking in a book that somebody gives you, there's ways to sit down and fix it.

CHAPTER III

-An Old Rascal, and a New One-

But back to the man snoozing behind a hay-bale whose name is *Peter Pond.*

Good old Peter Pond. Now, *his* is a life worth hearing about. I could have woken him right then and heard his collection of tall tales for the thousandth time, but I didn't. I yelled, "Gusty!" and ran straight to the stalls.

I found the big brown horse drinking snow-melt, just like I had been. He looked up, took his head out of the bucket, and nickered. I scratched his ears, and petted him down his long nose. He closed his eyes and pushed against me. We were both so happy to see each other.

Peter Pond came up beside us; I must have woken him after all. He smiled so big I could see all five of his teeth.

Rame, rame, rame donc,
Le tour du monde, le tour du monde.
Rame, rame, rame donc!

He sang loud enough to shake the rafters, stamping one foot to keep time, and I couldn't help but laugh at the sight of him. Gusty didn't startle, he was used to these kinds of concerts. He just laid his big head on my shoulder while I buried my face in his mane. He smelled like wet wool and old leather, just like a warm horse should.

"*Mademoiselle Marie Jeanne!* Did I ever tell you of how I escaped ze French army after defeat on ze banks of ze Monagahaley?"

"*Oui,*" I answered him.

"But what about ze time I stayed twenty-nine days with ze Yanktonai tribe sleeping in a tent between two baby buffaloes?"

"*Oui.*"

"Certainly I never did tell you about ze time that I . . ."

"*Oui! Oui! Oui!*" and he had me laughing. All my life I'd been hearing stories about Peter Pond, mostly from him, but from a fair number of other people as well.

Morfar says he has a Cree wife named Aggatha living up on the shores of Lake Winnipeg with two or three of his kids. Ma says he's always intemperate, often intoxicated, and altogether intolerable.

Towards me, Peter Pond is always kind and jolly, and so I love him for that. I even got so I don't mind his smell, from a distance, that is. I do think there's some value in liking folks for the piece of them that you, yourself, have seen, regardless of all the pieces you haven't.

"Say, *Marie Jeanne*, take up ze rag and rub ze arthur-itis outen Gusty's hips. He's stiffened up, so has he."

I put one hand on Gusty's back, and took up the rag in my other one. It was slathered in what smelled like three-week-old butter. I laid it on Gusty's hipbone and rubbed big circles all around.

"Oh, he loves it!" said Peter Pond, smiling at both of us. "Just hear him purr!"

Gusty is just gorgeous, to me anyway, but Peter Pond is a sight you won't forget. He's a full head shorter than me—not more than five feet—and built like an upside-down pyramid. Great big shoulders tapering down to the skinniest, sinew-iest little legs you ever saw.

His face is bright red and I don't mean flushed like a Scotsman, I mean painted bright-scarlet red. Every day he takes out a little tin of clay and smears it all over his face. Peter Pond looks like a *bona-fide* Devil just rode up from Hell.

I already told you about the quality of his teeth.

"*Monsieur* Gusty's getting too old for ze *hivernant* life." Peter Pond put his ear beside the horse's mouth. "What's that, Gusty? You'd rather be ze pet pony of a little girl?" He turned to me and asked, "What would you say to this, *Mademoiselle*?"

Peter Pond offers Gusty to me about once a year, but nothing comes of it. Ma says to give up on a promise from a man like that, and I've tried to, but in my heart I'm still hoping that one day, it'll come true.

"That's how they get you," says Ma.

Peter Pond isn't your run-of-the-mill voyageur: after he gets up North in the fall, he *stays* up North until spring. We don't know how he survives the winter out alone roaming the Territory but it isn't easy-living, you can bet that.

He always returns to us just before the ice breaks. Ma doctors his wolf-bites, then trims off what's frost-bit beyond healing. I fatten up Gusty for a few days or weeks or until whenever Peter Pond takes him and disappears until the next fall.

"Peter Pond, can I take Gusty out for a ride tomorrow?"

"Oui, oui, Mademoiselle!" Peter Pond let me, just like he always did. *"Oui! Oui! Oui!"* He picked me up under the armpits and bounced me onto Gusty's back, then lifted me back up in the air, and jumped me down again. It was our game, and we'd been playing it since I was tiny, asking *Up! . . . Up!* whenever I saw him walk by. It's still fun, even though I am fourteen now.

We heard a ruckus behind us, back near the door. I patted Gusty and told him I'd be back, gave the rag to Peter Pond, and ran to see the fuss.

Two ragged voyageurs had come in from the snowstorm, dragging a mighty sick man on a sled behind them.

"This fella here is come all the way from out East," one of them was explaining to Ma.

"He done pretty well, too, until Sault Ste. Marie, when he had a burning fever but got on the boat to Fort William anyway," the other man added.

They tipped the sled and what was in it slumped to the ground looking like a heap of old potatoes wrapped in a black robe. The cargo, weak as he was, put up one hand and waggled a finger:

"Father—you may call me *Father*."

–A Visit from Father Potatoes–

That sick man was in a bad state. He was sweating up a storm and the color of his face—I don't know if it was too yellow or too green but it was too something, that's for sure.

He could still talk, though.

"I am Father Nicolas Marie Joseph Frémiot of the Society of Jesus . . ."

"A *Jesuit*," Ma said, and sighed. She looked like she had rolled dice and come up snake-eyes.

Jesuit is a flavor of Catholic, and it's not her favorite. Ma doesn't exactly have a favorite, when it comes to churchmen. According to her, each one is worse than the other.

Father Potatoes turned to me. "Dear child, have you been baptized?"

"Yes," Ma told him, her voice flat.

He looked me up and down.

"Ugh! Are you *certain*?" he asked Ma again.

"I should be," she answered. "I'm the one who baptized her."

Potatoes outright scoffed at that. "And I suppose *your* mother baptized you?"

"No," she told him. "I, myself, am a heathen."

They were both riled up and willing to go on like this, when a sharp pain hit the priest like a bolt from the sky. He clutched his belly and passed out, landing in the shape of Christ on the Cross, except he was on the ground and made of potatoes.

"Go and fetch the wheelbarrow," Ma told me. "And try not to touch him. He's caught something, and he's brought it here."

I knew what that meant. Ma was going to doctor him. She'd doctor anyone who limped into the Forks, as best she could and as best they'd let her. She didn't know all the ways the Ojibwe have for curing folks, but she could make a sick man feel better, or at least not worse, and you can't always say that about doctors in civilized places.

It took all five of us to hoist him up, and while we were doing it, something inside his nose split a seam. Ma turned his head such that he'd bleed onto the ground and not back into his windpipe. We got him over, then heaved him onto a straw ticking, and the two voyageurs high-tailed it out of there.

And didn't Father Potatoes sleep for two days straight? Then he woke up and ate a little gruel, and got hopeful about it. But by night he'd turned back to poorly. Ma said she'd move Father Potatoes to the far corner of the barn to nurse him and keep his contagion a ways off. When I said I would help her, she didn't say *No*. She didn't say *Yes*, either. She didn't say anything at all.

I go out of my way to try to please Ma about once a week, but nothing comes of it. Some would say to give up on her ever liking me much, and I've tried to, but in my heart I'm still hoping that one day, it will come true.

That's how she gets me.

Our patient coughed all night and we gave him dogbane for it, but it didn't help. His belly was big, and hard, and hurt him awful. He took to swearing at us, using curses that'd make the Devil run for cover. Ma said his fever had got so high that he either wasn't in his right mind, or he finally was. She sat at his sickbed anyway, soothing his nerves and dosing him with mugwort whenever he would take it, morning, noon, and night.

One evening his big belly started to rumble, and then—I'm sorry to tell it—he spurted like a fountain out of his back end. Ma and I were beyond tired by then, but we still had to cope, so somehow, we did.

My job was to carry his slop pan down the hill and dump it, then come back and scrub myself up to the elbows. While I did that, Ma stirred maple syrup into the water we'd boiled the day before and forced it down his gullet while balancing his hind end over the bedpan. It wasn't pretty but Ma said we needed to get as much into him as he was putting out, else his insides would dry up and he'd be a dead man.

Whether we went on like that for three days or twenty, I couldn't tell you, but I was practically sleepwalking by the end. I remember finding myself dumping a fresh pitcher of maple-water into the slop pit, and I don't want to know what Ma might have been trying to get him to drink at the time.

"Death is on him," Ma sighed to me one evening. "There's nothing more we can do." I nodded. She knows it when she sees it.

"Would he want us to pray over him?" I asked her.

"Go tell Morfar to find a voyageur who remembers his *Agnus Dei*. You go on to bed; I'll sit up to watch and wait to the end. Everyone deserves that."

And didn't I wake up to find Father Potatoes better in the morning? And before noon wasn't he sitting up in bed drinking turkey broth? He looked kind of hollowed-out, but he was strong enough for talking, and proved it right off.

"I am *healed*! I sing out the *Glory*! Again hast Thou chosen *me*!" They could hear him yawlering outside the barn.

"How long has he been doing this?" I asked Ma in a low voice.

"Only since he opened his eyes," she told me, with a weary look.

He raised up both hands and started waving them about. "I give *all* thanks to *Thee*, O Lord!"

"I don't suppose he gave any thanks to you, who hath also had something to do with it," I said to Ma.

She answered me with one look.

"And here you nursed him, and there he is so ungrateful." It had been a waste of human kindness, in my opinion, but Ma thought different.

"A woman doesn't nurse someone to feel thanked, Mary Jane. She nurses them because that's what a nurse does. A woman feels and a nurse nurses. You've got to keep them separate if you're going to do it right."

In rushed the two voyageurs that had drug the priest into the Forks in the first place. Where they'd been all this time we hadn't a clue.

"Up and ready, I see!" one of them cheered to the other. They were anxious to get him back on the road as they wouldn't get paid until he got where he was going.

Father Potatoes rejoiced at the idea. "The Lord hast healed *me* that the *heathens* may know themselves to be *men*!" he said with a wild glow in his eyes.

"What in the world is he talking about?" I asked Morfar, off to the side.

"The Ojibwe," he answered me.

Father Potatoes was raving, but this time with no fever and a clear head. "Thou shall *blot out their ways* for ever and ever! Thou shall . . ."

I couldn't listen any further, as my ears were ringing. Why was I so dog-tired just then? And confused and overcome? I stood up from the table, and stumbled from it.

Ma caught me and laid a hand across my forehead, then pulled my eyelids down and looked in. "Get to the sick-bed," she told me. "Whatever *that man* brought here, you've caught it."

–In Which I Am Not Myself–

I can't tell you much about the next few days, it's all shadowy, like a dream I had but can't quite remember.

Mostly I recall a terrible pain in my stomach that moved up to my head every so often, then went back down again. It was a pain I couldn't do much about besides moan. I know they tried to get me out of bed once, and it was all I could do to stay upright for a few paces.

Ma says she was in and out with oatmeal and medicine and maple-water. "You'll feel better in the morning," she'd say to me every night, but her face told me it was more a hope than a belief.

Ma thinks I caught sick from the priest, but I didn't get anywhere near as bad as he had. In the end, she broke my fever with just one cup of tansey-flower tea.

"How come you never gave Father Potatoes any of this?" I asked her, sitting up in bed and feeling better.

"We don't have over-much of it," she answered.

To this day, that same fever comes and goes in me. It's like an echo—the same sound, over and over, but never as loud as the first time. It's a fever that doesn't keep me from doing what needs done, so it can't matter much.

But it sure is strange.

CHAPTER IV

–Back to Work–

The morning after my fever broke, I went back to work. There's always something needs doing at a trading post, even a burned-down one.

Morfar and some voyageurs pulled the still-good pelts out of the storehouse and aired them out. The kitchen, the workshop, and the living quarters got de-smoked and scrubbed down, and Ma was in charge of that.

I was just finished wiping soot from the bright-shiny for-sale items we keep displayed up front when Morfar came in, looked around, and said:

"Ev'ry needler, ev'ry glass bead, ev'ry ev'ry-ting here vill be blown like dandelion seeds in ev'ry direction. To be eaten or used or broken an' mended, then traded back an' fort, far away from here, an' amongst other clerks an' trappers, so on 'round the world 'til it comes back to us."

We spend a lot of time behind that front desk, Morfar and me. That's where he sets the price for what the trappers bring in, and we pay them in trade. I've been helping since I learned my numbers, and I'm good at it, if I do say so myself. Everyone else says so, too.

We're honest, Morfar and me. It doesn't matter if you're a seven-foot tall Sioux warrior or a one-armed porkeater, we'll give you the same deal. And we'll work with you, too. If you haven't got a beaver, we'll take two minks or three martens or even eight rabbits if that's all you've caught. We draw the line at squirrels, though. They're good for planting acorns and not much else.

Some would say my morfar is the most important man at Fort Garry. We wouldn't say it, though, because we don't call it *Fort Garry*. Or *Fort Gibraltar* or *Fort Douglas* or whatever the Company was calling it before that.

The Ojibwe call this place *the Forks* since it's where the Assiniboine River joins up with the Red River and they set off north towards Hudson Bay. Ma, me, and Morfar—we call it *the Forks*, too.

I was born at the Forks and I grew up here until I turned seven and we started spending the summer down at Fort Snelling with me in the schoolhouse, Ma in the laundry, Morfar in the Agency, and Robbie running wild. This particular year we'd be going down early, like I said.

The next evening, I was stood by the fire, scraping the underside of a deerskin. I was just starting to feel the softness come out, when I heard a sound like thunder far away, then lightning striking close.

Rumble ... Crack!

It was the ice breaking on Lake Winnipeg.

Me and Morfar and Ma, we all stopped what we were doing and looked at each other.

"Big day tomorrow," Morfar said, winking at me.

I unlaced the deerskin from its rack, and rolled it up tight. It would be one of the ten-thousand-plus things we'd load up in the morning, and drag with us down to Fort Snelling.

Then I laid down and slept the night at the Forks for what I didn't know was the very last time.

—On the Red River Trail—

Shhhrrrill-eeech! Shhhrrrill-eeech!

I woke the next morning to the whistling of the voyageurs. They'd been up for hours patching the canoes and were ready to put the pieces in. Whistling is their language for telling who to put what where. I closed my eyes and listened, keeping warm under the covers as long as possible.

Ma came in and started banging pots and pans around. Clanging cookware is her language for telling you that you should have been up by now. I dragged myself out of bed, washed, and put on my old calico. It was the dress she'd made for me, and the only un-burned one I had.

By the time I got myself down to the river, Hansel was splashing around in the shallows, itching to get moving. He and Morfar would go in the canoes, along with twenty-odd voyageurs and however much fur was spared by the fire. Me and Ma would go in the ox-carts, as we always did. It's better because you don't have to paddle, but worse because Ma expects you to keep useful the whole time.

Ma doesn't like separating from Morfar, even for a few days. She was fussing over him in *hjemmeland*-language, which I can't speak, but can understand when other people do.

"*Har du nok klær, Faren min?*" she asked him.

"*Ja, ja, det har jeg . . . ,*" he told her.

"*Sikkert på dette? De har ikke nok mat til å holde deg . . . ,*" she pressed him.

"*Jo, jo jenta mi, du må ikke bekymre deg på meg, jeg har livet slike langt før du var født, Datteren min,*" he assured her.

Ma treats Morfar more like a son than a father. She frets over him like he's some fragile thing and he lets her. Meanwhile I can't toughen up fast enough for her liking.

We said *Goodbye-for-now,* then climbed up and waited for the crack of a whip up ahead. All together we were twenty wooden ox-carts set to trundle across the prairie.

"Here's your mending, Mary Jane," said Ma as she handed me a wad of socks. She'd already threaded my darning-needle.

We traveled thirty-five miles that day, and made it to Fort Pembina late the next, where we gave out the blankets and wire and musket balls come down from York Factory, and took on enough pemmican to gag a herd of goats on. That's what we'd have to eat until we got to Fort Snelling.

If you've never tried pemmican—don't. Just don't. What it is, is old buffalo meat, pounded to a pulp, festered and sold to anybody unlucky enough to need it. It's the worst-best thing, trust me. Morfar isn't hardly picky about food, and he only says it's better than *most* shoes.

That day passed, and by the next one we were well onto the prairie. It's broad and flat and open and beautiful in its own way, like an ocean of grass.

The day after that, Ma said, "No need to do that over," after inspecting my mending. My goodness, wasn't she in a good mood? I was almost tempted to think it could be because of me, when I remembered about the mail.

Fort Snelling gets regular mail delivery every New Year's Day. My aunt Evelyn always writes us a Christmas letter and sends it in November. This year, we'd be reading her letter early, and Ma was bursting with joy over it.

Just when you think the prairie will never end, you smell the wet mud of the marsh. Then the trail goes soft, and the cart stops, and when they come to scrape the muck out from between the spokes, it occurs to you that you really, *really* have to pee.

Now I'll explain to you something that people never talk of: When there's no trees or bushes to go behind, how do you go pee? Boys, you can guess, but what about girls? Well, there's a set of rules that everybody goes by, and I'll tell you what they are.

You walk out alone, towards the east, and you march at a good strong speed, like you are going to get something and you know just where it is. When you get out to what feels like far enough, you squat down, bunch up your skirts, and pee.

Then you stand back up and look at the horizon a good long time, in courtesy of the people who are peeing behind you. Only when you hear them *Hooooe*-ing the oxen do you turn around and go back. I don't remember anyone teaching me this, it's just something you pick up on the trail.

From where I peed that day, I could just see Red Lake in the distance. I don't think anything could be as lovely as a northern lake sparkling in the spring sunshine when you've just busted out of winter, and I took a minute to gaze around. I thought I could just make something out up ahead in the cattails, and I set out squishing through the bog, to see what it might be.

When I got close to the lakeshore, I saw a family all sat together on a patch of high ground.

–A Family Picnic–

It was only women sitting there. Grandmas, mas, and girls—sisters, aunts and cousins, too. Plenty of little babies, probably both kinds, since everybody needs their ma at that age. They sure looked comfortable, there in the sunshine. One of the aunts was teaching some girls how to weave reeds, from what I could tell, and a grandma was telling stories. Something good-smelling was bubbling in a pot hanging over the camp-fire. All taken together, it looked like a fine way to spend the afternoon.

The tall reeds rustled just next to me and out walked a girl with a big sharp knife. She was startled by the sight of me, though she was the one with the blade. She looked me up and down, then put her knife into her belt and set down the bundle of bulrushes she'd been cutting with it.

I could tell by her dress that she was Ojibwe, and she looked about my age; tall and strong as me if not stronger. She wore two deerskins sewed together at the top, with a gap for her head to poke through. Her hair was in one braid that wrapped all the way around her head. I wouldn't have worn it that way, myself, but it looked nice on her.

We stood face to face until she got bored of it, I guess. I watched her go back to her mother, sisters, aunts, and cousins and felt jealous that a girl could have so much family around her. There was the look on her face, too. I don't quite know how to put it, but she looked like she knew who she was, and where she belonged. Me, on the other hand, I have no idea.

I heard the traces jangling and I knew it was time for me to be on my way.

As we bumped on down the prairie, I thought about how, all my life, I'd been hearing folks talk about Indians. That they have magic and can speak to the buffalo. That they know the Earth and the Earth knows them, and because of it, they'll be fine wherever they're moved off to. Or that they're heathens and savages that don't know how to eat polite or dress modest. That they need day-schooled or residentialized because a life never hearing about Jesus is no life at all.

There in the reeds I hadn't seen anybody especially magical *or* savage, just a group of folks having a nice time and getting some things done while they were at it. It made me wonder how many of the things I'd heard grown-ups tell each other could be maybe not-true.

We got across the prairie in sixteen days, which is nothing special, and by the time we arrived at Fort Snelling, there was no snow to be seen anywhere. The late-afternoon sun shone strong the day we pulled in, promising to make it even warmer tomorrow.

And what do you think I heard before I even got my two feet on the ground?

"Miss! Mar-y! Jane!"

Why, if it wasn't Miss Frances Ramsay herself come to meet us, complete with a silk parasol and two lace gloves on.

CHAPTER V

-A Happy Reunion-

"Miss Fran-ces Ramsay!" I yelled back.

"Now, now, I am Mrs. Frances *Simpson,* as you well know," she tutted up at me.

Miss Frances—I'll always call her so in my own head—was as beautiful as ever: violet-trimmed parasol, two fine gloves—and her dress! It was silk, with red and blue lines marking out a plaid pattern over a creamy background, and I knew she'd made it herself. Miss Frances is a genius of a seamstress, and can make a dress just off a newspaper article telling what's in fashion. Plus, I don't have any idea how she does it, but she gets her hands on the very best: silk cloth and fancy buttons. And she's generous with it, too. Why, she gives us girls all her leftovers just for practicing on. Can you imagine?

"Our little girl has become quite a young lady!" she said to Ma. "How tall you've become, my dear! I am so proud of you!"

she added, as if I had done something besides eat and sleep to make it happen.

I had a thousand questions for Miss Frances. Did she like being married? Did the Officers' Quarters really have a grand piano in it, sent all the way from Boston? Mostly I wanted to ask her if she'd kept any of my dresses, the ones she'd helped me to pattern and sew.

"Oh, my," said Miss Frances about something behind me.

I turned and saw Ma looking down at a soldier that had passed out in the vegetable plot. She rolled him over with one foot and bent down to check if he was breathing. I guess he was, because she didn't doctor Private Thirsty any further, just kicked his empty bottle out of her way.

Miss Frances wrinkled her nose at the smell of whiskey, then turned back to me. "Mary Jane, I'm so glad you're here. I'll come by to see you in a bit, after Evening Prayer." She gave my two hands a squeeze before she left.

Miss Frances hadn't changed, and I was happy about it. She was still both plain and fancy at the same time, which I think is a wonderful way to be. Sure, she'd been promoted from school-teacher to wife, but that was bound to happen sooner or later anyway.

As we waited for the carts to unload, I helped Ma pick through last year's garden, which had gone to seed and beyond. Dried-up cucumber vines lay in a snarl and the soil was all hoofed up, like they'd kept pigs in it. Ma started yanking weeds as if she had a score to settle.

And who do you think came running up behind her just then?

"It's That-cat!" I yelled, pointing down.

"Well, *Hello* there. What number life are you on these days?" Ma greeted him. "Eight and a half by the looks of you."

The big orange cat rubbed himself in a figure eight around her ankles, his stumpy half-tail sticking straight up in the air.

That-cat was one of the many stray cats that hung around Fort Snelling trying to get fed. The year before last, we'd found him sneaking into our living quarters. I would give him a pet and he would give me a purr, and Ma would walk in and yell, "You get *that cat* out of here!"

Ma says cats get up on the table and eat the butter, then throw it up under the bed and she isn't going to have it. She kept chasing *that cat* out, and *that cat* kept sneaking back in and we never could leave the butter out.

That-cat is the biggest and the fastest of his gang and he knows better than most how to run and hide when the soldiers get in a kicking mood. Even so, his luck ran out and one Sunday morning he staggered in with a boot-mark on his belly, dragging what was left of his tail behind him and trying to find a quiet place to die.

You wouldn't believe how Ma took to doctoring That-cat. She cared for him better than she did Father Potatoes, and I already told you how that was. She washed him in iodine, wrapped him in a rag, fed his face with duck fat, and watered him every hour. Cats generally don't care for being handled, but That-cat never said a word, he just lay there looking up at Ma with love in his eyes.

After That-cat healed up, we figured he'd go back to his gang. But didn't he take to following Ma around: down to the well, up to the laundry, and out to the garden? He never did try to come into our kitchen again, but we'd find him outside our door every morning. I don't know what That-cat does all night, but we never see a single mouse around our place, I'll tell you that.

They unloaded the carts and we dug our bundles out of the pile, with That-cat *me-yowling* happily all the while. We went into the barracks and found our rooms just as we'd left them. There was my empty perfume bottle, handed-me-down from Miss Frances, sitting on the bedside table. Next to it was a smudgy portrait of Pa, looking just like Robbie only in a uniform. I stopped to look at it, and try to remember.

Ma didn't stop, though. She went straight for the envelope sat on the kitchen table.

–Letter from Aunt Evelyn–

"Go down and see if the canoes have come in yet," said Ma, as she rummaged for her silver letter-opener with "S.M." engraved on it. We don't have a clue who S.M. is or was, by the way. Morfar got the thing in trade years ago. Ma takes it out but once a year, to open the letter from Aunt Evelyn.

I found Morfar down near the river, sorting furs. He and the voyageurs had come just that morning. Of course, Hansel was there, too. We hugged all around, happy to see each other again.

I brought Morfar up to Ma, and we all sat down at the

kitchen table, ready to hear about life at Fort Edwards. That's where Aunt Evelyn lives with Uncle George and their two girls.

Ma carefully unfolded two sheets of onion-skin paper, inked all over in a loopy hand, through the margins and right up to the edge. She took a sip of water, cleared her throat, and read the little-sister writing in her big-sister voice:

> Jan—New Year's day Fine & bright but cold, walked a little in the yard—had not been out for a week. 26th George brought your very kind letter its the first letter I have had since your last year's came Sun: 31 Went to Church—Rev Short severe to those who came late. Little Joanna, her heart breaking in the thought he meant <u>her</u>.

The letter was part diary, and part memory; in good spirits and affectionate as always.

> March—Thundering & lightning all night—everyone says they never knew <u>so early or so fine a Spring</u> Sun 12th The little lamb died & Susan cried but Joanna went to comfort her & my mother's heart was glad to see it—the girls so different but love as Sisters should, as we do, Dearest Ida. You were the strong heart that guided me & guides me still, though far away.

You hear a lot about people's *hearts* in a letter from Aunt Evelyn. Ma raises one eyebrow when she reads out the word, to show she wouldn't have written it that way.

April Friday 3rd—Yesterday & today A man & his son here at work making pig Stys & working in the Garden, they came from County Cork but have been living 5 years in Montreal. Asked them if they ever heard tell of Thorvald Thorvaldsen & no they didn't but it made my heart happy to say Morfar's name & feel a little closer to You there.

Morfar blew his nose into his handkerchief and rubbed his eyes. I don't think there's anybody in the world he loves more than his two daughters, Ida and Evelyn.

Sat [May 23rd]: a very nice Breakfast with strawberries & cream. It is my Birthday & I know in my heart you remember me. Joanna can draw such a likeness & Susan learned to plunk out "Beautiful Dreamer" on the church Piano.

June—Thursday 18th saw a hummingbird! Killed two pigs & made some pies. The girls love so to bounce & dandle the pastor-wife's new Baby, my heart sings when they do. I think of baby Mary Jane who was such a Delight . . . .

Here Ma stopped, and skimmed down the page. Aunt Evelyn's letters always come around to discussing me, despite that she hasn't seen me since I was two years old. Ma never reads those parts out whole, anyway. She says it would give me a big head and none of us need that.

July—Sun: very fine weather, saw some Woodpeckers &c makes my heart happy.

Mon: 20(th) George measured height of a Tree lying near the road, found it 142 feet & will have fine lumber made of it.

Ma had finished the page. She turned it over, and her eyes got quizzical.

Nov 23(rd) been having Hard Times lately but I try not to complain, and keep a brave heart.

Ma's face went worried.

Then a *Farewell-and-God-Bless-and-Keep,* and after that was scribbled,

Ida we sure could use a helping hand for a couple weeks or so though I hate to ask.

Now, what you have to understand about people from the *hjemmeland* is that they say about one percent of whatever it is and don't talk about the rest. It works most of the time, since the people getting talked to can guess what the other ninety-nine percent is. I looked from Ma's face to Morfar's and knew they weren't guessing anything good.

Ma turned the letter over, then over again. After a good long minute or three she took a deep breath, looked straight at me, and said, "You'll have to go."

There may not have been any snow at Fort Snelling, but I went frozen anyway, like ice all through.

My mind started spinning around why I couldn't go. First, I didn't even know Aunt Evelyn but from letters. Second, I never in my life had been gone even one night from Ma, and hardly more than that from Morfar. Third, I had never been south of Fort Snelling, and Fort Edwards was four hundred miles south of there.

To beat everything else, I was—no I *am*—all of fourteen years old.

When I saw the way Ma folded up the letter and put it back in its envelope, I knew there was no use in contradicting. She was wearing her look that means it's already decided—as good as done, really—and I better give up on my reasons. I still couldn't help from asking:

"But Ma, are you sure they *need* me?"

"No," she answered. "They need me. But you're my daughter, which makes you the next-best thing."

-Evening Prayer-

Dong! Dong! Dong!

The church bell rang for Evening Prayer, so near and so loud that it jangled Aunt Evelyn right out of my head. By the time we had got to the chapel and found our pew, everything was so familiar that I didn't know if me leaving was real, or something I'd dreamed the night before.

Ma always has to sit in the front row, and so I always have to sit there, too. Morfar never comes at all, and I don't know how he gets away with it. Robbie never went, either, that I remember.

Pastor Martin came in, and I was glad to see him, even if Ma wasn't. He's a Lutheran, which Ma doesn't approve of because they use real wine for Communion. Us kids like him fine because he plays jacks with the girls and stickball with the boys and marbles with anyone. We do have to let him get ahead a few points now and then just to keep the game going.

"That man's got a touch of the stupid" is what Ma says about him, but it doesn't matter to us, as long as he keeps turning the jump-rope.

He's also got a wife, who we call *Pastor's Wife*, and she's equally fun. They are something, those two. They act like first-best friends, in spite of being married to each other.

I don't know what Pastor's Wife had been feeding him, but Pastor Martin was even wider than when I'd last seen him, and he wasn't exactly small then. No matter, he hopped up the stairs like a robin going for a worm, squeezed himself behind the pulpit, and banged down the Bible, ready to go.

We sang one of the hymns we all knew by heart:

Love Divine, all Loves excelling,
Joy of Heaven to Earth come down,
Fix in us thy humble Dwelling,
All thy faithful Mercies crown!

It's one of my favorites because it's got somebody getting a crown in it, which naturally makes me think of queens; that night it was Isabella who was only twelve years old when she got coronated on the eighth of October, 1200. After we sang we sat down and settled in for the sermon. Ma took out a pencil and got ready to jot down notes. Pastor Martin gets excited and takes liberties with the text, which Ma cannot abide.

He was off like a racehorse, telling about Jesus going a-visiting and finding everybody running around like chickens with their heads cut off instead of lining up to get healed or forgiven or whatever it is you're supposed to do when Our Savior shows up.

Then he kind of lost the scent and got to describing the games they might have played back then and how Jesus' team probably won most of the time. I looked over at Ma, who was scribbling hard enough to set the paper on fire. I looked over at Pastor's Wife in the row behind us, waiting for her to yank on the reins. She cleared her throat *Uh-ah-HEM!* and the sermon more stopped than ended.

We sang the closing hymn, then shuffled over into the multitude. You can't get released until you say *Good night* to Pastor Martin. He shakes your hand with that big leathery paw of his, then moves on down the line, careful to act equal glad to see everybody.

Don't get stuck behind Ma because she's got to give him her corrections and that can take a while, especially when the Gospel is involved. That night she only had a couple pages, so we made good time.

When we came outside, Venus had just showed herself as a bright star in the southwestern sky. Jupiter was right next to her, glowing his own lustery light. I knew it wouldn't be too long before *Virgo* would show up and take over for the night.

Ma didn't notice any of it, for she didn't look up at all. I expect she was still fretting over Pastor Martin, because she didn't say a word the whole way—until we got to our door, that is. As she turned the knob and pushed her way in, she sighed and said:

"You know I've been correcting that man for years, and he's never once thanked me for it."

—A Yellow Dress, a Green One, and a Pink—

An hour later, Miss Frances came to our quarters just as she'd promised, with the Colonel in tow. He was the stock-stiffest man I'd ever seen, and all fitted-out in a uniform with a sash. He didn't smile or nod or say *Hello*, just stared straight ahead like he was on sentinel.

They'd brought with them two plates of stew, the kind with thick gravy and big chunks of meat in it. It was wonderful to have hot food again after weeks of cold pemmican.

"Thank you for taking the trouble," said Ma.

"Oh, it's not so much," Miss Frances said, shaking her head, "just the Colonel's left-overs. I'm always cooking these days! I have to contend with a hungry husband morning, noon, and night!" She looked up at Colonel Waxworks like she'd finally discovered her true calling was to boil his potatoes.

Miss Frances pulled a parcel out of her basket. "One more thing! I mean *three* more things, really!"

I knew what it was as soon as I saw it. "My dresses!"

There they were, all three, wrapped in tissue and tied with

ribbon. I remembered every detail, for hadn't it been me who'd made the designs? The golden-yellow one with ruffles on the skirt, the mossy-green one with a high collar—and my favorite: weft-gilded silk that gave a shifting rose-gold color.

They were grown-up-sized, but eyeing them afresh, I wondered if they might not fit me soon, the way I was growing. It didn't really matter, as I had no cause to dress up, but I did love those dresses—probably even more than *A Child's History of England,* truth be told.

"I finished the rosy one for you with a slip stitch through the hem," Miss Frances told me. "I do believe it turned out just as beautiful as we imagined it."

"It certainly did!" I held up the dress, then hugged it to me. "Thank you so much!"

She smiled, then blushed. "There's also a letter inside from me . . . to help you consider, well, your *virtue* . . . I mean, when you begin to think towards a . . . home and a *family.* You carry it with you, just in case you meet a young man . . ."

How does she know I'm leaving? Boy-oh-boy, does word travel fast in an Army fort.

She glanced at Ma, then said, "But it's more likely you *will* come back, and when you do, I thought perhaps you could be the one to read the girls *Uncle Tom's Cabin* this year? Would you like that?"

Would I? Uncle Tom's Cabin *is only my second-favorite book in the whole world* is what I thought. "Oh, yes, Miss Frances. It would be an honor . . ." is what I said.

Uncle Tom's Cabin is so *moving*—you really can't not-cry at certain parts. Miss Frances reads it to us every year, and it's turned us girls into Abolitionists, every one.

"Well then, *Goodbye* for now, my dear. You take care of yourself." She kissed me as the Colonel gave a great big salute, and then they were gone.

"Isn't Miss Frances wonderful?" I said to Ma afterwards.

She answered me: "You *do* know it's a sin to worry over your looks as much as she does . . . and that there's a lot more to being an Abolitionist than reading a book."

Ma likes Miss Frances just fine, but Ma *liking* is different than Ma *approving*.

"But Miss Frances is also kind, and generous, and—" I was repeating what us schoolgirls said about her all the time.

Ma cut me off. "Being handsome makes every good thing you do seem extra good, and makes people overlook everything else."

That was Ma all over: she knows right from wrong and never sees anything right. But hadn't she spent her summers scrubbing laundry so I'd be free to embroider with Miss Frances? I let her have the last word, which she would have gotten anyway.

"There's a few things you should realize before you get to Fort Edwards," said Ma. I stopped in my tracks as it all came back to me at once: Aunt Evelyn's letter and me going away.

Ma kept on: "You've got two cousins down there: one smart and one sweet. Susan, who is a year older than you—she's the sweet one, but Joanna is smart enough for both of them, and she's about your age.

"Evelyn's husband—George—he's a *good* man." I had heard Ma talk about *good* men before, but I think what she really means is *Not like your pa.*

"And your aunt: she's a little too cowed by the Church, in my opinion, but then the Methodists got to her early on."

Ma is a big believer in reading the Bible for yourself instead of letting somebody read it to you. She might be fond of a certain preacher, but she's not joining up, no matter how many times they ask. She says a man telling you he *knows* God is only a short step away from him telling you he *is* God, so you've got to keep those people at arm's length.

Then she said something that really knocked me back: "You'd better get some sleep, Mary Jane. The steamboat to Fort Edwards leaves early in the morning."

At that, I didn't just feel a jolt go through me, I felt an entire earthquake. I'd be leaving—that much had sunk in. But . . . but . . . *tomorrow?*

I looked out the open door, towards the south. It was the direction I'd be heading tomorrow, but my view was blocked by a big stone wall. I couldn't imagine my future any better than I could see it.

I went to shut the door and when I did, That-cat got up and walked away, instead of settling himself on our doorstep for the night, like he used to do.

"Ma! That-cat is wandering off."

She didn't even look up from what she was doing. I went outside and followed him a few steps.

"Ma! That-cat went into the munitions shed," I yelled back into our quarters.

"Not my business," she yelled back.

"But Ma . . . he's in there lying on a gunpowder keg . . ."

Ma stuck her head out the door. "Listen, if he wants to get to Jesus that badly then who am I to stand in his way?" She untied her apron, and folded it in half.

"And come back inside, Mary Jane. It's time for bed."

-A Night at Fort Snelling-

I couldn't sleep. I just lay there thinking of tomorrow. When the first light of dawn came through the window, I slipped out of bed.

Outside everything was so still and quiet, and wrapped in that unearthly glow that feels like dreaming except you're awake. I saw the Officer Houses, and I knew Miss Frances was sleeping in there somewhere. I saw the hospital where Ma goes, as she's the best at holding a soldier's hand while they do something awful to him.

I saw the schoolhouse where I had read pamphlets on *The Moral Conduct of Young Ladies*. I'd also sat there bored out of my melon reciting and re-reciting the sums that I'd known since a baby. I saw the schoolyard, where I'd had such a good time with Annie and the others. Up at the Forks there weren't any other girls to play with, that's for sure.

Dawn was on its way, and it cheered me some. I always feel that way: at night the world closes down and you've lost your chance for that day, but morning opens up a new possibility for anything to happen.

I climbed up the half-moon battery to where I could get a good look at the world. I saw the Mississippi River flowing south, draining the prairie behind it. The Dakota call this place *Minnesota,* and I think it has a nice ring to it. It means something about *water,* and they're right. To those of us who live here, the land of Minnesota is not land at all: it's rivers and lakes and marshes in between.

I walked the trail all down the side of the bluff, passing the chalky rocks up high, the sandy ones down low, and the flaky stuff in the middle. I was going down to see what the river was that year.

Some years the Mississippi is low and you can practically walk to Pike Island, some years it's high and the trees on the banks are drowned up to their armpits. This year the water was so high, steamboats were already running clear up north to Fort Snelling.

Something on the ground moved, and didn't it turn out to be a garter snake? They are the friendliest of snakes, greenish black with a long yellow stripe down each side. That snake was on his way somewhere, but he stopped to stick out his tongue at me. Then he turned around and lunged forwards and the rest of his body followed. Garter snakes act like it's nothing to go where you want by just sticking your neck out.

I hiked myself back up the bluff just as the morning sun was peeking into the world. I saw someone walking towards me, and when they got closer, it turned out to be Morfar.

"See over yonder, *Mari-yane*? The sun is not full-up. Come now valking with your old morfar, one last time before you go a-vay."

Hansel was so happy to see me, it made Morfar seem all the more sad by comparison. Didn't he know I'd be back just as soon as everything at Aunt Evelyn's was squared away? No more than a month at most—maybe less—a couple weeks, I was sure.

We walked together as the sun climbed itself up over the horizon. As we passed the chapel, he asked me:

"Dear *liten Mari-yane*, when was I born?" His voice was soft and low.

"Seventeen eighty-nine," I answered him.

"When was your mormor born?"

"Seventeen ninety-three."

"When was your mother born?"

"Eighteen-oh-nine."

"When was your father born?"

"Eighteen-oh-four."

"When was your brother Robert born?"

"Eighteen twenty-five."

"And when were you born?"

"Eighteen thirty-two."

"Exactly right, *jenta mi*. The story of our lives is not only in words, it is in numbers, too—never forget that."

There was a wetness in his eyes, which was maybe even tears. He went on:

"Your way with numbers will help you in your life. I know

because it is the only talent I ever had, and so it's the best thing I have to give you. But I hope it will also help you remember the *who* of your life, *Mari-yane,* the Lord knows I do."

He looked at me in the kindliest manner, and we joined hands to walk home. I felt brave, like I could go away and handle it all, but I also felt afraid, like I might get lost forever.

It was good and bad, all at the same time. Something can be, it turns out.

–The First Goodbye–

We came around the corner and there was Ma, stood in the doorway, drinking coffee out of a mug. She saw us and went back inside, then came out with a mug for me. I'd never had coffee before, as it would stunt my growth, according to her.

She also had with her a rolled-up cloth. "In there's three needles, a spool of silk thread, a sharp chert, cheesecloth, a vial of spirits, a teaspoon, and a tin kettle stuffed with wild pea leaves, five-finger root, horsemint, and what's left of the tansey-flower tea.

"From out of that, you'll be able to pull a tooth, balm a burn, lay a poultice, quiet a convulsion, stop a bleeding, and stitch shut a wound. I don't know what else I can give you . . ." She looked around, as if searching the room. Then she said:

"Now come inside and tell me: What are you taking of yours?"

I did, then showed her. "My three silk dresses and my Charles Dickens, of course." I picked up *A Child's History of England* and ran my finger up and down the spine.

And just like that, our coffee moment was over. She gave me a look like I was still a little girl who needed reminding of putting shoes and socks on every morning, and I didn't like it.

"Aren't you taking your Bible with you, Mary Jane?"

"Why?" I answered innocently. "Doesn't Aunt Evelyn have one?"

She clamped her mouth shut, turned her back, and walked away.

Morfar stepped forwards and gave me twenty-five dollars, all in one-dollar bills, so quite a bundle. I put it into my pocket and pinned it shut.

Then he gave me the rolled-up bundle of fur that he was carrying, and said:

"This here's fjourteen made beaver—the very best ones out of all the skins that came in this year. It's worth eight dollars an' fjorty-five cents, right here, right now, but don't you trade it for less than ten dollars.

"Now, that's emergency money, that is," he said, pointing at the furs. "I don't hope you find trouble, but if you do, you use it as you must."

He nodded to show he was done talking; I nodded to show that I understood.

Ma came out of the kitchen. "One last thing, Mary Jane. This is for you, to take with."

She handed me a glass jar full of crimson balls bobbing around in burgundy liquid. It was the sour cherries that I love so much, the ones we preserve in August and I eat all up before November.

"You saved that for me?"

"I did, and it's a lucky thing, too, for at the time I had no idea what this year would bring. You hold on to it and eat it when the time is right."

I put the medicine bundle into my bag, then I wrapped my dresses around the cherry jar, wrapped the furs around my dresses, and tied it all together with a rope. I tucked my book under the rope, just at the knot.

Leaving home is an odd thing. You feel like somebody should do or say something grand, but what is there to say? What is there to do, but *go*? Somehow we walked down to the dock, though I don't remember doing it. Somehow there must have been other people waiting to get on the boat, but I don't remember any of them.

I only remember Ma telling us that it was time to say *Goodbye.*

I hugged Morfar and said "I love you" in his ear as I sometimes did, but not very often.

"As you I do, *Mari-yane,* as you I do." He patted me on the head. Then he stood back and looked me up and down, like he was trying to paint a portrait for his memory. He whistled for Hansel, and turned to go. A hundred paces on, he stopped to wave at me and I waved back.

I watched him walk away.

I knew everything there was to know about how Morfar would spend his day. I knew he'd be in the storehouse past dusk, getting organized for the springtime rush. I knew what he would eat for supper, and which dishes he would use. And yet, when I turned back to look at him that last time, it seemed like the first time I'd ever really seen him.

51

When had he gotten so *old*? There was a heaviness in his step and a bend in his back that I'd never noticed before, even in all those walks I took with him every day. And not just him, either: when I looked close at Hansel, he looked old, too. Why had it never struck me how skinny and limpy he'd become?

I found the ticket-man—or rather he found me:

"Where are you bound for, Miss?"

"Fort Edwards, Sir."

"And you brought money for the fare, did you?"

"Yes, Sir. What is the price?" I asked him clear and open, the way the traders ask Morfar.

"I'd have to calculate . . . how much money do you have today?"

"Twenty-five dollars, Sir."

"Yes—that's it. Twenty-five dollars for a fare to Fort Edwards."

He took my money, and right afterwards, a bell rang and a voice barked out:

Ticketed passengers! Come aboard!

Ma took my face in both her hands and looked at me hard. She smiled a calm smile, then turned around and walked away. She didn't look back. She didn't say *I love you*.

But maybe her love is not something you say.

Maybe it's baptizing you herself instead of turning you over to someone she doesn't believe in. Maybe it's gluing you back together when you're sick enough to die. Maybe it's not letting you drink out of pewter and giving you the last of the tansey-flower tea.

Standing on the deck of the boat, facing down-river, I hugged my bundle tight to my chest. Under those layers of soft fur, and wrapped in silk, I could feel the glass jar of my favorite sour-cherry preserves. I didn't know exactly where I was going, but I knew that I would carry with me a heavy, bulky, and somehow fragile thing to remind me whose daughter I am.

CHAPTER VI

–Aboard the Minnesota Belle–

I looked around me and all I could think was *Sit down!*

The first, middle, and last rule of the canoe is *Never stand up*. Standing up in a canoe rocks it plenty, and overturns it likely. But on the *Minnesota Belle* nobody sat, they just milled about like lazy horses in a pasture.

You see, I'd never been on the river but in a canoe. I'd seen the *Minnesota Belle* pull into dock every summer, with her two big wheels and coughing engine. A herd of rich people would spill out to go behold the St. Anthony Falls—that's the sum total of what I know about big boats.

A whistle blew loud enough to take my eyebrows off as we left the dock. Soon we were moving fast enough to out-do a trotting horse. I'll never forget that first feeling of being carried away so free and fast.

The crew came out to set flat-white chairs all over the deck because Heaven forbid fancy people should ever sit on the natural ground.

Then who do you think I saw?

It was Pastor Martin, walking about, lifting chairs and banging them down again, trying to find one strong enough to hold him, I guess.

"*Hullo!* Mary Jane!" He skipped over. "You're on board, too? Oh, what fun! I brought some rocks from the shore, let's have us a throwing contest . . ." He yelled backwards, "Say there, Mrs. Pastor! Little Mary Jane will be on the boat with us!"

"Or *not* so little," she corrected him. "My goodness—how *tall* you are now!"

"Yes, yes!" agreed Pastor Martin. "Why, Mary Jane, you must have grown a foot!"

"Yep! Now I have *three*!" I answered, and we all laughed.

Pastor Martin raised his big hands up towards Heaven. "Praise the Good Lord who made you! Praise Him, indeed!" He hop-scotched down an imaginary pattern.

Pastor's Wife tried to steady him. "Now, now. Save some energy for the Camp Meeting."

"And won't we have a rousing good time?" cheered Pastor Martin. "The Coach Whip Band is going to play! Oh, I hope they play 'Prairie Queen' . . ."

"*A-hem* . . . We are given to good works, Mary Jane, and we go there to save lost souls . . . ," she said to me, while looking at him.

"Oh, yes," agreed her husband. "We'll have a jolly time. We'll sleep in a tent, and eat in the boardinghouse . . ."

"And pray that the sinners be lifted up to Christ . . . ," Pastor's Wife slipped in.

"And I brought horseshoes!" he added.

It did sound like more fun than whatever was happening at Aunt Evelyn's, and I was jealous for a minute or more.

I spent the whole morning leaning on the rail, watching the river go by. That swirling water didn't make a peep—no rushing or splashing sounds like the falls and creeks up North. No, it lolled around, bumping up against the side of the boat. You could see the pebbles at the bottom, blotted out now and then by a fish lumbering by.

I stood there for hours and didn't run out of things to watch. Rounded trees on the riverbanks with great flat leaves—not the needly-pointed pines I was used to. Bald eagles flying high overhead in great wide circles. Millions of mulberry bushes overflowing with early fruit, and two million birds eating it like Thanksgiving dinner.

Standing there, watching those things, felt strange to me in a way that I couldn't put my finger on. I stood and watched for a few more hours and saw even more.

Then it occurred to me: It was the first morning I'd ever spent not *doing* something.

Once I'd gotten old enough to be of use, I'd been washing, boiling, sifting, kneading, baking, weeding, watering, milking, carrying, tending, and mending, while Ma also worked and Morfar did, too. If you wanted to eat, you had to work—that's how they saw it. Staring out into the distance all day long wouldn't get the dinner cooked.

Riding on that boat, working my eyes instead of my back, was quite a thing. I'd heard voyageurs tell how they love being on the river beyond anything, and I finally knew what they meant.

The *Minnesota Belle* was pure luxury from one end to the other. I had heard there was a dining room full of cut-glass chandeliers where they served Green Turtle Soup and Roast Partridge and swapped out your silverware in between, and guess what? It's all true, and then some.

Me and Pastor Martin and his wife sat down at mid-day and feasted on something's tongue. Then we had strawberries with a dish of white sugar that you could take as much as you wanted from. It wasn't any of our birthdays but we felt like it should have been.

When they went up to join the pinochle, I stayed in the open air, and I'm glad I did. A band of swallows came out at dusk to have some fun. They swooped at me, chased each other, and played around in the air.

Guh-guh-guh! Hissss! . . .

I heard the boat's engine choke and sputter. One of the paddle wheels slowed its turning, then stopped. Soon after, the other one stopped, too. We were adrift.

Only in the quiet that followed did I notice the owls . . .

Whooo . . . whooo . . .

. . . and the bats . . .

Flitt-flitt . . . flitt-ta-flitt-flitt . . .

. . . and the frogs . . .

Kee-ruck-uck . . . kee-ruck-uck . . .

. . . and all the other sounds that signal the start of twilight.

It felt so peaceful to be floating like that, something in my mind let go of tomorrow and the next day and . . . I sat back and let the river take me where I was going, like how you can do with a smart horse late at night.

–Very Different Country–

"Ho! Port-side!"

Two men marched across the deck towards the lame paddle wheel. One of them jumped into the river and pulled gunk from the hub; another inspected each paddle, found a split one, and set out to replace it.

Traveling on a steamboat saves you time, in that you never have to stop and let it eat grass or drink water, but you lose that time in having to stop and fix things, is what I've learned.

We pushed off, and turned the bend, where we found open water that stretched out with no end in sight. It looked for all the world like Morfar's description of the sea.

"Is that . . . the *ocean*?"

I must have said it out loud, because the person next to me answered, "*That* is Lake Pepin."

I looked over and saw the captain in his smart white uniform. "It's twenty miles long and two miles across, the biggest lake on the Mississippi," he said, "save Lake Pontchartrain down at the mouth. Take a good long look, Miss, for we'll be in very different country soon."

We passed lily pads as big as dinner plates, each one holding a turtle stuck in a daydream. Waterbugs skated across the surface, stopping every so often like they'd forgot something but couldn't remember what it was. There isn't anything so free and easy as an animal at home on its lake.

That night I slept on a feather bed and washed my face with a white rag so fine somebody could have used it for a wedding veil. The things you can do if you've got twenty-five dollars, I swear.

The next morning, when I came onto the deck, Pastor Martin and his wife were already at the rail.

"*Good morning,* Mary Jane!" chirped Pastor's Wife.

"*Good morning!*" I answered.

"This is the day the Lord has made," declared Pastor Martin. "We will rejoice and be glad in it!"

"Look, it's Prairie du Chien!" Pastor's Wife was delighted. "There's St. Gabriel's!—a lovely church, even if it is a Catholic one."

"Oh, now, Cathy, we are all God's children. . . ."

Cathy? As in Catherine? I'd never heard Pastor's Wife's real name.

Catherine might be the queeniest queen's name of all; you can hardly flip a page in *A Child's History of England* without finding one. King Henry the Eighth had *three* Queen Catherines. I didn't tell Pastor's Wife where her name came from, though. I'd tell a girl, but wouldn't bother with a lady. Grown-ups are never properly impressed by stories of queens and their castles; they lose the ability, somewhere along the way.

Pastor's Wife pointed to the East. "This is where we say *Goodbye* and *Good luck* to you, Mary Jane. Your Fort Crawford is just there, see? Oh, look at their big flag waving!"

"Ahh, the stars and stripes!" Pastor Martin was in raptures. "Rest assured, you will be among *good* Americans at Fort Crawford."

"No, it's *Fort Edwards* I get off at," I corrected them.

"Fort *Edwards*? I thought you were going to Fort Crawford!" said Pastor's Wife. She was alarmed.

Pastor Martin asked, "They sound rather the same: *Craw*-ford, *Ed*-wards—Mary Jane, are you *sure*?"

"It's Fort Edwards, Pastor Martin, I'm sure."

"Well, now I am very concerned . . . ," said Pastor's Wife.

"Why? What's wrong with Fort Edwards?" I asked them.

"I hate to say, as we are given to good works . . ." Pastor's Wife was set to tread lightly, until Pastor Martin busted in:

"Why, there's Mormons there, that's what's wrong with it! That county is clear overrun with Mormons. And Fort Edwards is right near Nauvoo—that's the belly of the beast when it comes to Mormons!"

"What's a *Mormon*?" I asked them.

"A Mormon is an *Un-American*, Mary Jane," Pastor Martin answered me.

Pastor's Wife went on: "The Mormons have proven it many times. They all vote together in one big block!"

"And as for their leader, Joseph Smith, well, people are saying that he got what was coming to him," Pastor Martin added.

Pastor's Wife stood up straight and squared her jaw. "When Missouri sends its Mormons, they're not sending their best. They're not sending people like you and me, Mary Jane."

"They're animals!" Pastor Martin yelled it.

I looked at him, shocked. It hadn't been five full minutes since we were all God's children.

Pastor's Wife saw the look on my face and shrugged. "And some, I assume, are good people."

I was more than surprised to hear them talk in such a hateful way, especially since I'd only known him as a jolly man with a friendly wife, and a Pastor to boot! I tell you I was almost scared of them, and Pastor Martin saw it on my face. Naturally *he* thought that what I was scared of was the Mormons.

"Now, now, Mary Jane, be not afraid!" He clapped me on the back. "You just need to know who and what to look out for, and Jesus will do the rest."

The things they said about *Mormons* wasn't far off from what I'd heard soldiers say about *Indians*—or what Morfar heard his Sioux customers say about the *Chippewa,* for that matter. I'd expected more from a man leading a church and the woman leading him. Maybe I should have argued, but at the time, it was easier to keep things friendly.

"How about you shuffle and I split the deck?"

Pastor Martin held out a deck of cards and offered to play old maid, hearts, and even whist. I said *No,* though I could have beaten him easy as he's good at none of it. He asked the captain for a length of rope so we could jump, but I said *No* again. It just didn't seem like fun anymore.

The next morning when we pulled into the Port of Dubuque, they were first-in-line ready to get off and looking forward to the

Camp Meeting—which had already started, by the looks of the ruckus on the dock.

We said our *Goodbyes* and I expected a *You take care of yourself* or at least a *Good luck to you,* but instead, Pastor's Wife nudged Pastor Martin and said, "Go on, now . . ."

He turned to me and asked, "Tell me, Mary Jane, have you been well and truly Saved?"

"No," I told him, my voice flat.

Why is it that priests and pastors and preachers and their wives are so interested in whether you've been baptized, confessed, saved, or anointed? They ask like it's important. They don't ask you if you're scared to leave home, or if you ever miss your big brother, or how it is having a dead pa.

I watched Pastor Martin and his wife skip down the gangplank and fold into the jubilating crowd, waving their Bibles and generally making a show of it. Then all at once, they were gone, off to sing and dance in the woods and tell each other how Heaven was waiting for them, all the while wishing everybody else straight to Hell.

-A Change of Plans-

There I was, watching the only people I knew leave, and knowing I wasn't going to miss them one bit.

The captain saw me and said:

"Hurry and catch up with your parents . . . Quick! They're nearly out of sight."

"Sir, they weren't my parents. I, myself, am going to Fort Edwards."

"Well then, you'd better get off anyway. This is where the *Minnesota Belle* turns around and heads back up the river to St. Paul," he told me, and my jaw dropped.

"What . . . what will I do now?" I sputtered out.

"Don't worry a bit, your ticket says right on it. Let's see . . ."

I showed him the ticket I had bought. It was a piece of yellow paper with MINNESOTA BELLE stamped on it, and "The New, Substantial and Splendid Steamboat" written above and "Capt. R. E. Hill" below.

"Captain *R. E. Hill*? Why, there's no such person!" he said.

In the middle was written, "This voucher hereby entitles the bearer to First-Class Transport to ___" and the words *your finale destination* filled the blank.

"Who sold you this?" he asked me.

"The ticket-man near the dock at Fort Snelling," I answered.

"Was he wearing a leather hat with the brim torn off?" I shook my head *Yes,* and good grief the captain got mad. "That *scoundrel*! We've caught him selling false tickets out Chicago way . . . How much did you pay for this?" he asked me, and I told him.

"*Twenty-five dollars!* To take such advantage of a . . . For *shame!*" He considered for a moment. "The *Minnesota Belle* company will take the loss. We'll return you thirteen dollars, for twelve dollars was the true price of the trip."

It was kind of him, but I still felt pretty hopeless.

"How will I get to Fort Edwards?" I asked.

"There's plenty of boats that leave here and go past Fort Edwards . . ." Then he got an idea: "Here's what you'll do: you'll wait for the *Galenian*. She's not pretty, but she's manned by *good* people. Yes, I do believe that you'll be fine with her."

He took me to the bursar, who paid out thirteen dollars, then pointed to where I should wait. "Be patient, she'll get here eventually. Make sure you buy your ticket from the captain this time."

I thanked him and left the boat with my bundle.

I waited all morning, and saw some things that I'll remember always.

An old-feller came stumping up beside me, leaning on his cane. His white beard reminded me of Morfar's, but his red-and-black plaid shirt was one I'd never seen before. He nodded *Hello* at me, and we stood together, enjoying the fresh air.

Didn't we see some funny birds, though? Great big ones, each with two bellies: one belly for a belly, and one for a chin.

I pointed at one of them. "What kind of bird would that be?" I asked the old-feller.

"Why, that there's a *pelican*! Hain'tcha ever seen one before?" he answered, and I shook my head *No*. "They're only the best fishermen you'll ever see. They can take a ten-pounder straight out of the water—See! There he goes!"

One of the birds dropped like a stone. As he flew low across the water, he opened his great beak and scooped a shallow fish into his wide pouch of a throat.

We watched as more and more rafts floated, each one carrying a mountain of dead pine trees. Every one of those trees must have been five feet around and at least thirty feet tall, by my eye. At the top of each pile of logs stood a man holding a long iron hook.

"I used to be him," said the old-feller, pointing at one of them.

He rambled on . . . to himself, or maybe to the river . . . but I could listen if I wanted to.

"Ah, the old pine forests . . . the ones whose seeds started growing at the dawn of time. Trees so high they touch the clouds. One after the other, we cut 'em down . . . hundreds . . . thousands . . . and shipped 'em down the river.

"I've seen countless trees fallen, and I've seen countless men fall felling 'em. One minute you're sawing that last cut and the next you're running for your life, and Heaven help you if you ran the wrong direction. Let 'em fall easy? Ha! They'd have you sawing down the next tree, not holding a safety rope on the one before. There's a lot more money in a dead tree than in a live man.

"And once it's down, that's when the real work starts. Saw the branches off. Clamp the tongs and wrap the chains. Wallop the horses to the river. Push the log in, hop on top, roll and skip. Don't fall in or you'll be crushed. I've seen enough blood on bark to last me two lifetimes.

"I don't know if I'm lucky or what. I do know I did the job for twenty years and still have both arms and all ten fingers and one good leg and that there's the sum total of my pension."

We stood silent for a bit, until he said quietly:

"They'll run out of forest to chop down one day."

"Do you really think so?" I asked him.

"I *do* think so," he answered. "We logged the pines of Maine, then the sycamores of Pennsylvania, then the spruce on Lake Michigan, and now the old oaks of Wisconsin. I've seen what a logging company can do with a thousand axes swung by two thousand arms, and I know that those companies will keep right on swinging until there's nothing left to swing at."

As for myself, I can't imagine the world could ever change that much. It's too big, and too old, and things are already how they are. When I try to imagine a Minnesota without endless pine forests and wigwam villages and herds of buffalo, I can't. What else could it ever be?

We stood together for a little longer, the old-feller and me. Then he held his hand out to shake mine. We did, and he was gone. I never even caught his name. I haven't seen him since, and I guess I never will again. We might have become friends, me and him, but we only just brushed past each other on our way to somewhere else.

Before I left home, I never realized the world is so crammed full of strangers. I swear, you find them everywhere you go.

CHAPTER VII

–The Strangest-Looking Woman I Ever Saw–

It was late afternoon and I was thirsty and hungry—and I had to pee, too—but I didn't dare leave the dock. I just gritted my teeth and stood there with my legs crossed, scanning the side of each boat for the word *Galenian.*

I saw the little *Wisconsin* struggle by, chugging up-river and choking on her own steam. The *Smelter* had a cannon on her prow and they fired it when she rounded the landing. Then came the *Uncle Toby* and wasn't she, of all things, empty? The *Warrior II* passed by at quite a clip, on her way down-river to bully someone or something.

It seemed like everything *but* the *Galenian* went by that morning, including a rusty little tugboat pulling a string of three barges behind it, each one half-sunk under a rubble that must have weighed more than the Earth itself. The things you see floating down the Mississippi, I tell you.

I had a nervous time standing on that landing, wondering what kind of rusty bucket the *Galenian* might turn out to be. And when she finally put into port, I can't say that I felt any better.

The *Galenian* was nothing at all like the *Minnesota Belle*. She didn't have two tall smokestacks or two great paddle wheels or a ten-man brass band or a statue of a peacock or any of the nice things that the *Minnesota Belle* did. No, the *Galenian* looked like a floating shack with a smokestack instead of a chimney sticking out of it.

The *Galenian* also featured the strangest-looking woman I ever saw.

She was standing on the bow as the boat pulled in, big as a full-grown bear, and waving her arms at a farmer-looking man on the shore. When he saw her, he waded out to hand her two big baskets. Then he tipped his hat, and turned away.

As the *Galenian* docked, I could see closer-up what she had to offer. Five bales of hay is what there were for deck chairs, and somebody had hung their wet laundry off the guard rails. I saw goats running free and a gaggle of soldiers playing dice. There was a hog chained in a pen suckling ten piglets and a man gutting a pile of fish with no apron on.

I saw the strangest-looking woman I ever saw put her hands on her hips, puff out her chest, and holler cheerfully:

"*Hullo*, Folks! Who's got a ticket, and who needs one?"

–In Which I Purchase a Second Ticket–

"Hey! No pushing!"

A rag-tag gaggle of boys jostled to the front of the line, flashed their tickets, and spilled up onto the deck. When I finally got to the front, the strangest-looking woman I ever saw asked me, "Where are you bound, little one?"

"I am going to Fort Edwards, *umm*, Ma'am?"

"And we'll be happy to take you! Stand here beside me and wait for your people, and when they've come, I'll ticket you all together."

Before I could tell her it was just me, a whole heap of boys mobbed up, wanting tickets. I was taller than all of them, so I had a bird's-eye view of the whole affair. I didn't like what I saw, not one bit.

"Ahoy! Good young Sir! Where are you bound?" she'd ask them.

"Me? I'm fer St. Louie!"

"Well then, you'd better have fourteen dollars and fifteen cents, young man."

"Here you are. There's fourteen-dollars-and-two-dimes-and-you-owe-me-a-quarter."

He said it with a sneer, and she dug through her purse in a flustered way.

"Oh! And . . . well . . . there you are . . . Next!" The boy jumped aboard, grinning like the cat that caught the canary.

"And you, where are you bound?" she asked the next one.

"Errr . . . just a bit down the river. I'll get off at Rock Island."

"I see! A lark, then. That'll be . . . umm . . . four dollars and sixty-five cents."

"There. There's five dollars and three dimes and a nickel. You owe me a dollar back."

"Well . . . all right, yes. I see. Here you go." He jumped up and ran to the boy before, showed him the dollar, and they both laughed.

It went on like that, and by the time they'd all paid their fare and claimed their change, the *Galenian* was down twelve dollars and forty-five cents, by my count.

What awful, dishonest boys! I thought to myself.

Not really *boys*, though. They were at that age where they're more *not-men-yet*. The age my brother Robbie was when he ran off and we never saw him again.

Those boys looked to be the running-off kind as well. Most of them were wearing some stray piece of an Army uniform— a torn-up vest here, a crumpled officer's hat over there. After they'd all got past her, she turned to me and said, "Oh, there you are . . . but where's the rest of you? They'd best hurry, for she's about to push off!"

I didn't know quite how to put it. "I'm only me, Ma'am."

"Only you? All alone out here in this whole weary world? All by yourself down to Fort Edwards?"

"Yes, Ma'am. I'm being sent to my aunt Evelyn, who needs me . . . *er* . . . who asked my ma for some help."

She looked at me, kind and concerned. "Family troubles is it, then? Well, aren't they lucky to be getting the help of such a brave young girl as you."

"How much is the fare to Fort Edwards?" I asked her.

"Thirteen dollars and twenty-five cents."

That was more money than I had, if you remember. I almost started to cry, until I recalled what the captain of the *Minnesota Belle* had told me.

"Ma'am, I'm not to buy a ticket from anyone but the captain of the boat," I told her, almost happy in the idea that she might be trying to cheat me.

"Why! I *am* the captain! What do you think of that? You can call me Mrs. Captain like the whole rest of the world does!"

She wasn't angry, but she sure was loud, in a fun kind of way. I liked her even more, and was doubly sad that I didn't have enough money.

"Mrs. Captain, I only have thirteen dollars." I turned my pockets inside out.

"For such a brave young girl as you? Thirteen dollars it is!"

I'll get her that twenty-five cents if it kills me, I promised myself, for if you look at it a certain way, I myself had stolen two dimes and one nickel off of her. Until I'd paid her in full, I was no better than any of those awful boys, and worse than some of them.

She took my thirteen dollars, then flung both arms on the rail and hoisted herself up onto the deck. She turned back around, and reached out for me.

What a big hand she had! I couldn't help but look twice. *Too big for her, really*, I thought to myself. I looked down and saw that her feet weren't small, either.

She stuck her hand out a little further towards mine: "Climb aboard, then . . . we're about to set sail! I'll get the *Galenian* running back on time today even if it's the last thing I do tomorrow!"

—Striking a Bargain—

I gave Mrs. Captain my hand, and she hauled me up onto the deck, bundle and all.

"Now, what in the world is *that* for?" She asked it like walking around with a big bale of fur wasn't a completely normal thing.

"It's for an emergency," I told her.

"What kind of emergency? The kind where you need to pass yourself off as the world's biggest muskrat?" She laughed, but in a good-natured way, not in a making-fun-of way.

"It's only the best-quality beaver fur that came into the Forks this year. My morfar sent it with me. I'm to sell it if it comes to that."

"Well, you'd better find somebody to buy it. South of here there isn't going to be anybody who wants that fur."

"They might not wear it *now*," I allowed, "but come winter there's nothing better."

She shook her head. "I daresay you are in for a summer to remember down in Fort Edwards."

She couldn't help but to reach out and stroke that fur—it's human nature, Morfar says. As she did, her eyes lit up: "Why, your for-mare is right, this is some darnded fine stuff!"

She pondered: "It's a dilemma, it is. The *Galenian* is already behind schedule . . ." Then she threw up her hands and said, "Blast it all! I'll hold the boat for you—after all, the captain does as the captain pleases!"

She pointed down the dock. "See over there, that chimney poking up? It belongs to the trading post. I'm not overly fond of the man behind the counter, but it's your only option that I can see."

It occurred to me that by selling those furs, I could get the twenty-five cents I owed her. I knelt down, unwrapped my bundle, and got ready to take the furs with me and leave the rest with her.

"Mrs. Captain, will you keep these things for me while I'm gone?" I handed her everything I had left, tied up in three silk dresses.

"Of course I will. But go quick as you can . . . and come straight back—Go!"

I jumped off the boat and ran towards that chimney. I stopped to pee, but I don't care to tell about that.

When I got to the trading post it didn't look like any trading post I'd ever seen. It wasn't a cabin or even a shack: it was more like a horse-stall. On one side was a candlemaker and on the other was a woman who'd sand the corns off your foot for a dollar.

That trading-stall had the barest shelves; a cracked teacup and a dented-in spittoon was the whole display. Sat in front was a little man reading his newspaper. He didn't have a beard, but his mustache more than made up for it.

I cleared my throat *A-hem!* and he looked up.

"My, my, my. *Hullo* there, Missy! Aren't you a picture? There must be something I can offer a pretty young girl like you."

He smiled a smile that made me uneasy in my gut, but I stomped it down. *He's just trying to be friendly,* I told myself.

I held up my bundle: "This here is a pack of fourteen made beaver pelts, trapped from Manitoba country. They're each of prime quality and I'm not to take less than ten dollars for the lot."

His eyes gleamed with interest; a trader knows good fur when he sees it. He twirled one side of his mustache while he considered.

"And ten dollars you shall have, little Missy!"

He took a leather pouch from deep in his trousers and opened it. He licked his lips while he pulled out a bill, stuffed it back, pulled out another, and so on, until he found the one he wanted.

"And here you are! Ten lovely dollars. A very good trade for you, young Missy!"

It was just one single paper—a real live ten-dollar bill! And wasn't it fancy? It had fat babies, all strumming on harps and smiling like Christmas. There was a flowery-looking *one-zero* stamped on each corner. I'd never seen anything like it.

I thanked Mr. Mustache and said *Goodbye.* He smiled a syrupy smile and winked at me. My gut rose back up, uneasy, but I pushed it back down again. Then I scurried myself back to the *Galenian.*

"Good for you!" said Mrs. Captain when I told her I'd sold the furs. She pulled up the anchor with one arm, and we began to drift down-stream.

She handed me back my dresses, newly tied with a rope for easy carrying over my shoulder. The rope was knotted good and sturdy, too: didn't stretch but didn't bind, either.

"Oh! First things first," I told her. "Will you please take this and give me nine dollars and three quarters in return?" I handed her my ten-dollar bill, awful proud. It felt so good to think that I'd be honest in my fare, and still have plenty left over for security.

Mrs. Captain put one hand on each of my shoulders. "Just look at this dear little one, thinking of *others* before herself."

As I handed her the ten-dollar bill, something on it caught her eye. She looked at it close, then flipped it over, and looked even closer.

"Who gave you this?" Mrs. Captain was not pleased.

"The man at the trading post where you said to go," I answered.

"That Devil! I knew he wasn't the best kind of man, but I never suspected him as bad as that." She was fuming. "You see what it says there, across the very bottom?" She held it in front of me, and pointed.

"'*New Orleans Banking Company,*'" I read.

"That's right. And do you know where New Orleans is?"

New . . . Orleans? Where have I heard that name before? I asked myself. Then I remembered that Henry the Fifth got vanquished in 1420 at a place called *Orleans* by Joan of Arc, who they burned at the stake in 1431.

"Is this . . . *French* money?" I asked her.

"It might as well be!" Mrs. Captain explained. "It may as well be a Pennsylvania shinplaster for all the good it'll do you."

"But it has a big number *ten* written on it—it's got to be real!" I pointed out the small details, in case she'd missed them.

"Oh, it's real enough," she told me. "It's just not worth a cent until you get down at least to Baton Rouge."

I felt like I'd just dropped the good-china gravy boat. I couldn't pay Mrs. Captain back, after all. Not only that, but it was starting to sink in just how pitiful I was. No money, no fur, no nothing—except for a French ten-dollar bill worth five cents less than a nickel.

Mrs. Captain must have seen it on my face. "You poor thing. All alone out here trying to get to your—what did you say? Gramma and grampa?" she asked me.

"My aunt and uncle."

"Oh, this world is too evil for a lone little one like you." Mrs. Captain shook her head in sorrow.

I wasn't halfway to Fort Edwards, and I'd already seen the world change out from under me. The trees were different, the birds were different, even the *people* were different than anything I'd known up North. Could it be that money is different every-place you go, too? And why hadn't Morfar warned me about it?

Then I figured out why. Maybe Morfar didn't know! Maybe even Ma didn't know! For the first time in my life, I might know something that neither one of them did.

Then it dawned on me that I was the only one of us who had ever been south of Fort Snelling. *From here on out,* I thought to myself, *I'm in uncharted territory.* It felt exciting, like going fast on a horse, and scary, like it might not listen if you told it *Whoa!*

The next thing I knew, Mrs. Captain announced to me, and

everybody else: "While aboard the *Galenian,* I declare you to be under the captain's special protection. From henceforth it is my duty to deliver you to Fort Edwards, as much as it is my duty to deliver two hundred tons of ore to the Memphis Orgill Brothers and Company established 1837!"

When she said that, my breath all came out in a *sigh,* like when you untie a too-tight shoe. The scared part of me calmed down and the excited part of me took over. It was a wonderful feeling.

I still didn't know what I'd be in for when I got to Aunt Evelyn's, but thanks to the strangest-looking woman I ever saw, I was finally sure that I was on the right boat, with the right people, to get me there.

CHAPTER VIII

—Aboard the *Galenian*—

"For now, you'll follow me like a new-hatched chick follows its mother hen!" Mrs. Captain was serious about her duties.

"I sure will," I agreed. Mrs. Captain made me feel safe, and from that I felt brave. I bet that's how a chick feels about its mother hen.

"Now then, my dear little Chickie—let me show you 'round the *Galenian*! She's a fine ship, I say—though a captain can't help but be partial. Once you've seen how sturdy and spunky and ornery she can be, you'll understand why she's the very best boat in this big weary world!"

"I know I will!" I liked Mrs. Captain plenty already, and the *Galenian* was part and parcel of her, so I'd made up my mind to like it, too.

"Follow me, little Chickie, and I'll take you all around and let you see what's what, and then you must meet Robert Fulton. We'll never overtake the ore without him, now, will we?"

We walked the deck, weaving our way around the boys-gone-soldiers. They were huddled around a dice-game, or a bottle, or a pack of dirty pictures, or all three. It never failed that when Mrs. Captain came close, one of the boys would point at her, lean in, and say something that made them all laugh. Some would whistle or make kissing noises at her as she passed.

I felt myself afraid . . . like those boys were dangerous to her, and to me, too, but I couldn't tell you exactly how. Mrs. Captain acted like she didn't even notice.

"The *Galenian* is a one-hundred-and-forty-one-foot stern wheeler. She's twelve years old, built at the Pittsburgh shipyards. I'll never forget that day when she first came into Galena. She was the third boat of the season, and it was love at first sight. Greeley & Blake gave me the backing, and I've been at her helm ever since."

She showed me the stempost, the bulkhead, the fairlead, the guard, the stanchion, and a lot of other things I don't remember. She explained how the *Galenian* was blessed with a square stern and a molded bow. She took me along the hog-chain to where I could get a glimpse of the big rudder under the paddle wheel.

Then she led me to a big square box on the lower deck. It had a smokestack coming out of its top, about twenty feet tall. The box had a door on it, wide enough for me to get through maybe, but questionable for Mrs. Captain.

She motioned at it like it was the *Mona Lisa*. "And this— this!—is the boiler room."

Mrs. Captain gave the door a couple good thumps with her shoulder, then pushed it open with a flourish.

"Robert Fulton, this here is little Chickie. And Chickie, meet Robert Fulton!"

–Robert Fulton–

Robert Fulton was short, and stout, and looked like he had seen better days.

"He doesn't look like much," said Mrs. Captain, as she knocked him on the top, *Clang, clang, clang!* "But when he's got a fire in his belly, there's no stopping him!" Then she sang:

Open up the throttle, let the ol' smoke roll,
Overboard goes the cargo, when we're short on coal.
If we don't get him boilin', said Mrs. Captain to her mate,
We'll be meeting Saint Peter at the Pearly Gate!

Robert Fulton was a big iron kettle with a hatch in the middle and wheely things sticking out every which way. She rattled off his appendages: piston, crank-shaft, connecting-rod, four-stroke cylinder, and more. I tried to keep up, but she lost me.

Finally, she said, "It's well-nigh time to start him up!" She turned to me: "Want to help? Every steamboat needs a boiler-master."

"Oh, yes, Mrs. Captain," I answered. If I couldn't pay her the twenty-five cents I owed, then maybe I could work it off.

"Take up that coal scuttle, then. Chickie, how's your shoveling arm?"

"Only good enough to move a blizzard's worth of snow. It was my job to dig the horses out." Suddenly I was proud of something that I'd complained over no end.

She took me 'round to the coal pile. "Fill that scuttle right full up and bring it over. You'll have to make ten trips, Chickie, so hop to!"

After I was done, Mrs. Captain said, "Let's go up and get the pitch."

We climbed a ladder up to the shack sitting on the roof of the boiler room. "In here is the pilothouse, where I steer the ship," she said as she showed me inside. "It's also where I sleep, and eat, and generally just be me."

The pilothouse was tidy as a pin. On the floor, near the big wooden wheel with rolling-pin handles, there was a mat to sleep on, a mirror, and a hairbrush, all tidy together. Off in the corner sat a pail of water with a ladle in it, and next to it was a big bucket; a clothesline was strung up over both.

Mrs. Captain pointed to the bucket: "Grab that pine-tar, and we'll go down and light him up."

I picked up the bucket—it was heavy! The black gunk inside it was thicker than molasses and smelled like old rubber. I heaved the bucket onto my shoulder, climbed down the ladder part-way, then jumped the rest.

"Oh, to be young again!" said Mrs. Captain, watching me.

"Now slather a good layer of pitch on," she instructed once we got back to the boiler room. I swabbed dark goo over the coals.

"Why, look at you! You're a natural, if I've ever seen one," said Mrs. Captain.

That was her all over. Every little thing I did was just the *best* anybody had ever done it, according to her. But the more I heard it, the stronger it made me. When somebody's built you up enough, you feel like you can take on the whole world.

"My dear little Chickie, I do think you'll be a first-rate engineer for the *Galenian!*"

"Only because you're a first-rate captain!" I told her.

"Oh, my, now! Here on the *Galenian,* I'm also the ticket-agent, the first pilot, and the second pilot, too! But all my favorite people call me *Mrs. Captain.*"

"And all my favorite people call me *Chickie!*"

"Well, how-do-you-do, first-engineer Chickie?" She stuck out her big bear-paw for a handshake.

"Ready and able and reporting for duty, Mrs. Captain," I answered her, doing my best soldier-salute.

We laughed and were friendly together, and it was just overall wonderful.

She turned serious: "That pitch bucket you've got—once we set light to Robert Fulton, we don't want it anywhere near the flame." She shook her head. "That's how boats burn up, you know, keeping the tar too close to the boiler.

"Some of these boats you see on this river are no less than floating bombs, Chickie. And when a boiler blows, it makes for an awful sight: people blasted apart and pieces of them floating in the water." She looked sad as anything. "And as bad as

Mississippi steamboats are, on the Missouri River they're ten times worse—good Heavens, that *Saluda*? Now there's a tragedy waiting to happen." She shook her head, so I shook my head, too.

"And *that's* why I won't let just anybody feed the fire, only expert engineers like you, Chickie."

"Understood, Mrs. Captain."

"Go on up and put the tar back in its safe place, and then we'll light Robert Fulton and see what he can do," she said, and I went and did it.

After I came back, Mrs. Captain showed me how to light a splinter with a flint, which I already knew, but I watched close anyway in case there was a special way she preferred me to do it.

When she touched the little flame to the pitched coal— *Whoosh!*—a big flame rolled through Robert Fulton. We fastened his door, and checked the latch twice.

"Now it's a waiting game," she told me, and we stood and waited.

By-and-by, Robert Fulton started to *hissssss* and a little bit of steam puffed out his top. It wasn't long before the iron rod sticking up was moving, or creaking, at least. When it went up, it pushed another rod down, and that one pushed another up, and so on. The last rod was attached to an iron wheel, that toothed into a littler wheel, that turned the paddle wheel at the axle.

"Oh, our *Galenian* complains at first, doesn't she, Chickie? But we'll get her oiled up and she'll be humming along soon, you'll see."

After we got the line whizzing along, I saw the paddles on the big wheel dive down into the water and give a good push to the boat when they came up again. The turning was smooth, and we soon found ourselves moving down the river at a good clip.

"You did it!" cheered Mrs. Captain, though she was the one who'd done most of the work. I was already hoping that next time she'd let me do it by myself, maybe.

"What now?" I asked her.

"Now I go up to the pilothouse and steer, and you feed Robert Fulton whenever he's low on coal. We'll do that until the sun starts to set. Sound good?" she asked me.

"Sounds great!" I told her.

While I waited for Robert Fulton to get hungry, I stood on the deck, looked across the horizon, and watched the farm fields go by. Up at Fort Snelling, Ma wouldn't be planting her garden for a month yet, but down in Iowa country, green sprigs of corn were coming up everywhere. When we crossed into Illinois, the corn had ears with silky little tassels on it already. Three days on the river is equal to three weeks on the ground, from what I can gather.

I was lost in the calculation of it when I heard Mrs. Captain call me from above: "Oh, Chickieeeeee! Come on up and pilot the boat for a bit, will you?"

—At the Helm—

Pilot the *Galenian*! I was so excited I practically flew up the ladder to the pilothouse. Inside, I found Mrs. Captain with both hands on the wheel, rocking back and forth, from foot to foot. She had her sleeves rolled up all the way to her armpits, to allow for freer movement, I suppose, and the skin of her arms positively glowed, it was so pale. Her face, her hands, the back of her neck—they were all tanner than tan. I guess that's what being on a ship's deck day in and day out will do to a person.

"The rudder's straight below me, and this what I'm holding here turns it side-to-side—enough to keep her in the middle, I reckon."

She gestured for me to take the wheel. "There, now rock a little . . . plant your feet, and move your knees," she instructed me. "You've got it!" she cheered, as if it wasn't something just anybody could do.

"Gives a nice high place to look out of," she added in a dreamy way, like she'd passed some of her happiest moments at the helm of the *Galenian.*

My stomach interrupted both of us with a long, loud *grrrrrrrummmmmble* and I remembered that I hadn't eaten since breakfast.

"Why, Chickie, you need some food in you!"

I was sad then, too, for I didn't have any, and I didn't have money to buy any—well, no money that was worth anything anyway. Then I remembered the jar of cherry preserves from Ma.

"Do you like cherries?" I asked her. "I have a jar of sugared ones, the very best kind." I was happy to have something to share.

"Is that . . . all you have?" she asked quite serious.

"That and some few useful things like medicine and thread and such."

"Then, Chickie, you hang on to it until you really need it. Today you'll have bread and cheese and buttermilk and an egg or two, courtesy of Farmer Jenkins and his wife back in Dubuque."

I checked in on Robert Fulton, and he did need more coal, so I gave it to him. Then we ate, me and Mrs. Captain, and felt companionable. The eggs were cooked to rubbery, but a pinch of salt brought them up fine. We drank from the pail, but ladled the water into our hands before drinking, in order to keep it clean between us.

"That tasted as good as anything I ever ate," I told Mrs. Captain when we were done.

"I do concur, I do indeed, little Chickie. The Jenkins farm is first-rate, and to think that every time I pull into Dubuque, they come with a basket just for me."

"That's awful nice," I said.

"Isn't it, though? And all because nine years ago I took their second son down to Fort Armstrong so he could join up. That young man didn't have a penny for his fare." She continued, "He offered to shovel and carry and do anything needed—such a fine and honest boy he was. I remember him and his folks remember me, and that's the best way to get along in this big weary world, Chickie."

"He does sound like a fine person," I agreed. "Is he an officer by now?"

"No, he's not, I'm sorry to say." Mrs. Captain shook her head sadly. "The Army marched him down Florida way and got him killed. Died on the banks of Lake Okeechobee, is what his parents told me, standing in the mud with nothing but a hatchet, hadn't even been issued a gun yet."

"That's *terrible!*" I said, and thought of Pa, who might have died similar. Then I thought of Robbie, who might have gone for a soldier in the end, for all we knew.

She continued, "For too many of these boys, their time on the *Galenian* is the last happy journey they'll ever make. I get them to where they're going, safe and sound, and I don't charge much for doing it—it's the least I can do.

"It doesn't cost anything to be kind, Chickie; you must remember that. It's not always easy to be a boy, or a man, even. There's an awful lot of killing organized by the men at the top, but it's the boys at the bottom who'll be made to do it."

"Well, it's *always* a mistake to be dishonest," I said, and I really believed it at the time.

"Maybe so, Chickie . . . Then again . . ." Something behind me caught Mrs. Captain's eye and she jumped. "Is it? Is it?" she asked nobody in particular. "Yes, I think it is!"

She pointed up ahead: "See up there, Chickie? There they are!" It was two specks off in the distance.

Whatever it was, the *Galenian* was gaining on it, and fast. "Thank you, Robert Fulton!" she belted out at the top of her lungs.

It turned out to be two barges, each carrying no more than an anthill's worth of blue-gray rubble, but looking ready to sink anyway. The barges were tied in a line behind a tugboat that was pulling for all it was worth.

"Take the helm, Chickie, and hold an even course; I'll go down and put us together and then you'll really see what Robert Fulton can do!"

I watched as she tied up her skirt, quick as a wink. She clambered down the ladder and jumped off the side of the boat, right into the water! Then she dove under and didn't come up again until she was at the tugboat.

Just watching her—wasn't it something? The captain of the tugboat was as skinny as his boat was fat, but he stuck out his hand and hauled her up aboard.

Mrs. Captain ran to the stern and jumped onto the barge behind, then undid the rope that tied it to the tugboat. That barge drifted off to the right, while the tugboat puttered on. Mrs. Captain jumped again and untied the next barge, looping the rope out-and-under until it slipped free, and drifted off to the left.

I was terrified by then, as the *Galenian* was coming up on those barges fast and Mrs. Captain was still skipping back and forth between them, knotting ropes here and there. I braced myself for the crash, hoping to Heaven that Mrs. Captain wouldn't be smashed to pieces.

Just as I felt the *thunk-nk-nk* of the *Galenian* ramming into the behind barge, I saw Mrs. Captain dive off to the side, just missing getting crunched in the middle. By the time she bobbed up a few yards away, the *Galenian* had settled down and was pushing both barges from behind, thanks to Robert Fulton.

I heard Mrs. Captain yell up, "You can come down now, Chickie—what a fine job you did!" She was back aboard the *Galenian*, wringing a gallon of water from her skirts.

She hollered *Goodbye* to the tugboat. "Thank you kindly, Captain Kirby!"

"My pleasure as always, Mrs. Captain! I'll see you at Rock Island!" The tugboat's smokestack coughed until it pushed ahead of us, slow and wobbly as a twelve-year-old dog going for its dinner.

"Mrs. Captain, how long will it take for us to get the *Galenian* into Fort Edwards?" I asked her.

"Three or four or five days. It depends on a lot of things. Next stop is Rock Island, where we'll take on passengers—and coal, too."

"Aren't some of those boys supposed to get off before then?"

"They're welcome to swim ashore whenever they want," she said with a nod.

"And in Rock Island you'll sell tickets again?" I asked her. I was formulating a plan, but I wasn't ready to tell her about it yet.

"Yes, many tickets, I expect. Springtime arrives and adventure calls!"

I thought about how it wasn't adventure that had called me, it was Aunt Evelyn. It didn't matter, because there I was aboard the *Galenian* anyway, just like those boys; and it didn't matter twice over, because I felt I must be having a better time than all of them put together. They sat around on deck, while I ran back and forth, piloting the ship and minding Robert Fulton and being Chickie to someone with as much goodness as Mrs. Captain.

"And now we'd better get moving towards sleep," Mrs. Captain said, with her hands on her hips. "But first, let's go and tend to Robert Fulton together, shall we? If we get him good and going—but not too hot, mind you—he'll keep us moving all night."

The boiler room was plenty warm inside, so we left the door open as I ran back and forth with coal while Mrs. Captain checked the seals and joinings and did general maintenance.

"We had a good day today, Chickie, and a good day is something to be grateful for." She motioned towards you-know-who. "And a steamboat is only as good as her steam engine. People forget that, they do." She patted him on his pump handle, just like you would a best friend on the arm.

"Thank you, Robert Fulton," she said, and I got a lump in my throat just from watching the two of them.

–Confidences–

We climbed up to the pilothouse, where Mrs. Captain gave me a flint and asked me to light the lamp. I got it on the first try, and she started up about what a smart, capable girl I was. She made up a cot for me, then laid out her sleeping mat.

"If you want privacy, you just go behind that wall, and if I want privacy, I'll do the same." She did so, and came back wearing a long night-dress made out of the sturdiest, stiffest cloth I'd ever seen. "It's sail-cloth, Chickie, it's what they make boat-sails out of, good strong stuff it is," she told me.

She brushed her hair, and chatted with me. "Chickie, you're a fine, brave girl, you are, but I'll say I'm surprised to see you moving across the country all on your own. Your for-mare is sending you to your aunt and uncle at Fort Edwards, where they are in need, isn't it?"

"Yes, Mrs. Captain, that's exactly it."

"And you're what? I'm guessing thirteen or fourteen years old."

"Fourteen is right."

"I see. Well . . . it was only you who could come, was it? Don't you have a sister or a brother? They're still babies, perhaps, and you the oldest?"

"No, no little ones. I have one brother, who was always much older than me." She nodded like she was interested.

"His name was—*is*—Robbie. He ran off when I was just turned eight. I hardly remember him anymore, except for his red hair. Ma misses him quite a bit, but what mother doesn't favor her son better than her daughter?"

I hadn't meant anything by it. It's just the way things are, at least everywhere I've been.

"I know, Chickie. Oh, how I do know," she said quietly. She put a night-cap on and stuffed her hair up into it. "Well," she added, "I am glad you're here now."

"And you? Mrs. Captain, was there ever a Mr. Captain?"

"There was." She sounded sad. "He sailed up and down the Missouri River, back in the day."

"I'm sorry," I told her. "Is he dead?"

"Not dead, just gone. And I don't miss him, I have to say. He's long gone."

"Well"—I said it the same way she'd said it to me—"I am glad you're here now."

We settled into our beds, her on one side of the room and me on the other, and Mrs. Captain blew out the lamp. I slept like a baby that night, only not in a cradle, but on a barely-rocking, coal-burning, paddle-wheel-turning, gravel-pushing, great-big wonderful boat.

CHAPTER IX

–On the Mississippi–

Didn't I have a good time there on the *Galenian*? And I don't mean a fun time, I mean a good time, because nearly every minute that I was aboard, I was working. But I felt good about the work, and that made me feel good about me.

After dinner, Mrs. Captain taught me knots. Soon I could do a square knot and a double-overhand with my eyes closed, then I started in on hitches: clove, timber, fisherman's-bend, taut-line, and slippery. The trick is to stop your fingers before they stop you.

One evening, she handed me a string with four knots in it, and quizzed me: "What are those, Chickie? Can you name them off?"

"Let's see . . . the first is a monkey's fist, the second is an axel hitch, then a round-turn, and at the end is a Yosemite bowline."

"And what does that spell?"

"Spell?"

"Yes, *spell.* Monkey-Axel-Round-Yosemite. What do the beginning letters spell out?"

"*M-a-r-y!* Oh, I get it!"

"Exactly right—aren't you a smart one, Chickie? Now let's add to it a jug-sling, another axel hitch, a noose-loop, and we'll tack on an eye-splice for the end."

After we finished, I fingered our new knots down the string: "Jug-Axel-Noose-Eye . . . that's me! *M-a-r-y J-a-n-e!*"

"Exactly," said Mrs. Captain. "And now you know what all good sea-farers know. You hand that string to any boatman worth his salt, and he'll read the message *Mary Jane* at first glance."

"What a neat trick!" I told her. "It's like a secret code . . ."

"It is, Chickie . . . that it is." She ended our lesson by blowing out the lamp.

I came to know Robert Fulton like he was family, so I could keep him at his best. If you want the *Galenian* to go faster, you've got to make some steam, and the quickest way to make steam is not to bring up the heat, it's to bring down the water. What you do is . . . well, I know a lot of things about boilers, but I won't bore you with it now.

In the mornings I was in charge of doing the *sounding,* which is when you stick a notched pole straight down in the water until it either touches the bottom or doesn't. Six feet is a *fathom,* and that's what you want, or deeper, so the boat won't run aground. When you can't touch the bottom you yell *No bottom!* When it goes down two fathoms you yell *Mark Twain!* which sounds like somebody's name, but it's not, as far as I know.

Between jobs, I had lots of time to watch the riverbank go by. I never got tired of being on the Mississippi River, for all the hours I spent. Aboard the *Minnesota Belle* I thought about where all the water was going to, but on the *Galenian*, I started to think about where all the water was coming from. I remembered the broad white sea of snow up North and how it melts before the world goes summertime green. All that snow was in the river now, it's what was carrying me along to Fort Edwards.

I was lost in the thought when Mrs. Captain came up beside me. "It's a pleasure just to be on the water, isn't it, Chickie? And what a fine engineer you've become! I'll say, you are a great help to me."

I was getting used to her telling me what a fine, smart, strong girl I was, and I didn't mind it one bit. In fact, there was a part of me that had started to believe it.

"Chickie, I love the river, but it's more than that. I *know* the river, every inch. I know each curve and every rapid—not to mention each sandbar and sunken wreck—and I can see them in my mind when it's deep dark night and it's like a wall of ink up front."

It was beautiful to hear Mrs. Captain talk about piloting a steamboat. It was like how I can do sums, or how Ma can find the right medicine, or how Miss Frances can sew a slip stitch using her left hand. Maybe every person in the world has something like that, all of us different.

Mrs. Captain continued, "Though I must say, every part of this boat is as good as gold. She doesn't heel or list, pitch or plunge, or yaw. She's never foundered, or capsized, or keeled over. If I'm honest about it, the *Galenian* keeps to the middle and mostly steers herself."

I can't say that I was surprised. All that sounding I was doing never came up less than six feet, and I'd been at the wheel enough to know that turning it didn't actually do much, and once I'd got the knack of him, Robert Fulton needed almost no tending.

But I had thought of a way that I could be good-and-honest especially useful, and I couldn't wait to spring into action when the time came.

-Trouble Coming-

That evening, Mrs. Captain was in a reminiscing mood, and I was comfortable and ready to listen.

"Before I became a captain, Chickie, I lived aboard one boat or another nearly all my life. Why, my first memory is standing on the stone wall with the other boys, watching the boats sailing back and forth from Lake Michigan. Keelboats and flatboats and barges there were, and of course steamboats, and I knew the names and captains of each one.

"It's in my blood. All the men in my family left home on boats, off to waters salt or fresh. They went for whales, they went for furs, and now I go for stone."

"I've been meaning to ask. Those piles of rocks she's pushing—what are they?"

"Leaden-ore and nothing else, my dear Chickie! Pulled from the ground under Fever River, crushed and smelted and loaded up. Do you know what that gravel'll be used for?"

"No, I don't."

"It goes to make wheels for railroad cars! So folks can get places quicker, and manifest our destiny. So here she is, the *Galenian*, hauling the very stuff that's going to eventually do her in."

"Or maybe that gravel'll do us all in, Chickie . . . maybe it'll be made into cannonballs down in New Orleans. I wouldn't be surprised." Mrs. Captain was downright sober. "There's a big war coming, and those of us who go back and forth across the Mason-Dixon can feel it. Pray you'll be nowhere near when it starts, Chickie."

"A war?"

"An awful war. North against South. Brother against brother, it'll be."

"What are they fighting over, Mrs. Captain?"

"What do they ever fight over, Chickie? Money. Property. Land. Who can own what, and who can own who."

We sat quiet for a bit. I think we were both a little sad.

"There now, that's enough trouble-talk for one day, we're safe and sound on the *Galenian* tonight, and we should be grateful." She blew out the lamp. "*Good night*, Chickie," she said from one side of the room.

"*Good night*, Mrs. Captain," I said back from the other.

"You sleep well now," she told me, and but for my dreams about cannon-fire, and musket-shot, and Robbie laid out with a bullet through his heart, I guess I did.

-Putting into Port-

The next morning brought fine weather, warm and sunny enough to qualify as summer up at the Forks. Rock Island was coming up, and I was so excited I was just beside myself.

"When we put into port, I like to go on land and have myself a good, long itch. Chickie, will you accept delivery from the coal-man?" Mrs. Captain asked.

"I will," I answered, "but how will I know who he is?"

"Oh, you'll know," she said.

When we put into Rock Island, I turned my head right and then left and that's all it took to see the whole town. There wasn't a trading post, there wasn't a blacksmith, there wasn't any of the usual things. There was a saloon, and sat next to it was a church, and that was it.

I scanned the dock looking for a coal-man. Mrs. Captain was right: he wasn't hard to find, and only partly because he was pushing the biggest wheelbarrow in the world, filled to the brim with nuggets of black, shiny coal.

But I recognized him more off his face, for he was a sight all to himself. All around his eyes was blacker than night, forming a mask that circled the upper part of his head, just like a racoon wears.

"Sir! Over here!" I waved both of my arms over my head.

He noticed me, waved back, and pushed his heavy wheelbarrow over using just one arm. His other arm carried along a giant basket.

"*Hullo!*" he answered, and handed the basket up to me, then grabbed the rail and pulled himself onto the *Galenian*. Goodness,

he was nimble, and muscley all over. He was also short, coming up barely past my waist.

"I'm Mary Jane, first engineer," I introduced myself with a smile.

"I do believe it." He smiled back.

"That basket is for Mrs. Captain, of course. It's got the things she's partial to . . . there's smoked meat, and double-smoked cheese, and a good supply of dried apples . . . enough to get to Memphis on, I'm hoping, even if her first engineer were to join in. A youngster as tall as you eats more than nothing, is my guess."

"You guessed right," I assured him. "Robert Fulton will be glad to see you, is what I expect."

"Oh, yes, we're long-acquainted, him and I."

He took off his hat and a whole mess of yellowish hair shook down. From up close I could see that black mask of his for what it was: his actual skin. It was permanently soot-stained, making the whites of his eyes look all the whiter.

"Stand well back, now." He pulled out a neckerchief and tied it over the lower half of his face. Then he tipped the wheel-barrow forwards and a thousand pounds of coal slid down, while another thousand pounds went *Poof!* up into the air. The black coal-cloud settled over both of us the way dew settles over a meadow at sunrise.

He brought another seven or eight more wheelbarrows' worth, and then did it all over again, until the deck of the *Ga-lenian* looked like the Black Mountains Queen Eleanor went to in 1188.

"You're all set now, I believe," he said when he finished. "There's nothing pleases a steamboat captain like having fine weather, a swift current, a sturdy boiler, and plenty of coal."

"Yes, Sir," I answered. "It's dusty work for you, though!"

"Well, now, there's nothing I'd rather do than make sure Mrs. . . . make sure *folks* are set up with the coal that she . . . that *they* need. You'd be amazed at the refuse some of these boilers are run off of: candle-ends, rotten boards, old shoes, you name it. The best captains, like the *Galenian* has, run their boats off good, clean coal, they do."

He wasn't looking at me when he said it, but at something behind me. I turned to see, and saw Mrs. Captain on the riverbank, rubbing her back against a big oak tree, itching herself like a black bear does against a pine, with bits of bark flying everywhere.

He sighed. "I'll wish you *Farewell*, and take my leave now."

"Do we owe you money for the coal, um . . . Mr. Coal Man?"

"Oh, no, you've paid us for the season already, in advance." He shuffled his feet. "You'll tell Mrs. Captain that . . . that Thomas sends his regards, will you? And . . . and . . . ask if maybe on her way back up-river she'll stop and spend the afternoon? Only if she's nothing better to do, that is."

"At the church or at the saloon?" I asked him.

"Well, I've never been in that saloon, I must say. I'm more of a spuds-'n'-gravy man, myself. I do go into the church every Sunday, though. After I spend all day Saturday scrubbing myself, that is!" He folded his neckerchief and put it back in his pocket.

I didn't know what a *spuds-'n'-gravy* man was, but it sounded better than a *gin-'n'-whiskey* man, which looked to be the only alternative there in Rock Island.

"You tell Mrs. Captain that Thomas will be glad to find two lemonades, and will look forward to when she comes."

"I will, Mr. Thomas."

"Haw, haw! 'Mr. Thomas'—listen to you! You better call me *Racoon Man*—everyone does, you know."

"Not *everyone*, I guess." I said it with a smile.

"No, not my *very* most favorite people . . ." He seemed a little shy about it, so I didn't say any more.

He looked over at Mrs. Captain, who was finishing her last itch. Then he turned to me: "She's got the most goodness of anybody what's ever been on this river, you know that?"

"Oh, I do, Mr. Racoon Man," I assured him. "I most certainly do."

I shook his sooty hand and said *Goodbye.* Then I hurried across deck to Mrs. Captain, to tell her all about it.

–In Which I Am Very Useful–

I admit I forgot all about the Racoon Man's invitation when I saw the mob of not-quite men shoving and pushing, all of them surging towards Mrs. Captain, wanting to get on board, and to cheat her in the doing of it.

I heard her ask the forward-most one her usual question:

"Ahoy! Good young Sir! Where are you bound?"

"Me? I'm fer St. Louie!"

"Well then, you'd better have eleven dollars and forty-five cents, young man."

"Har y'ar. Twelve dallars. Ya'owe'me three-quatters-'n'-a-dime," he said, shoving the money in her hand while looking shifty as all get-out.

"She does not!" I stepped up from behind. "Mrs. Captain, you owe him exactly two quarters and a nickel."

The boy turned to glare at me. "Naw, thar! Who're you t'be bustin' in? Why, yer a *girl*, y'are!"

"Why, yes she is, my good young Sir!" said Mrs. Captain. "She's also my first engineer."

"Ahh, a fancy young lay-dee y'ar . . . ," he growled.

I was scared down-deep, but then I looked at Mrs. Captain, and thought of all her goodnesses, and decided to be brave up-shallow, for her sake. I stepped in between them, and faced him eye to eye.

He growled again. "I tell yer once an' once't only, yer fancy Miss . . . keep clear o' what yer don' unnerstand."

"Oh, I understand good and well what you're trying to do. You're trying to run off with thirty cents that don't belong to you. Now, you can give the captain another six nickels and get 'three-quatters-'n'-a-dime' back *or* you can take two quarters and a nickel, like I said. It's your choice."

"Har naw, I've got plenny more choices 'an that . . ."

He had that look in his eye that a dog gets when it's itching to bite.

"You most certainly do," I told him. "You can give her another quarter plus two dimes and get a dollar back. *Or,* you can give her another five dollars and get fourteen quarters, thirty-eight nickels, and fifteen pennies back.

"You can even give her a fifty-dollar bill—should such a thing exist—and take the seventy-nine quarters, one hundred and thirteen dimes, one hundred and forty-seven nickels, and fifteen pennies she gives you up the Hudson Bay and trade it for twenty-one beavers, forty-two badger-skins, four hundred and forty-one squirrel furs, thirty-seven plugs of tobacco, one bear trap, a double handful of gunpowder, and sixteen eggs!

"You have any number of choices, but at the end of it, you *will* have paid the captain eleven dollars and forty-five cents."

I was red in the face by then, and I was almost seeing red, too. He, on the other hand, had turned almost white. He went to mope back at the end of the line, but before he did, he looked at Mrs. Captain sideways.

"Freak," he called her, under his breath.

The next boy answered politely and paid his fare exact, down to the penny. And the next one did the same, and the next one, too. All except for an exceptional-ragged one with no shoes and a bruise across one eye. He turned his pockets inside out for Mrs. Captain, who looked at me sideways.

I quickly counted up what he had and spit out a ticket-price for less than half of it. We let him keep his rabbit's foot, slingshot, and what looked like some kind of hairball, which he'd also offered up. He paid his money and jumped up on board, then ran across the deck to pet the piglets.

Just before we pulled up the gangplank, that first boy came

'round again, acting sheepish. He paid his eleven dollars and forty-five cents exactly, and kept his head down while he did.

Mrs. Captain nodded at him, and even said, "Welcome aboard, young Sir."

I was still hot about it, and all set to grumble, when she reminded me: "It doesn't cost anything to be kind, Chickie. Just because he's mean, doesn't mean we have to be. For all we know, he's got a hard road ahead of him, and we're the last piece of kindness on it."

I knew she was right, and even felt a bit ashamed after I remembered that I, myself, still owed her that twenty-five cents.

After we had shoved off and given Robert Fulton his afternoon feeding, we went up to the pilothouse, where I counted up the money, sorted the bills, and bundled up the change.

"Mrs. Captain," I asked her, "how do you decide on the prices for these tickets?"

"Oh, that's easy to answer. One of the Orgill Brothers and Company established 1837 down in Memphis has a son who is a fine accountant—*Obadiah* is his name. He sat down with me and worked out the exact prices based on five cents a mile. I've memorized each one of those numbers until I can spout them off front and back. Oh, he's a fine boy, that Obadiah, I do hope he's thriving up there in Chicago . . ."

"When was this, that you set the prices?" I asked her.

"Let's see then . . . seven years ago? Or was it seventeen? Some time, but I still know those numbers by heart, there was a little song he came up with to help me learn 'em . . . as I recall . . ."

"And you haven't increased your prices since then?"

"No, I stick to them numbers Obadiah gave me. He's a good, smart, capable boy!"

"Do you think you could raise prices to the nearest dollar? Just make an eleven-dollars-and-forty-five-cent ticket into costing twelve dollars even? That would simplify it some."

"And stop using those numbers that Obadiah worked so hard on? Well, never! He figured them just for me, it took him the better part of a week to map it all out. No, I'll keep them in service just as they are, and he'll be proud to see it when we meet again."

I wanted to keep arguing, but I also knew nothing would come of it. She'd decided, and she had her reasons.

I still wanted to fix things up for her my way, but it was because I cared for her, that's all. When you care for someone, you want to make everything just so for them, you can't help it. It's part of the caring, I suppose.

We finished up our tasks for the day, and I said no more about it.

–Questions and Answers–

It was only after we had eaten our fill of dried meat and hardtack and a whole host of other good things from the basket, that I remembered to pass on the Racoon Man's invitation to Mrs. Captain.

"Oh! I am to tell you that Mr. Thomas the Racoon Man wishes to cordially invite you for a lemonade the next time you come into port at Rock Island."

"He said that, did he?" She was all-a-fluster. "Did he say that? Or did he say *Well, it is nice to drink a lemonade now and again, a person ought to try one sometime*?"

"No, Mrs. Captain, he was talking about you. An invitation from *him,* to *you.*"

She colored up bright red. "Are you sure? Perhaps he said *Drinking a lemonade all by myself is quite a nice thing . . .* Yes, he very well might have said *I do enjoy a lemonade on my own and in my own kitchen.*"

"No! Mrs. Captain, he wants to have a glass of lemonade with *you,* I am sure of it. Likely at the church in Rock Island."

"The church! Oh, who would think of such a thing? You must have heard wrong, Chickie."

"Of course I *heard* him! He specifically said the church, because he's not much for the saloon."

"Well, that puts an end to the matter! That church doesn't want the likes of me in it." Mrs. Captain folded her arms and let out a big *Harrumph.*

"A glass of lemonade, at a Sunday Social on the lawn? Anybody's welcome to that."

"Not *any* body, Chickie. Not *this* body."

"Well, that's a shame," I said, and I meant it. "It's too bad for you to miss out on a nice afternoon just because you're too stubborn to go to services," I told her.

"Oh, Chickie, you are just a little chick, aren't you? Not hatched enough to have seen the meanness of the world yet. When you do, I hope you'll not add to it."

Then I asked her, to the point: "Mrs. Captain: Are you a Mormon?"

She laughed until she more-than-laughed, holding her belly with both hands like she was going to chuckle herself in two.

"No . . . no . . . oh, goodness . . . *that's* what you thought I meant?"

"I've known church-people who think Mormons aren't any good, and wouldn't have them, that's all."

Mrs. Captain nodded. "Church doesn't always bring out the best in people, Chickie, it's true. You wouldn't think it, but it's true."

"My morfar says people mainly go to church to see who's not there."

She laughed again. "You're for-mare sounds like a wise man . . . My own parents looked religion up and down, tried out the options, and settled on being Millerite."

"What's a 'Millerite'?" I asked her.

"Oh, dear, you haven't heard of us, then? Oh, my . . . A Millerite is a follower of William Miller. 'Billy Miller' as my parents called him. Studied the Bible, he did—studied it until his eyes crossed over.

"The Book of David, especially—he was like a dog with a bone on that Book of David, drug it around and gnawed on it and worried it and buried it and dug it up again for years upon years. Found a bunch of stuff in there that nobody had ever noticed before, not in the two-thousand-odd years of saints and sinners puzzling on it before him.

"*Jesus is coming back again,* he told us, *so you better get ready*. Well, everybody says that, but old Billy Miller, he knew *when*, *where*, and *how*.

"First, we're gonna see a big ol' bright spot in the sky, and then we'll hear a host of trumpets blast out. Then us Millerites are gonna be sucked up to Heaven and good luck to the rest of you left down here behind on this weary world.

"Yes, it'll be quite a thing, I assure you. And that Billy Miller, he knows the exact day—calculated it using the Book of Daniel—right out of the Bible itself. Chickie, do you want to know what day the world is going to end?"

I nodded.

"October twenty-second, 1844."

"But . . ."

"That's the day. That's the day I go to Glory. I believe it and I know it. I know it like I know my own name."

"But Mrs. Captain . . ."

"Chickie, don't you say a word against it. Don't let the Devil dance on your tongue. Better to cut it out, says Billy Miller!"

"Mrs. Captain, wait!"

"Well, what is it, Chickie?"

"Mrs. Captain . . . it's 1846."

"Who told you *that*?"

"Well, everyone. I mean, everybody knows it."

"Oh, ho! Not us Millerites. We know better, we do."

"What?"

"Well, when the world didn't end on October twenty-second, 1844, the only thing it could've meant, was that it *wasn't* 1844 after all!"

"You mean Billy Miller got it wrong?"

"No! Heavens no! Why, it's obvious that the whole rest of the world got it wrong!"

"Now I know you're funning me . . ."

"Funning you? Far from it, Chickie! Why, we put on white robes and climbed up into trees to be part-way ascended in advance. Sure, it was a bit of a blow when the big day came and went and nothing happened, but the idea was right, even if the number was wrong. You see, Billy Miller forgot to remember that October twenty-second, 1844 wasn't going to *be* on October twenty-second, 1844, that year."

"So where are your ma and pa now, Mrs. Captain?"

"I don't rightly know, it's been so many years. We lost touch after they threw me out. But wherever they are, I'm sure they're still itching for the world to bust apart. Once Billy Miller tells them when October twenty-second, 1844, will finally be, they'll be counting down the days like waiting for Christmas."

We stood together, listening to the *Slap, slap, slap* of the paddle wheel.

"Mrs. Captain, if October twenty-second, 1844, turns out to be today, there's no place I'd rather be for the end of the world, than floating down the Mississippi River."

"Same, Chickie. Same here."

Reee! Reee! Reee!

We jumped, then laughed. From behind us, the piglets had all begun squealing their hearts out.

Maybe it was because that raggedy boy had found some turnip tops to share. Or maybe it was because they agreed that

109

there is no better place on Earth than aboard the *Galenian,* and felt the need to say so.

–Good Luck and Farewell–

"We're coming to the end of the line, Chickie—no, it's the *beginning* of the line for you. Tomorrow we'll put into Fort Edwards and you'll meet your auntie and uncle," Mrs. Captain said to me, as we were turning in for the night.

"Like I said before, my dear Chickie, they are lucky to be getting the help of such a brave and smart girl as you."

"I'm awfully sad to leave you, Mrs. Captain. Who's going to help you sell tickets when I'm gone? I just hate to think of those boys cheating you out of the fare."

"Now, Chickie, you're not to worry about me. I've been on the river a long time, and a nickel here and there ain't going to ruin me. If there's cheating to be done, I'd rather be the one getting cheated than the one doing the cheating. That's just who I am. That's who I want to be."

"*It doesn't cost anything to be kind*—somebody once told me that," I said to her.

"That's exactly it, Chickie. We don't know what that boy had to do to get a nickel into his pocket, and we don't know how long he needs to make it last. They don't have an easy life, those boys, and I'm not going to make it harder while they're aboard the *Galenian.*"

Mrs. Captain had a good soul. Maybe a better soul than mine. I saw the whole thing in black and white, like Ma would've, while Mrs. Captain saw it in past, present, and future. She could see the person in front of her, how they got to her, and where they might have to go next.

Then she added: "I also know what it's like to leave a place where there's no one begging you to stay."

And that's the thing about Mrs. Captain: there was something sad in her past, I could tell—some kind of problem, bigger than I could understand or solve. So I said what I felt, because that's all you can do in situations like that.

"Well, I am glad you're here now, Mrs. Captain, and I am mighty glad to be the one with you."

"Oh, me too, Chickie, me too. And you just know that if you ever need me, you can find me on the Mississippi River. Somewhere in the thousand-mile stretch between Dubuque and New Orleans, to be precise!"

She sat up and stretched both arms towards the ceiling, then leaned over. "I'm blowing out the lamp—ready?—we'd both best get some rest before tomorrow."

I lay still in the darkness, thinking to stay awake and feel the waves a while, to better remember the *Galenian* by, but I didn't last long. I slept hard and don't remember dreaming of anything.

The next morning was the last morning of my life when the sun got up before I did.

A bit past noon, I spotted the little tugboat up ahead, ready to take on the ore so that we could put into Fort Edwards. I ran up the ladder to Mrs. Captain and asked her, "Can I untie the barges this time? I want to try, and I think I can."

"You want to cast off? Well, what a bright, eager girl you are. And you can swim, can you?"

"Yes, I can. I can swim real well, Mrs. Captain."

"All right, Chickie, we'll chance it. Swim out and jump on, just like you've seen me do. You can't miss the knot—it's a wagoner's hitch with a butterfly loop on it—just grab the dolly on top and give a pull. Captain Kirby'll be there to catch 'em and tie 'em up right."

"Got it!" I told her.

I tied up my skirt and dove off the side of the boat, into the Mississippi. I felt that magic instant when you go from being all-dry to being all-wet. Then you're sliding through the water. You breathe out as you glide, then let yourself bob up for air, then push back down again.

The water was so warm, it surprised me. There's two kinds of lakes up North: frozen, and almost-frozen. The icy water punches you in the chest when you dive in, and you come back up gasping for air. The warm water of the Mississippi made me feel like I could stay under forever.

After I felt my hands bump up against the side of a barge, I hoisted on, and ran for the knot. I undid one barge, then jumped to the next, just as I'd seen Mrs. Captain do, back before Rock Island. I dove off of the last barge just before impact, and swam back to the side of the *Galenian* in one breath.

Mrs. Captain stuck out her hand and hauled me up onto the deck. She told me for the hundredth time what a good, smart, strong, capable girl I was, and by then I almost thought so, too.

When Fort Edwards appeared, I could see Army buildings and stables and a main street with stores and houses all around.

It wasn't as big as Fort Snelling, but it was a thousand times bigger than Rock Island.

"Well, Chickie, looks like we're here!" Mrs. Captain clapped me on the back. "Time to start putting the *Galenian* into shore," she said, then added, "*Fare-thee-well*, little one!" She hugged me, and ran off towards the rudder.

There was a crowd waiting on the dock: people either wanting to get on or wanting somebody to get off. Towards the back of the crowd stood a girl who was about my height with curly yellow hair and a plain blue dress on. She was looking up and down the length of the boat.

"Mary Jane!" she was hollering all around, this way and that. "Mary Jane! Mary Jane!"

I waved both arms but she didn't see me, and then I lost sight of her in the milling mob.

I jumped down the gangplank, and dove into the crowd, searching around for her, this way and that, while at the same time, looking back, trying to find Mrs. Captain so I could wave a last *Goodbye*. I was about to give up, when suddenly, standing right in front of me was a girl about my height, with curly yellow hair and a blue dress on.

"*I'm* Mary Jane!" I said to her.

"Oh, yes." She smiled and slipped her arm through mine. She gave it a little squeeze and added, "Yes, you are. Welcome home."

I took my next step, and stumbled. The ground felt way too solid under my feet, too fixed and there-to-stay. It would take me some time to get used to not being on the river.

I turned for one last look at the *Galenian* and found Mrs. Captain standing proud next to the paddle wheel, ready to welcome everybody aboard, whether they deserved it or not. I raised one hand in the air, and waved it back and forth.

When I was sure she'd spotted me, I yelled out—loud and clear—"Thank you, Robert Fulton!"

CHAPTER X

–Friends and Relatives–

When I looked closer at the girl by my side, I saw that her hair was duller than I first noticed, and that her dress was clean, but thin and worn. Her arm through mine was strong, however, and not at all bony.

"I'm glad you're finally here," she told me. "I've been meeting every steamboat, hoping to find you. They said you'd be on the *Minnesota Belle,* but there's no such boat comes into Fort Edwards."

"Thank you, then, for waiting . . . Say, which of my cousins are you?"

"I'm not your cousin," she told me, plain and simple. "I am your friend."

She led me away from the dock, past the ticket-sellers, past the Army recruiters, and past the porters who'd offer to carry your bags for money, until I found myself standing, face to face, with . . . a pair of knees.

I looked up and saw the biggest horse on Earth! Bigger than any I'd seen before and bigger than any I've seen since. The biggest horse that God ever made, I'll wager.

I reached up to pet his muzzle—for he had kind, soft eyes—when another muzzle pushed me back. There, standing next to him, was the second-biggest horse that God ever made.

"Oh, now, be nice . . ." The girl took the mare by her bridle. "This is Mary Jane. She's going to be our friend."

The mare pushed her nose against my chest. I felt her two nostrils suck in a deep breath, smelling me all through. She blew the air back out in a long shudder and swung her great head away from me. I could tell by the way she held her ears that I'd passed the test.

The bigger horse, having got the go-ahead, brought his head down and I wrapped my arm around his neck and stroked his muzzle, the way a horse likes you to.

"This is Samson and Delilah," the girl told me. "Samson loves everybody, but Delilah only likes people who love Samson." She laughed and I laughed, too, because aren't horses funny, each in their own way?

"They've worked together, side by side, since before I was a baby. Delilah is the boss, aren't you, Delilah?"

Delilah nickered as an answer. Darned if she wasn't one of those horses who can understand every word you say.

"They're Clydesdales. Have you ever seen a Clydesdale before, Mary Jane?" she asked me.

I shook my head *No*.

"Cold-bloods, they are," she explained. "Clydesdales can pull up whole stumps, and break rocks. But these two, they *haul*. They could drag the sun itself if you could only get a rope around it."

One look at Samson and you'd believe it, plus there was Delilah to boot. The two of them put together added up to one dinosaur, more or less.

"And Delilah, she's the one who keeps Samson sound, she's so smart. If the load's unbalanced, or the wheels aren't greased right, she won't budge until it's fixed. When Samson gets a rock stuck in his shoe, it's her who stops, not him. The way she fusses over him, you wouldn't believe!"

I could tell Samson was one of those who would work himself to death just to please you, and I was glad he had Delilah making sure it could never happen.

"So, these two are Samson and Delilah, and I'm Mary Jane, and your name is . . . ?" I asked her.

"Oh, me? I'm the Schmidt Girl."

An older boy stepped up beside us, with a pail of water for Delilah. And wasn't he tall? And broad, too.

"Oh, *Hello*!" I said to him, "You must be the Schmidt Boy."

He gave me a nod that meant *Yes*. And that was the closest the Schmidt Boy ever came to conversing with me.

"Yes, that's my brother," said the Schmidt Girl. "And up driving, is my father, Father Schmidt. And sat next to him, is my mother . . ."

"Mother Schmidt?"

"Of course! We're the Schmidts, and there aren't any others, at least not since everybody loaded up and started West."

"Climb up now, girls. It's time to go," said Mother Schmidt.

Father Schmidt took up the traces and whistled. Next thing I knew, I was sat in between the Schmidt Boy and the Schmidt Girl, rolling along in a wagon that only Samson could pull. It was double-long and iron-framed, and must have weighed near as much as the *Galenian*—but Samson pulled it as if it was a pillowcase full of feathers.

I turned to the Schmidt Girl, and told her, "I'd still like to know your first name."

"My Christian name? It's *Margaret*."

"*Margaret!* Oh, how wonderful! Queen Margaret was the grandmother of the Queen Mary who I'm named for! Well, one of them anyway, because Mary Jane is actually two names for two queens . . ."

I was just done telling her about how Queen Jane got blamed for Wyatt's Rebellion in 1554 and about to launch into how Mary Queen of Scots might have killed Darnley in 1567, when we turned off of the main road, onto two dusty ruts, and a house came into view.

It was a wooden cabin, simple and handsome, but forgotten-looking. It didn't have a cow for the barn, nor a hen for the coop, nor vegetables in the garden, nor anything. One lonesome house smack-dab in the middle of nothing, with no signs of life anywhere.

That is, until Aunt Evelyn came running out with her arms spread open wide.

-A Full Basket for an Empty Pantry-

I didn't recognize Aunt Evelyn by her looks, that's for sure. She was as tall as Ma is short, and as thin as Ma is stocky. No, I recognized her by what she said.

"Oh, *my heart*! My *heart*!—Oh, look at you—oh, you're *here*—here you *are*!"

She wrapped me in her arms and rocked me back and forth, shedding tears of happiness. A person can't help but be glad to see someone who is that glad to see you, but I have to admit that I could hardly hug her for the bones. Under that loose dress, her ribs stuck out like a wash-board, I was sure.

"Girls! Girls!" she yelled back towards the house, then to me: "I'll go and fetch your cousins . . . they'll be so happy to see you!"

While we waited, Mother Schmidt handed me down a huge basket. "This is for you and your family, and may it preserve you all," she said to me.

"A welcome present? You are too kind . . . ," I told her.

Mother Schmidt looked at me, and I saw worry on her face. "I'll pray for you," she added, and nodded at Father Schmidt to signal their leaving.

As Delilah turned Samson back towards home, Margaret said to me:

"Mary Jane, I'll be back on Saturday. You keep well in the meantime, won't you?"

"Of course, Margaret. It sure is nice to have a friend already made when you land in a new place."

She gave my arm one last squeeze and climbed up. Delilah whinnied, and Samson began to pull.

Aunt Evelyn came running a second time. "Thank you, Father Schmidt! Thank you, Mother Schmidt! Thank you so much!" Margaret turned and waved, and Father Schmidt held up one hand to say *Farewell.*

Two shy girls came out of the house, holding hands. One was tall and blond, the other short and brunette, and both nearly as skinny as their ma.

"Susan, Joanna . . . this is your cousin, Mary Jane." Aunt Evelyn introduced us, smiling all around.

"*Hello*, Mary Jane," said Susan, and smiled a little. Joanna said nothing—one of her hands was in front of her face—but I saw hopeful eyes behind her dark bangs.

"*Hello*, Susan. *Hello*, Joanna." I was glad to meet them. I'd never had sisters, and girl-cousins are the next best thing.

I handed the basket to Aunt Evelyn. "The Schmidts are such big-hearted people . . . I thank Heaven for them every day," she told us.

We went 'round the house, and into the pantry, to put the things away. When I opened the cupboards, I saw that they were empty. And when I say *empty* I don't mean *not much*, I mean *empty.* There wasn't a half-jar of molasses, or a tin of baking powder, or a sprig of rosemary. There was *no-thing.*

"Aunt Evelyn, your supplies are very low!" I said to her. "But don't worry, tomorrow you can give me some money and I'll go into town and stock us up."

Aunt Evelyn said, "Well, you sweetheart, you! Wouldn't that be nice, if you could." Her voice was cheerful, but her eyes were sad.

Wasn't there a strange mish-mash of things in that basket Mother Schmidt had given us? One sack of oats and another of flour. Twenty-three eggs and a peck of green beans. A hunk of lard and a bag of salt. A darning needle and some thread.

I wouldn't have packed a welcome basket that way, all full of practical things only. I'd have thrown in a couple of lemon drops, at least. But Aunt Evelyn was moved to tears:

"The Schmidts and their generous nature. It goes right to my heart, every time," she said, dabbing at one eye.

At the bottom of the basket, I found a slip of paper with words written on it:

Feast upon the words of Christ, for behold, the words of Christ will tell you all things what ye should do. 2 Nephi 32:3

"What is this?" I asked Aunt Evelyn.

"Oh, that's a verse from their Bible. A little odd, but it does speak to the heart. They are Mormons, you know."

"Mormons!" I said, and nearly dropped the empty basket.

If that wasn't something. I hadn't been gone a week from Pastor Martin and I'd already crossed paths with real, actual Mormons, and even made friends with one of them.

Aunt Evelyn took me 'round to the front. "I'll show you the house now," she said, opening the carved oak door.

Theirs was a log cabin, of good size and so well built. The heavy front door hung sturdy on its hinges, and a fine set of hickory panels lined the walls. But just like the pantry, those rooms were empty.

I didn't see a butter churn, or a spinning wheel, or a laundry barrel, or any of the things I thought every house had. Except for a table for eating and a bench for sitting, the place was bare. The more Aunt Evelyn showed me around, the less I saw.

When I had seen what there was to not-see, she led me down the hall, towards the main room with the fireplace.

"You'll meet your uncle George now, Mary Jane. He's been looking forward to this for weeks—he mentions it every day. Oh, my, won't his heart be joyful to see that you've finally come?"

-Meeting Uncle George-

Whatever had happened to Uncle George, he probably shouldn't have lived through it.

He was sat in a kind of flattened-out chair and the right side of his head was caved in, smashed like a dropped egg. One whole side of his body was no good: it hung off his skeleton like a suit of clothes on a hook.

When he saw me, he hollered and blubbered and stomped one foot—trying to stand?

"George, Dear Heart, here she is!" said Aunt Evelyn, her voice just as sweet as anything. "That's right, it's our niece, Mary Jane—Ida's girl, come to lend us a hand."

"Uh . . . *Hello*, Uncle George."

Uncle George bellowed and a wad of froth came out of his mouth—trying to talk?

"Oh, yes! Dear Heart, she *is* a treasure, I quite agree!"

Aunt Evelyn bent down and wiped the drool from his chin, and he went on gaping and making barking sounds.

"I know, Dear Heart—she has grown and is a baby no more, just like our girls . . . you're very right, it *is* a wonder to see her so tall and fine."

Aunt Evelyn stroked his cheek and pushed the hair out of his eyes. She murmured now and then as he whooped and bawled, as if they were talking back and forth. After a bit, he flopped back in his chair, having worn himself out. She wiped his chin again, and then his nose, too.

I thought he was frightful. I thought she'd gone batty. I thought a lot of things that day, but only because of things I didn't know. I didn't know how deep and strong and true the love between two people can be.

Aunt Evelyn leaned in to him and said, "That's right, Dear Heart, I'll show Mary Jane the girls' room and get her settled. You can visit with her tomorrow, after you're both rested up."

We left Uncle George and went to the nook where Susan and Joanna slept at night in a cozy wooden bed built into the wall. Aunt Evelyn pulled a ladder-like thing out from under, and it unfolded into its own little cot. *What a clever invention,* I thought, as she unrolled a mattress ticking and laid a quilt for me.

I untied my bundle and gave her the tin kettle with the medical supplies inside. "Ma sent this with me."

Aunt Evelyn's eyes shone like I had just handed her a purse full of diamonds. "Oh, how I've missed having one of these!" she said, holding it up to the window. "Well, we'll use it tomorrow— and every day." She hugged it to her like a little girl with a new dolly. I never saw someone get so excited about a dented old tea-kettle.

Then she opened the top, took out the medicine, and placed it on a shelf. "Your mother has such a talent for healing—she always has. She puts her whole heart into it, I know." She sighed. "I do wish she was here to look at Uncle George. I know she'd have him all fixed up and back to himself again in no time."

Now, Ma is a force of nature and I'm the first to admit it, but there are a few things she can't do, and one of them is to un-dent somebody's head.

"Put your things down under your bed, and make yourself at home, for you *are* home when you are here," she said, and turned to go. "My heart's telling me that your uncle George needs me just now."

My "things" amounted to three silk dresses, a bad ten-dollar bill, and *A Child's History of England,* and I would have been hard-pressed to tell you which was going to be the most useless there at Aunt Evelyn's. Then I remembered the jar of sour-cherry preserves, with the letter to me from Miss Frances wrapped around it. I wasn't in terrible want of any of those things—at least not yet—so I slid the bundle under my bed and got started forgetting all about it.

I went back to join the family, but on my way, I peeked into what turned out to be . . . a water closet! Built right into the house was a little room for a person to get cleaned up, maybe after doing your business, so to speak. A mirror hung above the commode, with hearts carved all around its wooden frame, and a lump of plain soap on its shelf. I saw my own reflection in the glass.

I don't look half-bad, I thought to myself. *A little more grown, and a lot more adventuresome, than the last time I looked in a mirror.*

In the family room, I found Aunt Evelyn crouched next to the stove, blowing on some embers. My two cousins were standing next to her and watching.

"Mary Jane, I am just making some oat-mush, and I think I could split four bowls into five . . . will you have any?" she asked me in between breaths.

"Oh, goodness, Aunt Evelyn! I ate up everything Mrs. Captain had before I got off the *Galenian,* for she was to take on more supplies at Fort Edwards, of course. A whole string of sausages, I must have eaten, and let's see . . . half a cheese wheel, and a pint of strawberry preserves . . ."

I stopped when I saw the eyes of the girls, who were looking at me like I had just described having rode into town on a unicorn. Something so fantastic, you're afraid to believe it could be true. But more than that, sad that it wasn't you.

I looked into the pot and saw barely enough oats to be worth stirring. Back at the Forks, I wouldn't have bothered shaking that much out of the bottom of the sack.

"Well, if you're sure . . . ," Aunt Evelyn asked me again. "You've traveled so far today, sweetheart . . ."

"Yes, I'm sure," I told her. "I'm not hungry."

It wasn't the last time I would say those three words to Aunt Evelyn, but it was the last time that I would say them and actually mean it.

–Ida's Daughter–

"Mary Jane, will you come over here and sit with me a minute before you go off to bed?" Aunt Evelyn asked me, and I did.

"You *are* Ida's daughter, I can see it in you." She ran her hand under my chin. "We were so glad when we got the letter that you were coming, my dear. I thought . . . I thought at first that Ida might come herself, but of course Morfar needs someone to take care of him."

Was Morfar as old as that? I asked myself, surprised by her words, and had to answer *Yes,* though I didn't want to.

"But you're here now, Mary Jane, and aren't we glad to have you? It will be good for the girls to have a cousin they can lean on, and look up to—and they will, just give them a little time. I fear these past months have been hardest on them, even harder than they have been on me and George . . . yes, Dear Heart, that's you."

Uncle George had begun to grunt when he heard his name. She paused to wipe his face, then continued:

"Those girls need their mother, but George needs me so much right now that I've had to leave them to themselves, and for too long. By now, they're both downright heart-sick, but it's not how they are naturally. Two better-spirited girls you couldn't imagine—except for including *you* of course, for you are their cousin after all.

"I've been trying to hold us together but it seems more than I can do. The Schmidts send a basket every Saturday—and we did have a visit from George's old sergeant, from when he was at Fort Edwards all those years ago—don't you remember how glad we were to see him, Dear Heart?"

Uncle George grunted again.

"And I am grateful, you know, but it's all too much to do, and the girls, well, I'm afraid they suffer, and harden, and I hate to think of it. And I've tried to find a way . . . but I can't seem to sleep well when I do sleep, and I just . . ." I thought she would begin to cry just then, she seemed so nervous about so many things, and just worn out in general.

"I can help, Aunt Evelyn. You just tell me what you need," I said, and took her hand.

"Oh, Mary Jane, there's so much of my sister in you." She wrapped me in another long hug, so close that I could feel her heart fluttering inside its cage of poked-out ribs, and let her cry a little.

"Perhaps you could sit with George now and then, for he does need some tending, and talking to, and being with . . . don't you, Dear Heart?" She turned to her husband. "And I know *you* will enjoy getting to know your niece, won't you?"

She turned back to me. "Then I could be with the girls more, and get the house in shape, and maybe even plant a garden before summer hits . . . Mother Schmidt sent us some seeds, they must be around here somewhere.

"What do you think, Mary Jane? It won't be forever, just until George is well enough and strong enough again to go back to work, to be his old self again . . . For that's your plan, isn't it, Dear Heart? Of course it is! Why, we still have your carpenter's tools . . . they are out for loan, but just for loan, until you can use them again."

I looked at Uncle George. He couldn't speak or walk or look you in the eye like he knew what you were talking about. He was nodding off in his chair, but his legs jerked him awake every few seconds. Aunt Evelyn took the pillow from her own cot and arranged it under his knees. That calmed him, and he was soon sleeping peacefully.

I watched as she kissed his forehead and told him *Goodnight:* "You sleep now, Dear Heart. You'll be stronger tomorrow, I believe it. And I'll be here, right beside you, as I always will."

–Making Do–

The next day I woke up and started drinking coffee for real. It was the only thing that I let myself have more than my fair share of. I knew I had to keep going at all costs after I heard the full story.

Six weeks after Uncle George got hurt, they sold the wedding china, and the two silver candlesticks, and such-like. Six weeks after that, they sold the horse and cart, and the piglets with their sow, and so on. Six weeks after that, Aunt Evelyn wrote to Ma.

In the time between her writing that letter and me getting here, they'd sold the flowers from the garden, and the barbed wire from the fence-posts, and the Schmidts had started bringing them baskets on Saturday. They didn't have anything to spare, and yet they did.

I already knew how it was to want things you don't need, like a lace collar or a fountain pen, but I had to learn how to live in want of the things you do need, which is a different way of life altogether. Turns out it's all about the numbers. *When you know the numbers, then you know some-ting,* as Morfar would say. It goes like this:

Thirty apples in the basket, twelve big and eighteen little. Twelve big for Uncle George, boiled and mushed. Eighteen little between the girls and Aunt Evelyn is one per day, skip Friday and two on Saturday night, and I can eat Uncle George's peels. Thirty cores to ferment for vinegar, one to set aside for Samson when he comes. Delilah will understand why there's not one for her, and her eyes will say "It's all right, no need to say Sorry."

Then you do the same with the eggs. And the nuts. And everything else. All this to say I made do. It's true, we didn't have much, but somehow, we had enough, and after all, we were a family.

And in the end, we were lucky. The rain came down and the sun came up. The beans sprouted, the cheese didn't mold, the roof held, my traps were full, and we got a new basket every week.

We did what we did, and we kept doing it. We didn't give up on each other, and we didn't give up on ourselves. And with every day that passed, making do got a wee little bit easier.

CHAPTER XI

–Two Queens and a Rabbit–

One morning, I found a baby rabbit trapped, but still alive, in one of my snares. I decided to bring it home for a pet, as a bunny can live on plain grass, if it has to. Aunt Evelyn had had to give away their shepherd-dog, as they couldn't spare enough to feed him, and it had shattered Joanna's heart—is how she put it to me.

The afternoon was sunny, so we sat outside and I French-braided Susan's hair while Joanna sketched *Mr. Hare-ington* using a piece of charcoal.

"Do either of you know who Queen Joanna was?" I asked them in the voice Miss Frances used in the classroom at Fort Snelling.

"No, who was she?" asked Susan.

"Just the cleverest queen that Spain ever had, that's all."

"She was?" Joanna looked up.

"Why, of course," I told them. "Queen Joanna could ride a show-horse and knew both French and Latin."

"I bet *I* could learn both French and Latin," said Joanna, "if I ever got the chance, that is." She reached out to re-position Mr. Hare-ington, who had hopped himself out of the light.

"Anyway, when Queen Joanna married in 1496, it was to a king named *Philip the Handsome* . . . honest, that was his real name!"

"Ugh . . . *married*," Joanna scoffed, "I'll never get married. Boys are clumsy and loud . . . I can do without."

"Well, so could Queen Joanna. After Philip the Handsome died in 1506, she was sole-in-charge for forty-nine years."

"That doesn't sound too bad . . . ," said Joanna. She returned to her sketch, and got so taken with it that her hand slipped down from her face. For a moment, I could see the wide, pink scar that runs from her nose to her lip.

"Was there a Queen Susan, too?" Susan naturally wanted to know.

"Almost," I told her. "Her aunt became Queen of France in 1498 . . ."

"Well, isn't that wonderful!" She said it like it was the best news in the world.

"And why is that?" I asked.

"Because having a nice auntie is even better than being a queen." She turned and kissed my cheek, then let me finish tying the end of her braid.

As I looked from one to the other, I felt so proud and tender towards both of my cousins. They're so different, but so love-able, each in their own way.

"Come now, let's go in and see your pa." I stood up, reached out, and took one hand from each into mine. "It'll do his heart good to have a visit from such two good, smart, strong, capable girls," I told them, and we went inside.

–My Family–

Our days had formed a pattern: I'd get up and drink some coffee, then go 'round to check my traps. By the time I got back, Aunt Evelyn had made us all oat-mush for breakfast, and we five ate together. Then she'd spend the morning with the girls while I tended to Uncle George.

In the afternoon, I'd take the girls for some fun while Aunt Evelyn cared for her husband. I taught them cat's-cradle and double-Dutch jump rope, and they picked it right up—Joanna maybe a little quicker than Susan.

Near sun-down, we'd start in on the garden while Aunt Evelyn made the girls their dinner. She'd call them in and feed them, and send them to bed, and stay with them until they were asleep, then she'd call me inside for our evening together. I'd make dinner for her and Uncle George, and after we'd helped him eat, her and me would stay up, quite late sometimes.

For as long as the twilight held, we'd work out a stain, or melt used-up candle butts, or other small work. Some nights she'd ask me to read aloud from the old Andrew Jackson pamphlets in order to give Uncle George something to think about. On other nights we'd sit quietly together and enjoy not being alone.

Staying up with their ma had made me more of an auntie to the girls than a cousin, but that was fine by me. After all, I had been raised by Ma, who was a far sight tougher with me than Aunt Evelyn was her girls. I didn't feel the need to be tough with Susan and Joanna, though. Those girls had things hard enough already.

Instead, we had footraces and caught butterflies and picked wild violets. Every so often they'd want to go in the house and see their pa, and he always opened his eyes and blinked fast when he heard their voices. They'd hug and kiss him just like they had ever done since they were babies, and Aunt Evelyn was right: it did your heart good to see it. I even got so I could tell his moods and him mine, and we became friends, of a sort.

It was the first full, proper family that I'd ever been a part of, with something like a mother and father and sisters and all the usual things, and it didn't take long for me to love being in it. Aunt Evelyn mothered me, and Susan and Joanna looked to me for encouragement, and we all took care of Uncle George.

My family needed me, and while I was there for them, I came to realize how much I needed them. I never once wished I was back at Fort Snelling, though I would have had plenty to eat up there, and a lot less work to do.

Maybe a person needs family even more than she needs food, when it comes right down to it. It sure feels that way to me.

–Unbelievers–

"See how well the seeds your mother gave us have taken? They popped up on a Wednesday after planting on Saturday. Think of it: green beans sprouting after only three days in the ground . . . ," I said to Margaret as we were putting up strings for them to climb.

"Three days is usual, Mary Jane. Haven't you ever done green beans before?"

"Of course I have!" I told her. "But up North we wait at least a week for them to show."

"Then you'll be glad to know that here you can have sweet corn, and summer squash, and even tomatoes ripe and ready all before the Fourth of July . . . and be just bursting with spinach in June . . . which you already are, by the way, in rhubarb," Margaret said, pointing to the overflowing patch.

"And we'll eat every bit of it, I promise you. It's already stopped the girls' gums bleeding."

We'd gotten to be the best of friends, Margaret and me. Father Schmidt would drop her off every Saturday to deliver us a full basket and collect the empty one. Then, he'd go into Fort Edwards and unload whatever Samson had been hauling that week, giving us a whole afternoon together before he came to pick her up.

"You'll see, Margaret," I told her. "I am going to fatten my family back up to where they should be."

"You'll need more than a garden for that, Mary Jane."

"I've got big plans," I said, pointing across the field. "I'll pickle those cucumbers, and dry the peas . . . roast the sunflowers' seeds . . . There's going to be radishes and onions and Swiss chard like you won't believe—enough to sell the extra—and watermelons, too. I keep the skin of every animal I snare, so I can sell them to folks traveling north. With the money that comes in, I'll get a cow and feed her on those pumpkins, which gives a golden cream that sells very dear . . ."

She didn't look at all convinced.

"I do know we can't stay here forever, Margaret, but Aunt Evelyn needs more time. She's convinced herself that Uncle George can be his old self again, and I must say, if it was love that could make it so, he'd be fit as a fiddle right now."

"Your aunt sounds like a good woman. And Father has always said that your uncle is a *good* man."

"And it's my job to take care of them. Once I get everyone strong enough to travel, and Aunt Evelyn eased enough to reason with, I'll write to Ma and move us all up North. I know that if I can just get them to her, she'll sort out the rest."

"I'm relieved to hear it, Mary Jane," she said.

"Trust me, everything's going to be f—"

Dizziness hit me hard just then, as I was in one of my fevers that day. I didn't faint, just sort of crumpled towards the ground, as Margaret went to catch me.

"I'm all right, I just need to let my head settle a bit," I told her. "There's no need to worry."

"I *do* worry about you. My whole family worries about you." Margaret was upset, I could tell; she had even started to cry.

"Margaret, there's nothing to cry over, this comes and goes— I'll be fine in a minute or two."

"But . . . it's more than that, Mary Jane."

"Well then, what is it?"

"It's that you're all . . . *unbelievers*! We think about the peril you are in with the end of days so near. You won't be kept together after the seventh day . . . it's just horrible what is waiting for you all."

She was genuine-crying by now. It was a frustrated, angry crying, as if there was something unfair about it all.

I took her hands in my own. "But we *do* believe—well, I know Ma definitely does, and Aunt Evelyn does—they read the Bible every day—Ma's got most of it memorized, for Heaven's sake. All three of us girls have been to church plenty . . . also, come now, the world's not going to end—not anytime soon, anyway."

"Oh, but the end *is* near, Mary Jane! All the signs have appeared. Creation can't go on like this, with so much evil in it, and more happening every day. No, the only thing we can do is ready ourselves for the final judgement. And *you* will not be among the saved—do you understand that? It pains me, Mary Jane. Truly, it does." She was deadly serious.

"Now, Margaret, it's not as bad as that. Why, look at all the *good* in the world! From Mrs. Captain, who got me here safe, to Aunt Evelyn and the way she sticks by Uncle George—to you Schmidts, who have kept us going out of nothing *but* goodness! It seems like evil doesn't have a chance against people like you."

"Oh, Mary Jane," Margaret said sadly. "You haven't seen the things we've seen."

We stood together for a moment, and I tried to think of

something cheerful to say. I saw Samson and Delilah in the distance, coming towards us and kicking up the dust of two elephants.

It was her pa, coming to fetch her, as his chore was finished and our day together was over. I put my arm through hers and we walked out to meet the wagon.

I gave Margaret a hug before she climbed up, and I thanked Father Schmidt for bringing her. He nodded at me and whistled to Delilah, who turned the wagon and set Samson moving towards home.

That was the last I saw of them—until the next Saturday, of course, when they came back with another basket, and saved us all over again.

-On the Mend-

Uncle George did get better.

He never got back to being what he had been, but he did get better while I was there. It was a wonderful thing to see. I think I saw it clearest because I didn't know him before, I only knew him now. And nowadays, he was always a little stronger today than yesterday.

Aunt Evelyn, for her part, had never stopped seeing him just as he was when she first laid eyes on him. *It was love at first sight,* she'd tell me, *Cupid's arrow shot me straight through the heart.* She'd take his hand in hers. *Double arrows in both directions, wasn't it, Dear Heart?* and smile so happy at his invisible answer.

They shared a secret language, those two, that went beyond what you could hear from the outside. I wouldn't have believed it at first, but I saw it every day, when I lived there.

One afternoon, me and the girls were sitting in the family room listening to Susan play the piano, which is what we called it when she plunked through her songs on the top of the kitchen table and sang out what it should have sounded like. They'd had to sell their piano early on, Susan said, and she looked so mournful telling me about it, I knew I had to try to make it right somehow.

I heated some tongs in the fire and used them to burn the outline of piano keys onto the wooden table. I fit on thirty-six black and forty-nine white ones, and Susan said that was good enough. She played on it every day after that, and most days more than once. I'm glad I did it, though I've heard all eight verses of "Beautiful Dreamer" in excess of what should be the legal limit.

One afternoon, Susan was just getting to the *Laura-Lee* part, when I heard Aunt Evelyn call out from the corner where Uncle George sat.

"Girls! Girls! See here, girls!" she shouted.

And wasn't Uncle George up and standing on his own two feet? He did have one arm draped over Aunt Evelyn, but he wasn't putting too much weight on her, really. The girls ran to him and hugged him around his waist, and we all cried some happy tears.

Uncle George was standing . . . I could hardly believe it, though I knew it had been Aunt Evelyn's goal all along. She knew he could get there, even if I didn't, and I was mighty glad I had done all she'd told me to.

Today you'll work on his hands, she'd say, *first close his fist for him—like this—and then open it again. Ten times on each hand . . . We've got to keep him moving,* she'd tell me, and I did as she said. He was trying, too, I got so I could see that. We were a team, Aunt Evelyn, Uncle George, and me, and we all did our best.

I didn't expect much at first, but as the weeks went by, he got so he could pinch onto a piece of cloth . . . then hold it up . . . then wave it up and down. After a while more he could turn his head and bring a fork up and down, though that one side of his always did work better than his other.

Aunt Evelyn spent her afternoons working on his legs, but I'd been skeptical about the whole enterprise. When I saw him standing that day, the first thing I did was promise myself never to doubt Aunt Evelyn again.

That evening, when we sat together sewing under the lamplight, wasn't Aunt Evelyn in the best mood I'd ever seen her?

"What a day we've had, Mary Jane! I couldn't ask for a better one. My heart couldn't be more full than it is right now. Mark my words, before winter he'll be able to sit up and whittle—won't you, Dear Heart?" She nudged Uncle George with her elbow, and looked in his eyes, gathering his answer. "Oh, my Dear Heart, I know how you're looking forward to that!"

I had an idea. "How about we ask for his carpentry tools back? It might cheer him to sit in the midst of them—don't you think so, Uncle George?"

I had gotten into the habit of talking to him while we were together, like Aunt Evelyn did. He would kind of answer, and if you knew him well enough, you got to know what he said.

"Oh, yes, Dear Heart, why, you just love the smell of sawdust, don't you?" Aunt Evelyn chimed in. "Why, when he first came home, back before he could open his eyes, I'd bring handfuls of it under his nose, then flowers, and vinegar, or soap, or anything else that might help him know that the world was still here . . . but it was the sawdust that brought you back to me, wasn't it, Dear Heart? Oh, how we both love the smell of sawdust now!" She chucked him under the chin, and smiled at the memory.

"Yes, the future is bright," Aunt Evelyn continued. "Once you can sit up and get back to whittling, Dear Heart, you can take on piece-work, and earn a little. Yes, things are coming back together, and having you here has made all the difference, Mary Jane."

I looked at Uncle George. I knew that he knew something of what was going on, but sitting up and doing a job for pay? That seemed like a stretch.

Then I looked at Aunt Evelyn. I'd learned that there was mighty strong stuff underneath that soft-hearted manner of hers, and also something between the two of them that was beyond what most people can imagine.

So maybe it was a stretch, but that's not the same thing as impossible. Who was I to say?

–My Me–

"Look, Mary Jane! I did it!"

Aunt Evelyn was holding her right hand up in the air, and pointing to it with her left.

"Hooray! Aunt Evelyn—you've got it!"

I'd been teaching her a neat trick: how to thread a needle using only one hand. It's not easy—try it sometime. You hold the spool between your thumb and pinky, and the needle between your two middle fingers. I, myself, can do it without thinking. Kind of a nervous habit, it's become.

We were sitting together by the empty fireplace, and I was scanning Uncle George's old political pamphlets, looking for a topic to bring up with him in the morning. I found something:

"Oh, Aunt Evelyn—see here, what he says further on:

"'Feelings of patriotism only shall direct me; for I am one of those
Old-fashioned men who *dares* to love his country . . .'"

"Ugh, I can't listen to any more about that Andrew Jackson. Put it away." Aunt Evelyn's voice sounded like Ma's for a minute, she was so disgusted.

"You know who was the absolute worst about that Jackson character? Your father, Mary Jane. *Good Old Hickory!*—he'd say—*Now there's a man who isn't afraid to speak his mind!*"

"Really? What else was my pa like?"

It was the clearest detail I'd ever heard about my father—not exactly complimentary, but it did make him out to have been a living, breathing person.

"Your pa would have thrown himself over Niagara Falls in a barrel if Andrew Jackson said to. Why, Morfar always hoped he'd done just that, or such-like, whenever he disappeared."

"You mean when he left Ma, after she got big with me . . ."

"Oh, Mary Jane, your pa did nothing *but* disappear. He was gone from your ma more than he was with her. Yes indeed, he stayed with Ida long enough to get your brother started, then came back long enough to get you started, and then he was gone for good."

She turned to her husband. "Dear Heart, remember how the two of you quarreled?" Then back to me. "It was just awful. They came to blows more than once."

"Sounds like they flat-out hated each other."

"Oh, sweetheart, you're too young to understand. Your pa and my George . . . well . . . they are two very different men."

Oh, I understand. There's "good" men, and then there's Pa, I thought to myself.

Aunt Evelyn kept on: "It goes to show how outlandish your pa was, that he couldn't get along with a good-hearted man like my George." She smoothed Uncle George's hair across his forehead. "Dear Heart, *you* came to Fort Snelling to be a carpenter, not to quarrel with a man like . . ."

"Why did Pa come to Fort Snelling?"

"To be a soldier, of course! But he couldn't be trusted with ammunition—too hot-headed, like I said—so he got tasked with keeping the garden plots. Well, it soon got to being Ida's job, like every other thing they tried to rely on him for.

"Now, my George has worked hard every day of his life—haven't you, Dear Heart?" Uncle George stirred, as he always did when he heard Aunt Evelyn say *Dear Heart.*

"I guess Ma should have never married him," I suggested to her. It wasn't a nice thought, and it didn't make me feel good, but that didn't mean it wasn't true.

"Oh, but she *had* to marry him, Mary Jane, she couldn't help it. She felt it in her *heart.* Nobody—but nobody—can control their heart, and hers was telling her to go to him."

I couldn't help but laugh at the idea of Ma all stars-in-her-eyes over a young man. "Aunt Evelyn, you know as well as I do that Ma's too . . . umm, like she *is* . . . to ever moon over anyone."

"That's not what I mean, Mary Jane. When I say you feel it in your heart, I mean that you *feel* it in your heart, all at once. That big wad of muscle gets worked up and starts pounding inside your chest; you can feel it up to your throat and down to your toes. That clanging you feel is your heart telling you to *go* to somebody."

"But what if your heart tells you the wrong thing?"

"What if it tells you the *right* thing?" She bent over and kissed Uncle George's forehead. "I wasn't there when your ma first saw your pa, but I'll never forget when I first glimpsed my George. We were in the ox-cart, just getting into Fort Snelling, and I saw him with the other tradesmen.

"His eyes, his hair, his square jaw—his smile!—When I saw him smile at me, I felt my heart thumping like it'd break a rib! It beat hard enough to rattle my brain until I didn't know up from down. The only thing I did know was that I had to *go* to him."

She was talking to me, but looking at Uncle George; their eyes were locked like he was remembering, too.

"And didn't I jump off that cart while it was still moving? I jumped with both hands held out. And didn't he drop his tools to catch my hands in his? I just wasn't myself in that moment—I was *more* than myself. It was a big step—no, a *jump*—forwards, towards who I wanted to be."

"That's crazy, Aunt Evelyn! What if he hadn't caught you?"

"There's risk in listening to your heart, Mary Jane—I won't lie to you. There's never any promise it'll turn out perfect, and even when it does, the hard times still come." She lifted Uncle George's head so she could get his pillow just right. "But *promise me* that when you feel your heart go off like mine did, you'll listen to what it's telling you. Lord knows it was the smartest thing I ever did," she said, and kissed him on the cheek this time.

"I will, Aunt Evelyn, but I still hope I don't end up like Ma."

"Oh, now, don't worry too much about that. Your ma was hardened long before she met your pa. She had to be. It's been one thing after another, all her life, since she was a little girl."

Truth be told, I'd never wondered why Ma was the way she was. I always thought she was hard so I wouldn't grow up soft. I knew that if I wanted to hear more about it, this was my chance.

"Aunt Evelyn, all I really know about Ma is that things weren't good in the *hjemmeland*, so she left there—you all did—and ended up at the Forks. Oh, and I also know she had to eat shoes. It's hard to forget that part."

"Oh, shoes was the *best* of what they had to eat back then." She nodded at me. "Did Morfar tell you how his little sister died from eating that rotten blubber they drug home? Little Aunt Agatha, only four years old."

"No. I didn't even know I had a great-aunt Agatha, dead or not."

"Well, Mary Jane, you get comfortable, and I'll tell you how the Thorvaldsens got to America, why don't I?"

It was one of those warm summer nights when the katydids come out and sing like they own the place, setting the mood just right for storytelling. I pulled my knees into my chest, leaned back onto a pillow, and settled in to listen to Aunt Evelyn.

She began: "I don't remember the *hjemmeland,* of course, but Morfar says that the whole place turned to starvation and misery in 1812 on account of having sided with Napoleon. They hung on as best they could until baby Carl—your uncle—passed from fever. Then they were beyond desperate: Ida was only eight, and our ma was heavy carrying me.

"Morfar went down to the docks and signed up for Canada, to make something of himself, and then send for us. They wanted men to clear land and plant potatoes, which is what he might have done at home anyway, had he had any land to do it on."

Aunt Evelyn was in a mood to keep talking, and I was in a mood to keep listening. I couldn't help but be amazed at all the things nobody had ever told me.

"The *Prince of Wales* came into port at York Factory just as the first snow was starting to fall. Morfar got off and walked straight to the clerk to ask if there wasn't a letter for him. There was one from my ma, of course, and it was three days before he found someone who could read it to him.

"It told that I was born, and a girl, and as healthy as could be expected. That little Ida was bringing in a few pennies working in the match factory. That our ma would try to hold us together until he sent for us, but please make it soon.

"Morfar folded it up and tucked it into his front pocket, next to his heart. It would be three full years before he got his next letter from home.

"During those years he worked and saved, and worked and saved some more. In eighteen twenty, he got promoted to junior clerk at the Forks, and he wrote to us to promise our fare. Our ma paid a man to read it to her, then write back that we were coming.

"I didn't meet my father—your morfar—until we ourselves sailed into York Factory a year later. He walked for twenty days along the Hayes River, expecting to meet his wife, his twelve-year-old daughter, and three-year-old me. When he got to the dock, he found only two of us: Ida herself so thin and hard-worn, and me clinging to her like a baby monkey."

"What happened to your mother? To my . . . *mormor*?" I asked.

"She died on the way," she answered me. "I don't know how she died, as I was too young to remember. Ida is the only one who knows, and she's never cared to talk about it. I don't know if you've noticed, but she has never again set foot on a boat, to this very day."

I hadn't noticed, until that very moment. I thought of all those miles she'd traveled on ox-carts, and how it was all just to avoid the river. Talk about taking the long way home.

"So we're the same in that way, sweetheart, you and me. I never knew my ma, and you never knew your pa."

I nodded, but inside I thought, *It's not the same, Aunt Evelyn. Your ma didn't want to leave you. My pa couldn't wait to.*

"It was Ida who *raised* me, Mary Jane. And wasn't I lucky to have such a sister? Now, my Dear Heart, he has brothers only— fine men, he says—the two that live back in England. There's also a third—the one who came over to America with him— who he never talks about. I've gotten the impression that they aren't overly fond of each other.

"But Ida—did you know that she taught herself to read so she could read for Morfar, and then taught me? Why, I didn't see the inside of a schoolhouse until I was eight, when Morfar decided we'd go to Fort Snelling for the summer."

"I tell you, Ida's the smartest of us all—she's smarter than anyone I've ever known, or even met. But she never got the chance to be a child, and she can't help but be angry about it, deep down. She's had to put someone else first all her life: first it was me, then you kids, and now Morfar."

Aunt Evelyn got sad and serious: "Ida was so hard with you kids when you were little. I know how it broke Morfar's heart . . .

But she does love you in her own way, Mary Jane. Sweetheart, you really *should* write her a letter. It's past time you did."

"I know I should, Aunt Evelyn, and I will. I don't know what I'm waiting for."

I *did* know what I was waiting for. I was waiting for when I could tell Ma that I'd fixed everything, and it all turned out good. Because maybe that would mean that I had turned out good as well. And then maybe she'd start to believe I'm not quite as bad as she told me I am.

"Oh my goodness! Look there, Mary Jane: the sun is peeking up over the horizon. What a strange night we've had . . ."

"Really?" I looked out the window and sure enough, a faint light was breaking in the East. "Why, that means it's already Saturday—the day that Margaret comes!"

"You make extra sure to have a good time together, for I don't know how long those Schmidts will be here. They are one of the last families left in these parts, and I expect they'll have no choice but to follow the others soon, and we'll be heart-sick with missing them."

She laid a hand on her husband's shoulder. "Those Nauvoo Mormons are some *good* Mormons, I'd say. *And some good Mor-women, too!* you'd answer, wouldn't you, Dear Heart?" Aunt Evelyn laughed like Uncle George had just told the joke himself.

I got up and stood at the east-facing window, so I could watch the sun come up properly, and I wasn't disappointed. A golden ball rose on the horizon and washed the world in pink, then yellowy, light.

I finally felt like I knew who Ma and Morfar *were*—not just that, either. I even knew something about who Pa *was*. That naturally got me to wondering who *I* am.

I made a list: *I am Ma's daughter. I am Morfar's granddaughter. I am Aunt Evelyn's niece. I am the girls' cousin. I am Margaret's friend.*

Eee-duhl-lee-ah!

Eee-duhl-lee-ah!

Out of the stillness, the thrush began her call, signaling a new day to no one in particular . . . or maybe to herself.

I'm a daughter, a niece, a cousin, and maybe someday I'll be somebody's wife . . .

Kwee-kwee-kah-kwee!

Kwee-kwee-kah-kwee!

A blackbird joined the thrush, and they sung together like they liked what I was thinking just fine.

I am so many things . . . but, underneath it all . . . I am Me.

Eee-duhl-lee . . . kwee-kah-kwee!

Eee-duhl-lee . . . kwee-kah-kwee!

Their singing grew louder, like they were saying, *Yes! Yes! That's just it!*

I am Me . . . I may be Ma's daughter, but I am, more than anything, my Me.

Chuh-chuh-chuh-chuh, twa-lee-lee-lee-lee-luh!

When the wren added her voice to the chorus, I knew that all of Creation agreed.

CHAPTER XII

–Standing By–

"*Honey*, Mary Jane! I saw honey! Not more than two miles back—a big rotted tree just full of it!"

Margaret was shouting from the wagon; I dropped my hoe and ran to meet it.

Joanna had got there first. "*Hello*, Delilah—may I give Samson this apple?" she was asking. Delilah lifted one foot, which I suppose meant *Yes*, as she'd developed a soft spot for Joanna.

Susan greeted them with her sweet smile, as always: "*Hello*, Father Schmidt. *Hello*, Margaret."

Margaret was excited: "Mary Jane, run in and ask your aunt if she's got tools for honey-gathering, and cheesecloth—oh, and jars, too, as many as you can find."

She didn't have to ask me twice, for my sweet-tooth had been aching since I'd got to Fort Edwards. *Honey drizzled on my oatmeal and stirred into my milk . . . cinnamon-sticks dipped in honey to chew on . . .* my mouth was watering.

I barged back into the house. "Aunt Evelyn, Margaret is taking us all to collect honey. She says I need cheesecloth and glass jars and, well, do we have anything else?"

Aunt Evelyn jumped to her feet. "Oh, *do* we! We've still got enough rusty old bee-chasing gear for you girls to go out harvesting for a week. Your uncle *loves* to go honey-ing."

She turned to Uncle George: "You kept me in honey since the day we married, Dear Heart. And you will again, I just know it." He drew up one side of his face into his own special smile.

I dug around the house for jars, pans, colanders, a pestle—and found it all. While I was packing up, Aunt Evelyn came in carrying a tin . . . well, *thing*.

"What in the world is this?" I asked her.

"It's your uncle's bee-smoker, sweetheart. Here's three twists of tobacco for it, as my Dear Heart hasn't smoked since . . . between you and me, I'm hoping he's quit for good," she whispered in my ear.

"All right then, here's hoping I'll be good and sticky when we come back." I laughed, looking at the strange contraption.

"Never you mind, sweetheart—that's the wonderful thing about honey: it washes clean away with water. You girls just have a good time."

I tied it all up in my big apron and ran out front. I grabbed the two sacks of onions that I'd harvested earlier, to give to Father Schmidt. He'd sold enough of my produce in town that I almost had enough money to buy that cow. I'd kept back a quarter for Mrs. Captain, though, on the slim-to-none chance that I ever saw her again.

When I got to the wagon, Margaret was organizing everyone. "Susan, Joanna: you climb into the back seat, and I'll sit between you," said Margaret. "Mary Jane: you take the things and sit next to Father. Everyone keep your eyes peeled for a dead cottonwood with bees going in and out like nobody's business."

After about a mile or so, Father Schmidt turned and asked me, "How fares Geowge?"

"Oh, very well," I answered. "He gets better each day. Why, only yesterday, he stood up onto his own two feet!"

The wagon halted suddenly, and Delilah swung her head round to look at me. I swear that horse could understand every word we said, through and through.

"He did? Now theyah's something. Maybe your aunt will be right in the end."

"She believes he will, and I believe it, too, by now. I'm hoping he'll be well enough to travel by Christmas, and then I'm thinking to go to Morfar, er . . . my grandfather and Ma, up at Fort Snelling."

"Theyah's a good plan. You're a right smaht gahl—like my daughtah, ya are."

"Father Schmidt, I can't say it too many times: we are so grateful to you for those baskets. I guess I don't need to tell you that before my garden kicked in, what you spared us was all that kept us going."

"Now, now, it's me that must be thankful. More than once

your uncle Geowge saved me from being cheated or wahse down at the sawmill."

"He did?"

"Ayuh. The gentiles hate us, for we ah the keepahs of the true whahd of God . . . but I've known your uncle for yeahs. Since he come down with your aunt and their two babies. Specially asked to rebuild Fort Edwards aftah its stables burnt down. He was . . . is . . . an exceptional carpentah."

"Is that how you know him? You hauling wood and him needing it?"

"Theyah's just it. He and I—we knew each othah from the sawmill. Me and Samson, we brought the wood, and sold it to the Company, who gave me almost nothing for it. Then the Company sawed it into lumbah, and sold it to your uncle for a ahm and a leg!

"And didn't those men bully me, too? Called me a no-good, dirty polygamous. Tried to poison old Samson heyuh with spoilt foddah, but Delilah, she knew bettah and wouldn't let him eat it."

Delilah whinnied an angry whinny, like she remembered and was still disgusted by it.

"But your uncle, he stood—stands—by me and takes my paht. We made a deal, your uncle and I. He'd buy the logs from me for a fair price before we got to the sawmill. Then he'd pay them to saw his wood into lumbah—only the sawing, mind you. We both saved money, and got to be good friends in the doing so . . . despite him being a gentile and not in possession of the true whahd of God, that is.

"But I must say: your uncle didn't—doesn't—drink or gamble

or sware. He doesn't talk dahty about women, specially about your aunt, of cauhse. Ayuh . . . I heard plenty about what an angel she is as we rode in this vary wagon, he couldn't help it. *My Dear Heart*, he always called her as.

"Your aunt had such trouble those yeahs, the heart-sick kind . . . two lovely gahls they've got—yes, but she wasn't able . . . to make their family *grow* like she'd hoped for . . . a boy or two, maybe . . . but Geowge, he stood—stands—by her of cauhse, regahdless.

"And Delilah liked—likes—him. She even let him drive Samson once, and she won't even let Brothah drive him, as of yet. Yes, indeed, that is a *good* man, your uncle. Though he's a gentile, as you all ah."

Father Schmidt lost his smile then, and frowned a sad frown.

"I'll nevah forget that day when the saw jammed and a plank shot off and hit your uncle right to the head. Awful, just awful. And him laying theyah, bleeding and bucking on the ground, and not one man in the Company doing a thing about it.

"It was up to me, so I carried him to the wagon, laid him flat-out, hitched Samson, and asked Delilah to take us to your place quick as she could, so he could draw his last breath at home with your aunt, for I knew that's what he'd of wanted.

"Your aunt heard the galloping and came, then she and his gahls drug him inside. And that's the last time I saw him. I had a notion I'd brought him home to die.

"And now you tell me he's up and standing on his *own two feet*! It's a credit to your aunt for standing by him, it ah. The

Good Lord's rewahded her with a miracle, despite her being a gentile, as you all ah."

I listened to Samson's heavy *clop-clop* as we rolled along, and tried to imagine what it would be like to see Morfar, or Robbie, drug home bleeding, and breathing towards his last. Would I jump in, trying to wrestle him back from death, or drop down and give up? Would I stand by him, whatever it took?

I'd known that Aunt Evelyn was strong, but I'd had no idea *how* strong. Come to think of it, maybe I didn't know how strong I was, either. Maybe nobody knows how strong they are, until they have to find out. And maybe not having to find out is the best luck you can wish for in this lifetime.

–Queen of the Comb–

"There it is! That's the tree—there it is!" I looked where Margaret was pointing and there stood a great cottonwood tree—well, half of one, anyway. Battalions of bees were buzzing in and out of a rotten knot on its side.

"Ayuh, Delilah," Father Schmidt said in a loud booming voice, and we clambered down.

"*Goodbye*, Father. You'll find us right here when you come back." Father Schmidt nodded at his daughter, then whistled to Delilah.

"We don't carry honey-trappings as a rule, so it was lucky your uncle had some," Margaret said to me as we walked towards the tree.

"Aunt Evelyn says it's good gear, too, though I haven't the least idea how to use it."

We set down a good twelve feet off from the buzzy bundle of bees all ganged-up on the trunk. I'd been stung enough times during my life to make me skeptical about going any closer.

"We're going to have to kill a lot of bees, Margaret, if we want to get into that tree."

"No, we won't, Mary Jane," said Margaret. "We're going to sneak right past them. Give me a twist of that tobacco and the smoking can, and you get out some matches."

She opened the top, and stuffed the bottom full of tobacco. I threw in a lit match, and then another, and she shut the lid. We took turns working the bellows until a thick heavy cloud of smoke came out with every pump.

"Mmmm, that smells like Pa," said Susan. Her and Joanna came over to sniff, and you could tell it made them think of the old days.

Margaret gave me the smoking can to hold while she covered her whole self in cheesecloth like a mummy. Then she walked straight up to the bees' front door, stuck in the nozzle, and pumped the bellows like no tomorrow. As she did it, the buzzing quieted down until there was less than a handful of bees flying about, and none too straight, either.

"Come on over, Mary Jane," she told me. "And bring that big knife."

"Are you *sure*, Margaret?"

"Completely. They won't sting us—or even notice us—trust

me!" She puffed a few more puffs of smoke inside, just for good measure.

When I got to the trunk, Margaret raised the knife above her head, and brought it down again, splitting the trunk and leaving a hole big enough for us to stand inside. Two saloons' worth of smoke came billowing out, and after the haze thinned a little, we could see billions of bees crawling around inside. They stuck close to the walls, though, and none came after us.

"See that side, over there?" I looked in and saw honey-combs in rows, layered like the pages of a book, including the big one she was pointing to. "We'll scrape the bees off, pull it out, and harvest the honey."

We carried the hunk of dead log back to the girls and began to slice the honey-comb off of it. First thing first was to eat some, so we did until we were sticky from our mouths, to our earlobes, to our eyebrows. I swear I enjoyed seeing the girls eat their fill more than I enjoyed the honey itself.

Then Margaret organized us into a line: she cut the comb, I cleaned it for bees, Joanna pounded it with the pestle, and Susan pushed it through the colander. The wax we put in a separate pile, as we'd melt it for candles when we got home.

I was already tallying in my mind just how many wicks dipped into how much beeswax I'd need to sell to finally get us that cow, when she called out to us:

"Girls, come here and look!"

We all came over, looked where she was pointing, and saw one bee twice as big as the rest, crawling about on the backs of the littler ones. It was different-looking from the others, too: not at all fuzzy, but smooth and pointy on one end.

"Wow, you're right," I said. "He's a big boy, that one."

"She's a big *girl*, Mary Jane! She's the queen, and she tells the rest what to do."

"She does?" I was surprised.

"Yes, she does, and most of what she tells them to do is to make more honey . . . and to make more bees!" We laughed, all together.

I peered in. "Oh, wait, I see another." I looked closer and saw that I was wrong. "Oh, no, it's too fuzzy, and small."

"Search all you want, girls: you won't find another in that comb. Why, there can't be two queens ruling one kingdom— you of all people should know that, Mary Jane."

"So we just wrecked her castle?" Joanna was concerned.

"Oh, no, girls. We'll move her to another tree, and the rest will follow, because she's the boss. There's no king in a beehive."

"Just like Queen Joanna!" said Susan.

Joanna brought her hand down from her face and pointed into the hive: "Except *that* queen has a *sister* who is queen of a tree nearby, and they spend every afternoon together."

At that, Susan put her arms around Joanna and kissed her. They wandered off hand-in-hand towards the wildflower patch, to pick posies and share secrets, just like sisters do, whether they're queens or not.

-A Turn of Fortune-

Seems like our fortunes have finally turned, I thought to my-self, sitting on the hill next to Margaret, looking at thirteen jars of spun-gold honey, all in a row. The bees had woken back up and were humming a happy tune. There'd be meat for dinner that night, George was standing, and the wildflowers were in bloom—what more could I ask for?

A little less sun, to be honest.

Fort Edwards in July was hot like I'd never felt hot before. Oh, I had known a warm summer day in Minnesota—or even a whole week sometimes—but there were days in Fort Edwards where it felt like I was being cooked by something, honest-to-God.

I try not to swear, but believe me when I say it was hotter than *Hell* on the day we found honey. The girls didn't seem to mind as much as I did; I guess they were used to it. They chased each other around the meadow, playing tag, until they were worn out, then settled down to make daisy chains.

Me and Margaret got up and moved to a spot in the shade where we could watch. "Isn't wild daisy season beautiful, Mary Jane?" she asked me. "The daisy is my favorite flower, you know."

"It's no wonder you prefer them. They're strong and pretty, just like you," I told her.

"Tough and weedy, more like—but so cheerful-looking, with their heads all pointing to the sky. Like they know Heaven is there, but aren't at all worried about getting let in someday."

"Then you are for sure a daisy, Margaret, for a girl so as good as you will have no trouble getting into Heaven, I'm sure of it."

Margaret turned very serious, all at once.

"I feel the same way about you, Mary Jane. Truly, I do," she told me. "Father does, too. He says he's never known a better man than your uncle, and that if your aunt is as *good* a woman as he says she is, it doesn't seem right that they should be separated and cast below just because they have not heard the words of the Prophet."

"It wouldn't be right, and I don't think it's true, Margaret. Ma says that we have to decide for ourselves what we believe. She doesn't hold with prophets or preachers or priests or popes or any of them."

"She told you that?" Margaret's eyes were wide.

"Only about once a day. Ma says God gave us a brain so we can use it, and not just follow someone else."

"But what about your salvation, Mary Jane? This world is only passing and the next one lasts always."

"Come now, Margaret, how can anybody know what happens after we die . . . until they're dead, too?"

She shook her head. "What you say troubles me, and coming from a gentile . . . but then, you're not like the other ones we've known . . . the ones who drove us out of Zion, and murdered our prophet . . .

"But, Mary Jane, what if Prophet Joseph wasn't right when he said that *we* are the only true followers and that nobody outside of us can have any claim to goodness? And if the Prophet could be wrong about something like that, he might be wrong about all of it. What am I supposed to believe then?"

"Between you and me, I couldn't tell you if I really believe there's a God at all. Ma says it might take me my whole life to figure it out; she says maybe that's what life is for."

Margaret was so shocked her mouth fell open, like she couldn't believe someone couldn't believe.

We heard Susan call out: "Margaret, your pa's back!" and turned to see Delilah and Samson kicking up dust while coming towards us. Me and Margaret sorted our gear, and after the wagon pulled up, we loaded the first part while the girls held out the colander for Delilah and Samson to lick clean.

We rode back at a comfortable pace, thoughtful but content, in a way—and pulled by two gigantic horses still sticky around the muzzle.

After Father Schmidt dropped us off, the girls and I ate and went to bed early, as we were tired and sun-burnt from our outing. I looked forward to only good things as I dozed off, and dreamt of soft, waxy candlelight and Christmas at Fort Snelling.

In the middle of that night, I heard a *thump* in the sitting room, like a bag of wood dropping from a shelf, so loud that it broke my sleep. I was out of bed and running to Uncle George before I was even full-awake.

I found them there on the floor, Uncle George in spasms and Aunt Evelyn knelt over him trying to keep his head from clattering against the floor.

"Oh, Dear Heart, Dear Heart, I am here, shush now, I am here," she whispered to him while holding his head.

"Aunt Evelyn . . . ," I said. I guess I thought that if I just started talking, the right thing to say would catch up with me. It didn't.

She looked up at me, and I won't forget her face anytime

soon. She looked less like a woman and more like a scared child, like somebody's little sister pleading for help, looking for something.

I could tell what she was looking for. She was looking for Ma.

And thank God for Mrs. Captain because right then I knew that I was going to have to be the good, smart, strong, capable girl that she had always told me I was.

CHAPTER XIII

–Monday, Tuesday–

Things got worse after that.

George's right side curled up on itself: his fingers into his palm, his hand up under his arm, his arm into his body. Aunt Evelyn sat for hours, rubbing his hands and trying to loosen the muscles, but it didn't do him any good, he just got stiffer and stiffer.

The stiffness began to spread, such that his neck froze up to where he couldn't turn his head, and then his backbone froze, too. His legs would sometimes kick at the knees, but they wouldn't let him stand anymore.

By Monday his face was blank, both sides just nothing. He stopped making even the little noises we'd grown used to. He could blink and he could swallow, and that was about it. I hardly knew if he was dead or alive, but Aunt Evelyn—she kept right on talking to him, *Dear-Heart-this* and *Dear-Heart-that.* She sang to him, and gathered the girls to him before they went to bed.

On Tuesday, Aunt Evelyn laughed gently, saying she'd caught his eye sparkling like it used to. It was the sheer force of her love that let her see and hear and know those things, and it about knocked me over to watch it. I do hope it was true, but I can't say that I saw it myself.

All I could see was a man turning into stone, while wave after wave of love washed over him, bashing itself endlessly against a rocky shore.

–Wednesday, Thursday, Friday–

Water from the well, flour from the sack, cheese from the wheel, and apples from the barrel—we kept right on doing the things that you do while you wait for things to get better. Aunt Evelyn was always saying things would get better, and I got so I believed her. To keep hoping is easier than giving up, in its own way. As tired as we were, to keep on moving seemed a lot less effort than standing still.

My fever came and went, but I kept it to myself, as we already had plenty to worry about. Susan and Joanna learned to feed and tend and entertain themselves, as Aunt Evelyn stayed by Uncle George's side day and night, and I stayed by her side while she did it. It was all I could do to get her to eat a few mouthfuls now and then.

By Wednesday, we had figured out a way to get a little gruel down Uncle George, but it was more than a pity that he couldn't shift around on his own. We were afraid of him getting sores where his weight lay against the chair, and we took to turning him every so often to try and take some of the pressure off.

On Thursday, Aunt Evelyn fainted while we were turning him from his back to his side. I brought her to with cold water, and made her go lay down on the girls' bed, for she'd had no sleep in days.

After I'd gotten Uncle George to swallow down some applesauce, I called the girls in to say *Good night* to their pa. I went to check on Aunt Evelyn, and found her whimpering in a high fever. I soaked a cloth in cold water and laid it on her forehead and wondered what in the world I was going to do now.

By Friday morning it was pretty clear that Aunt Evelyn was afflicted with whatever Father Potatoes had brought to the Forks. She coughed and coughed and her belly was big and hard, and it clearly hurt her some.

It might confuse you, but once I recognized her sickness for what it was, I felt relieved. *I've seen this before,* I said to myself, *and I know how to cure it.* I told the girls as much, and sent them to sleep on the floor of the sitting room, near their pa. I kept up all through the night that night, dosing her with dogbane and mugwort and honey-water, all the time waiting for sunrise.

She was worse by morning, and was spurting her insides out through her back end, to be blunt about it. It wasn't anything I hadn't seen before, and so I dug in and doctored her even harder.

I boiled coffee, I drank coffee, I ate the grounds after, and I kept myself going. Losing Aunt Evelyn was not an option.

–Rocky Ground–

"What's wrong, Mary Jane?"

Margaret was still on the wagon, but she could see clear from the road that I wasn't all right. Susan and Joanna ran past me, and when I saw them hugging on Samson, and Delilah letting them do it, and Father Schmidt holding the traces—for a passing moment it seemed like any other Saturday.

Margaret came closer, took my hand, and looked at my bitten-down fingernails. She smoothed my snarled hair, then asked again, "What is it? What's happened?"

"Aunt Evelyn's sick, but she's resting now."

"Is it bad?"

"I won't say that it's not, but I've seen it before, and I've seen it cured, too."

"Tell me her symptoms. Tell me *everything*."

I told her about the fever and the coughing, and she asked *What more?* I told about Aunt Evelyn not making sense and her stomach hard and full of wind, and she asked *What more?* I described what came out of her back end and when it did and didn't have blood in it, and how her eyes had yellowed up, and that her tongue was swollen to where she couldn't swallow.

She asked me, "Have either of the girls had fever?"

"No, I keep them separate and make them fend for themselves."

"Well, thank goodness for that." She paused, and then continued: "Mary Jane, you sit down and rest while I go talk to Father."

I slumped down, sliding against the house, until I was sat on the ground. *Just five minutes,* I said to myself, *I'll shut my eyes and let them worry about it for five minutes.*

Margaret came back with a plan, but I wasn't ready for it.

"The girls need to come with us, Mary Jane. They can stay at our place until . . . until this . . . resolves itself."

"No, Margaret, no. They need to be where their ma and pa is, even if they can't be close—they're just girls, still."

"Mary Jane, this is a fever that kills people. *They must not catch this*—do you understand? You've been well and truly exposed by now—but the girls—they might escape it if they get themselves gone."

"No, no. You're wrong, Margaret. I've seen people get better from this, maybe even including myself. I've seen it with my own two eyes."

"And I've seen people *die* of it with my own two eyes—*lots* of people, Mary Jane—whole families. Once it gets to circulating, this fever spares no one. As of now, Susan and Joanna still have a chance to dodge it, and you must not take that chance away from them."

What she said stunned me. It was as if her very words had slapped me in the face.

Margaret turned and walked back to the horses, where she told the girls to hurry inside and get their things, for they would be coming to stay at the Schmidts' for a while.

"Make sure you say a special *Goodbye* to your mother before you go. We'll wait for you." Then she added, "But don't kiss her, girls. Not this time."

Margaret came back to where I was sitting and put both of her hands out to ask for mine. I gave them over and she pulled me to standing.

"Susan and Joanna will be safe with us, Mary Jane, don't worry yourself over them. You stay here and see your aunt through this."

"I'll try . . . if you're sure it's best . . ." I couldn't help myself from crying a little, I felt so lost and lonely just then. "Everything was getting better, too. I just don't understand why this is happening. I pray she'll get better, even though I don't know if anyone's listening . . . Margaret, you believe there's a God, don't you?"

"I do, Mary Jane, but I believe it because I *feel* it. And feeling can be more powerful than knowing, at times like these."

I looked inside of me, trying to find what I felt. I thought of the stories and poems that Ma had read to me before I could read them for myself. The ones about scattered seeds and lost coins and peaceful waters and milk and honey and rocky ground and the valley of the shadow of death, where I shall fear no evil. It seemed as if those stories finally made sense, now that I could hear them echoing through my own life.

"I think I feel it, too, Margaret," I told her.

"Cling to that feeling, Mary Jane. You cling to that, until we come back next Saturday," she said.

The girls came out with their bundles. Margaret told Susan to put them in the wagon, and sent Joanna back inside to fetch a scissors and some ribbon.

"Susan and Joanna, both of you, come here and let your

cousin cut a lock of your hair, each, so she can give it to your mother to hold during her tribulation."

I did so, and they both cried a little during, while I told them not to worry, that no matter what happened, I'd be here the whole time.

CHAPTER XIV

-Keeping Watch-

I stood a long time after the wagon rolled off, just looking in the direction it had gone. I was suddenly homesick, and longed for the Forks where everything had been so simple with Hansel and Morfar and especially Ma, who always knew what to do to make things come out all right.

It was Ma who should have been there, to help Uncle George, to cure Aunt Evelyn, to fix all this trouble. I felt myself unready and small, like what I was wasn't nearly enough for what was coming. I felt scared . . . I felt so many things, until I remembered what Ma had told me, while she was in the thick of it nursing Father Potatoes:

A woman feels and a nurse nurses. You've got to keep them separate if you're going to do it right.

I went inside the house and drank one glass of water, then

another. I ate the end of the bread loaf, chewing it carefully. Then I downed five big spoonfuls of honey, and wiped my face afterwards. I was preparing myself for battle.

I will cure them, I said out loud to the face in the mirror. The face in the mirror looked back and added, *I don't have a choice.*

The next several days are a blur of watching, wiping, watering, and feeding my aunt and uncle. Of giving tinctures and making poultices and dressing wounds. I was using up the medicine fast, but I kept going. *I will cure them,* I kept saying to the face in the mirror, and it kept answering, *I don't have a choice.*

I saw my medicine supply dwindling before my eyes. First the goldenseal ran out. Then my store of yarrow root. Then pawpaw, licorice, horseradish, spurge-weed—all of them gone. I took out the tansey-flower tea and said a prayer over it. I gave it to Aunt Evelyn, and it did nothing.

Still, I clung on and wouldn't let go. I didn't have a fever myself, thank goodness. Or maybe I had an awful fever, but I was too busy to feel it. *A woman feels and a nurse nurses.*

It was growing harder for me to walk back and forth between them, keep them straight, one from the other, and recognize which room I was in. I decided to move Aunt Evelyn's bed into the sitting room, so she could lay nearer to Uncle George, where I could sit between them and tend more easily to both. I placed a quilt on the floor, then rolled her off the bed and onto it, trying not to hurt her as I did.

She writhed some on the floor and wouldn't settle. She kept moaning five names over again and again—at least I think that's what they were. "Susan, Joanna, Baby Boy, Baby Girl, Littlest Baby . . . Susan, Joanna, Baby Boy . . ." and so on. I couldn't figure it out, until all at once, I knew who they were.

They were her children. The children she'd had, and the children she'd lost. The children she'd kept alive in her heart, and loved—then, and now, and forever.

-Words to Live By-

Once Aunt Evelyn and Uncle George were quiet, I went back for the bed, and when I pushed the frame away from the wall, I found my bundle underneath, covered in dust. Three silk dresses, a bad ten-dollar bill, and two hundred and fifty-two pages of *A Child's History of England*—not to mention one jar of sour-cherry preserves. Then I remembered the sealed letter to me from Miss Frances.

It's funny where your mind goes when you haven't had enough sleep. Miss Frances was the only person I ever knew who had two different of the same shoes, one shaped special for the right foot, and the other for the left.

Shoes, I thought to myself. I looked down at my own feet and tried to remember what it felt like to care about shoes.

The outside of the envelope had my name on it. It was for *'when you begin to think towards a home and a family,'* she'd said while giving it to me. Wasn't that what I was trying to do by keeping Aunt Evelyn and Uncle George going just then? Trying to make a home and a family? I had no idea how to do it, was the problem.

Surely someone who wore two different of the same shoes would have an idea of what to do. I broke the seal, and read:

My Dearest Mary Jane,

    Upon our parting, I wish to impart the most tender and urgent advice I have to give. Be it known that there is <u>nothing</u> more important to the happiness of a family, than a cheerful <u>temper</u> in the woman who is housekeeper, as illumined by her <u>smile.</u> On the contrary, wearing <u>a countenance of dissatisfaction</u> more than destroys all comfort . . .

I dropped the letter to the floor. *Is she telling me to . . . smile?*

I couldn't believe it. There I was just trying to keep everybody alive for one more day. I laughed despite myself, because it all seemed so ridiculous.

I went and fixed the bed so that it was set across from Uncle George's chair, and got Aunt Evelyn settled into it. A few more hours of watching, wiping, watering, feeding, turning . . . I don't know, maybe it wasn't hours. Maybe it was days. I had let go of time. Then I let go of everything.

I was knelt at Aunt Evelyn's bedside and sponging her forehead. Her eyes were open, but they were looking far past me, like she was watching something I couldn't see. These words came to me then, as clear and real and true as any ever had.

I believe God made her.
I believe God loves her.

I believe God wants her back.

I believe God can take care of her better than I can.

I felt peaceful with the hearing of it, like every time I'd ever been to church was finally making sense. I stood up and went to wash my hands. When I looked up and into the mirror afterwards, my face showed a new kind of calm.

I wiped around my eyes and rinsed my mouth. I smoothed my hair and took off my apron. I lit the lamp, sat down beside her, and got ready to let her go.

-My Witness-

I sat and watched her die.

You might think it was hard to do, but it wasn't. It doesn't take anything special, really. You don't have to be strong. You just have to choose. When someone is slipping into dying right in front of you, you have two choices: to get up and walk away, or to sit down and stay put. I could have left. I could have gone to the well, or walked around the farm, or stood and looked out the window, or just anything. I didn't choose that. So by default, I chose to stay.

You might think it was awful to sit there watching her die, but it wasn't. It was the end of something for me, but not for her. I was watching her go, that's all. She was leaving, and it was not yet time for me to follow. So I stayed.

It actually felt like an honor to be there, next to her, during those hours. Like something empty inside of me was being filled. It was like watching the sunset: you know it won't last, but it is so beautiful while it is happening.

You may not understand me, but that's all right. You will understand if it happens to you.

Her breathing went from its easy slow rhythm to a scratchy stop-start type of pant, like she was running up a hill. Then her lungs began to make a crackling sound, like a baby shaking a rattle. It might have lasted hours. It might have been day. Or night. I don't know. After she stopped breathing, she was so quiet, everything was all so quiet. She died with her eyes closed, and for that I am grateful.

I sat there for a long time. Then I got up and held a wet cloth to George's lips, wetting his mouth a little, his teeth and his tongue. He was frozen stock-stiff, except for a little jolt now and then when I turned him. I set him flat on his back, like Aunt Evelyn had always said he liked, and arranged the wads of sheepskin here, and there, until his breathing was easy.

Then I laid down between them, on the floor, and I slept long and hard.

When I woke, it was Saturday, the sun was shining, and Uncle George was dead. His last act was no less than a miracle: that frozen man had somehow turned himself onto his side, and died facing Aunt Evelyn.

I went over and turned Aunt Evelyn's body to face his, so that in death they'd be just like they had been in life. Two dear hearts reaching for each other.

CHAPTER XV

–Homecoming–

Life is for the living. And I lived. And Susan and Joanna lived, too. And for that, I will never stop being grateful.

After someone you love dies, you feel like the whole world should stop, just because yours did. But it doesn't, and you don't either, really. You make coffee, and put the can back on the shelf. You see a crow pecking at your garden and go to shoo it away. You bend down to check how the pumpkin is coming along, and for a split second, you look forward to that cow you wanted to buy. Then you catch yourself and remember how little the pumpkin, the coffee, the cow matter because of how much you want them back.

It was only a few hours ago that they were still warm and breathing. Why should they have stopped? It doesn't make any sense. They just stopped breathing.

Relief washes through you like a tide coming in. Your choice is simple now. You'll move. You'll take the girls and move up North. It will all be okay. It is for the best, really.

It is not for the best. They died, how could that be for the best? You are afraid that you are a terrible person for thinking it is for the best.

You are afraid of so many things. You are afraid that it was your fault. You think of how he coughed on honey-water just that morning and you are afraid you might have held the spoon wrong. If you had only held that spoon right, he might still be here, warm and breathing.

You are afraid you will forget them—how they were—now that they are gone. It hurts so much that you are afraid it will hurt like this forever. You are afraid it will stop hurting because that will mean that you forgot them—how they were—now that they are gone.

Uncle George and Aunt Evelyn's bodies hadn't quite gone cold when I heard the Schmidts' wagon pulling up. I came out on the porch, and stood looking towards the road. The house was empty of life, and I must have looked empty myself, for as soon as Joanna saw my face, she climbed off the wagon, took three steps forwards, and crumpled to the ground.

I dropped my coffee and I ran. My feet started moving before my brain even started thinking about it. I ran to Joanna, lowered myself to the ground, and held her. She was wailing, like a baby, like a little girl, saying "Mama . . . Mama . . . Mama!" I pulled her weight onto me and rocked her back and forth with my left arm.

I held my right arm out towards the wagon and called, "Susan, Susan, here . . ." Then I was holding both of them, rocking them back and forth while they howled.

I pressed my face to the top of their heads, and I spoke. My voice slid down through our loose hair and tears and sweat and snot, hoping to reach their ears.

"Your ma and pa died peaceful, girls. I was with them every minute," I told them. "Until the very end . . . your ma . . ." *Susan and Joanna,* she said, over and over again . . . those were her last words on this Earth.

"They are gone, but I am here, and I will take care of you now. Your ma taught me all about how to take care of somebody. She said you were to go with me now, up North, to our side of the family. It is what she said she wanted."

Is a lie still a lie if it feels more true than the truth?

Margaret interrupted us: "Girls, go in to your ma and pa one last time, tell them all you need to say, then say *Goodbye.* We will wait for you here, as long as it takes." When Susan and Joanna had gone inside, she said to me, "I feared I would find you such. We brought the girls today, just in case there'd be a chance for them to . . . but it's just as well we brought them regardless."

"It wasn't awful, Margaret," I told her. "But I don't seem to know what to do with myself now. I made some coffee, and that's about as far as I got."

Margaret spoke gently: "We need to move them and get them buried, Mary Jane. The sun is going to be terribly hot today, and likely all week."

I nodded.

"Some might say it's a mercy that Evelyn won't have to live through the death of her dear George," she suggested gently.

I felt numb. "I know that I'm supposed to believe they're in Heaven now, but I . . . I don't know where they are, I just know they're gone," I told her, then considered: "In a way, it's none of my business. What was between those two was something mysterious, I tell you."

Margaret took a deep breath: "And we are the ones left behind, and alive. And what do we do now, Mary Jane? Can you answer me that?"

"We live, I guess."

"No, Mary Jane. We *love.* We give love and we receive love. We put love above all else. That's what we do now."

That was my friend Margaret. She was wise and loving and so smart and so deep. And she hugged me while I cried. When the hug was over, she kept her arm around me, and I leaned my head on her shoulder while she sang:

So let us love, dear;
love, like as we ought;
Love is the lesson which the Lord us taught.

I'll never forget her voice—it sounded so clear and simple, like the ringing of a bell.

It was a hymn that I'd never heard before, but I guess the Mormons have their own set of hymns. It wouldn't surprise me one bit.

—Ashes to Ashes, Dust to Dust—

Margaret came out of the house with a handful of apples and a glass of water. She gave me both, and went back in. I drank the water down and fed Samson the apples, but it was Delilah whose head I hugged that day. And it was Delilah who stood and let me, and breathed her warm breath down my collar, and soothed my aching heart.

"Do you know wheyuh you'll go?" Father Schmidt climbed down from the wagon.

"We'll go up to Ma and Morfar, north to Fort Snelling," I told him. "As soon as we can find passage on a steamboat, that is."

"We'll drive you into Fort Edwards, wheyuh you can ask aftah a pension. All those yeahs in the Ahmy, they ought to pay for Geowge's burial, at least," he said, then followed Margaret into the house.

When I went inside to help the girls decide what to take and what not to, I found Susan playing our pretend piano and Joanna pretending to listen to it, one last time. The girls were leaving the only home they'd ever known, and I know how that feels. A person needs to say *Goodbye* to a place, so I went back outside to give them some time to do it.

I lifted Mr. Hare-ington out of his pen—the girls already knew we couldn't bring the bunny—and set him down in the vegetable patch. He hopped straight to my carrots and started in feasting like he couldn't believe his luck. I was glad to know he'd have a bit of enjoyment before his hard times kicked in.

After a bit, Susan came out with her songbook and Joanna

with her drawings, and they climbed up onto the back bench of the wagon. Father Schmidt came out of the house next; he was carrying Aunt Evelyn like a baby. She looked so small and thin in his arms, and light as a feather, too. It made the girls feel easier—I'm sure of it—seeing her in the strong arms of a man who had been so kind to us, and who she'd been so fond of.

The Schmidt Boy came out after that, carrying Uncle George the same way. Until then, I hadn't even noticed he had come along with his sister and pa. And when I did notice, I still couldn't hardly believe it was him. It was the same boy as when I first arrived, but taller and bigger, somehow. *He's going to be the human version of Samson,* I thought to myself. It did us good to see the careful, dignified way he carried Uncle George. *He's on his way to being a good man,* I thought to myself.

Last came Margaret, carrying all the bedsheets she could find. It was the only time the Schmidts ever entered a gentile household, she told me afterwards.

The men laid Aunt Evelyn and Uncle George out on the wagon, and Margaret shrouded them in their winding sheets. She had a sponge, and a basin of good clean water, and she washed them as she wound. She was so gentle as she wiped them clean, right down to each toe and finger, as if their bodies could still feel her touch.

It was like watching angels work, seeing those three care for our dead. Preparing the dead is the Lord's work if there ever was. Heaven knows me and the girls weren't in any fit condition to have done it; we were huddled off to the side shedding a tear now and then. But it was never so bad as that awful moment when I first saw Joanna come down off the wagon. It's amazing to say, but we had already healed a little since then.

Delilah whinnied and turned Samson onto the road away from Aunt Evelyn and Uncle George's house for the last time. She kept her head high and walked slowly and, as always, Samson followed her lead. It felt like a real funeral-march, so grave and ceremonial, and that healed us some more.

I'm willing to bet Delilah understood when she saw those bodies loaded on, and the girls climb up, so sad and weeping. She was hands-down the smartest horse I ever knew.

—All Sorted Out—

We rode for an hour before we got to where the honey tree was. There it stood, all gutted out; you could still see the fresh gash where Margaret had cut it. When I turned to point it out, I saw a sight I didn't expect.

It was Susan smiling. Granted, it was a small, shy smile that didn't last long. It passed over her face like how a cottony cloud softens the blazing sun as it drifts by.

It was the Schmidt Boy that was making Susan smile. He was sat next to her, the backs of their hands just-about-almost touching. He looked strong and dependable, like someone you could lean on, and I think Susan was, just a tiny bit.

Those two must have become some kind of friends during her stay, I thought to myself.

Joanna sat on the other side, deep in prayer with her hands

folded. She looked earnest enough to make up for everyone who had ever just gone through the motions at church, which included me more often than not.

Maybe a week with the Schmidt Family has changed her too, I considered.

Before the afternoon was over, we came to what had been Fort Edwards's headquarters until the Army left it "high and dry," as Father Schmidt put it. The old guardhouse had a sign on it that said *American Fur Company Counting House.*

"Me and the girls will go in and look for someone . . . for anyone, that is," I said to Father Schmidt.

"Ayuh. We'll wait outside, then," he answered.

It felt good to be at a trading post, makeshift as it was. I walked in not quite like I owned the place, but at least like somebody who'd been there before. All at once, the smell of musty record-books and grimy dollar bills took me back to better days.

"*Good afternoon*, Sir. Are you the clerk?" I said to the little man standing behind the desk.

He nodded. "I am Archibald Swapson, but you can call me Archie. How may I help you?"

If anybody ever had the look of a store-clerk, it was him. He was bald as a billiard cue, and the top of his head shone bright like he'd spent all morning polishing it. But in his eyes, I saw a man who was interested in keeping good records, and un-interested in cheating anybody.

"*Hello*, Mr. Archie. We have come from George Wilks's

place. These are his two daughters, Susan and Joanna, and I'm his niece."

"I see the resemblance. Very nice to make your acquaintances. How is George doing, by the way?"

"He died, Mr. Archie, just last night, I'm sorry to say."

He shook his head. "I knew he was mighty banged-up, but I'm still sorry to hear it. George was as *good* a man as I ever met. We traded regularly, this-for-that, and I was always glad to see him coming through the door. And Mrs. Evelyn, now a widow, that is too bad," he said with much sympathy.

"My aunt Evelyn is dead, too, Mr. Archie. A fever took her."

He looked from me to Susan to Joanna and back again, and his eyes went misty. Then he cleared his throat, and told us:

"Girls, you need to know that Mrs. Evelyn Wilks was very special. She had a *gift*, that woman did, like nothing I'd ever seen before, like nobody else in the world, not woman nor man—nor nobody. She could tally goods, and price them out, and sum, and divide, all in one breath, offhandedly-like. She'd come into my storeroom, take half a look at the shelves, and tell me right down to the penny how much my inventory would bring in.

"She saved my bacon when I was getting started, for they put me down here without one day of experience—why, I was working bellows for a blacksmith when they made me clerk! Mrs. Evelyn Wilks: she'll be missed, and she'll be remembered. I can promise you that."

Didn't my jaw drop open just then? But then I closed it just as fast: of course Aunt Evelyn could work numbers, why, she'd grown up at the Forks just like I had!

"Thank you for your kind words, Mr. Archie."

"Girls, is there any way I can help you?" he asked us.

"Well, I would like to sell these two silk dresses to you, finely hand-made, in the hopes of making three steamboat fares back up North to Fort Snelling."

I handed him the yellow and green dresses for inspection. I couldn't bear the idea of parting with the rosy one. Don't tell anyone, but I had already dared to dream it'd be my wedding dress someday. You see, living with Aunt Evelyn and Uncle George had changed me, in more ways than one. Marriage didn't seem like too bad an idea, provided it was with the right person. Aunt Evelyn always said that living, loving, being with someone, forever and through anything, is what this life is for, when it comes right down to it. Seems to me like something important as that, you might as well kick off in your favorite dress.

"You'll go back to Evelyn's people, then? Yes, I remember the year those two came down. George and Mrs. Evelyn Wilks, the love-birds. Him carrying one baby daughter on each arm and her toting a big bundle of beaver skins! Tell me, is Mrs. Evelyn's . . . hmm—what was it? . . . mo . . . morf . . . is her father still alive?"

"Our morfar. Yes, he's still alive. We'll live with him and my ma."

"Oh, that's good to hear. You'll be all right then, you three." He looked at the dresses. "Do you know whereabouts how much money you'll need for th—"

"Seventy-two dollars and ninety-three cents," I answered him.

His eyebrows went up in surprise, then relaxed down again when he smiled at me. "You have her gift, I see. A different piece of Mrs. Evelyn lives on in each of you, I'll wager, and the world will be a better place for it."

Mr. Archie was a good soul, but he was making a little much of my abilities. All I'd done was taken the fare from Fort Edwards to Dubuque and added five cents a mile between Dubuque and Prairie du Chien, then six cents a mile between Prairie du Chien and Fort Snelling, and multiplied the whole mess by three.

"Here you are," he said, taking the money out of his register and counting it carefully, "seventy-two dollars and ninety-three cents. Now you keep your dresses, and consider it payment for all the hours Mrs. Evelyn spent helping with my books.

"She wouldn't take a nickel for it when she was alive, and you would be doing me a great honor by letting me make things right for you, now that she's gone."

"Thank you, Mr. Archie. I owe a debt to them, too, for all they taught me."

"Then you pay it back by getting those girls up North and making yourselves into a happy family again, won't you?"

He smiled at me, fatherly-like. The girls each shook his hand, and we said *Goodbye.*

And just like that, the future was sorted out, in its way. We'd sail up-stream, and when we got to Fort Snelling, we'd all get off and start over. I'd put everything as right as it ever could be, now that Aunt Evelyn and Uncle George were gone. I'd have to break that news to Ma and to Morfar, but I'd wait to do it in person, as gently as anybody ever could.

In the end, I'd lost her sister, but I'd found her nieces, and Ma was going to have to be satisfied with that. I knew I was, in a way that's not easy to explain.

CHAPTER XVI

—An Unfriendly Conversation—

I came outside to find a sheriff talking to Father Schmidt, who was looking down at his feet, saying nothing. A littler sort of sidekick-sheriff was there, too, listening in and dancing around.

"A gang of Mormons ride into town with two dead bodies in their wagon? And the driver doesn't want to talk, eh? Well, you'll start talking if you know what's good for you, because before sun-down, there's going to be a lot more questions."

I couldn't believe what I was hearing. A ma, a pa, and two teenagers—a *gang*?

The Schmidt Boy was sat up behind the horses, gripping the reins. I could see the veins popping out on his arm from where I stood. Seemed like he wanted to say something, but was trying not to.

I jumped myself in between Father Schmidt and the sheriff: "That's my uncle George and my aunt Evelyn there in the back of the wagon, Mr. Sheriff, Sir. They died yesterday, him of stroke and her of fever, and I was there with them when they passed."

"George and Evelyn? Wilks, you mean? The carpenter? Place out east?"

I nodded *Yes.*

"Why, my Maud knows Evelyn from church. A good Methodist, she says. And you three girls are Methodists too, I hope," he said, looking from Susan to Joanna to me. "Religion is a mighty necessary thing for a girl."

I nodded. What else was there to do?

"And what are you doing with this lowlife Mormon, then?" He pointed at Father Schmidt.

His sidekick chimed in: "Keep sharp or he'll marry all three of you while you're not looking, hee-hee!"

If I had been Ma at that moment, I might have given those bullies what-for. But I wasn't Ma at that moment. I was Mary Jane at that moment: fourteen years old and trying to get two other fourteen-year-olds onto a steamboat, except for that Susan was fifteen.

"Mr. Sheriff, Sir, we were desperate to get into town, and get them buried, because of the heat." That seemed to satisfy him, so I added: "Please, Sir, do you know where I might ask after an orphans' pension for the girls? Uncle George was a carpenter for the U.S. Army."

"Haw! Hee-hee! You might be in luck, and you might not . . . ," said the sidekick, who'd never heard of anything funnier than two girls being orphaned.

The sheriff explained: "The Army left their lawyers behind,

189

and they're the ones who do all the deciding. Nine times out of ten it's less than sensible, but that's the federal government for you: rules, rules, rules."

He shook his head like obeying the law was the biggest burden to be borne by man. It's an odd way for a sheriff to look at things, but that's just how people are on the frontier.

"Go down and fetch one or two of those lawyers, Cruxton. I'll stay here and keep an eye on these Mormons."

Cruxton couldn't believe his good luck at being told to do something that his boss didn't want to. He jumped up and down a couple of times, then turned and ran down the alley like the sheriff was on fire and it was up to him to find water.

-The Trial-

It wasn't long before we saw three figures hustling towards us, looking like two black crows chasing a sparrow. Closer up, it turned out to be two men in long black robes behind Cruxton, who held a hopping lead.

Closer still, the crows wore old dusty wigs: one had his on right-side front and the other had his on wrong-way back. Closer yet, I saw they each carried a gavel. Here they were, two human crows, come to judge the living and the dead.

"Tell the court and state it plain! Whom are the deceased laid out before us?" the black crow with his hair on forwards called out.

"That's George and Evelyn Wilks," the sheriff told them. "The carpenter and his wife. Place out East. Used to be an Army man."

"And is there a witness to said demise?"

The sheriff pointed at me. "She was there."

"She-was-there, *What?*"

"Your Honor," groaned the sheriff, rolling his eyes.

The black crow with his hair on backwards turned to me: "You may approach the bench!"

What bench? I thought to myself, but stepped forwards anyway.

"What manner of death befell them? Speak!"

I spoke. "He by stroke and her by fever. It was only last night, Sir . . . um, I mean *Your Honor.*"

Now, a lawyer's not a judge and I know it, just like I know a patch of dirt in front of a trading post isn't a courtroom, but I was willing to play their *Your-Honor* game if that's what it took to get the three of us onto a steamboat heading north.

Forwards Crow took a thick book out from under his robes, some kind of registry, or similar.

"Yes, here it is. Ahem . . . Let it be known! 'Serviceman George Edward Wilks, U.S. Army Foundryman, in service from 1825 to 1838; awarded Distinguished Service Ribbon 1837; married and in possession of two daughters, born 1831 and 1832.'"

Backwards Crow screamed out: "Here it is written and here it shall be!"

The two lawyers turned and bowed to each other like it was 1565 and they'd just read out the banns of Queen Mary.

Forwards Crow had more to say: "The court finds Serviceman George Edward Wilks deserving of proper burial and eternal rest within the confines of Oakland Cemetery."

"South of town!" added Backwards Crow.

They leaned together and conferred, then went back to cawing at us.

"The court is in favor of keeping families together whenever possible, and of keeping thrift at all times. Thus we shall cast the wife of the deceased into the same grave as her husband before her," said Forwards Crow.

"As the rib shall be cast back into Adam!" added Backwards Crow.

They were a real piece of work, those two, but I didn't say anything against it. Knowing Aunt Evelyn and Uncle George as I did, being twined together for eternity was exactly what they would have wanted.

I've got to hand it to the lawyers on that one. Sometimes people do the right thing for the wrong reason, and it all works out.

Backwards Crow moved right along. "And now, the division of property!"

Forwards Crow took another book out from under his robe and began flipping through its pages. "Silence in the courtroom as we consult the Revised Statutes of 1846! Let's see . . . Section 554.4."

He cleared his throat, and continued. "Estate of Inheritance— Land . . . Domicile . . . Animals . . . Ahhh, here it is: 'Female Daughters are to remain the holding of their father's line.'" He banged his gavel in the air three times for emphasis.

It came to me then, that as we were cousins linked by sisters, Joanna and Susan and I were of different "father's lines." Sure, *I* might be inclined to think of us as Thorvaldsens because we all had the same morfar, but the law didn't see it that way. Officially and on paper, I was a Guild because of Pa, and the girls were Wilkses because of George.

Forwards Crow continued: "Two daughters of the female persuasion are evident within the record of standing. A one: Susan Ida Wilks, born of first and only wife to George Wilks. A two: Joanna Evelyn Wilks, born of first and only wife to George Wilks. Yes, it is written here: two daughters, both alive and in good standing."

If I don't do something fast, those two lawyers will split us up forever, I realized.

"Three daughters—I'm the third daughter!" I cried out. I added, "Your Honor, Sir," for good measure.

Backwards Crow furrowed his brow. "No, you are not. You are an omission. From the record."

Forwards Crow raised one hand in a *stop-everything* kind of motion. "Objection!" he roared. "The defense submits that the omission most likely comprises a rare but common error."

"Sustained!" roared Backwards Crow right back at him. "I'll allow that the quantification is best regarded as a rough estimate only."

"So ruled!" yelled Forwards Crow. "Let the record be amended to describe two daughters plus or minus one."

It was Backwards Crow's turn to bang a gavel on nothing, and after he'd done it, he took up the registry and asked me, "For the record then, your name?"

"Mary Jane, Your Honor, Sir."

"Mary Jane *Wilks*, yes?"

"Yes, Sir, Your Honor. I'm a Wilks."

I had clearly said *Aunt Evelyn* and *Uncle George* to those two sheriffs, and never any *Ma* or *Pa,* but they said nothing, and I figured they either weren't paying attention before, or they didn't care, or both.

I noticed Margaret's face, alarmed as all get-out. It's wrong to lie, of course, and there I was doing it so natural and quick. She would never have, I'm sure—she'd have stuck to the straight and narrow. But just like I wasn't Ma at that moment, I wasn't Margaret, either.

-The Inheritance-

Forwards Crow had taken the registry back: "Ah-ha! Next of inheriting kin stands as Mr. Peter Osbourne Wilks, proprietor of Wilks Tannery, and resident of Greenville, Mississippi."

"Next of kin?" I must have sounded scared and confused, because I was. "Please, Sir, Your Honor, Sir, we don't know any Mr. Peter Wilks in Greenville, Mississippi.

"My aunt Ev—I mean *Ma*—she came down from Fort Snelling, where our morfar—our grandfather still lives. He'll happily take us all in, and we want to go to him, Sir, Mr. Lawyer Sir, Your Honors, Your . . ." At that point, I was happy to call them Lords God Almighty if it helped.

"The court has ruled! It is to Mr. Peter Osbourne Wilks,

proprietor of Wilks Tannery, and resident of Greenville, Mississippi, you are bound!" boomed out Backwards Crow.

Forwards Crow added, and not unkindly: "Miss Wilks, as you've no guardian more than eighteen years of age, you are obliged to go to your uncle, Mr. Peter Osbourne Wilks.

"Now, there it is . . . *Mary Jane Wilks.*" He ran his finger across the columns of the registry, then looked up and asked me, "What is your Date of Bir—?"

"February-twenty-third-1827," I said, so fast that the words practically tumbled out on top of each other. Something in my brain saw a chance and I took it, and my tongue had to catch up later.

"Ahhh . . . which makes you . . . let's see . . . hmm . . . nineteen, doesn't it?"

Nineteen years, five months, and three days, I thought to myself, inside my head, *'28, '32, '36, '40, and '44 being leap-years, that is.*

I watched as he wrote the date I'd given beside my new name. With that one swipe of a pen, I aged five whole years.

The sheriff butted in, sounding concerned: "If she is an adult, does that make *her* the girls' guardian?"

"Mayhaps! The court shall now deliberate!" hollered Backwards Crow. The two of them riffled through Section 554.4 and came to some kind of agreement between themselves.

Forwards Crow pointed his gavel at me. "While *you* are of an age to go where you please—"

Backwards Crow cut in, "—your two younger female sisters

remain the property . . . er, *responsibility* . . . of their father's brother, Mr. Peter Osbourne Wilks."

And with that, the world collapsed underneath me. I looked at Susan and Joanna and I could tell they were falling off the same cliff.

The sheriff stepped up: "Listen here, *Your 'Honors.'* Why, you've just sent these two girls more than five hundred miles down the river, all by themselves . . . I hope you at least have some kind of orphans' pension for them to travel on. It sounds like George Wilks was a good soldier, and I know his wife to have been a good Methodist."

The crows consulted each other again, then announced: "As Serviceman George Edward Wilks was awarded Distinguished Service Ribbon in 1837—nine years ago—you two girls are each entitled to a one-time pension of five dollars." I forget which one said it.

"Five dollars each?" the sheriff cried out. "Why, they won't even make it to St. Petersburg on that!"

Forwards Crow explained: "Had the Distinguished Service Ribbon been awarded in 1836—*ten* years ago—each would be entitled to a full twenty dollars annually."

"I guess George Wilks shoulda considered that when he picked a date to die," growled the sheriff, then turned to the girls: "Give the steamboat captain ten dollars to guarantee the two of you, and this 'Mr. Peter Osbourne Wilks' can pay the balance when you put in at Greenville."

He turned to Father Schmidt: "You'll drive the girls to the

dock, and I'll follow close behind." He said it awful mean. "Then you'll take those bodies over to the morgue. Cruxton will be waiting, so make it quick, or we'll all be out looking for you."

Then he spoke to Susan and Joanna, much kinder: "I'm appointing myself your temporary guardian until I get word from this 'Mr. Peter Osbourne Wilks' that he's got you. Today's Saturday, so they'll be boats a-plenty on the river trying to get their cargoes in by Monday. I'll get you aboard one, and expect you to send word of your arrival the moment you get there, else I'll be sending the authorities." He looked sideways at the Schmidts, and not too kindly, either.

The Crows rustled up ten single *Bank of the United States* dollars and gave five to Joanna, and five to Susan.

"Two passengers going south and one passenger going north!" Cruxton announced it as if the ticket-sellers a mile off could hear him, then skipped off cheerful towards the morgue.

I looked into the girls' faces and saw my own. Both wore the face I'd worn when I learned I was leaving Ma and Morfar—times twenty, I'm sure. I decided that, while I couldn't do anything about my own face back then, I could do something about theirs right now.

"I'm going south with them," I said, stronger and clearer than I'd ever said anything in my whole life.

Forwards Crow thought for a moment, then shrugged and nodded. "The court has precedently ruled that you are of an age to go where you please, Miss Wilks. Thus you are free—free to submit to either patriarch line, that is."

Backwards Crow banged his gavel in silent agreement, and disappeared the books back into his robes. "The court has ruled in the dispersion of the Estate-in-Full of the Serviceman George Edward Wilks, deceased, to Mr. Peter Osbourne Wilks, living, proprietor of Wilks Tannery and resident of Greenville, Mississippi."

"Hear Ye! Hear Ye! The court has spoken. May its ruling stand for all time!" proclaimed Forwards Crow, and that was the last piece of nonsense we were to hear out of them.

We watched the two robes become one as they trotted away, back to the same place they had come from, wherever that was.

–Another Goodbye–

"Come on, girls, let's get you to the dock," said the sheriff. "Don't fret about your ma and pa; I'll make sure George is buried in good Methodist fashion and that the Army writes condolences to the extended family. Evelyn's father lives up at Fort Snelling, did you say?"

"Yes, Sir. Thorvald Thorvaldsen, care of the American Fur Company."

"They'll break the news in proper fashion, with a signature and seal at the bottom—and I'll make sure they slip in something about to where and to who you're bound."

In my head I was thinking, *I'll travel south with the girls, and first thing when we get to this "Uncle Wilks" person, I'll write to Ma. She'll know what to do next, I'm sure of it.*

At the dock, I petted Delilah and Samson extra-long, as a sort of *Thank You*. Samson pushed his big head into my chest and Delilah tugged at my collar with her lips, as her way of saying, *Keep your chin up, my dear.*

I saw the Schmidt Boy take his coat and put it around Susan's shoulders, saying to her, "This'll keep the rain off, when it comes."

"Thank you," she told him. It was quite a look that exchanged between them.

"It'll fit both you and your sister—and Mary Jane, too." He looked briefly from Joanna to me, then right back to Susan. "But it's mostly for you," he told her.

The sheriff was standing off to the side, staring at the Schmidt Boy like a cat ready to scratch.

I turned back around, and kept my voice low when I said, "You be careful, Father Schmidt. These people don't like Mormons."

"Now theyuh, I know that, children. If theyuh's one thing I know, it's that," he answered me, and we both felt sad.

Mother Schmidt handed me one last basket, and I thanked her. Then it was time for *Farewell-and-Goodbye.*

We shook hands all around, one by one. "Girls," Margaret asked Susan and Joanna, "do you want to go and say *Goodbye* to your ma and pa, one last time?"

Joanna looked at Susan, then answered, "No, Margaret. It's not them in the back of that wagon. It's just their bodies, and they don't need those bodies anymore."

Susan added, "We've already said what we needed to say," and they all hugged each other for a long moment.

Then I turned to Margaret, who had been such a good friend

to me and taught me so much. I couldn't bear the thought of never seeing her again, but then again, I had to bear it, so I did.

We hugged just as long, and afterwards, she was still holding my hand.

"I'll pray for you," she told me, looking straight into my eyes, and I nodded.

She didn't need to say it. She'd told me many times that she prayed for us all regularly. Still she said it to me, out loud, on that day.

Maybe that's what you say, when you've run out of everything else to say. It's what you grapple for when you need something beyond *Goodbye.*

Margaret climbed back up beside Father Schmidt, who whistled to Delilah, who nosed Samson, and they started for home. I turned my back and faced the river, so none of them would see if I started to cry.

I stared off down-stream, because that's where we were headed. I wanted to go north, but I didn't have a choice. The world with all its sheriffs and lawyers was forcing the girls south, and it was all I could do to grab hold as the current pulled them away.

I felt a splash, and looked down at my old friend, the Mississippi River, sloshing against the dock. It was heading south, too. It didn't have a choice, either. Just like me, it had started way up North and traveled here; and now it had to go further, unable to turn around.

I said to myself, *We'll go together, this river, the girls, and me.*

We'll go south, to this next place, and we'll see what it's like when we get there.

I wiped my eyes, raised my face, and turned back around. I opened my arms and brought Joanna to my right side, and Susan to my left. I closed my arms, and held my family tight.

CHAPTER XVII

–A Familiar Face–

I stumble into luck sometimes, and I positively wade into it now and again. I knew I was in it up past my knees when I looked up-river and saw the *Galenian* coming towards us.

I jumped up and down and waved my two arms and yelled, "Mrs. Captain! Mrs. Captain, it's *me*!"

She came up port-side and yelled back: "O Chickie! My Chickie!"

The sheriff came over, looking uneasy. "Who is that . . . *person*? And how does she . . . um . . . how do *they* know you?" he asked me.

"That's the captain of the *Galenian*—it's the same steamboat that brought me . . . um . . . that we used to visit at the dock . . . um . . . with *Pa,* back in better days."

It was a quick save, and clever, I thought, but the sheriff looked at me like he knew my story wasn't water-tight.

The *Galenian* docked with Mrs. Captain stood at the top of the gangplank, but before I could run across and hug her, the sheriff put himself between us. "Is it true that you are acting as the captain of this vessel?" he asked, and none too kindly, either.

"One hundred percent! Why, I'm Mrs. Captain, after all. Don't act like you haven't heard of me, Sheriff." She held out her hand like they were old friends. The sheriff kept his in his pocket, like they weren't.

I took Susan and Joanna aside: "Girls, be ready to go along with whatever I say . . . we all know that lying is wrong, but . . . well, it's going to be me and you two against the world for a stretch, and I need to do what's best on a dime."

I won't lie, they both looked bothered, especially Joanna. But they didn't say *I won't*, so I took it as *I will.*

"Does either of you have a piece of string?" I asked them.

"No, but I brought some yarn," said Susan.

"Better yet. Give me a length of it, won't you?"

She measured out a length, bit it off, and gave it over. I tied seven knots into it, quick as I could. First a butterfly loop, then eye-splice, lobster-buoy, icicle hitch, eye-splice again, Vineyard's bend, and eye-splice at the last.

I double-checked it after I finished. *B-e-l-i-e-v-e*, it spelled out, just like I wanted.

I stepped up: "Mrs. Captain, remember how you taught me those sailors' knots all those *years* ago? Well, I've been practicing ever since! *Look here.*"

She took the yarn from me and ran her fingers down the

length of it slowly. "You've done these knots just right, Chickie, and you've put them in a *fine order,* too."

"I'm sure you remember my *little sisters* Susan and Joanna . . ."

"Of course, of course!" she said instantly. "My, what fine, strong girls you've all grown to be!"

"Sweet and smart, too," I added. Joanna had one hand up over her mouth like she always did when someone new came around.

"I don't doubt it for a minute! Now tell me, how is *everything* with you?"

"Not so good, Mrs. Captain. We lost Aun—*Ma* and *Pa* to fever and stroke, the two of them. They passed just last week."

Last night, I corrected myself in my head. It felt like a thousand years ago.

"Evelyn and George, wasn't it?" Mrs. Captain asked, and I nodded *Yes.* "How terribly sorry I am to hear it! They were fine people—*weren't they?*"

"Yes, they *were,* Mrs. Captain. We loved them both, very much."

"And they were lucky to have three such good, smart, strong, capable girls as you. No better girls in the world, than theirs."

"Oh, but Mrs. Captain, I'm not a *girl* anymore," I said quickly. "Since you've last seen me, I've had my *nineteenth birthday.*"

The sheriff looked back and forth, unfriendly-like.

"Oh, my, *yes!* Well, that makes sense . . . and your sisters?"

"Fourteen and fifteen years old, they are." I said it without any twinge, as it was the actual truth.

"Ease your minds, girls, I'll get you *wherever* you need to go, be it *north* or *south* . . . the *Galenian* sails from one end of the Mississippi to the other and back again."

"Thank you, Mrs. Captain," said Susan with a smile.

"Now, *where* is it that you are bound?" she asked us.

The sheriff busted in: "They are to be delivered to Mr. Peter Osbourne Wilks, proprietor of Wilks Tannery, and resident of Greenville, Mississippi."

"He's . . . he's *Pa's* brother," I added. "Since Pa is gone, the girls belong to him."

"They belong *in his care*," the sheriff corrected me.

"I see," said Mrs. Captain, again. "And I will be very interested to learn what kind of man he is when we put into port down in Greenville next week."

"And I will be very interested to learn from *him* that these girls have been delivered, safe and sound," answered the sheriff.

I changed the subject: "Mrs. Captain, I know the fare is more, but we only have ten dollars of orphans' pension to give you, but . . . our *uncle* is to pay the rest when we get to Greenville."

"We'll square up later, Chickie; I'll get you there safe and sound, just put your minds at ease," she said.

I saw the tugboat coming towards us, pulling a barge stacked with fresh timber. "*Hello*, Captain Kirby!" I shouted.

"Ye—yes, Chickie. It's still Captain Kirby driving the tugboat. Same from all those *years* ago," she said, raising one eyebrow at me. Then she turned to the sheriff. "Sir, I'll thank you kindly for bringing me the girls, and say *Goodbye* to you, as we're due to shove off once the cargo's hitched."

Mrs. Captain stretched out her hand towards him again, and

again he didn't shake it. Instead, he took us girls aside and told us, "Get aboard the boat, then, girls—but keep your wits about you while you're on it."

Truth be told, I had already suspected that hanging on to my wits would get me further than letting them go, but I thanked him for his advice anyway, and we parted, cool but friendly.

-The Honest Truth-

"Oh, Mrs. Captain," I said, after I was sure the sheriff was gone and out of hearing. "We *can* pay your full fare." I fished out the money Mr. Archie had given us. I held it out: "Eighteen dollars and fifty-five cents to ride from Fort Edwards to Greenville; here's three times that."

"No! I say *No!* I'll not take a cent from you girls."

"You *have* to take it. I won't have the girls see me cheating you, like those boys try to do."

She took the money, but not eagerly.

"Don't fret, Mrs. Captain, this leaves us with seventeen dollars and twenty-eight cents, so we'll be fine. And the girls *do* have five dollars each, that part is true."

Mrs. Captain turned to Susan and Joanna: "Aren't you girls lucky to be in the good hands of my Chickie! Why, she's the best kind of girl there is—same as you two, I'm willing to bet."

Susan smiled and Joanna even brought her hand down for a minute, she was so pleased.

Just then, I put my hand in my pocket, and felt the quarter I'd saved for Mrs. Captain, knotted at the bottom. I pulled it out.

"Oh, Mrs. Captain . . . and this! This is that quarter I owe on my first ticket. I put it aside after I sold the very first of my garden in Fort Edwards, just in case . . . just in hoping I ever saw you again."

And didn't it feel good to put that coin in her hand?

"Oh, Chickie, I'll keep it always. Such a good, kind, *honest* girl you are." She put it in her own pocket, along with the yarn knotted to say *Believe*.

"Not so honest as you might wish, Mrs. Captain. But for now, at least, these two are my sisters and I am nineteen years old. It's what's keeping us together, so it has to stand."

Joanna's braid had come undone, and Susan took her off to redo it. Mrs. Captain and I stayed where we were and talked some more.

"Stick to your story, Chickie, if it feels like the right thing to do," she told me. "Some of the things people call lies are truer than the truth."

"I think I understand, Mrs. Captain. I came to understand a lot of things since you dropped me off at Fort Edwards."

"It was only last spring, wasn't it? Well, I daresay you've had something of a summer. Aunt and uncle both gone to their reward—suddenly, was it?"

"Yes, I did my best, but I couldn't . . ."

"Death comes for all of us, Chickie. And when our day comes, what we wish for most is a hand to hold, and if we're lucky, that hand is attached to someone we love. It sounds like George and Evelyn got that wish."

"I hope they did."

"And the girls? What of them?"

"They're bouncing back, I think."

"That's good. And now to Greenville?"

"They are minors, and bound to their pa's brother, as their ma was only the sister of my ma."

"Keeping to the father's line, then . . . that's the law for you."

"That's why I've claimed to be their sister, and also nineteen. I thought it would make *me* their guardian, but no luck. I'd asked to take them back up North, but the lawyers said *No*. So here we three are, heading south and going with the current, instead of against it."

"You did well, Chickie, given the fix you were in, but you've bit off a lot to chew. Tell me, what do you know of this Peter Wilks? Beyond that he owns a tannery in Greenville, Mississippi, I mean."

"Actually—we don't know anything else about him, Mrs. Captain." I shook my head. "Not a darn thing."

–Finding Our Place–

"Come aboard, girls! The *Galenian* will be shoving off as soon as she's gained all passengers."

Behind us, a line of rag-tag soldier boys had formed, and were getting ready to cheat their way on board.

"Mrs. Captain, let me help you with selling tickets . . ."

"I thank you but *No*, not this time, Chickie. Why, you must show the girls around the *Galenian*! But first, go and stake out your place on the deck, and quick."

I hated to walk off, but she was right: claim your place early or end up next to the pig-pen. *Next time she does the ticketing, I'll be right beside her,* I promised myself.

We took our time finding a dry spot starboard, so we could watch the river go by. After we set down our things to claim it—there's not much stealing on a steamboat, as you can't get far—we walked the length of the *Galenian.*

I pointed out the stempost and bulkhead, then the fairlead, guard, and stanchion. The girls followed behind me like they were *my* Chickies, and glad to see it all, but I must say Joanna caught on better than Susan.

We talked while we walked, and I said to them, "How do I put this? Mrs. Captain is not very *lady-like*—some would say she isn't a lady at all—but I'll tell you one thing: she's as good a *woman* as you will ever meet in this life, or the next."

"Mary Jane, you don't have to explain. If you like her, then so do we," said Susan, who I swear got sweeter every day.

Joanna agreed. "I feel quite home here on the *Galenian* already. I still miss Ma just awful, but I'm not overly sad today. Mrs. Captain, in that motherly way of hers, does make me feel good."

"She doesn't just make you feel good, Joanna, she makes you want to *be* good, all because she believes you already are. Isn't it amazing?"

Mrs. Captain came over, dripping wet. "The barge is tied fast and we are moving! Wave *Goodbye* to Captain Kirby, girls. We won't see him again until St. Petersburg."

We jumped up and down and waved, and he waved back.

"My dear Chickie, let's introduce the girls to someone *very important* in the boiler room, shall we?" I busted into a smile, knowing she meant Robert Fulton.

"Of course! Susan and Joanna, I think you'll find someone just wonderful in there who will be *very* glad to meet you . . ."

As we walked, the wholesome smell of steam took me back to my first-engineer days, and I smiled with the remembering of it. Once we got to the boiler room door, I reached for the handle, and told the girls, "On the other side of this door is one of the most wonderful folks you'll ever meet."

I knew I was right, but I didn't know just how right I was.

-A New Friend-

I expected to see Robert Fulton in the boiler room, and there he was, in his usual spot. But the real surprise was standing there *next* to him: a little boy, not more than eight or nine, and grimy as all get-out.

And when I say he was *grimy,* I mean *gri-my.* His bangs turned out to be ground-in dirt on his forehead. His shoes turned out to be road-tar stains on two bare feet. Underneath the grime, he wasn't in too good shape, either. He had one eye sewed shut and not scarred over yet. It was healed past the worst of it, but still. And he was too darn skinny.

I will say that he did have the best smile, so big it split his face in half, ear to ear. It was the smile of somebody who'd just won the sweepstakes. He could outdo the happiest children I'd ever seen, there was that much joyousness bursting out of him.

I liked him right away. I quite approve of a good measure of dirt on a healthy boy, or girl, for that matter. Sometimes the very most unkempt kids are also the cheerfullest, and I've got to wondering if true happiness doesn't come from the freedom to get yourself dirty.

He wasn't the only one smiling: Mrs. Captain was positively beaming at the little fellow, like he was every Christmas present she'd ever wanted, pantsed in filthy corduroy.

I stuck out my hand to him. "Pleased to meet you! These are my sisters, Joanna and Susan, and I am Mary Jane."

He grabbed my hand and wagged it up and down with all his might, trying to show extra friendliness. "I am the Rooster!" he said, loud and proud. "And I just finished tending Robert Fulton."

"Isn't he the finest, smartest, strongest, helpfulest boy you've ever seen? I tell you I've never seen his better," said Mrs. Captain.

I wouldn't have guessed that boy could smile any bigger than he had been, but Mrs. Captain brought it out of him.

"Rooster, this here is Chickie!" Mrs. Captain motioned towards me. "The very same Chickie you've heard me tell of. She'll be aboard with us to Greenville, and her little sisters with her. Aren't we lucky to be all together?"

"Oh!" said the Rooster. "Then, I'll shake your hand again. I'll shake all of your hands if you'll let me!" We did, and eagerly, until he'd worn himself out a little.

Susan said, "We are glad to know you, Rooster," and Joanna had both hands down from her face. They liked him just as well as I did.

"He didn't have a *good start*, the Rooster didn't," said

Mrs. Captain. "But he's on the *Galenian,* now. He worked his way up to first mate, quick as lightning. Nobody, just *nobody,* could be more pleasant and kind and helpful than my Rooster."

"I can haul coal and stack it, I can carry water and pour it, I can mix pitch, I can blow the whistle, I can hold the rudder, I can refill the lamps . . ." The Rooster was proudly listing off all his helpfulnesses.

"And you keep Robert Fulton tended, almost as good as you did, Chickie—no, I'd have to say just exactly as well, on my honor."

"Are you traveling somewhere, Rooster?" I asked him.

Mrs. Captain cut in: "The Rooster's home is right here on the *Galenian* for as long as he cares to be here, and pitch in—or not pitch in—whenever he feels like it. This is a place where he's wanted, and this is a place where he's appreciated. Certainly, he'll have adventures up and down the river, but he's to think of himself right at home when he's here with me."

"She tells me that once a day," said Rooster, proud and happy as anything. "More than that, if I ask her to."

"He's coming right along, my Rooster is. He wasn't given a *good start,* and that's a shame, but we're going to make up for it now, and from here on out, too. Learning everything so quick and ready, and so kind and considerate, a better, smarter, stronger, capable-er boy there never was!" boasted Mrs. Captain of the raggedy little fellow, who was smiling right beside her.

-A Good, Smart, Strong, Capable Boy-

"Do you want to watch me doing the sounding?" the Rooster asked us.

We followed him around the deck as he thrust the twelve-foot pole straight down in the water until it either touched the bottom or didn't, then yelled out the depth. I'll admit he was better at it than I'd ever got. He didn't even look at the numbers on the pole, he could tell by the feel of the *thump* how deep it'd went.

"Do you want to come up and see my first mate's quarters?" he asked next. "I'm to drink a cup of milk after every sounding. It's to strengthen up my bones. Mrs. Captain says they aren't what they should be on account of me not having a *good start.*"

He led us up the ladder to a sturdy shack built onto the side of the pilothouse where Mrs. Captain slept. The shack had its own door, and a real pane of glass for a window.

"This is where I drink my milk, and have my things. Mrs. Captain made it special for me so I wouldn't have to sleep on the deck. Tonight I'll see the moon out that window. The place where I slept before didn't have any windows." He shook his head at the bad memory, then poured himself a cup of milk and drank it in one swallow.

"Do you want any?" he offered us.

"No, we're just fine," I told him.

"Suit yourself!" he said, and downed another cup.

"So, Rooster, how did you come aboard the *Galenian,* if we may ask?"

"Oh, that's easy. The Racoon Man showed me the way. He's the one who unswelled my eye and paid the doctor to sew it shut, too."

"He did?"

"Yes, he did. I'd taken to sleeping in the saloon's coal cellar, as it was quieter than the saloon. He found me laid out in the coal one morning—she'd been a-raging just terrible the night before—and said, *Don't you have some other people you can go to, my little friend?*

"I told him, *Thank you, Sir, but if I had, I would have gone to them a long time ago.*

"Then he said, *Little Friend, I hate to say it, but I'm afraid she's going to downright kill you one of these nights.*

"So I asked him, *Mr. Racoon Man, Sir, do you have some other people I could go to?* and he scratched his chin and thought about it.

"That same day, when the *Galenian* came into dock, the Racoon Man brought a pile of coal on, stood me beside it, and asked Mrs. Captain to take me down to Memphis where I could maybe join up as a bugle boy because I wasn't getting a *good start* there in Rock Island."

"I see. And how do you like being aboard the *Galenian*? You sure are good at helping to run it."

"Don't I just love it? I love everything about it. When I first got on board I was all braved up to go fight the wars, but when we found the recruiter-man, those soldiers all looked so tricky and mean that I—well, I started to cry. The recruiter-man slapped me and said *Shet yer blubbering.*"

"Oh, no!" said Susan, her eyes blazing.

"It was Mrs. Captain who took me aside and said, *Rooster, forget this man. Would you rather stay on the* Galenian *as my first mate?* and you can imagine how long it took me to say, *Oh, yes, I would!*"

"Of course you did," added Joanna.

"So now I am first mate of the *Galenian*—for as long as I want to be, Mrs. Captain says. She doesn't even own a belt, did you know that?"

"Why would she, Rooster?" I asked him. "You don't need a belt on a dress like hers."

"My mum wears one always. She'd take it off and wallop me with it, buckle end, most every day. Everybody says she's a bad'un."

"Then I'm glad you're here now," said Susan.

"And I know Mrs. Captain is glad you're here, too," added Joanna.

"I wasn't the Rooster before I came here; I wasn't anything. But now I am the Rooster, and everyone tells me that it is something fine to be, and I think so, too."

We took a look around the room, while the Rooster stood proudly and let us. Aside from the milk-can, it was pretty bare.

"Do you have any games, Rooster?" asked Susan. "We can play marbles if you have any."

"No, I don't, but I could. Mrs. Captain gives me three nickels every Saturday to keep all for myself. It's my share of the family wealth, she says. One of these times when we put into Memphis, I'm going into town to buy anything I want."

Joanna turned and asked me, "Will we be stopping in Memphis?"

"Yes, and before the week is over, likely."

"Then I will take you into town, Rooster, and help you do your shopping," she told him.

"Will you, Miss . . . ?" The Rooster's eyes lit up.

"*Joanna* . . . and yes, I will. I'll buy us both a lemonade, as well, as I have five dollars of my own to spend. I'll look out for you, if you'll look out for me. How does that sound?"

The Rooster ran straight to her, wrapped his arms around her waist, and hugged her for all he was worth. She patted his head in a sisterly way, never minding the grime.

Now that I think about it, it makes sense that Joanna took a shine to the Rooster right off. All her life she'd had a scar on her face as a cross to bear, and she knew better than anybody that after his stitches closed, he would, too.

In fact, none of us could help but feel sisterly towards the Rooster. There he was, a lone, eager little one who wanted nothing more than love from somebody who didn't wear a belt. I was Mrs. Captain's *Chickie*, and he was her *Rooster*. We'd both found safety under her wing just when we needed it the most.

The Rooster's one eye suddenly got bright. "Did you hear that? Robert Fulton needs me. Miss Joanna, and Miss . . . ?"

"*Susan*," she told him with a smile.

"Miss Joanna and Miss Susan, then. Do you want to come with me, and see what-all I can do?"

They followed him off, convinced that he was the most

wonderful little boy in the whole world. I went to find Mrs. Captain, hoping to learn more.

"Say, that Rooster is a good, smart, strong, capable boy, and I think he knows how lucky he is to be on board," I told her, after I found her at the wheel.

"It's me who is the lucky one, for a better boy there isn't to be found anywhere. He didn't have a *good start*, and that's mostly down to his mum, but I won't have a word said against her, for what's the use in that? And we don't know what kind of troubles she's had, we haven't walked in her shoes, as they say."

"*It doesn't cost anything to be kind*—somebody once told me that," I reminded her.

"Exactly that, Chickie. Nonetheless, it's for the best that my Rooster flew that particular coop, if you know what I mean."

"He won't go for a soldier, he told us, but what will become of him, do you think?"

"Oh, now, Chickie, I'm getting older, I am. I reckon I've got about five more years in me as a steamboat captain, and then, well, the *Galenian* can't have just any captain, can she?"

"Do you mean you'd give the *Galenian* to the Rooster?" Mrs. Captain was good-hearted, but this seemed like a lot, even for her.

"Who else have I got to give her to, Chickie? I'm not going to sell her for parts down in New Orleans, or to some miscreant who'll blow Robert Fulton sky-high. No, we've been through too much together, the *Galenian* and me."

"The Rooster does seem to have picked up plenty of boating skills," I mentioned.

"Hasn't he, though? Yes, the *Galenian* will be his one day, if he wants it. And who better to captain her after I've retired myself?"

"*Nobody* better, I say."

"It's down dirty hard being unwanted in this weary world, especially for a child. But the more the world doesn't want him, the more I do. I'll tell you something that I think you'll understand, Chickie. I am that boy's ma in the same way that you are those girls' big sister."

"I can see it. It's truer than the truth," I said.

"My Rooster might not have got a *good start*, but I'm going to make darned sure he gets a *good middle*."

I couldn't help it, I was that overcome. I went straight to Mrs. Captain and hugged her for all she was worth, like the Rooster had done to Joanna, more or less. Mrs. Captain patted my head the same way Joanna had done to the Rooster, too.

More or less.

–Listening Good–

Being aboard the *Galenian* made me feel downright optimistic about things. And the more I thought about the future, the brighter it got.

Why shouldn't the girls be happy in Greenville? I asked myself. *Peter Wilks is their flesh-and-blood uncle, after all. His brother George was a good man, and they must've gotten the same good start. Plus, he owns a tannery, and Morfar always said that's a good business. He couldn't hardly help having more money than Uncle George and Aunt Evelyn did at the end.*

It occurred to me: *After I get the girls good and settled with their uncle, I could make my way back north to Fort Snelling, and have my old life again! Live at the Forks with Morfar and Hansel, and Ma would see how I'd sorted everything out after all.*

Me and Mrs. Captain were chatting one night, when I said, "Seeing you here, taking in an orphan, so good and kind, and both of you so happy, gives me hope. I'm inclined to believe that Peter Wilks is a *good* man, just like his brother, and that he'll take good care of those girls."

"Make up your mind after you get there, Chickie. People deserve your kindness, but they have to earn your trust," she told me.

"Mrs. Captain, if there's one thing I've learned since leaving home, it's that there's *good* people everywhere. Aunt Evelyn and Uncle George were the most lovingest people there's ever been. The Schmidts—if anybody ever did love thy neighbor, it's them for certain. And you, Mrs. Captain, always building me up in that motherly way of yours. And the Racoon Man, and the old-feller on the dock, and the captain of the *Minnesota Belle*, I found friendliness in all of them."

"Chickie, you're right in that there's good inside every one of us. Trouble is, you can't count on it being in use at any given moment. Remember that man who cheated you into taking a New Orleans ten-dollar bill back in Dubuque?"

"Of course I do! But that was my fault: I should have known better."

"Now listen to me, Chickie, and listen good. It is *never* your fault when someone takes advantage of you. That's a low-down dirty thing they do of their own choosing."

"Maybe. You know, I *was* uneasy in my gut the whole time I was trading with him."

She raised her eyebrows. "Don't *ever* ignore that uneasy feeling you felt. I don't mean to scare you, Chickie, but it's not a sea of angels out there waiting for you girls. Lord knows, I wish it was, but Lord also knows, I know it's not. The best protector you've got, when it comes right down to it, is your gut. So promise me you'll always listen to what it tells you, and never ignore it again."

"I promise, Mrs. Captain."

The girls came back and we shared out our basket, putting the best bits towards the Rooster. While we ate, Susan told about the Schmidt family, and put extra emphasis on the niceness of the Schmidt Boy. Joanna told how they'd helped her find religion, but that she'd stopped short of joining up. I told about how the sheriff had bullied Father Schmidt, and Mrs. Captain shook her head and said it's not safe for Mormons anywhere, nowadays.

When we looked to the horizon, we saw the last golden light of the day. If the sun was going to bed, we figured we might as well go, too.

The girls followed the Rooster up the ladder, where Susan made sure he drank his milk and even got him to wash his face a little. Then Joanna told him Bible stories until he fell asleep, the ones about helping strangers and finding little lost lambs and that sort of thing. Meanwhile, Mrs. Captain walked the deck, lighting the lamps, and I went down to turn out our three bed-rolls.

The girls met me at our place on the deck and we laid down, side-by-side-by-side with me in the middle. We watched the moon rise up and listened to the *slosh, slosh, slosh* of the river. Just as the Milky Way was coming clear, my eyes got heavy, and I drifted off to sleep.

CHAPTER XVIII

–The Teller of Tall Tales–

Scrrraaaape-thump!

I lifted my head that next morning to the strange feeling of the *Galenian* not moving. Not rocking, not turning, not drifting—just plain not moving. I had slept so deep that I hadn't heard the whistle blow! It took me a minute to blink my eyes open and realize we'd already put into St. Petersburg.

What a pretty little town, I thought to myself as I looked about. Next to the dock stood a little fountain, spitting water into the sky and catching it again for no reason. Next to it was a bandstand, where citizens could come to hear important people or politicians.

I stood up and brushed off my dress, then rolled up our bedding. Susan and Joanna were at the other end of the deck, fixing each other's hair and laughing together, like sisters do.

Mrs. Captain had just finished putting down the gangplank when she saw that I was up and doing.

"Mary Jane, can I ask you to go into town and take a basket from a Mr. Samuel Clemens? You can't miss him. He's got a mop of white hair and three bushy mustaches: one over his mouth and the other two above his eyes. An old friend of mine, he is, and a more generous soul there's not to be found," she explained, and I set off directly.

I didn't have to go far off the dock before I found an extra-eyebrowed man holding the biggest darn basket I'd ever seen, with what was surely his wife standing beside him.

"Would you be Mr. Clemens?" I asked the man. "I'm Mary Jane."

"*Ahh* . . . Private Chickie, reporting for duty?" he asked me, rather louder than what was necessary.

"Why, yes—I guess that's me."

"Your reputation precedes you, Corporal Chickie. I've heard great things of your glorious campaign advancing on Fort Edwards."

"You have?"

"Oh, yes, from my brother-in-arms, Mrs. Captain, no less. We served together on the *A.B. Chambers* back in thirty-seven, up and down the Missouri River. We had complementary detail: I exploded the boiler every morning, and he—*err,* she—unexploded it every evening, and between us we kept it in prime condition."

"And what was *that* boiler's name?"

"I'm glad you asked, Sergeant Chickie! He was Andrew Jackson when he was blowing up, and John Quincy Adams when he was cooling down. Two-faced, like any good politician."

He told a few more tall tales that he thought were mighty funny, and I laughed like you have to do with men of a certain age who like to talk.

". . . those were the days! I'm telling you, Major Chickie, you should have been there . . ."

"Umm, is that basket for us, Mr. Clemens?" Truth be told, I wanted to get back to the boat before he promoted me to general in a ceremony of fresh stories.

He snapped to attention, and barked out, "Reinforcements for the warship *Galenian*!"

I took it and thanked him kindly, and he saluted in reply.

"Permission to speak freely before discharge?" he bellowed. "There's another basket! One more! Admiral Olivia, present arms!—if you please."

Mrs. Clemens gave me the second basket, even bigger than the first, and smelling of wonderful newly baked bread.

I was all ready to say *Goodbye*, when he launched back in.

"Colonel Chickie, have I ever told you about a frog by the name of Webster? I first heard tell of him from the bartender at . . . oh, what was that hotel called, my dearest?"

He put his arm comfortably around his wife, who answered him with kindness and affection, but not before she sighed and rolled her eyes at me.

–Lesson on the Riverbank–

When I got back, I found the Rooster on the shore. He'd been skipping stones, he said, and chasing dragonflies.

I set down the baskets and took off my shoes, wanting to feel the wet sand squish between my own toes. It was still early, but the day was hottening up like it was angry about something.

"Miss Chickie," he said, offering me a stick. "Will you write my name in the sand?"

"Sure I will. Do you want *Rooster* or your given name?"

"The name Mum gave me is *Daniel*. She wasn't always a bad'un, you know. So write that one, if you please."

I was all set to tell him about King Daniel who drove the Mongols out in 1245, when I thought about my own time with Mr. Clemens, and decided to hold off.

D—A—N—I—E—L, I scratched out in big clear letters. "Now you try."

And didn't he do it just right? Then I asked him:

"Rooster, do you know how to count?"

"Up to twenty—and that's farther than the sounding pole goes," he said, and looked proud.

"Excellent," I told him. "Do you want to learn how numbers *work*?" He'd make a good ship captain, but being able to cipher would make him an even better one.

"Oh, yes, Miss Chickie. I want to learn *everything*."

"First things first, we need to dig down to get at the good mud." We did, and after a few minutes, we'd brought up a good-sized pile of red-brown clay.

"Now, Rooster, I am going to teach you the same way Morfar

started with me—only we used snow!" He laughed, then settled in to pay attention.

"Now—pinch off five bits of clay. Good. Now smash the five bits together to make a ball. Okay, let's call that ball *five* even though it isn't in bits anymore."

"You're a *five*," he said to the ball, as if it could hear him.

"Exactly. Now, pinch off three more bits and lay them next to the ball—and what does it make, all together?"

He puzzled for a minute, then said, "Eight?"

"Yes! That's exactly right, Rooster."

"Now what?" he asked eagerly.

I got him up to *ten*, then *fifty*, then *one hundred*, all in balls and pinches. Then we went backwards to *twenty-three* and *sixty-seven*, and such. Then forwards to *forty-two* and . . . you get the idea.

"There, Miss Chickie! I think I got it."

"You're sharp as a tack, Rooster. If you keep practicing, soon you'll move the *idea* of clay around inside your mind, and you won't need it in your hands at all."

"Wow!"

"You'll get it, Rooster, I know you will. I had to close my eyes at first, but now I can do it with eyes open."

"I'll practice. I'll practice every day!"

We heard Mrs. Captain whistle, then holler: "Get yer tickets—it's now or never!"

I put out my hand to help him up. "C'mon, Rooster, let's go help Mrs. Captain."

I stood beside her, making sure the going-to-be soldiers each paid a fair ticket, except for one or two friendless-looking chaps who got a hefty discount without knowing it.

"Do you think I could help like that someday?" Rooster asked me, when we were done.

"Absolutely you could! You just need to know how numbers go to money. See here . . . each *pinch* of clay equals a *penny,* the *ball* equals a *nickel,* and . . ."

I explained quarters and dollars, and so on, and I could tell by his face that he understood it all. He really was something special.

Every day, I'd find him sat on the deck, moving bits of coal around, and getting quicker and quicker. I felt so proud seeing him at it, which is strange because it was him who was doing something, and not me.

Maybe that's how it is after you teach somebody something: you get a share of the pleasure that they get from knowing something new.

-Your You-

In St. Louis, I did the ticketing with the Rooster beside me offering numbers now and then. By Cairo, wasn't he doing it without any help at all, piling the dollars and coins just so?

As pleased as I was, Mrs. Captain was even more so. "Didn't I tell you, Chickie? My Rooster is the finest, smartest, strongest, helpfulest boy that's ever been!" I agreed, then tousled his hair.

Susan had taught him how to wash it with soap, and it had come up in thick black waves that brought out his one blue eye just lovely. It was his Irish coming through, we were sure.

On the night before we were due to come into Memphis, I found the Rooster leaned over the stern rail with his hand stuck in the water, watching the eddies that flowed around it.

I leaned over beside him. "Penny for your thoughts, my friend."

He looked up. "I come here sometimes and wonder about Mum. Racoon Man told me I should forget her because she's a bad'un who didn't deserve me, but he didn't know her before she took to the saloon."

"I'm sorry, Rooster. You've had it tough, and that's a shame."

"I heard him tell Mrs. Captain that Mum is a bad'un who'll come to a bad end. I don't want her to come to a bad end."

"Of course you don't, Rooster. But it *is* better that you're here now, with her being . . . not able to take care of you properly."

"I do love it here, and I love Mrs. Captain, and you girls, and Racoon Man, and everyone who's been so good to me, but sometimes I worry they're wasting that goodness. What if down deep I'm a bad'un like my mum?"

I didn't know what to say, but then I did.

"Rooster, let me ask you: Am *I* a bad'un?"

"No, Miss Chickie, you never could be! You taught me numbers and . . . You're not a bad'un—why, you're a best'un!"

"My pa was a bad'un, Rooster. As bad as any there ever was. Everybody says so—Ma, Morfar, Aunt Evelyn—everybody."

"But how could he have been, with you so good?"

"We're different from those who borned us, Rooster. We are ourselves. We will always belong, before anything, to ourselves. Just like I am *my* Me, you are *your* You."

"I am my Me . . . ," he said to himself, considering.

"We can make ourselves into who we want to be. And you're someone who can tend a boiler, do the sounding, sell tickets, and make your friends happy, just by being who you are. *You* are a best'un, Rooster. It's true, as true as anything I know. You remember that I'm sure of it, until you are, too."

"Time for bed, Rooster. Ready for a story?" I heard Joanna's voice behind us.

"You want to wash up extra tonight, as tomorrow we've got a big day in Memphis," added Susan.

We followed him up the ladder, where he changed into a sooty night-shirt that had once belonged to Racoon Man. Susan helped him scrub his elbows, which took some time and patience, not to mention soap.

Joanna told him the story of Daniel in the Lion's Den, which I thought would be too scary—a lone little boy thrown in with a beast. But she told it in a way that reminded me it's not how Daniel got *in* with the lions that matters, it's how he got *out.*

She laid one hand on his forehead. "So in the end, dear little Rooster, Daniel didn't kill the lion and the lion didn't kill Daniel. They sat in the darkness, separate but together, and shared the long night. And when morning came, they had found peace."

We waited until he was in deep sleep before we blew out his lamp, and tiptoed away. He was dreaming, but I don't know if it was about Memphis and marbles and strawberry taffy, or about the strong soft paw of a lion, wrapped around his shoulders and keeping him safe. It didn't matter: he'd have time for both.

-A Day in Memphis-

People say the Mississippi gets lazy south of St. Louis, but I say it's more like it gets confused. It looked to me like it couldn't remember whether it's supposed to be flowing south or north—or east or west, for that matter. It didn't even know whether it's a river or a lake, seemed like. But the egrets and the herons and the gulls—they didn't care what it was, so long as it's full of fish.

By the time we pulled into Memphis, both the Rooster and the girls were desperate to spend their money before it burned any more holes in their pockets. I'd gotten the feeling that Main Street would be like nothing I'd ever seen before, and when we got to it, I wasn't disappointed at all.

The Rooster wanted to go into the Calico Jack's Nautical Shoppe and look at sailors' things, so we did that first things first, as it'd have been cruel to make him wait any longer. I stood at the counter, while the girls walked him up and down the aisles. After he'd given the stock a good once-over, he came up beside me, and said to the clerk, "That map up there, Mister. The big one of the Mississippi River. How much does it cost?"

"A dollar fifty," sniffed the man. He was the snooty type who doesn't have time for a child-customer, as if their money isn't as good as any other, and sometimes better, if you catch my drift.

I leaned down. "It's too much—it's a cheating price," I

whispered to the Rooster. If there's one thing I know the price of, it's a map. More people than you'd think can get themselves to the Forks with no idea how to get back.

"But I want to buy it for Mrs. Captain! She loves maps, and all of hers are old and torn. But I only have seventy-five cents." He looked sad enough to cry.

"Rooster, you don't have to buy Mrs. Captain anything. You being you is present enough, I'm certain of it."

"But it's . . . it's her birthday tomorrow! I've been thinking on it, and I'm *decided*. It's a map I'm wanting—*that* map." He pointed.

I stood up and squared my jaw. "He will give you sixty-five cents for it," I told the man.

"Ha! It's worth a dollar fifty. Take it or leave it."

"He will take it, and he will pay you sixty-five cents for it, which is a more-than-fair price, as a survey of the whole North-west Territory can be had for a dollar, and you know it. We don't look like much, us two, but we're mighty tight with a steamboat captain, who's mighty tight with all the others. Wouldn't it be too bad if the boats suddenly stopped bringing you your inventory?"

I smiled at Rooster, and he piped up, mighty brave. "You heard her, Mister. Sixty-five cents. *You* take it or leave it."

"Errr, all right . . . sold. But I'm not happy about it."

"Your happiness is not what we were after, but we thank you kindly for the map. Please roll it up ready for sale . . . and then you'll get your sixty-five cents."

I watched so he didn't slip us a blank page while the Rooster counted out thirteen of his nickels. He was just handing it over when I stopped him and said, "Say, Mister, why don't you tie it with a ribbon, as it's for someone special?"

"A blue one, please. No—green!" added the Rooster.

After that, we decided we'd better get a move on, since the Rooster wanted to get back in time to sell tickets. Susan and Joanna took him and they walked off in order to find something that pleased them, while I walked off in the other direction for the same reason.

I didn't get ten yards before I got tempted by a fancy-soap shop with a French name I don't remember. I went inside, closed my eyes, and smelled all the roses in all the gardens in all the world, cut and gathered into a pile, and put under my very nose.

"*Bonjour, Mademoiselle! Bienvenue!* You have smelled the roses, *peut-être*?" A girl with dark hair and dark eyes, and not much older than me, was stirring a huge pot positively over-flowing with rose petals.

There were thousands of petals—maybe millions—bushels and bushels, anyway, every shade of pink and red, crushed and bruised and floating in a swirl atop a few inches of water just threatening to boil. I watched her place a thin tin plate on top of the flowery mess and close the pot with a heavy lid.

"And now we wait, *Mademoiselle*! *Un petit* moment, then from the vapor comes treasure!" She smiled at me and her eyes sparkled.

It was almost like watching her dance, seeing her reach for this and that, readying for the big moment. There was a roaring furnace in the furthest corner of the shop, and I saw her open its little door just long enough to slip a pair of tongs into the glowing orange coals.

"*Attendez, Mademoiselle . . . c'est* the time *de la* magic!"

She opened the lid, lifted out the plate, and on it I saw a tiny droplet of oil. I don't know what I expected to see, but it took my breath away, it seemed so special. Then she used a tiny spoon to scoop the oil into a tinier glass tube. She pinched the tube on each end with the hot tongs, trapping the little glob in the middle.

"*Voilà!*" She held the glass up high, where it caught a sunbeam and split it into a thousand little rainbows that danced around the room. I was star-struck. To say I wanted that rose oil was an understatement. I *had* to have it.

It might sound strange, but by then, I needed to have something that I didn't need. Something not useful, not for cleaning, or cooking, or doctoring. Something for *me*.

"How much, errr, *Madame*?" I asked her, not really caring—I was set to pay anything she asked.

"Five dollars, *Mademoiselle*, is *le prix*," she told me, with a smile that looked like an apology. "*C'est écrit* there . . . just there." *Huile de rose—cinq dollars* was written on a slate hanging above a barrel of pink petals.

I had seventeen dollars and twenty-eight cents in my pocket. *Spending five dollars would bring it down to . . .* I was figuring, until it hit me again just how much I wanted it.

"I'll . . . I'll buy it, please. That one, in your hand, if I may."

"Ah, *Mademoiselle*, you will not see *les autres*? Many other beautiful *fleurs* we do . . . *ici* we have the same, only violet, for three dollars. *Et* this, *ici,* here we have geranium . . . only one dollar . . . scent is *très jolie."*

She was being kind, and I knew it. From the looks of me, I'd be better off spending five dollars on a new apron and a pair of shoes. I would have said the same to her if it had been me behind the counter.

I told her: "It's all so nice. But I want the rose, thank you."

"Oui, oui, of course . . . but . . . *Écoutez, Mademoiselle:* the glass can only be broken once! You can use *le parfum* only one time—*une seule fois."*

Truth be told, that made me want it even more. Just once, for one special day.

For my wedding? I smiled at the question that popped into my head. *I already have the dress, might as well go ahead and store up a few more things I might need for marrying nobody,* I told myself as the cash register went *Ding!*

—All Good Gifts—

I made my way back onto the *Galenian* and found the Rooster sat on the deck playing marbles with Joanna and Susan.

"Ah-ha! I think I can guess what else you bought," I said to the Rooster.

"Aren't they the best marbles in the world?" he asked me. "Miss Joanna and Miss Susan bought them for me! I'm going to keep them always and never trade even one."

"Look, Mary Jane, look what I bought!" Susan pulled out shiny new sheet music for "Beautiful Dreamer." I groaned—but on the inside, not so she could hear.

"And I got this . . ." Joanna showed me a tiny brass cross hung on a thin chain. "It's real gold, I'm sure of it . . . at least, that's what I think it is," she added, looking close.

Early the next morning, I found Mrs. Captain down near the paddle wheel, rubbing tears off her face. She was holding the map given to her by the Rooster, with the ribbon untied.

"Oh, isn't he the most wonderful, giving, caring, thinking-of-others-ist boy you ever knew? I'll just never get over it. What a gift he is to the world, my Rooster."

"Oh, yes! Your map. I'm glad you like it. He paid no more than a fair price for it, I made sure."

"Like it? Why, I *love* it—a hundred times more than my other maps. Why, they're nothing to me now. I'll burn 'em. This is the only map I'll be needing for the rest of my days."

"Oh—and Happy Birthday, Mrs. Captain!" She looked at me quizzically, and tilted her head. "He said it was for your birthday. Today *isn't* your birthday, then?"

"It is now!" She yelled it out as if louder meant truer. "It ever will be, after today."

"Well, if he gets to choose the day, then I get to choose the year. I say 1814, which makes this your thirty-second birthday—that's a good age."

She laughed. "It's all settled then, and thank you, my dear Chickie."

"Where is the Rooster gone to?" I looked around.

"Oh, he's off with Robert Fulton, they're up to the usual. You know, I've a hankering to go up to my quarters and enjoy my new map properly for a bit."

"You go ahead, Mrs. Captain. I remember enough about the *Galenian* to keep her afloat for a couple hours. You go, go on and enjoy yourself with your new map."

"Maybe I will go up, just for a bit," Mrs. Captain said. She was re-tying the ribbon when something up ahead caught her eye, and she pointed to it. "Ahoy! See that big willow with the funny branch, there? Means it won't be too long before we put into Greenville. There you'll meet some new characters, I'll wager."

–Moving On–

Way down upon the Swanee River,
Far, far away,
There's where my heart is turning ever,
There's where the ol' folks stay.

I noticed an old-timer at the rail, singing his heart out. *I'll go keep him company for a bit,* I decided. *There's good people everywhere, and why shouldn't he be one of them?*

I went to stand beside him, where I could listen better.

". . . Oh, gal! I didn't see you there. I'm disturbing you, then?"

"No, not a bit, Sir. I heard your fine voice and came over to say *Hello.*"

"You're too kind to an old man, I only sing to help pass the time," he said. "But I *am* very glad to meet you. Say—join me for the chorus?"

"Oh, no, I can't sing, myself . . . but I do like to watch the river go by."

"Well then, gal. Let's us watch the river for a bit, shall we?"

It was the usual sights along the Mississippi: trees and more trees, for the most part. There's a long wagon trail that goes along beside the river, and you notice the odd person on foot or on horseback. But on that day, I saw something altogether different go by.

Two men on horses went first, each of them carrying a gun. Three other men walked behind them: they each had a gun on one hip, a cane in one hand, and a whip in the other. Those men had pale skin—except where their faces were red with the effort of it. The people who came after had dark skin—except where their backs were red from a whip's cut. People owning other people was just as evil as I'd always heard it was, from Miss Frances, or from Ma, or from anybody. But the sheer bloodiness of it, I hadn't been told of, not really. Not anything like what I was seeing for myself.

Behind those red-in-the-face men, at least a hundred wretched men, and boys, limped along, lined up in twos and chained so close they couldn't hardly turn a head. Each was pressed up against the hair of the man in front, the nose of the man behind, and the shoulder of the man beside.

A hundred women and girls—even more wretched—trudged behind the men, their hands, waists, ankles, even necks, tied together and to each other by rope. Some were swollen with carrying, some with nursing, some were dragging along, some being drug.

Some were singing somehow. Some were crying. Some were both.

Six big wagons followed them, loaded with cornmeal and lard, rope and chain, babies and bodies.

I wondered if I was dreaming. Or nightmaring. I looked over at the old-timer, and his face was just as cheerful as it had been.

"What . . . Why . . . Where are those people going?"

"People? Oh, you mean *property*, gal. At least ten thousand dollars' worth, I'd reckon. And it's not going anywhere, it's just moving."

"But those men *can't* barely move, chained like that."

"It's property *being* moved, gal. How did you think people get their property from one place to another? By riding it in a Surrey carriage with a fringe on top? *Ha ha!*"

"Moved *from* where, then?"

"Out East, I imagine. Agents buy the property and drivers move it to the South."

"Those men on horses, they're the drivers, then?"

"Well, of course they are! Now there, gal, where were you raised that you don't know that?"

"I just came down from Fort Snelling this spring."

"I *see* . . . ," he chuckled, "north of North, then. And pray tell what did they teach you about slaveholding, up there at your Fort Snelling?"

"That it's a terrible sin, and a moral depravity."

"*Ha ha!* Cut and dried as that, is it?"

"Of course it is! I'm an Abolitionist. My whole family is, really. Morfar—my grandfather—says people held in bondage— and the Indians, too—are deep-down just like you and me."

"He said that, did he?"

"Oh, yes. And my ma goes to a Tuesday Ladies' Tea where they read out of *The Liberator*."

"Oh, does she?"

"All the girls in my school are Abolitionists, too, every one of them. We all started being it after Miss Frances read us *Uncle Tom's Cabin*. There wasn't a single one of us who didn't cry when Little Eva died. Annie made herself so sick over it that her pa brought home a kitten."

"That *does* sound like an Abolitionist, I'll give you that."

He was listening like I'd caught his interest, so I went on. "Slaveholders don't feel any Christian love in their hearts, that's the problem. Once they do, they will *naturally* do the right thing—that's what Miss Frances says."

"Sounds like you've got it all figured out, gal. You're off to New Orleans, I imagine? Maybe on from there?"

"No, Sir, I am bound for Greenville, Mississippi, where my . . . where *our* uncle lives. He owns a tannery."

"Oh, he does, does he? *Ha ha!* Well, maybe you'll get yourself some occupation putting Christian love into his heart."

"Thank you kindly—I guess . . . May I ask where you are going?"

"Down to Natchez, gal, where my wife, Essie, rests ever-lastingly in a graveyard near her people. *My* people are from Liberty, where my one son and two daughters live. And Lord only knows how many grandchildren, *ha ha!*"

"That sounds like a nice place."

"Indeed it is, gal. I own two thousand acres of the most beautiful country God created. Inherited it from my daddy, who inherited it from his daddy before him."

"Do you keep horses?" I asked, as I'd been missing Samson and Delilah.

"Do I? I've got horses, 'n' donkeys, 'n' goats, 'n' dogs, cats—all manner of critters. And, what's more—I've got *property*! Four hundred head—fifty-some moved to me from Savannah just last year, driven just as you see before you."

I was dumbfounded. He had seemed nice enough at first. I could have even mistook him for a *good* man.

"I'll give you something to ponder, gal, and then I'll leave you in peace," he said. "Where do you suppose the cotton that made your dress came from? Or the tobacco for your granddad's after-dinner pipe? Or the sugar for your mama's ladies' tea? You can thank the hard-working property-owners of the South for most of what you Northerners like to sit on your bee-hinds and enjoy yourselves with, gal."

It made me sad to see how he just didn't understand. The answer to slavery is right in front of our faces: just stop doing it, and set everybody free. Everybody knows that. It's not that complicated, after all.

The old-timer took up his tune where he'd left off, and walked away, before I could explain how simple it is. Before I could tell him how everything would be completely different if it was me down here in his shoes.

-Lesson on the Deck-

Mrs. Captain came over just then, looking concerned. She must've heard what we were talking about, because she told me:

"Chickie, you have to understand that these Southerners have their own ways, and they started doing them long before you were born. I've been sailing the *Galenian* in and out of the South for years, and I've . . . well, I've seen some things.

"When you get off at Greenville—which won't be long now— you keep your head down and worry about yourself and those girls. You've got plenty on your plate in taking care of them, and you aren't in a position to go saving anybody else."

"But, remember how there's good people everywhere, Mrs. Captain? I said it and you agreed with me."

"Yes, that's true, Chickie, but . . ."

"These *good* people—I want to be one of them."

We heard a hooting and hollering coming from the shore. I looked ahead and saw what must be Greenville. There on the dock was a man in a white suit waving his hat like he'd never seen a boat before and couldn't contain the joy of it.

I couldn't make out his face, and anyway it would have been a face I'd never seen before. Even so, I didn't have to wonder who it was. Something inside of me already knew that it was none other than Peter Wilks.

CHAPTER XIX

–Goodbye and Hello–

It was time for us to get off the boat. Mrs. Captain and the Rooster saw us as far as the dock, then let us go.

"It doesn't do any good to say *Goodbye* to you, Mrs. Captain," I told her. "I tried it before and nothing came of it—found myself right back on the *Galenian* after all!"

"And that's just the right way to put it, dear little Chickie! Why, I couldn't love you better than I do—all of you! Susan so sweet, Joanna so smart, and my Rooster—he's just plain wonderful backwards and forwards!"

"Um . . . you forgot someone," I said to her.

"Did I? How could I have . . ."

"You, Mrs. Captain—*you!* You've been so good to all of us that we don't know what to do . . ."

". . . Except to love you back, which we always will,

Mrs. Captain," Susan broke in. Joanna nodded, and I noticed that both of her hands were down from her face.

The man that I already knew was Peter Wilks came over, pleased as punch. "Lasses—*Eh-eh*—Our three lassies! *Eh eh-heh, gah, eh-heh!*" he said.

Mrs. Captain stepped up, eyeing him all around like he was a steamboat she was deciding whether or not to get on.

"M'lady, we present to thee Peter Wilks!" he said to her about his own self. Then he swept out a hand and bowed, bending himself nearly in half and touching his toes. Mrs. Captain shook his hand, friendly as it was, and even gave him a smile.

"Pleased to know you," she said in return. "I am Mrs. Captain, and this is my vessel the *Galenian*, what brought these girls here."

"An' lucky are they to have had such a lady as thee looking out for 'em."

"I'm your niece Mary Jane," I told him. "And these are my sisters, your other nieces, Susan and Joanna."

"Stars 'n' garthers! What names, what lovely names! Su-san! Jo-an-na! *Eh-heh!* Just to think o' it."

"Thank you, Mr. Wilks," answered Susan.

"*Eh-heh eh, gah, eh-heh!* Now thee three lasses must call us *Uncle—eh-heh!*"

Mrs. Captain seemed satisfied at this. She hugged us girls all around, then dried her eyes on her apron. "What I said last time still goes, Mary Jane: if you ever need me, you can find me on the Mississippi River."

"Me too!" the Rooster piped up. "Somewhere between Dubuque and New Orleans." Joanna told him what a good, smart, capable boy he was, while Susan smoothed his hair out of his face and kissed his cheek.

Then we were on shore watching the *Galenian* shove off. Her next stop would be Natchez, one hundred and seventy miles down-river. In the space of a few minutes, Mrs. Captain and the Rooster were gone from our sight.

"Oreight, lasses—thee are *home* now, consider theeself so. Our lassies three!—*eh eh-heh, gah, eh-heh! Three!*—We thought our George had only two—but it were *three!*"

Didn't he have a strange way of talking? It was like nothing I'd ever heard.

Now, let it be known from the start that Mr. Peter Osbourne Wilks was odd—*extra* odd—and that means something, coming from me. Growing up at the Forks as I did, I can count on one hand the number of people who came through that *didn't* seem odd. Even so, Peter Wilks was a unique specimen.

He was remarkable tall—must have topped seven feet—and very thin, except for a big belly that stuck out like a balloon. He was bald except for some very few white hairs, though what they lacked in number they made up for in length. He wore a bright white shirt with brown tobacco stains all down the front, just where a man dribbles when he chews and talks at the same time. His white shoes were polished to a shine, like you'd expect to see on a man leading a marching band.

He stood with his arms crossed, smiling at us so proud: "Our lassies three!—*Eh-eh*—Just to think o' it! *Eh eh-heh, gah, eh-heh!*"

244

"He sounds just like Pa!" I heard Joanna whisper to Susan, and they hugged and cried a little, both of them.

In all the time I knew Uncle George, he could no more than grunt and squawk. Then I recalled how he'd been born in England, and supposed it's just how children learn to talk over there. It's unfortunate, but you can't blame them because they're too little to know better.

Joanna's eyes were lit up and Susan was smiling. *Maybe they feel like they've found family,* I thought to myself, then considered: *No matter how odd he is or isn't, Peter Wilks is their uncle.*

Didn't I want those girls to be happy? More than that— I wanted them to be so they didn't even *know* they're happy, like they were back before their pa was hurt, and the money ran out, and their ma got sick, and all the rest. Back like I was just a few months ago, walking through a snowy pine forest with Morfar.

I decided I'd give Peter Wilks a fair shake and keep an open mind, if only for their sakes. The girls had had to bear up under a heap of sadness in Fort Edwards, Illinois. Maybe Greenville, Mississippi, would be the place where they could finally set it down.

–A Short Detour–

"Come, then! We'll whisk thee to thee new home—*eh eh-heh, gah, eh-heh!*—Oh, won't it be lovely to have thee?"

We climbed into Peter Wilks's carriage and started off. It wasn't a mile before we pulled up under a fancy wooden sign that said *General Store*. Underneath was painted *Groceries &*

Dry Goods & Sewing Supplies and above was painted *Telegraph & Post*, in smaller letters, but just as fine.

"Look here, Widow—our lassies have come to us! Send word to Fort Edwards telling they've come, will ye?"

The woman seated behind the counter nodded. She was tall and wide-ish, with short curly hair and the face of someone you don't want to argue with.

"*Good afternoon*, young Misses. I infer that you are the Wilks nieces come to live with their uncle, is that correct?"

"Yes, Ma'am, we are. My name is Mary Jane, and these are my sisters: Susan and Joanna."

She set down her knitting, and rose to shake my hand. "I wish you welcome, Mary Jane. And to you as well, Susan and Joanna. I am the Widow Bartley. I own this store and I run it, too. I don't lock the door because I'm always here."

"Time for presents, lassies! *Eh eh-eh, gah, eh-eh!*" Peter Wilks clapped his hands. "Go on now 'n' pick what thee want. *Eh-heh!* Aye, how wonderful to have presents!"

Susan and Joanna followed him, a little confused, but willing to oblige. I stayed at the counter, and kept talking to Widow Bartley.

"You're missing out on presents, Mary Jane," she warned me.

"Never mind that, Widow Bartley, those girls need *food*. Up at Fort Edwards, we had less than nothing, most days."

It hadn't been all that long since they'd left home, and the girls were still skinnier than was good for them, not to mention me, too. "What should I ask him for?"

She glanced over at Susan and Joanna. "Eggs," she said. "Three eggs a day for each of you." She came out from behind the counter and walked the aisles, finding what she wanted. "Whole milk and dark rye bread. Cheese and spinach and sugared plums and molasses. Smoked pork hocks and don't boil them, fry them in lard—or better yet, in butter. And duck—not chicken—but duck, fried the same way."

As she talked, she threw a good amount of each into a wooden box. "Here's enough for a week, but if it's gone sooner, you come right back to me," she said, handing it over.

"Thank you, Ma'am, I will."

She yelled over her shoulder towards Peter Wilks. "Twelve dollars, all together, for the food!"

It was a fair price. I liked the Widow Bartley. She was no-nonsense.

Susan returned to the counter carrying a music box and Joanna had a set of drawing pencils. They laid them out for purchase.

"Seventeen dollars—new total," said Widow Bartley.

"Nay, nay! Lassies! We must have more! *Eh-heh-heh!*" He turned to me. "Now then, luv, thee must have a present as well."

I wasn't much bothered about it, so I asked for a peppermint stick from the jar behind the counter.

"Nay, lassie, nay! Not like that—ask for sommit grand, sommit wonderful! *Eh-eh!* Think, now. Think o' what thee want, lass."

I glanced over at Susan, then took a chance.

"A piano!" I told him. "We want a piano at home."

"Thee shall have it! An' what else?"

I looked to Joanna. "Pet rabbits!" I added. "All different kinds, a long-haired and a lop-eared and a spotted—and some of them babies, too."

"Oh, wonderful! Won't it be a lark? Rabbits 'n' a piano— *Eh-heh*—order 'em, Widow Bartley, order 'em now. *Eh-heh, gah!*"

"Done," she said, handing him a receipt. "Half-payment now and the other half upon delivery."

"Put it on our account, Widow Bartley, th' *Wilks* account!" She did so, but not before he added a few more things we didn't need.

"I thank you for your business as always, Peter Wilks."

He pointed at me. "This one will be back tomorrow for sundries—if thee think we can trust her wi' th' dosh 'n' dollars, *eh eh-eh, gah, eh-eh!*"

"We'll be open," she said, ready to see us out.

At the last minute, she took me aside. "Like I said, Mary Jane, I don't lock the door because I'm *always here*. You remember that."

—La Douce Tannerie d'Wilks—

"Thee new home be not far now!" Peter Wilks yelled at us over his shoulder while driving. "An' aren't we just a-tinglin'? *Eh-heh!* Three fine lassies at home, just for us! *Eh eh-heh, gah, eh-heh.*"

A minute later, we rolled under a trellis with *La Douce Tannerie d'Wilks* painted across the top, and dead wisteria hung all over. The vines had gone to seed long ago, just like the rest of the tannery.

The worst was the smell. It smelled of rotten guts and raw manure and soured cheese and burnt soap and every bad smell you ever smelled, stirred together, warmed up, and let out straight into your face. Me and the girls couldn't help gagging a bit when we pulled up.

"Can't see th' brass for th' muck, eh? I spy leather boots on thee pretty feet, lassies. Thee do know leather be skin, nay?" Peter Wilks chortled as he put down the reins.

"An' how does skin go from covering a living beast to covering thee two tad feet?" he asked us, and we didn't know.

"Ahh . . . they don't teach that in th' schoolhouse, do they? *Eh!* That's our lad George, throwing dosh away on schoolroom schooling. *Eh! Eh!* We always knew his sweet Everlyn would bring our lad to ruin—tried to tell him so more than once."

I glanced at the girls, who looked like they'd been slapped in the face.

"Tanning hides isn't easy or pretty, but it needs done 'n' it pays well. It's for men wi' aspiration 'n' ambition—men like Peter Wilks! *Eh!* Not for men drug down by their *Dear Hearts* . . .

"Success like ours is for men what have th' guts to take a risk now an' again. *Eh! Eh!* Sell for profit 'n' buy from loss, that's what Peter Wilks knows how to do, and Peter Wilks did not learn it inside o' some mithering schoolroom, that's for certain. *Eh! Eh!*"

The carriage stopped with a jerk. "Aye! There's a tanyard for thee, only th' most prolific in th' bleedin' county, it were . . ."

Before us lay two deep pits, one crusted around with a milky-colored rind, the other half-full of brown slime oozing in from a festering pile of all-sorts: moldy persimmons, black-walnut hulls, shaved-up tree bark, alder cones, and acorn caps.

Next to the pits was some salt-looking stuff that burned

the inside of your head with its fumes. But worst of all was the brains. A big-old mound of gray and wrinkly and cheesy brains off to one side, with flies and maggots having a field day on it.

"O'course, we haven't tanned a hide in a year or more—don't need to! *Eh! Eh!* Made a regular fortune buying low 'n' selling high, *eh!* Now we just scrawm about as we wish, doing what we will, when we will. Until one day last week when th' gov'mint tells us we've three lassies coming to us! *Eh! Eh!*"

Something on the horizon caught his eye: "Look ye there! What do thee suppose it be? *Eh!* It's MONEY! *Eh! Eh!* An' likely more than thee think, too. Aye, that's where th' real dosh be. *Eh!*"

He took up the reins and drove towards the red dust that was kicking up across the far field. As we got closer and closer, I began to understand what he meant, and to see what he wanted us to see.

–Peter Wilks's Property–

Making that red dust were two people dragging something behind them.

When we arrived at the main house, he shouted at them, "Stop here, stop here! We're in th' mood to get a look at thee." They unyoked and came to stand before us.

Peter Wilks pointed at them: "Behold, lasses! Two fine pieces o' property, all ours."

It was a ma and her daughter, I could tell from the resemblance. They shared the same eyes, with high arched brows, just alike. The thing most different about them was their skin: the ma's was the color of coffee without cream, and the daughter's was the color of coffee with cream. I might have taken them for sisters, they seemed so near in age, but for the way the little girl looked up at her ma. Aside from that, both wore broadcloth smocks, and neither one had shoes. They were muscled and skinny all at the same time: the kind of muscles built by too much work and too little rest, and a lifetime of it.

"We could get three hundred dollars in a quick-sale for th' full-grown, no questions asked. Less for th' ungrown one, maybe a hundred or so," he told us, then added, "We don't use 'em hard as we could, but it doesn't cost much to have 'em around. They cook 'n' carry, 'n' fettle about. Perhaps thee lassies will find some use for 'em."

The little girl bit her lip, and reached for her ma's hand. Her ma took it and pulled her closer.

I was stunned. I wasn't exactly keen on Peter Wilks by then, but I hadn't suspected him so bad as this. Susan and Joanna's eyes were like saucers, not knowing *what* to think about it.

Something wet touched my hand, and I jumped. When I looked down, I saw that a dog had sidled up beside me. He was so big and brown, you could've taken him for a bear. I was glad for the distraction.

Joanna put her hand out, and he dog-kissed her, too. "Mr. . . . Peter . . . Uncle Peter," she said, her voice shaky. "Does he have a name?"

"They both got names, luv! This one's *Sugar.*" He pointed

straight into the grown woman's face. "We call her that because she's so sweet, ain'tcha ain'tcha?" He made kissing noises at her.

"An' that"—he pointed to the little girl standing next to her mother—"we call her *Candy*—know why? Because she's made out o' Sugar! *Eh eh-heh, gah, eh-heh!*

"Look sharp! *Garrrr!*" Peter Wilks lunged towards Candy, threatening to snatch her up, like some mean thing from a fairy-tale. Candy stepped behind her mother, who met his gaze straight-on for almost a second, then looked away.

"*Eh eh-heh, gah, eh-heh! Eh eh-heh, gah, eh-heh!*" Peter Wilks laughed hard and long, then he yelled out: "Get a move on, th' pair o' thee! Go on now!"

Sugar and Candy yoked themselves back up and drug their burden off towards the tool-shed. I tried to smile a kindly *Hello* at them, but they didn't see. They were careful to look down, and not at me.

–The Story of a Quick-Sale–

"We used to own more property—a whole stable o' property. Until we ran into a bit o' luck, it were," Peter Wilks said, and got himself fixed to tell us all about it.

"One day—might be a year ago—we come out to find a piece o' our property floating in th' tanning vat, tongue stuck out an' eyes bugged. Overseer had not an idea what happened, *heh-eh!* 'Twasn't full-grown property drown in th' vat, but still, a loss be a loss.

"Damned if a door-to-door trader didn't stop by just then

to try to talk us into buying new. We told him, *Not today, mate. Can't thee see we're in th' middle o' it?*

"Oh, no, kind friend, don't get me wrong! I'm not a trader parsay, I'm a speculator," he told us like it were sommit nice. *A fine place this is . . . what have you got here in property?*

"*There's our property right there—crying an' a-wailering over what's in th' vat,* I told him.

"He tallied them up. *I count two adult males, one broodmare, four ungrown males, and three ungrown females. Those ungrowns will make good-sized adults, I'll measure.*

" *'Cept that one floating in th' vat, he's as growed as he's gonna get. Eh eh-heh!*

"*I'll give you fifty dollars for that dead boy!* He told us he buys dead ones, packs 'em in ice, and carts 'em down to New Orleans, where they load 'em into boats and sail 'em up to Philadelphia, where they cut 'em up and look at th' insides, in fancy medical schools! *Eh eh-heh, gah, eh-heh!*

"So we told th' lad, *Sounds like th' arse-end of th' deal for thee, but we'll take it!* And he puts five golden-eagle coins into our hand, on th' spot! Now *gold* be worth sommit, lassies—paper money can go to naught in a heartbeat, but not gold.

"But that door-to-door lad weren't done yet. *I'll make you an offer, I will! What would you say to a full six thousand for all ten, including the dead one? Six thousand in gold right this very minute!*

"We looked over our property all in fits over th' dead one, begging us for a preacher burial 'n' not sell to th' medical. Ungrowns screaming 'n' clutching at their mar-mar. I tell thee, swapping that mess for a big bag o' gold didn't sound too shite right about then.

"So we impulsed it, because we always were an impulsive self-made man. *Mate, thee can have 'em!* I answered. *But we'd just as soon keep th' female for company! Eh eh-heh, gah, eh-heh!*

"*Of course! A man like you needs his supper cooked for him, and say, I'll even let you keep back an ungrown to cook your dessert!*

"He gave us a flat six thousand for th' lot, except th' two I showed thee. An' now I've got a fat bag o' gold inna oyle down th' ginnel!"

The Southern sun is mean. It was the hottest day of my life so far, but I stood there shivering. My jaw was iced shut, and I said nothing because I couldn't think of what to say.

Peter Wilks kept right on. "We don't miss what we sold, not a bit. It aren't easy managing property, for here's th' thing: *Damn if they don't resist us, every which way we turn!* Any bleedin' thing a body's out here trying to get done, they'll resist it. Sometimes it's small, like not walking so fast as we know they could. Sometimes it's big, like ruining a set o' skins with too long a soak. A body can bray on 'em all day 'n' all night, 'n' it hardly does any good. Just one thing after another wi' property."

He shook his head at it, like it was the hardest luck anybody ever had.

–Cold Nose, Warm Heart–

I set out to change the subject. "Joanna meant the dog, Uncle Peter—what's his name?"

"Oh, *his* name? His name be *dogmeat,* for all he's fit for. Can't seem to be rid o' him, 'n' we don't feed him, neither; he goes off a-bleggin', is likely.

"Th' old man what brought him down said he were a duck-hunter up on th' Chesapeake Bay. Boasted that hound could bring in a hundred ducks a day, in shite weather, too. When th' old bloke died we couldn't get to th' body for three days, that loppy dog wouldn't let us near."

The dog had moved on from Joanna, and was politely nosing Susan, who returned his greeting with a pat on the head. I think Peter Wilks got jealous.

"He's a mangy gowly cur, not a hound for us, lasses." He went to kick him. "Sling thee hook, ye bloody pest!"

The dog stepped to the side and Peter Wilks's foot went right past him, up into the air.

Whump! He landed flat on his back, cursing.

The dog was unbothered. He walked off with his head held high, probably to find himself a nice shady place to lie down.

After Peter Wilks rose back up and brushed himself off, he had a look on his face like *That never happened,* and we went along with it.

"Let's get thee inside, now," he said. He climbed the porch steps, then turned and waggled a finger at us: "Never forget how lucky thee are to have someone take thee in, lasses. We didn't have to, it's charity that compels us, o'course. But still, we're well happy thee are here, 'n' that you're to be ours. *Eh eh-heh!*"

He pushed the rusty screen door open. "Come in, ye lassies!" he said to us over his shoulder. "Come 'n' see thee new Home Sweet Home—*Eh! Gah, eh-heh!*" He went inside, expecting us to follow after.

Susan looked up at me in a worried way. Joanna leaned in and asked in a low voice, "Is that right, Mary Jane? Is this to be our home?"

I looked around us, from the rotten vats to the falling-down house to the place in the dirt where the ma and her daughter had stood.

"No, girls. This ain't home," I told them. "You'll know it when we get there."

CHAPTER XX

–A Room of My Own–

Peter Wilks's house was just packed full of space. The girls forgot about what happened outside in the yard once they saw inside in the parlor, all full of fancy things. They begged that each of us should have our own bedroom, for it was a luxury they'd never had. And why shouldn't we? The whole upstairs was nothing but sleeping rooms. In the end, even my silk dresses got their own room, though the three of them did have to share.

I kept us right next to each other: down the hall it went Susan, Joanna, then me. On the far end was Peter Wilks's room, but he told us never to go in unless we were asked. I thought, *Why in the world would we want to?*

The girls insisted I have the biggest room, the one with lace curtains and a porcelain sink. I gave in but made them promise to come in and out as they pleased, then sent them to unpack.

I put my *History of England,* my rose oil, my near-empty medicine bag, and my jar of cherry preserves under my bed and sat down to think about how I was going to get us out of there. And where I was going to get the courage to even try.

You see, by then I had my mind set on getting Sugar and Candy free. That's what a real Abolitionist would do, anybody would tell you that. And they are some *good* people, those Abolitionists, no doubt about it.

So there it was: I had to get Peter Wilks to let me leave *La Douce Tannerie d'Wilks* and take my family with me. I also had to get him to wake up and free Sugar and Candy from the bondage he was holding them in. In short, I'd have to convince him to give up some of his things and a lot of his money—that's how he'd see it, I was sure. What I didn't know, was how to even start. But I thought maybe if I put my wits to it, I could figure it out.

So I put my head in my hands, and I tried. Before I got much of anywhere, I heard Peter Wilks downstairs, hollering for his dinner.

-Yorksheer Ways-

"Lassies—suppertime!"

I came downstairs to find the parlor door open such that I could see into the kitchen. Sugar was putting the last touches on something good to eat, and Candy was right beside her. I saw her slip her daughter a piece of roast duck, some of the sweet meat at the neck, the very best part. Then she began to sing:

As I went down in de valley to pray,
Studying about dat good old way,
When you shall wear de starry crown,
Good Lord, show me de way.

She kept her voice low, but clear, and her daughter swayed beside her, looking up at her mother and studying her face, like you do with the person you love most in the world.

Then Sugar saw me out of the corner of her eye, startled, and stopped. I winked at her, just to let her know that I was on her side, but she didn't wink back.

"Suppertime! Suppertime for our lassies!"

Peter Wilks was shouting again. The girls came downstairs and we joined him at table. "What a day we've had!" He was in a right good mood. "We're knackered 'n' famished . . . 'n' could eat us th' oven door if it were butherd."

He banged on the table and shouted into the kitchen, "*Sugar!* Get in here 'n' bring us breadcake 'n' mash. *Look sharp, goddamn ye!*" He sounded so mean, the girls and I jumped in our seats.

Sugar came in and loaded up the dinner table with the roast duck and all the other good things she'd made. "Go on, lassies, go on! Thee all need to slap some timber on." Peter Wilks dug in, and we followed his lead, as we were hungry, too. The food was extra good, and we piled our plates high and drowned them in butter, cream, and gravy.

Ding! Ding! Ding!

Midway through his plate, Peter Wilks tapped his glass with a fork.

"Now I'll tell thee how it's going to be, for it's going to be a certain way. Us Yorksheer folk have Yorksheer ways. *Eh eh-heh, gah, eh-heh!*

"First, don't bother us in th' morning as we like to have a nice lie-in. Next, we're generally off into town to check th' bank stock exchange—not that we're fool enough to put our own dosh in it. We'll have a bit o' scran after, then out to th' barn—'n' don't come mithering in, any o' thee, 'tis *forbidden*—understand?"

I nodded, as did Susan and Joanna.

"Lastly, afore we sleep, we drink a glass o' milk. Always have, always will. We need it for th' health, which ain't never been strong.

"Aye! We need our milk to keep us hale. Milk wi' cream innit! One glass every night, just after we're tucked into bed. Our Candy were always th' one to bring it, but comes with a sulk on . . . *Eh!* One o' *thee* must bring it from now."

"It will be me, I'll be the one," I said. *That's when I'll convince you to let us all go,* is what I was thinking.

"Oreight, oreight, no need to fight over us, lassies. *Eh eh-heh!* Thee can all have a turn. Come in with a smile on 'n' we'll have us a nice visit, then off to bed when we send thee."

I smiled and nodded to show I understood.

"An' now . . . where'd we put our hat?" He looked and didn't find it, then left the room to search around.

Sugar was on her knees sweeping up the crumbs from our supper. I wanted badly for us to start off on a good foot, so I knelt down and put my hands on her shoulders.

"Sugar, can I tell you something important?"

"Yes'm, Miz," she answered, but didn't quite look at me. She more looked through me.

"I want to be your *friend*," I told her, kind as could be.

"Yes'm, Miz," she answered, but not grateful, like I had expected.

Peter Wilks walked in with his hat on and didn't like what he saw.

"Lassie—lassie, *nay!*" he hollered. "Up off th' floor, 'n' remember theeself!"

I jumped up. "Yes . . . Uncle Peter."

"Thee are to be *Mistress* 'n' I'll have thee act like it, or pay th' price, I promise thee." He looked from me to Susan to Joanna, with as angry a face as I'd ever seen. "We'll have three *respectable* nieces in our house, not a passel o' clarty bitches."

I was afraid. "I'm sorry, Uncle Peter," I said.

"Go on 'n' fix us our milk now." He pointed at me. "We're out to th' barn, then upstairs to don our nightclothes. Thee'll come in just after."

Once he was gone, Sugar grabbed Candy by the arm, and they cleared out without looking back. I turned to Susan and Joanna: "You'd better get yourselves to bed. It's been a long day, and the sun is already on its way down."

I said it plain and calm, like I wasn't shaken out of my wits—like I knew what we'd do next. I think it worked, too, because they both kissed me and did what they were told.

–Off to Bed–

I went into the kitchen and found a pitcher of milk on the windowsill. I poured out a glass for Peter Wilks, then stirred in some cream with my finger. It looked so tasty, I admit to taking a gulp or two before bringing it upstairs.

Peter Wilks was laid in bed, wearing a night-shirt and night-cap, both of yellow seer-sucker. I plumped his pillows, like he asked, and handed him his milk.

"Eh! Lass, we won't have thee faffin' about wi' our Sugar, understand? An' don't let us catch thee *coddling* our Candy, neither, for being soft wi' property brings naught but trouble. An' if we can't trust thee around th' property, how are we to trust thee with th' grocery money?"

Peter Wilks's heart was two cups less than empty of Christian love, from what I could tell. I did what I thought might help.

"Uncle Peter, have you ever read *Uncle Tom's Cabin*? It's a fine book. Say, I could read it out loud to you when I bring you your milk . . ."

He sat up straight. "*Cabin? Ha!* Who'd want to hear about a manky ol' cabin? Not a self-made man on our own grand *estate*! An estate worth nine thousand a'least—some would say ten! *Ten thousand dollars* o' capital, pure capital all around us, lassie. Thee never heard o' so vast a sum, now did thee?"

I had heard of so vast a sum, but had never met any one person who had it. All the trapped furs we brought into Fort Snelling in a year didn't come to half of that. The *Galenian* had to sail a thousand miles of Mississippi River with a full docket, twice over before she collected a quarter of it.

"*Eh eh-heh, gah, eh-heh!* An' there's six thousand dollars gold besides, inna oyle down th' ginnel." He grabbed me by the chin. "Don't let us catch thee poking around trying to find it. We'll skin thee alive if we do, 'n' we have the tools sharp and ready to do it." He let go of me, then laughed, "*Eh eh-heh!*"

I have no earthly idea what a *ginnel* is, nor a *oyle*, neither, but I didn't need to in order to be scared out of my wits.

"An' don't go greedy on us, neither. We never made a will 'n' never would, thee'll do well to remember that." He pointed straight at me. "I reckon little brother'll get the lot one day, th' twonky waller."

"An' now we must have our milk, otherwise we won't sleep happy. We need our milk to keep us strong. We aren't hearty, it's our only flaw. Catch any contagion reet quick, we do—or might have, if we didn't. A year ago, we did no more than walk by Ben Rucker's broken foot an' wasn't our own foot sore by th' end o' that day? Aye!

"But tonight–tonight wi' our three lassies just for us? Tonight we're in fine fettle! *Eh eh-heh, gah, eh-heh!*"

He reached for his milk and drank it slow, making slurpy sounds. Just past his fifth swallow he stopped to sing out just for the giddiness of it, and swung his glass back and forth to keep time.

I married a wife in th' full o' the moon,
A thrifty housewife to be,
Each night I have trouble to put her to bed,
Rank as a sow is she!

Then he drank down the last drops, handed me the empty glass, and patted the bed. "Come sit, lassie. We won't bite, 'n' our ditty's got a deal more verses to it."

I sure didn't want to. I gave out a big yawn and said, "Uncle Peter . . . I think I should go off to sleep. We've got a big day tomorrow."

He looked me over, then waved me away with one hand. "Oreight, oreight, put wood t'oil 'n' begone with thee—'n' keep to mind what's been said about th' property—thee'd best not let us catch thee getting ducky—we won't have thee plotting against us, we'll cut it off right quick—'n' that's a promise!"

I left his room, shutting the door behind me.

-A Taste of Home-

On the way down the hall, I stuck my head into Susan's room and found both of the girls curled up together. I wasn't surprised; in fact, I was glad of it.

When I got to my room, I laid down, and discovered I wasn't at all sleepy. I thought about Ma and Morfar and Hansel. I thought about Fort Snelling and Annie and Miss Frances. I thought about the Forks and Gusty and Peter Pond. I thought about the chilly lakes and crisp air up North. About winter snow, and spring rain, and summer flowers, and autumn fruit . . . *like cherries*! I remembered the preserves under my bed, the ones Ma had given me to take along.

Why not? I asked myself. *Tasting home might help me figure out how to get home.*

Downstairs the house was quiet. I opened the front door, then the screen door, and sat myself outside on the porch front steps. It was dark thick night and the fireflies were blinking and dancing in the darkness.

Out of the shadows came a lumbering beast. It was the bear-dog! He laid down in the dirt a few yards off, and flopped over on his side. *In case you want company,* he seemed to be saying. He didn't bother me at all. In fact, it was friendly having him there.

I screwed open the jar of preserves, and looked up for the moon. No luck, but a breeze came up that felt nice and broke the hot for a minute or two. I reached my whole hand into the jar and ate, squeezing the cherries between my teeth and letting the juice run down my gullet. They tasted like far away and a million years ago.

It did help me think. Peter Wilks was never going to *let* any of us go, least of all Sugar and Candy. If we were ever going to get out of there, we'd have to run away. So I made a plan.

I'll ask him for grocery money, as often as I can. Then I'll shop, and put it all on Peter Wilks's tab. I'll pocket the cash after, until I've saved up . . . let's see . . . three hundred and thirteen dollars should do it.

The day I've got that much, we'll pack our things . . . and run.

We'll hide in the riverbank and wait for the first steamboat of the day. I'll buy us five tickets going anywhere: Susan, Joanna, Sugar, Candy, and me. We'll hop on and off steamboats, sailing up and down in a zigzag, to throw everybody off our scent. Sooner or later, we'll land in Fort Snelling, and find Ma. She'll know what to do next.

It was a good plan, I thought: three young ladies traveling with their "property"—three young ladies who never stuck around long enough to raise suspicion.

I ate myself past full, until there was only one cherry left, stuck to the bottom of the jar. "Come here, boy," I called to the bear-dog, and he shambled over. "Go ahead, boy, you have the rest."

It only took one lick of his huge tongue to clean out that jar. He dog-kissed my hand *Thank you* up my elbow, then laid down on the step just below where I was sat.

I looked him over. Wasn't he the most powerful-looking dog I'd ever seen? Big-chested and more than a hundred pounds if he was an ounce. He saw me looking and picked up his head. Didn't he have the most unusual eyes, the color of maple syrup? I flattened my palm and he slid his head under it. He had rich, coffee-colored fur all down his shoulders that went wiry, like a sheep's wool, on his back. He had a tail big as a willow branch, and webbing between his big brown toes.

"You need a name," I told him. "I'm going to call you *Cherry* since you liked those preserves so well. You don't mind that it's a girl's name, do you?"

He shifted his big head and looked at me with so much love in his eyes, I could have named him *Beelzebub*, as long as it was me doing the naming.

I yawned for real, finally sleepy after all. "I'm off to bed,

Cherry. I'll see you tomorrow if you come around." I gave him a few pats before I stood up and went inside.

And wasn't he lying there in the exact-same spot when I came outside the next morning?

That big burly dog hasn't left my side since. Except for when he's with the girls, that is.

CHAPTER XXI

–My Part–

I didn't say a word about my plan to Susan and Joanna—the less they knew about it, the better, for now. It'd take me months to build up three hundred and thirteen dollars, so I told the girls to settle into Peter Wilks's place, and trust me to figure something out.

It was easy living there at *La Douce Tannerie d'Wilks.* We had plenty of food, and we didn't have to cook it. We had plenty of house, and we didn't have to clean it. A body doesn't need much time to settle into that.

To stamp out any suspicion we'd ever run away, I was playing the part of the Southern belle, and acting like I was born for the job. I'd loll about on the porch waving a fan with the girls lazing around next to me. You'd think I'd've gotten bored out of my melon as the weeks went by, but my time at Aunt Evelyn's had taught me how to appreciate the pleasure of doing nothing.

The only thing I *had* to do each day was fix Peter Wilks his glass of milk and then listen to him ramble, which wasn't exactly work. Otherwise, I didn't need to lift a finger. I even gave up picking flowers for the dinner table, after he caught me and cussed me out for doing work better fit for property.

The next day—right when Peter Wilks was handing me the three dollars for groceries—I told Sugar to go pick some magnolia blossoms, and to *Look sharp!* in the exact same voice that he always used. He nodded at me, well satisfied, and gave me an extra dollar.

Later that day, I slipped up and said *Thank You* to Candy for bringing me my shoes. He had an unholy fit over it and told me he wouldn't stand for me making alliances with the property and that he'd skin us all alive before we could plot against him. I don't mind telling you that it scared the liver out of me, just like the first time he said it.

To keep on the safe side, I took to criticizing every little thing Sugar did, and Candy, too, whenever he was close enough to hear me. According to me, the lemonade was stirred too fast, the furniture was polished too shiny, the tablecloth got washed too clean, that sort of thing. I can't say I was happy when the girls started doing it, too, and I began to worry in earnest about what this place was doing to all of us.

Then one night at dinner, Candy spilled the gravy boat all over Peter Wilks, and I had to take a swipe at her, but only because he would have done much worse if I didn't. I missed on purpose, but from the look on her face, I knew she thought I'd tried for real. I did feel sorry about all of it, especially later when

I saw Candy struggling with our slop pots and Sugar coughing over the fireplace. Us being there was making their lot even harder, and I felt just awful about it.

But then I'd remind myself, *It won't be much longer until I get them their freedom,* and the feeling would mostly pass.

-Second Thoughts-

I had a routine: I'd get up early and get the girls started in on another day of leisure. After lunch, I'd head over to the General Store, pick out three dollars' worth of goods, and ask that it be charged to the Wilks account. In the evening, I'd bring Peter Wilks his milk and ask for another three dollars, go to sleep, get up, and do it all over again.

One morning, I was on the porch, paging through the *Godey's Lady's Book* while working up the courage to ask Peter Wilks for ten dollars that night, in order to get things moving a little faster. Susan and Joanna were there, too, doing nothing useful. Cherry was snoozing across the threshold, keeping track of who-all came in or out. Need I say Sugar and Candy were all over the place, working as hard as we could make them?

A delivery van pulled up and on it rode Susan's piano, bound by at least a thousand ropes and pulleys. Peter Wilks came out from the barn and made them set it down in four different places before he found the spot in the parlor that suited him best.

"There's a piano for a princess," he said, satisfied, as we all finished our lunch. "Go on now, lassie, get thee music papers 'n' give us a tune," he ordered Susan, and she ran upstairs. Looking at Joanna, he said, "Don't thee pull a long face; thee rabbits'll be along any day now. *Eh eh-heh!*"

Joanna tugged at my elbow. "Mary Jane, I don't want rabbits anymore," she whispered. "Cherry will eat them, and then he'll be in trouble." She had taken quite a shine to the big dog, and he to her, as well.

I cleared my throat. "Uncle Peter, it's a beautiful piano. So much so that we can do without the rabbits."

"There's not to be bunnies? But we must have presents for all th' lassies! *Eh eh-heh, gah, eh-heh!*"

"It's enough that you let us keep Cherry on the porch, Uncle Peter," I said, looking over at our big dog, laid across the doorstep.

"*Ahh* . . . ol' dogmeat's got a proper name now, does he? Thinks he makes a fine pet for fine ladies, does he now? Oreight then, 'tis beneath us to care. A self-made man on our own grand *estate* can't be bothered wi' a manky ol' hound.

"But thee ever tire o' th' cur, just say th' word, lasses. We keep a special bullet loaded 'n' ready for th' mongrel. Don't we, ye gowly brute?" he growled in Cherry's direction.

Cherry opened one eye and looked at him, then closed it again as if Peter Wilks wasn't worth the notice.

Susan came back downstairs with an armload of sheet music, all atremble with excitement. "Joanna, dear, please come and turn the pages, will you?"

Now, you know I love those girls, but I did want to get out of there before "Beautiful Dreamer" started up. I also saw my chance to add to the money-jar.

"Uncle Peter, I'll go and cancel the order for rabbits. And . . . and may I have . . . um . . . ten dollars for the groceries?"

"Aye, aye, lass . . . Go, thee go!" He handed me the money and waved me off towards the door. "An' won't we have fun with our two young lassies here on th' new piano? *Eh eh-heh, gah, eh-heh!*"

–A Trip into Town–

"I'll be gone less than a minute," I said as I tied my bonnet. "Cherry, let's go for a walk, hey, boy?" The big dog looked back and forth between me and the girls like he wasn't sure.

"We won't be long, Cherry," I assured him. "Now *come!*" He trotted right to me, still looking over his shoulder towards the house.

The Mississippi River runs right by the General Store, wide and muddy as it is. When we got to it, Cherry took himself down to the water, swam a few big circles, then laid himself down in the shallows. That dog can't stand not being wet if there's the least chance of it.

Outside the General Store sat a group of men playing checkers, chewing tobacco, and what-have-you. They introduced themselves around—Misters Shackleford, Hines, Lothrop—or was it *Apthorp?*—and the rest. I've a sharp memory for faces, so I stored theirs up for future reference.

"So you're one of the new nieces out to Peter Wilks's place?"

"Yes, Sir, I am *Mary Jane*, the oldest."

"How is he today? Sick-to-die from an ingrown hair? *He he-heh, gah-gah, uh-huh gw'an!*"

They all laughed at the impersonation, and it wasn't a bad one, I'll admit.

Splash! . . . flap-flap-flap-flap!

I turned to see Cherry standing in the water, staring up at some ducks as they flew away. Then he turned and looked back at me as if to say, *Don't just stand there—shoot!*

"That dog must like you, Mary Jane. He hasn't left the field where we buried old what's-his-name since . . . have you ever seen him in town, Hines?"

"No, I haven't, but I'm not surprised. I've heard about that breed: lamb if they like you, and a lion if they don't."

"I'd believe it," I said. "He sure has taken to us girls."

The Widow Bartley came out onto the porch. "What can I do for you, Mary Jane?"

"*Hello*, Ma'am. I just came by to tell you that we don't want the rabbits anymore, and to cancel the order."

"Easily done. There's always a market for the meat, anyway."

I decided not to tell Joanna that part. "Thank you kindly, Widow Bartley."

"Is there anything else you're after today? Some groceries, maybe?"

"Oh, yes, ten dollars' worth of the usual things. Sugar will be along to fetch it later." The more I spent, the heavier the groceries, and I'd taken to sending Sugar to fetch and carry it all.

"Your uncle has racked up quite a tab feeding three growing

girls. He's good for it, I know . . . likely has enough gold to buy my whole store ten times over."

"Say, Mary Jane—is it true that Peter Wilks sold all but two of his property for six thousand in gold?" one of the men asked me.

"That's what he told us," I answered.

"Haw haw! Hear that, boys? Peter Wilks ain't got the good sense God gave a rock."

A different man struck in: "Peter Wilks won't ever think about the long term, that's his problem. You've got to consider the future income from property, not just the value of its quick-sale. Take that thirty-year-old male he had, for example—the bigger one. A full-growed male in the fields can easily make you ten thousand dollars before he wears out."

"More from a female, because of breeding potential."

"Of course. But even ungrown property can earn you six or seven thousand dollars before it's all over."

"That's if the creek don't rise. You have to project some amount of loss with the ungrown ones."

"A lot depends on how you feed 'em."

"Just enough cornmeal to walk, not enough fatback to run," said one of them, and all the others nodded in agreement.

"So let's see now . . . the two adult males and six ungrown that Peter Wilks sold off, over time, would have brought in at least . . ."

". . . Fifty-six thousand dollars," I cut in automatically.

One of the men added it up on a newspaper and declared, "Ho! She's *right*! Ten more years and Peter Wilks would've been living in some real high cotton!"

The whole of the American Fur Company didn't make fifty-six thousand dollars of profit over an entire year. The slaveholders of the South were getting richer than Croesus, I realized. Maybe slavery does have something to do with empty hearts, but it seems like it has just as much to do with full pocketbooks.

The Widow Bartley cut in, "Mary Jane, you'd better get back to your sisters, don't you think?" She acted disgusted by the property-talk. I thanked her again, and said *Goodbye* all around.

Then I whistled for Cherry and walked back to *La Douce Tannerie d'Wilks* with a ten-dollar bill in my pocket to add to the jar under my bed.

–In Which My Kind Offer Is Refused–

I walked under the *La Douce Tannerie d'Wilks* sign to find Sugar at the pump with Candy, who was handing her mother empty buckets and taking them back filled up. Both of them were occupied such that they didn't notice me.

Candy set an overfull bucket down kind of clumsy, splashing her mother up to her ankles. But instead of getting mad, like Ma might have done, Sugar reached her hand down into the half-full bucket and flicked five fingerfuls of water at her daughter, and Candy shrieked and giggled in that way you do when your favorite grown-up obliges to play. Sugar smiled and went on flicking water at Candy, who dodged and danced and squealed with the fun of it.

"On a day hot as this, making your own rain is the right

idea!" I said it as cheerful as anything, hoping to join in, but my words didn't just stop the game, they outright ended it. Candy stepped behind her mother, who looked at me, and then down. They weren't laughing anymore, that's for sure. Why, it was as if I'd ruined the moment just by being there.

Cherry's collar slipped my hand and he lunged for the tap—like I said, if there's water around, you'll find him in it—and when he did, Sugar and Candy both took a quick jump back. They always kept their distance from Cherry, but then again, not everybody likes dogs. It's too bad, for it's never a mistake to make friends with one when you get the chance.

I needed Sugar to know that I wasn't really the person I was whenever Peter Wilks was around, but I couldn't tell her outright that I was going to rescue her—and Candy, too. The less they knew about it, the better, for now. Then I got a different idea:

"Sugar, does Candy know how to *read*? If not, I could teach her."

"Oh, *no*, Miz Mary Jane, you don' need to go wasting your time on setch a thing. We get along as we are."

"It's no trouble, Sugar. Why, I could teach her numbers, too— I'd enjoy it, even. She could be with me in the afternoons—"

"No, no . . . *I'se* take care of her." She looked straight at me for the briefest of moments, and then away again.

I don't mind telling you that it stung a bit, she was so set against the whole thing. "Well . . . whatever, then," I told her. "Say, tonight, after dinner's cleaned up, will you go to the Widow Bartley's general store and pick up the groceries I just ordered?"

"Yes'm, Miz. But I'll be needing a pass to travel after sundown."

"Nonsense, Sugar!" I answered her. "The Widow Bartley already expects you, and it's no more than a stone's throw away. Why, she'll be glad to see you—why wouldn't she be?"

Sugar didn't answer, just looked through me in that way that she does.

I tried one more time to be friendly: "All right . . . well, *Goodbye*, you two, and I hope you have a nice day. I suppose I'll be seeing you later."

"Yes'm, Miz," was all she said as she picked up a bucket, then motioned at her daughter to follow, and they walked away.

–Murder in the Afternoon–

"Aye-yeeeeeeeeeee!"

I heard a scream come from inside the house, a bloodcurdling scream. Cherry ran full-throttle into the house, tearing his way through the screen door.

I heard one big snarl come from the parlor: *Rawr-rawrrawrf!* After that, there was silence.

I ran inside to find Susan standing on the piano bench, and Joanna pointing to the far corner of the room. There was Cherry with a great, big rat pinned under one paw. He picked it up in his jaws, shook it once, and we all heard the neck go *Snap!* He put it back down, bit it on the scruff, and ripped its skin clean off in one motion.

Then he went to the girls and sniffed them up and down for a good long time. Once he was satisfied that all danger was gone, he went and laid himself across the threshold as usual.

"I know some trappers that would give an arm and a leg for a dog like that," I said in amazement.

Joanna ran to Cherry's side. "Rats are filthy creatures. I hope he doesn't come down sick." She began checking his gums all through for bites and scratches. He laid down quiet and let her, knowing he wasn't hurt in the least.

"I'm . . . I'm not scared of rats, Mary Jane, really, I'm not," said Susan. "That one just surprised me is all. I would have thrown my shoe at it, but Cherry got there first."

"I know, Susan. You and Joanna are as strong and brave girls as there ever were. Still, it's nice to know that we don't have to worry about . . . well, *anything* with Cherry around. If he isn't a darned good dog."

"He's the *best* dog that ever lived," said Joanna, giving him a little kiss on the cheek.

All in a day's work, said the look on Cherry's face.

"I'll make Candy take the carcass out and clean up," I told them. "By the way—where's Peter Wilks?"

"Off to the barn," Susan answered.

Then, for no reason we could tell, Cherry sprung up and stared out towards the gate with his ears set high. A few minutes later, a figure came into view, and he bolted out to meet it. I saw him sniffing 'round and 'round, sizing things up. When I saw his great tail wagging back and forth, I knew that whoever this person was, they were friend and not foe.

CHAPTER XXII

–The Peddler–

Up to our front door came the most interesting-looking person I'd ever seen, though I couldn't see much right then, just two skinny legs stuck out the bottom of a gigantic mountain of luggage.

"*Hullo!* I'm real glad to meet you," echoed out through the Alps.

"*Hello* there. Can I help you somehow?" I asked.

"I present Ezekiel Applebaum, at your service. But do call me *Eddie*—everyone does." He shed bags, one by one, until I could see the boy inside the mountain, who was not far off from being a man.

And wasn't he dressed in this, that, and the other thing? He had on a blue shirt that looked two sizes too small, under a black suit that looked three sizes too big, above a pair of brown shoes that looked four thousand miles worn-out.

When he pulled off his hat to take a bow, a big mess of curly black hair appeared. From top to bottom, he looked un-like anybody I'd ever met, but somehow just-like himself.

"And what may I call *you*?" he asked me, smiling the kind of smile that makes you smile back.

"You can call me *Mary Jane,* and *Good afternoon* to you."

He popped up one finger like he'd gotten an idea, then dug through the one bag still hanging off his neck. He pulled out a small wooden contraption, clacked it a couple of times, and asked me:

"Tell me, Mary Jane: Do you need a pair of false teeth?"

"No, I don't, Eddie."

"Well," he said, with a twinkle in his eye, "someday you will!"

It might have been the first time he made me laugh, but it certainly wasn't the last.

—A Strange Invention—

Eddie Applebaum carried copper pots and tin pans and other useful-but-not-pretty things in his bags. He carried lace collars and opera-glasses and other pretty-but-not-useful things in his other bags. All of it was for sale, he said, but only after we came to a price that made all parties feel good.

We didn't buy anything from him, but we did enjoy a nice afternoon together. I made Sugar bring out some lemonade, and Joanna showed off how fast Cherry can bring back a ball, then a stick, then anything you can throw. We went into the parlor and sang while Susan played the piano, and you can guess what song that was. The whole time, Eddie told us jokes until we all had a belly-ache from laughing.

It's true that Eddie Applebaum didn't sell us anything that day, but he gave us something worth more to us than everything he carried put together. A good laugh can make a person forget their troubles; I swear it does more for your health than a doctor can. Before Peter Wilks came back for dinner, we walked Eddie to the gate and told him he'd be welcome back anytime.

All that next week, I was happy to find him behind the counter when I walked into the General Store to buy groceries.

"*Hullo!*" he said one day, reaching out to shake my hand. "Say, can you help me, Mary Jane? I've found two holes in my good trousers." He pointed to some pin-striped pants, folded on the shelf.

"Sure I will, Eddie." I felt into my pocket. "Why, I've got needle and thread right here with me."

He handed me the trousers and I looked them up and down, inside and out, but I couldn't find any holes. "They look all right to me, are you sure these are the pair?"

"Oh, yes, those are them. Look again, Mary Jane, the holes are mighty big."

I looked again. "For the life of me, Eddie, I can't find them."

"You can't? It's the two big ones, where I put my feet through!"

That was Eddie all over, making me laugh first off before anything. Wasn't it a nice way to start my day?

Eddie knelt back down, picked up two thick copper wires, clamped the ends together, and started to twist.

"What in the world are you doing?" I asked him.

"I'm helping the Widow Bartley rig up a *telegraph*—it'll be up and running tomorrow, with any luck."

"A *telegraph*? What's that?"

"*Goodness,* Mary Jane! It's only the miracle of our age, is all! You can send out a message of twenty words for . . . what are you planning to charge, Mrs. B?"

"Five dollars," the Widow answered him, after she'd nodded me a *Hello.*

"Five dollars! Well, that's more than fair," said Eddie. "Up in Memphis, they're charging ten."

"Twenty-five cents to send one word?" I thought it was ridiculous. "No one's ever going to pay that. Why, I know for a fact that you can send a three-page letter from Fort Snelling all the way to Philadelphia for just ten cents!"

"I'm sure you're right, Mary Jane—but how long does it take that ten-cent letter to get there?" asked Eddie.

"Generally, three weeks—but sometimes two, if good weather." As a clerk, Morfar knew such things, and he'd passed them on to me.

Eddie puffed up his chest. "What would you say if I told you that the folks up at Fort Snelling would get your message in the very same *minute* if we sent it using this telegraph?"

"I'd say that's your funniest joke yet, Eddie, and that's saying something."

The Widow Bartley broke in: "Come now, Eddie, less flirting and more stringing those wires."

"Yes, of course, Mrs. B—but one more question: What will you charge to *receive* messages?"

"No charge, Eddie."

"What? Are you sure, Mrs. B?"

"Absolutely. Can you imagine me decoding and knowing the reply, then charging folks money to tell it to them? It wouldn't be right, and I'll not do it."

"You're one in a million, Mrs. B, a heroine for the ages!"

"No, I'm not, Eddie. I'm just a simple Quaker, that's all."

"What's a Quaker?" I asked.

"Someone who tries to keep their mouth closed so that their heart may open," she answered me.

"Oh. That sounds like a fine way to be," I said. "I do believe in God, I've realized, but I can't say as I'm particular to any one church over the other. First and foremost, I consider myself an Abolitionist."

"*Hush*, girl!" the widow hissed at me. "That's not funny, Mary Jane."

"I *am* an Abolitionist, truly, and I don't care who knows it. I started being it after Miss Frances read us *Uncle Tom's Cab—*"

"Mary Jane, *get in here!*" The Widow Bartley pulled me into the back room of her store, and closed the door tight after us.

"You're not from here, which makes you ignorant. But you need to know that kind of talk is *dangerous.*"

"What kind of talk? About Abolition?"

"*Stop saying that word,* Mary Jane. I'm serious." I looked down at my elbow where she had it gripped tight. "You need to keep your head down and worry about yourself and your sisters. You've got plenty on your plate already, living with that Peter Wilks."

It was just like what Mrs. Captain had told me before we got off the *Galenian*. All these *good* people I knew—why were they so dead set on me doing nothing against the worst sin on Earth?

My eyes adjusted to the darkness such that I could look around, and what I saw in that room confused me. Three big closets stood against the wall, one kept shut with a padlock. The shelves didn't hold anything but a few mediciney-looking packets. One cupboard door was ajar, and in it was a pile of quilts.

"Widow Bartley, you sure keep some strange stock. Why sell quilts in Greenville, where you can't sleep for the heat?" She saw me looking in the cupboard and shut it quick.

"Mary Jane, if you have any Christian love in your heart, you will forget that you were ever in this room."

"I won't tell anybody, Widow Bartley." She clearly didn't want it getting out that she ran her inventory so low; traders and shopkeepers are funny about things like that.

"Good girl," she told me. "Now let's go back out and see what Eddie's doing."

–Under the Weather–

Eddie was loading up his gear when we came back out of the storeroom. He slung a leather apron over one shoulder, and stuffed a pair of rough leather gloves into his pocket. Both were blotchy, like they'd been soaked around in something blue and green.

"Say, Mary Jane! I'm headed out to check on a battery, it's off towards your place. May I walk you home?"

"Certainly, Eddie. I'd like that."

The Widow Bartley called to me as we left, "Can I count on Sugar to come by and pick up your purchases, Mary Jane?"

"Yes, as usual," I answered her.

"As usual, then," she answered me back.

Not a trace of wind nor a bit of shade held back the heat that day. "You'll have to slow down, Eddie, I'm positively baking, and I can't keep up!"

"Gladly, Mary Jane! The slower we walk the more time we'll have together."

"Seems like I walk slower, I talk slower—I even think slower down here. The only thing I do faster is sweat."

Eddie took out his handkerchief, and mopped his face. "Aaaah! I'm sweating like a river—no, three rivers! The St. Croix drains my armpits, the Missouri drains my back, and they both join together in the Mississippi valley of my *tokhis*!"

I didn't know what a *tokhis* was, but the way he said it made me laugh, and it made him laugh to see me do it. It was one of the many things I liked about being with him.

We strolled on until we came to a barrel, with a jug set beside it.

"Do you know how a battery works, Mary Jane?" Eddie asked me, using a schoolteacher voice.

"No, I don't."

"*Feh!* I was hoping one of us did. Would come in handy right about now!"

I watched as he ever-so-carefully removed a glass jar that was filled with something blue at the bottom and something not-blue at the top. He took up a funnel and asked me, "Say, Mary Jane, pour in a few drops from that jug, will you?"

I did as he asked, and bubbles began to rise.

"Behold! The *half-amp* appears!" he declared.

"*Half-amp?* What's that?" I asked him.

"That bit of copper at the bottom, and the other bit of zinc at the top—somewhere between them is where the *half-amp* is born, and goes out through the wires."

"These wires?" I pointed.

"Careful, Mary Jane! Never touch the *half-amp*, for it gives a shock that can kill. First a great *zzapp!* Then a *sizzle . . . Oy!*"

"*Oops*—sorry! But the telegram-message—the twenty words— it rides on the half-amp through those wires?"

"Exactly! Did you see the thing I put on Mrs. B's desk? By pressing the button on the top, Mrs. B stops the *half-amp*."

"Turns it off?"

"For a half-second only, for it's the off-on, on-off that makes the message."

"What do you mean?"

"Like so: To send the letter *A*, you do a quick off-on followed by a long off-on, *click-cliiiiick*. For letter *B*, *cliiiiick-click-click-click* . . . different for every letter of the alphabet. She sends your twenty words as *clicks*, and a reply comes back in *clicks*, also."

"Just through that one wire?"

"Exactly! Through wires connected from battery to battery, all across the land. Omaha, Memphis, St. Louis, Chicago, and beyond. Someday a wire will cross the Atlantic Ocean."

"And you'll be the one to get it up and running, I'll wager! Gosh, you know a lot about it, Eddie. Where did you learn it all?"

"Oh, I picked it up along the way. I was a newspaper-man, then a pamphleteer, now I install telegraphs, and peddle what I can as I go. I'm far from home myself, so I'm all for anything that helps folks keep in touch."

I thought of the letter I should have written by now. "Do these wires go all the way to Fort Snelling? Where my . . . our morfar lives?"

"Yes, of course! But . . . what's a *morfar*?"

"A grandfather. *Our* grandfather."

"Ahhh, you miss him terribly?"

"It's strange to say, but it isn't so much that I miss the people as much as it is that I miss the place itself, and the way we have of doing things."

"Ahh, the North. Tell me, Mary Jane, are the northern lights real? Great ribbons of green that wave across the northern sky?"

"They are real, Eddie. They look like God is putting a new coat of paint on Heaven."

"*Ah-ha* . . . like the great pink sunsets above the wheat fields of Omaha."

"I suppose. Is that where you're from, Eddie—Omaha?"

"I come from everywhere, Mary Jane."

"Now, Eddie, what do you mean?"

He looked at me, thinking. "I wouldn't tell just anybody . . . but you are a friend, I believe."

"Of course I'm your friend. And my sisters, too. We all like you real well, Eddie, and you're welcome with us any time—I hope you know that by now."

"All right then, dear friend. You ask about my home? Mary Jane, I am a Jew: my *people* are my home. How can I explain? We have our own way of doing things . . . ways of praying and dressing and eating and speaking—*tradition*—that's the word!"

"Oh! But why didn't you ever tell me before?"

"Because it's dangerous to be a Jew among gentiles, more than you could understand. Even still, I keep our traditions, as best I'm able, and that's what links me to my people, no matter where I roam."

"Roam? Oh, you mean *travel*, I think."

"No, Mary Jane, traveling is about getting somewhere. Roaming is about the road itself and I . . . well, I was *born* to roam, Mary Jane. I know it as well as I know anything."

"I see . . ."

"I came to Omaha, from Nashville, and there from Cincinnati, and there from . . ."

"But what about your own grandfather, and the rest of your family? Don't you miss them?"

"Oh, yes, they are everything to me."

"So why did you leave?"

"How to explain? My father came from the Old Country, where

there were always rules: where a Jew may live, work, travel . . . but here in America, his son is free to roam as he wishes."

"And you roamed all the way down to Greenville, Mississippi!"

"Why not Greenville, Mary Jane? I like it, for now. How could I not—it's where I met you!"

"Well, I *don't* like Greenville. I don't like living with Peter Wilks, even if he's the girls' . . . our uncle. I don't like the way he . . . manages his property."

"Then why don't you leave, Mary Jane? That's what I do when I don't like a place. Back to the open road!"

"You do make it sound wonderful, Eddie. But tell me, on those open roads you've roamed, have you ever once seen a girl out by herself, wandering as her fancy takes her?"

"Well, no, now that I think about it."

I thought of Pa and my brother Robbie, then I thought of Ma and baby Evelyn. "It's boys that travel seeking adventure. Girls travel seeking safety," I told him.

"Eddie, after my . . . ma and pa . . . died, we were *ordered* by two lawyers and a sheriff to come down here and live with Peter Wilks. Girls have to belong to some man or other—a father, an uncle, or a husband—and the law keeps track."

"*Ahh*, if only I could whisk you away from here. We'd fly through the wire together like the *half-amp*." I smiled at the thought.

Then he took my hand and said, "Mary Jane, I would do just about anything for you."

I looked at Eddie, and saw a good friend, maybe the best

friend I'd ever have. In his eyes were all the good things he'd seen in the places he'd been, and I don't doubt that in his heart were many good people. A life on the road had made him kind and caring and open: he wasn't running away from places, he was roaming amongst them.

He took my other hand in his other hand, and I sensed a big moment coming on. It felt like my whole world was turning upside down, and I got dizzy. So dizzy that I almost fell down.

CHAPTER XXIII

—In Which the World Falls Apart—

"Mary Jane—Oh! Are you all right?"

I felt my own forehead and it was hot as a poker. "Eddie, I'm not well . . . I've got this fever that comes and goes . . . I've had it for months."

"*Achh!* Fever is a curse! Let me get you to your sisters: climb on and I will carry you."

"Thank you, Eddie, I'd be glad for it." He helped me up and I rode piggyback. As we made our way, I perked up some. By the time we got to the tannery, I was walking on my own two feet.

"You're back!" cried Susan, and ran to give me a hug. "Oh—*hello*, Eddie!" she added.

"*Hullo,* girls!"

"Hi, Eddie," Joanna chimed in. "Mary Jane, you missed all the fun. Cherry pretended he was sick and I pretended I was his doctor and look at him now!"

Cherry stumbled over, a cloud of dust following him. His big tail was set in a splint and tied with old bedsheets, and it scraped the ground back and forth as he wagged it.

We all laughed. "Awww . . . What's the matter, friend?" said Eddie, patting the dog's furry head.

We heard Peter Wilks inside, yelling for his dinner: "Lassies, our lassies!—come an' sit. I'm knackered an' famished an' could eat us th'oven door. . . ."

"We'd better go, Eddie. I'll see you tomorrow, I hope."

"Mary Jane, you can see me whenever you want. *Shalom.*" He said it with a kind smile, just for me. Then he turned to the girls. "Say there, does anybody know how Moses makes his tea?"

"No, Eddie, tell us!" they said.

"*Hebrews* it! Get it?"

We all laughed. Eddie walked away, stopping near the gate to give us one more friendly wave *Goodbye.*

After the supper dishes were cleared, Peter Wilks took himself off to the barn, to do what, we never knew. Just after he was gone, the fever came back and hit me hard.

"Mary Jane, you're awful pale." Susan's voice sounded worried and Joanna's face looked it.

"Let me sit quiet for a bit, out on the porch where it's cooler. It's the old fever, so it'll pass soon, I know." Susan helped me to a chair, sat me down, and put a pillow behind my head. Joanna told Cherry to lay at my feet and guard me.

I must have dozed off, for the next thing I heard was Peter Wilks upstairs yelling for his *glass o' milk wi' cream innit!* I tried to stand, but sank right back down, my head spinning.

I felt Susan at my side. "You rest a little more, Mary Jane, I'll take it up to him. Joanna's upstairs in your room, already asleep."

I went to object, but my head throbbed such that it hurt to open my eyes.

"Mary Jane, let me take care of it, just this once," Susan told me. "You need some rest."

"All right, Susan, you go ahead. . . . But I'll come up before too long, I promise."

"Go ahead and close your eyes, Mary Jane. Cherry is right here by your side."

I did close my eyes, and it felt heavenly to drift off again. When I woke it was still dead-night, and I had the peaceful feeling that comes after a fever passes.

Then a strange sound came from beneath my feet.

Grrrrrrrll hmmm grrrrrrrlll . . .

I'd never heard Cherry growl before. And such a funny growl, too! Not angry, more like a warning . . . or a worrying . . . about what, I didn't know.

"What's the matter, Cherry? Is something out there?" I searched the yard, but couldn't see much in the darkness. *It could be a wolf,* I thought to myself, *and a wolf can kill a dog.*

"Cherry, you'd better sleep upstairs with me tonight. I don't care what Peter Wilks says, Joanna would never forgive me if I let something happen to you."

We were tiptoeing down the hallway, moving towards my room, when Cherry planted himself in front of Peter Wilks's door and wouldn't move. I tugged at his scruff to come along but he wasn't going anywhere.

Instead, he put his nose to the floor and sniffed all along the doorstop. Then he lifted his head, looked straight at the doorknob, and let out another, *Grrrrrrrll hmmm grrrrrrrlll.*

My gut folded in two and I felt the uneasy-est feeling I'd ever felt in it, times a hundred. *Never ignore it again,* Mrs. Captain had made me promise, and so I didn't.

I grabbed the doorknob, turned it, and pushed my way into Peter Wilks's room.

An electric shock went through me, worse than if I'd touched a hundred *half-amps.* There, on the bed, I saw Peter Wilks doing something I don't ever want to see again.

He had Susan on his lap. One of his hands was up between her legs. His other hand was between his own legs, and he was rubbing himself. His eyes were squeezed shut and his mouth was wide open.

Susan's eyes were wide open and her mouth was squeezed shut. Her arms were stiff at her sides, and her fists were clenched. Her spine was as straight up-and-down as the cross they hung Jesus on.

She had frozen, like how a doe stands stock-still in front of a hunter, hoping that if she doesn't move, doesn't blink, doesn't breathe, he will lower his gun and walk away.

-Girls Seeking Safety-

I grabbed her by the elbow and I pulled. My arms started moving before my brain even started thinking about it. I pulled her down the hallway to my room—I might have dragged her, I don't know. I just knew we had to get someplace where I could shut us all in and bar the door.

The only thing I said was "Cherry, *come!*" but I didn't need to, he was already at our heels. I opened the door to my room, pulled Susan inside with me, and made sure that Cherry came, too. I glanced around the room and found Joanna sleeping in my bed. After I pulled the door shut, Susan slumped to the floor.

I don't know how I did it, but I pulled the oaken dresser away from the wall, and then pushed it against the door. It had taken all three of us to move it just one inch on the day we moved in, but on that night, it was no problem for just me.

"Cherry, *guard!*" I told him, and he laid down in front of the dresser and locked eyes with me. "If anything—or *anyone*—tries to come through that door, *you kill it,*" I told him. He blinked at me once without breaking his stare, and I daresay it meant that he understood.

I sat down beside Susan, who was rigid and blank. "You're safe now, Susan. He can't come in here; Cherry will kill him if he tries. Peter Wilks will never hurt you again. I won't let him. I promise."

Susan began—ever so slowly—to melt. First she leaned against me, then she put her head on my shoulder, then she crawled into my arms. I rocked her back and forth and whispered, "You're safe. You're safe now, Susan. You're safe." I said it over and over again. I don't know if she heard me. I don't know if she cried. I only know that she clung to me.

"Susan, I will take care of you," I said, a little louder this time. "I will take care of everything," I told her, "I know what to do."

I didn't, of course.

I held her in my arms and waited for the sun to come up. At dawn, I gently moved her into the bed, next to her sister. Somehow Joanna had slept through it all.

I stood over the wash-basin and looked at myself in the mirror. I won't forget my face anytime soon. My eyes stared out towards me in raw panic. I looked like a scared child, like somebody's daughter pleading for help, looking for something.

I could tell what I was looking for. I was looking for Ma.

–An Urgent Message–

By the time the sun was high enough for it to be proper morning, Susan was asleep, and Joanna was awake.

"Joanna," I whispered to her, "you need to take care of your sister, she's been hurt. Let her sleep as long as you can. If she wakes up and wants to talk, go ahead and listen, but if she'd rather be quiet, just sit nearby.

"Don't either of you leave this room, and keep Cherry with you. I have to go to the General Store, but I'll be back just as soon as I can, with some breakfast. Now, help me move this dresser just a bit, so I can get to the door."

We pushed and pushed until we got the thing to budge just far enough for me to slip out. "Cherry, *guard*," I told him. I didn't need to, though. He was laying on the floor next to the bed, one eye on Susan and the other on Joanna. I knew I wasn't the only one who hadn't slept a wink that night.

I grabbed our money out of the money-jar, then crept out into the hall and pulled the door shut behind me. I carried my shoes, so as to make as little noise as I could. I stopped in front of Peter Wilks's door to think for a minute.

It was still early, and I knew he was inside. Should I bust in and yell? He'd deny it all, say they were only playing, say it was her idea . . . my stomach turned.

I saw what I saw, I reminded myself, *and I believe my own eyes.* Peter Wilks had crossed a line from which there was no returning. But what was I supposed to do about it?

I didn't know, but I was sure that Ma would. *The likes of Peter Wilks is no match for her. Why, she'll probably come straight down and deal with him herself,* I decided, and it gave me hope. I'd gotten this far by myself, but it was time now that I really needed her.

I pulled a single hair out of the top of my head, wrapped it around Peter Wilks's doorknob, and laid one end inside the keyhole. If he turned the handle, the hair would break and I'd be able to tell he'd gone out.

I tiptoed downstairs and out the door, then put my shoes on and ran all the way to Widow Bartley's General Store.

I burst through the door to find her practicing her alphabet codes. She looked up at me over her reading glasses.

"Mary Jane, *Good morning!* Eddie's off tending the battery, he'll be sorry he missed—"

"Widow Bartley, I need to send a telegram to Fort Snelling." I took five dollar bills out of my pocket and slammed them down on the counter.

She looked down at the money, then up at me.

"Of course, dear, I'll try. We've done test signals, but this will be the first private message I've sent."

"Twenty words, yes?"

"Yes, is it ready?" I shook my head *No.*

"Here, write them on this piece of paper. In clear letters. Twenty words."

I thought for a moment, and then I wrote:

```
Mrs Guild Fort Snelling We are here
Peter Wilks Greenville What should I do
He ain't safe with the girls
```

The Widow Bartley folded the paper in half, then took it from me. She sat down at her desk, and opened a book. She began to tap the button on the telegraph, then paused to stretch her fingers. More tapping, and waiting, and hearing clicks, and noting them down, and then looking them up in her book.

Finally, she turned to me and said, "I've made contact with Fort Snelling, now I'll send your message."

She unfolded my note, pulled her book to her, and I saw her pencil in the dots and dashes under each word. She checked it twice, then three times, and finally tapped it out on the telegraph. She waited, then tapped some more, then listened.

After she closed her book, she came back to the counter. "I've sent it twice, Mary Jane, and I've had double confirmation that it got to the Fort."

"Now what happens?" I asked her.

"The operator at Fort Snelling needs to find Mrs. . . . the *addressee*, and personally relay the contents. Then we wait for her . . . for *an* answer to come back to us." She was taking a lot of pains to seem as if she hadn't read my message, even though we both knew she had.

"Widow Bartley, one more thing: I need food, for me and the girls, picnic-type food, enough for two days, even." I thought, then added, "To be charged to the account, as usual."

She pulled out a basket and began to fill it with good things in large amounts: whole cheeses and loaves of bread and strings of cured sausages and such.

"Here you are," she said, handing it to me. "I could have put in eggs, but they don't travel well."

"And a roll of paper and some pencils, please," I blurted out. Our eyes met. She had a deep worried look on her face.

"Of course." She found the things and added them to the basket.

"Thank you, Widow Bartley, thank you for everything. I have to go. I need to get back to my sisters."

"Yes, you go on . . . when a reply comes, I'll get it to you immediately."

"Thank you, I appreciate it." I walked towards the door, carrying the heavy basket with both hands.

As I closed the screen behind me, I heard the Widow Bartley call out, "Mary Jane!" I poked my head back inside, and she came over. "Do you want me to call the sheriff out to Peter Wilks's place?" she asked, her voice lowered.

My thoughts raced. What would I say to a sheriff? What

would Peter Wilks say to him? What if the sheriff called in the lawyers and they split us up? Or what if they did nothing? No, I didn't need a sheriff, what I needed was Ma.

"Not yet," I told her.

"Understood. For now, then." She nodded. "Go on, back home. I'll stay right here next to the telegraph, and send Eddie to you with anything that comes in. Or you come back and bring the girls, if you think best."

"Thank you, Widow Bartley, thank you for everything."

"Don't mention it," she told me, and sighed. "Honestly, tomorrow's when I expect you'll get your answer. Are you girls going to be all right tonight? I have to ask . . ."

"Yes," I told her firmly. "I daresay that dog would kill for me if I asked him to . . ."

"Good, Mary Jane, that's good." Her eyes flashed with anger. "Now, dear—go back to your sisters."

I walked home as fast as I could, lugging a basket with at least three days' food beside me.

-Sheltering in Place-

I returned to find the house quiet. Breakfast was laid out on the table as usual, but nobody had so much as touched it. Grits, bacon, eggs, toast, jam . . . I added it to the basket.

Upstairs I noticed that the one red hair was still balanced across Peter Wilks's doorknob. *He hasn't gotten up yet,* I thought with relief.

I needed to see how the girls were doing, especially Susan. I hoped she'd open up and tell me everything, but I wasn't going to push her. First things first, and that was to make her feel safe.

I'd opened my bedroom door just a crack when Cherry stuck his face right through. He wasn't angry, as he'd smelled it was me. He peered up and down the hall, then backed away so I could come in. As soon as I shut the door again, he planted himself in front of it.

"*Good morning*, girls, I'm back." I said it as cheerfully as I could.

"Susan's still sleeping," Joanna whispered, pointing to her sister, who was laying in bed with her face turned towards the wall. "Though between you and me, she might be faking. I think I saw her with her eyes open."

"Girls, let's eat something," I said. "We'll make a picnic right here on the floor, I have a whole basket of good things. Susan—Susan! Don't you want to come eat with us?"

Susan rolled over and looked at us, but didn't say anything.

I said, "There she is! *Good morning*, Susan . . . I have something special for you."

I took out the roll of paper, spread it two full yards, and ripped it free. Then, using the pencil, I drew piano keys across the bottom, white and black. "Susan, I can't remember, it's three black keys, then another three?"

"No, Mary Jane. It's two and then three."

"And the black plus white equals ten keys total, before it all starts over again—right?"

"No, no." She climbed down out of bed and knelt beside me. "There's twelve, twelve keys and then it starts over—here, let me do it."

I gave over the pencil and we sat side by side with our shoulders touching. Watching her draw one octave down the paper, then the next, I felt a rush of relief, like when you lift a bandage and find the bleeding has stopped.

Joanna was eating. "Anything good in that basket?" I asked her. "What should I try?"

"I put cheese on a slice of bread, and put jam all over it. It's good, but sticky." She laughed as she licked her fingers. "Do you want me to make you one?"

"Make two, please," I told her, hoping I could get Susan to eat.

"Can I give some of this sausage to Cherry? He looks hungry."

"Joanna, when *doesn't* he look hungry?" I asked her, laughing at the thought. "But yes, you can. Cut the sausage up into tiny little pieces."

"Why?"

"Because we're going to teach him tricks. As many as he can learn. And Susan's going to play her paper piano. Later we'll draw, or braid each other's hair, or make up stories, or play cards—or all of it. We'll stay in this room all day today, and pretend we're camping, all three of us warm, dry, together, and *safe.*"

"Plus Cherry makes four!" added Joanna.

"Of course," I said, petting his big square head. "Cherry makes four."

We spent the day in that room, playing, drawing, braiding,

and more. Somehow along the way, Susan perked up, like how a crocus pushes itself up through the snow.

When we laid down to sleep, the girls took my bed and I laid on the floor, putting myself between them and the door. Cherry laid down, putting himself between me and the door. Between him and the door was the big oaken dresser blocking the entrance.

I don't think Cherry slept a wink that night. Drowsy as I was, I saw his two glowing eyes, unchanging and unblinking, reflecting the light of the moon every time my own eyes flickered open.

We can't stay in this room forever, I told myself, as our troubles rumbled like distant thunder.

But we can stay here tonight, I answered myself, holding them at bay, as I drifted off to sleep.

–The Answer–

Hiimmmmh, hiih, hiih, hiimmmm . . .

I woke to the sound of Cherry whimpering. He was shifting about uncomfortably, and it came to me why. He needed out.

"Oh, sweet boy, I'm so sorry," I told him. The girls and I had the chamber pot, but he'd had nothing, and I'm sure he was ready to burst by then.

"Run outside as quick as you can, then come back to me, yes? Good boy!"

I shoved the dresser a few inches and cracked open the door. Cherry rammed his head through and pushed his way out. By the time I got to the window he was already out in the yard.

I don't know if you've ever seen a dog pee on the ground and drink out of a rain-barrel at the same time, but Cherry did it all in less than a minute, moving at least three gallons in both directions. I heard him bounding up the steps, and turned just in time to see his big skull push through the door, shaking the dresser on his way in.

The first thing he did was jump up on the bed to sniff both Joanna and Susan, making sure no harm had come to them during the ninety seconds he'd been away.

"Cherry!" Joanna woke up giggling, tickled by his whiskers. He responded by giving her a huge kiss *Good morning* across one cheek.

I whispered, hoping not to wake Susan. "Joanna, I am going to run to the General Store, like I did yesterday. I need you girls to stay in this room while I'm gone, just like you did before. Cherry will protect you, you know that."

"Of course he will! But Mary Jane, I'm bored. Are we going to stay inside all day *again* today?"

"No . . . yes . . . maybe . . . I don't know yet." I added, "Don't worry, Joanna. Just wait one more morning—I promise I'll be back before lunchtime with a plan."

I burst into the Widow Bartley's General Store to find her in front of the telegraph with her eyeglasses on.

She said to me, "Nothing yet, my dear. I've been close by all night, and would have heard something come in. You're welcome to sit and wait here in the store."

I thanked her and sat down in the corner, and soon enough, waiting turned into wishing, then wishing turned into hoping.

Ma will save us, I'm sure of it. Maybe she's already got herself on a steamboat and will get here in . . . hmmm . . . ten days? Can I hang on that long? Wait! Maybe she'd started sooner, after they got word from those lawyers in Fort Edwards . . . Maybe she'll get here today! Maybe in a few hours! Soon, she'll come through that door knowing just what to do. She'll take over and make everything right, and I can just . . . go back to being me.

Seven o'clock passed, then eight o'clock, then nine . . . and I kept waiting, wishing and hoping.

"Do you want some coffee, Mary Jane? I think I need some," the Widow Bartley asked me just before ten.

"Yes, please, I think I do, too."

"I'll go up and make some—I won't be gone more than a minute."

When she returned, she was carrying a big cup for each of us. We stood together for a minute, slurping it down, until we heard . . .

Cliiiiick-cliiiiick-click, click-cliiiiick-click, click, click, cliiiiick-click . . .

The Widow Bartley grabbed her pencil. I watched her jot down a string of dots and dashes, then take out her book and look carefully back and forth, figuring the letters one by one.

To me, it took forever, but she finally did come over and hand me a folded paper. "Here's your answer, Mary Jane," she said, her face as blank as stone.

"Wonderful!" I thanked her. "I'm going off to read it, if you don't mind."

"Of course, Mary Jane, you do as you like. But promise me

you'll come back and . . . check in . . . and bring the girls, if you think best. The door's unlocked and I'm always here . . ."

"I know, I know. Thank you, Widow Bartley."

I hustled down to the riverbank and sat under a willow tree growing half-in and half-out of the water, like willows do. A fair bit of weight was lifted from my shoulders when the Widow Bartley handed me that paper, and I was ready for the rest of it to be lifted, too. I was ready to be rescued.

I unfolded the paper and it said:

```
Mary Jane Guild Morfar and  I are both
good health
Hansel died at Easter He went easy Do
your best
```

The shock that went through me couldn't have been less painful than touching that wire Eddie told me not to. I was hurt enough to die, and it wasn't half-an-amp that had killed me, it was twenty words. Or at least they killed some part of me.

"Do your best"? My best? Me? All alone? All alone, down here?

My heart felt something, something fuzzy in the distance. As it came closer, I recognized it for what it was. I was ashamed. Ashamed of having believed myself to be worth saving. Ashamed of the little girl inside of me who had simply wanted her ma.

"Do your best"? My "best" is what turned those girls into orphans. My "best" is what landed us in this horrible place with this horrible man.

I closed my eyes and clenched my fists, and was angry. Angry at myself for ever believing I'd be rescued. Angry at the little girl inside of me who had simply wanted her ma.

That little girl inside of me died on that day, killed by twenty words. And she wasn't the only one, for that little girl's ma died as well. I might still have a mother, but I no longer had a ma. Not someone who would take care of me. Not anyone to go back home to.

CHAPTER XXIV

—An Unexpected Proposal—

I sat there under the willow, with my head in my hands, feeling the most alone I'd ever felt, missing myself, even. I missed the little girl who had a ma and someone to go back to. I missed how trusting she was and how simple she saw everything. I knew I'd never see that little girl again, and she hadn't even told me *Goodbye.*

I don't know if an hour passed, or two, or four, but my thoughts were broken when I felt the earth jostle beside me. I looked over to see Eddie sitting on my left.

"Here you are—I've been looking all over for you! *Hullo,* Mary Jane. *Ahh!* You are sad. . . . What is the matter, my friend?"

"I used to be different, Eddie." I heard a new darkness in my voice, even as I said it. "When I was younger, life was so much less . . . complicated. And I was a happier person back then, because of it."

Eddie sighed. "Weren't we all, my friend, weren't we all . . ." He paused, then he began to sing:

Kinderyorn, zise kinderyorn
Eybik blaybt ir vakh in mayn zikorn;
Ven ikh trakht fun ayer tzayt,
Vert mir azoy bang un layd.
Oy, vi shnel bin ikh shoyn alt gevorn.

Eddie's voice rang out across the river, strange and lovely. It was both bold and tender. It was sad, but strong. It was just what was needed to calm my soul.

After the last note faded, I wondered aloud: "Eddie, when you talk you are always laughing, but when you sing you sound as if your heart will break."

"*Achh,* Mary Jane. I am a Jew. My heart was broken long before I was born. We laugh because it is a miracle that we are even alive."

"What was the song about?"

"The words tell of a man's sadness when he thinks about the years of his childhood, and how they will never come back. He misses his home, his mother, his *chavrusa.*"

"A *chavrusa*? What's that?"

"You would say 'best friend,' I think. The person you can talk to about anything."

"Friends like us?" I asked, and felt grateful, it was so nice to find myself understood.

"In a sense, perhaps . . . ," he answered me.

"I'm so glad you're here, Eddie. Having a friend beside me makes everything seem a little better right now."

"Does it, Mary Jane—do you really think so?" I looked up and found his eyes searching mine. "Join me on the open road, then! We'll be best friends—no, more than friends—we'll be . . . husband and wife—why not?"

"You can't be serious, Eddie."

"Sure I am! I've just thought of it, and it solves everything. Let me take you away from this place—this Greenville that you do not like, and makes you so sad."

"But we don't even—"

"Hear me out, Mary Jane. One week—seven days from now—I will leave for New Orleans. From there, I will set sail to a beautiful city that hangs over a crystal-blue ocean, a city called *Rio de Janeiro,* in a place called *Brazil*—where my uncle has started a shipping company.

"Come with me, and be a girl seeking adventure—but not by herself—with her . . . umm, *chavrusa* by her side! We will forge our own future! Sailing from harbor to harbor, tramping through the forests and the jungles, trading treasures with the Tupi tribes . . ."

"Eddie, I can't. What would Susan and Joanna do without me?"

"They will have each other, until they, too, find husbands, as you all must—it is the way of the world, Mary Jane. Tell me, how old are you now? Sixteen?" he asked me.

I told my usual lie; what else could I do? "Nineteen."

"*Nineteen!* Well beyond the proper age . . . Mary Jane, there's nothing here for you, you told me yourself. Come with me, far away from here, such good friends we'll be!"

"You're asking me to leave my *family*, Eddie."

"No more than I'd be leaving mine! You can't imagine my mother when she finds out I married a gentile. Why, she'll never talk to me again, I will be cast out as if I'd never been born. But we will have each other, Mary Jane. We will be each other's family—we will be each other's everything."

"I'm not sure I'm ready for that, Eddie."

"But of course, this is sudden for you. You must have some time to consider." He stood up, and pulled me up, too.

"You have heard my proposal, Mary Jane. Think on it for one week, my . . . yes, my *chavrusa*. Seven days! I will count them and when they have passed, I will come to you and you will give me your answer."

He took off his hat, placed it over his heart, and made a deep bow. Then he turned around, and walked away.

He was gone before I could tell him *Yes*.

-My One and Only Chance-

I was in a strange situation, having to choose between running away with a young man who I knew to be a *good* man or staying behind with a criminal of a man and the mountain of hurt he'd caused.

I could go to Eddie, right now, and ask him if we could leave tomorrow. He'd call me his *chavrusa* and make me laugh and we'd go off together to see the world. And how else was I ever going to see the world? What if this was my one and only chance for a life of adventure?

Or I could go back to the girls, who needed me as much or more than they ever did.

But why did it have to be *me*? Why did finding a solution always have to fall on my shoulders? I'd been *doing my best* for months now—starving, nursing, worrying—so that those two girls could go on being children. *I was fourteen years old*—the exact same age as Joanna and a whole year younger than Susan. What if I said to them, *I did my best, now you do yours*?

I could divide the fifty-two dollars and twenty-eight cents I'd saved up between Joanna and Susan, and give it to them on my way out of town. It'd be nowhere near enough to get them to Fort Snelling, but it was more than double what I'd left home on. They were smart girls and they'd find a way to get themselves free . . . and didn't I deserve some freedom, too?

I started walking. I was glad for the dusty road, and the mile ahead of me, for it'd give me some time to think on how to break it to the girls.

—On the Road—

It was quite a mile I walked that day. As the road got dustier, my thinking came clearer. I wanted to run away with Eddie—that's what I'd thought. But the real truth was two words less: I wanted to run away . . . period.

I liked Eddie. I liked him more than any boy I'd ever met, and I knew he liked me, too. He had it all: personality, brains, and good nature. We could make a good life together, full of fun and adventure—that's what my brain was telling me. There was only one problem: my heart wasn't telling me anything at all.

Ba-boom, ba-boom, ba-boom . . .

My heart was beating like it always did—like it does when I set the table, or take down the wash, or give Cherry his supper. Like how it does when you don't notice it beating at all. Like how it did whenever I was with Eddie.

My heart sure wasn't beating the way Aunt Evelyn said it does when you find the person you have to go to—or go *with*, in this case. If I was to go off with Eddie, I'd miss my chance to listen, someday, when my heart did have something important to say.

I'd stick with the girls, I decided, for so many different reasons that I couldn't explain all of them. The only one I can tell you for sure, is about what my heart didn't tell me. And that's what made all the difference.

It wasn't very nice knowing that I'd still be in Greenville next week and not getting on a boat in New Orleans bound for the glittering shores of *Rio de Janeiro.* I put one foot in front of the other anyway, until I found myself right back where I'd started, at *La Douce Tannerie d'Wilks.*

–Unafraid–

I went in the house, climbed the stairs, and started down the hall towards my bedroom. I stopped at Peter Wilks's door, surprised at what I saw. There was my single red hair around the door-knob with one loose end in the keyhole. It had been two whole days, and Peter Wilks had not left his room, nor dared to show his face.

He knows what he did, and he knows it was wrong.

I had been so scared of him, of the idea of him, when we were hiding in that room, but I wasn't afraid of him any longer. Rage flushed through me, almost knocking me off my feet. I wanted to scream at him, *I know what you did.* Then I would say, *I'll have my dog rip the skin from your body like the rat you are.*

I turned the doorknob, snapping the strand of hair in half. I heard furniture crash behind me as Cherry bashed his way out of my bedroom. I put my shoulder to the door and pushed my way inside.

I wanted to scream at him, but I didn't scream. I gasped, instead.

—A New Plan—

Peter Wilks was in a state, laid up in bed. I could feel the heat of his fever across the room.

"Ahh, lassie, thee came. Some water, for th' love o' God, some water."

To be honest, it didn't move me much. *Let him suffer,* I told myself, and turned to go.

"Oh—stay! We've been gippin' 'n' gozzin' here in our own lop for days . . . Lassie, please stay wi' us—We'll pay! We'll pay thee wi' gold."

I stopped in my tracks. "How much?" I asked.

"A hundred, nah—two hundred! As much as thee want. Please, lassie!"

That changed everything. If I could heal him up, I'd surely get enough gold to buy five steamboat tickets and then some. It was really the same as my first plan, only us leaving with plenty of money and a whole lot sooner.

I gave him a glass of water and left. I went to the girls, and told them, "Peter Wilks is sick with fever." I glanced at Susan, not knowing what to expect. All her face showed was relief.

When I got back to Peter Wilks, he had sicked up those two glasses of water, all down his front. Then he began to cough like he was tired of his lungs and wanted to get rid of them. It dawned on me that I was in for a miserable couple of weeks tending to an outright criminal. Then I thought of someone who could take it on, at least for a while.

"Girls, go to the Widow Bartley's store and ask her to send . . . oh, what was his name again? . . . Robinson! To send Doctor Robinson . . . and take Cherry with you." They couldn't have any better protection than him.

As soon as they left, Peter Wilks sicked up again, only this time it was more bile than water. I knew it wouldn't stop until he got some food settled in his belly. "Sugar! Bring some oat gruel, grits, or whatever!" I yelled downstairs.

By the time Sugar came in with oatmeal, a third round of sick came up out of Peter Wilks, and an even fouler sick came out of his lower end, and I was in it up to my elbows trying to get him to the basin. It was a damn mean thing to be stuck in

Greenville covered in Peter Wilks's sick, and it made me want to be damn mean in return.

I couldn't be mean to the girls since they were in the same boat as me. I couldn't be mean to Peter Wilks because I wanted his gold. But there was someone in that house that would have to let me be mean to them, who couldn't fight back, even if she wanted to.

"Rags, Sugar, get rags!" I hollered right at her. "Ugh . . . Now!" I'm ashamed to tell you, but after that I started in cussing and cursing, and said a bunch of things that I would never have said to anybody else.

I didn't mean it, I told myself later, *I was at the end of my rope. I'll make it up to her,* I promised in my head. *We'll soon be free of this place—all of us.*

—The House-Call—

"Well, well, well. Peter Osbourne Wilks has taken to his bed! Whatever could it be this time?" Doctor Robinson sounded right cheerful when he came to our door.

"Thank you for calling, Doctor," I greeted him.

"Always a pleasure to visit *La Douce Tannerie d'Wilks,* my dear. Only place I can be sure to find a healthy patient. What's he bellyaching over this time?"

I took him upstairs and showed him into Peter Wilks's room.

"You'll see he's poorly. Fever, unbroken, one day, possibly two," I told him. "Can take a little water, but can't hold it down.

Can't hold down gruel or corn-pone, either. What does get in doesn't stay long before we see it out the back side."

The doctor pulled up Peter Wilks's eyelids, then listened to his lungs rasping in and out. "He does look worse than usual, I'll grant you that." Then he bent down, right next to Peter Wilks's ear, and shouted like all get-out.

"Peter, now, GIVE UP THE GAME!" The sick man winced, but didn't much come to.

"I'm almost tempted to take you serious this time, Peter Wilks," said the doctor. "Many a time I've come running to this Tannery because you were a-dying, got to be every Wednesday for a while. Once it was you'd cut your toenails and what came off didn't smell quite right . . . laid you up in this bed for a week, *DIDN'T IT, PETER?*"

It *was* serious this time, anybody could see that. Except Doctor Robinson who, when it came right down to it, didn't much care.

"It's always something with him, Mary Jane. He puts on a good show, but it's attention that he wants, not medicine. The point is to get everybody worked up, near and far."

He turned back to Peter Wilks. "It wasn't two months since that you bullied the Widow Bartley into sending an urgent letter all the way to England, begging your brothers to come and see you, just once before you died. *JUST ONCE BEFORE THE TOENAIL TOOK YOU, EH, PETER?*

"Here's my diagnosis: Peter Wilks will get better when it suits him—just like always. In the meantime, he's darned lucky to have someone like you, who feels enough affection for him to nurse him through his little *charade*."

You're wrong, Doctor Robinson. I hate him worse than the Devil. But a woman feels and a nurse nurses. I've got to keep them separate if I'm going to do it right, because doing it right means getting enough money to get us out of here.

We needed to get ourselves gone soon, too, in case those English uncles did show up, putting that much more on my hands. I decided I'd heal Peter Wilks up just enough so he could pay me, and as soon as that gold touched my hand, me and the girls would pack our things and run.

And by "the girls" I meant Susan, Joanna, and me. Oh, and Cherry, too—we weren't going anywhere without him. For Sugar and Candy, I'd figured something else out. After me and the girls got away safe and sound, I'd write a letter to those professional Abolitionists out East—and send some money, too, asking them to escape Sugar and Candy out of there. That's their speciality, after all.

For now, I'd keep my head down and worry about myself and the girls, just like Mrs. Captain and the Widow Bartley had told me to. They'd been on to something, I was starting to think.

Doctor Robinson closed his bag; he was done doctoring Peter Wilks. "Best of luck to you, my dear," he said to me before he left. "Don't let him take you for a ride, for this is all a theater act. I've personally seen it too many times to buy a ticket, if you know what I mean."

He walked out the door before I could tell him about Aunt Evelyn's sickness, or mine before it, and how Peter Wilks's suffering matched up to the very same things. Probably wouldn't have done any good anyway.

–Doing Poorly–

The rest of that day wasn't a happy one for Peter Wilks. He'd get a smidge better, then a lot worse, then a half-smidge better, then a whole lot worse. Off and on, I'd hear the piano downstairs, and Cherry barking the short little barks that meant Joanna was teaching him to *Speak!* It was more than fine by me, as it kept them away from Peter Wilks and his contagion, not to mention his other derangements.

At sun-down, I settled him as best I could, hoping to get some sleep myself. In the morning, I found his breathing ragged, and naturally got worried about getting my payment.

I opened up my medicine kit and dosed him with dogbane and mugwort, and had Sugar get some mayapple from the yard. I boiled down a poultice of onions and licorice seeds, but I made Candy spread it on his chest. Nurse or not, I couldn't bear the thought of touching his body.

And by afternoon, hadn't he bounced right back? Still weak, but sitting up, sipping honey tea, and talking a blue streak. Seemed like the right time to collect payment, seeing as he meant go on living after all.

"I can see you're improved, Peter Wilks. Plenty healed up enough to pay me what you promised," I said to him with my hands on my hips.

"*Nay, nay*, lassie, thee can't want pay. Look around thee! Our lassies already have all thee could want, here wi' us! Lap o' lux-ury thee are in, our three lassies. Pianos 'n' rabbits if thee want 'em. *Heh-eh!*"

"But you said you'd pay me in gold if I stayed 'til you were better, and now you *are* better, thanks to me."

"Comes an' goes! Comes an' goes! We aren't hearty, it's our only flaw. But a self-made man rallies, we does. An' we're a self-made man on our own grand *estate* worth nine-thousand-some-would-say-ten! All for our lassies to enjoy, wi' naught to do but bring us our glass o' milk wi' cream innit every evening when we're to bed. *Eh eh-heh, gah, eh-heh!*"

I walked out the door and slammed it behind me.

CHAPTER XXV

–My First Dilemma–

For the hundredth time, I needed a new plan. A plan where three people could travel a couple thousand miles on fifty-two dollars and twenty-eight cents. I was awake all night, laid between Susan on one side and Joanna on the other, trying to figure out the impossible and getting nowhere.

Early the next morning, I left to go downstairs, hoping against hope that a cup of coffee might clear my tired old brain. As I passed Peter Wilks's room, I heard a cough. Not just any cough, either. It was the dry, rattling cough that Aunt Evelyn had in her very last hours. The kind of rattling cough that rattles *you*. The kind of cough that stops you in your tracks, outside the bedroom door.

I'm not going in. I've had enough. Enough of his meanness and his sickness . . . enough of him. That's what I felt.

A woman feels and a nurse nurses. That's what I thought.

I myself don't know all the reasons why, but in the end, the nurse in me heard the cough and went into his room, leaving the woman in me outside in the hall.

-The Cure-

Peter Wilks roused himself just enough to clutch onto my arm when I came near. He gripped me like he'd fallen through the ice and I was his only chance to get pulled out.

"Lassie, we are woeful sick an' we know it . . . 'n' we know we're a sinner, an awful sinner . . . a sinner afore God . . . but *please . . .* please don't let us die!"

Please don't let me die. You don't forget it after someone says those words to you. I hear it in my mind to this day.

I won't let you die, I said to him. What else could I say?

I sat down at the foot of his bed. I couldn't bring myself to do more than swab his forehead and help him drink now and then, but I stayed beside him for the rest of the day, and all that night, and listened.

Granted, most of what he said didn't make any sense, but I got the gist. He kept going on about wanting to see his brother *Harvey* who was some kind of preacher. He went on about a brother *William,* too, who'd been born different such that he couldn't hear or talk. I suppose those two were the ones still in England, unless they really were on their way here, that is.

He even mentioned George, in a way that made me think he was sorry how things turned out. That got to me some, I'll admit. Hard as I am, maybe I'm still soft inside somewhere.

Deep in the night, I woke the girls and sent them to the Widow Bartley to ask for tansey-flower tea. I didn't know what else to do. "Don't worry about waking her," I told them. "The door's unlocked and she's always there."

Before an hour was passed, I heard a knock at the door. "It's me, Widow Bartley. I've come to help."

"Oh, do come in."

She took an inventory of Peter Wilks: felt his pulse and cupped her hand over his nose to feel his breathing. He gave a great cough, and turned on his side, moaning. She looked at what he'd spit up, and found it mostly blood.

"He's bad off," she told me. "The girls said your ma had something similar?"

"Uh . . . Yes, just like," I said. "And we lost her."

"That's a shame . . . for down here, we have a cure. A cure for exactly this."

"You do? The doctor didn't say anything about . . ."

"Doctor Robinson? Oh, he's a fine doctor if you're already healthy."

"What is this cure?"

"It's in this blue bottle I brought you. A full dram of it. That's plenty. Give it to him, give it all, just to be safe. I'll tell you: it doesn't always work, but it can."

"How do I give it?"

"Just screw off the white cap and pour it in. If he coughs it up, don't worry, it'll be enough already 'sorbed in through his gums."

"I understand."

"And this—this is important—once you've given him this cure, you'll have done all you can. You've done all that *anyone* could possibly do for the man. The cure doesn't always work, but it just might in this case, I've got a feeling. But you promise me, Mary Jane, that after you give it to him, you'll rest easy in knowing you've done all you can."

"I promise."

"Then I'll leave you to it," she said, and handed me the bottle.

"How much do we owe you?" I asked her.

"No charge," she told me. "It's free. This one is free."

-My Second Dilemma-

I sat beside Peter Wilks to watch and wait to the end, because everyone deserves that. In my hand I held the blue bottle with the white cap. In it was the power to cure that man. All I needed to do was pour it down his throat to bring him back to the world.

The nurse in me was in favor of the idea, but the woman in me was not.

What would our lives be if Peter Wilks rose from that bed and found himself again? We were his—the lawyers and the Army had both said so. We legally belonged to Peter Wilks and we were his to do with as he liked. And I knew what he liked. Could I keep him off of Susan forever? What about Joanna? What about *me*?

Probably yes. Maybe no.

Morfar once told me that you can't retrain a dog that bites and won't let go. Once they do such a thing, you'll never escape knowing that they can. You have to shoot a dog like that, he'd told me. You shoot the dog not because you want to, but because you don't have a choice.

I didn't turn the white cap, I didn't open the blue bottle. I told myself I didn't have a choice, and I sat and let Peter Wilks die.

You might think it was hard to do, and it was. It was awful.

Hours passed. Or was it days? I kept him clean and I kept him comfortable, as best I could. I brought cool rags for his forehead and changed the sheets and even helped him drink the tansey-flower tea. Every ten minutes I looked at the blue bottle of medicine on the nightstand, and I thought about turning the cap and pouring it into his mouth. And every ten minutes, I did not. *I don't have a choice*, I told myself, every single time.

And then Peter Wilks was dead.

He had asked me *Please don't let me die.* And I had let him die. Maybe I had even killed him. Depends on how you look at it.

I didn't have a choice, I kept telling myself.

But it wasn't true. I did have a choice, and I made it. I made the choice to keep my family safe.

I did my best.

CHAPTER XXVI

-The Next Day-

For the living, there is always a next day. A next day full of hours that you don't quite know how to fill. A next day when you begin to notice how many *things* he had. His things are everywhere. Somebody should do something with all these things.

It's all so sad. The hairbrush next to the basin is sad. The toenail clipper on the windowsill is sad. His dead mother's bones in the ground far away, they are sad. If there is a God in Heaven after all, I'm sure He is sad, too.

You get some boxes and walk around his room, filling them with things, this and that. You don't know who you are saving them for, but they can't just be thrown away, like he never existed. Or can they? You put the full boxes in the attic. You'll throw them away tomorrow. Not today. It can wait.

I put the little blue bottle with the white cap into my pocket, still unopened, walked out, and shut the door. It could wait, too.

When I told the girls that Peter Wilks was dead, they asked me what they should do now. *I'm not sure it matters*, I wanted to tell them, because I wasn't sure it did. They'd—*we'd?*—be passed on to the next stranger in their father's "line" and I'd have to *do my best* all over again.

Instead, I asked them if they could keep themselves busy while I went over to the General Store in order to tell the Widow Bartley and the others. They said *Yes,* and I left them on the front porch with Cherry standing guard.

Out in the yard, I saw Sugar walking with Candy. When I told them that Peter Wilks was dead, Candy was happy enough to smile and clap her hands and I couldn't blame her. Sugar stopped her daughter, pulled her close, and *shushed* her, and her face looked more worried than I ever thought anybody's could.

I don't remember walking to the General Store. I must have done it, because I do remember everyone who was sat out front stopping in their tracks when I told them that Peter Wilks was dead.

I saw Mr. Hines hang his head over the checkers he was playing with Ab Turner. They shook their heads, both of them sad. I think I even saw a couple of tears hit the board.

Before I knew it, all of those men were broken up and howling like hound-dogs, crying to the Heavens asking *Why? Why?* Just as their wailing reached its peak, a great heavy man stood up, took off his hat, and banged his fist on a barrel.

"Seein' as the Rev'rend ain't here, and seein' as I am Deacon of our good Baptist con-gergation, it is befittin' that I should say a few words. *Ah-hem.* Peter Wilks: modest, edur-cated, generous, and a faultless example, was he. Each-and-ever' one of us loved him like a brother, and will miss him sorely."

A man came forwards, wringing his hands. "I can't see how we can go on without Peter Wilks, nor how we'll want to. The whole county'll be in a sinkin' spell oncet they y'all get wind of his departin'."

"He was finer'n frog hair 'n' better'n chicken lips!" shouted someone in the back. The exact same set of men that were making fun of Peter Wilks when I first arrived answered, *Hear! Hear!*

The Widow Bartley came outside and announced, "This girl right here, Mary Jane, she nursed that Peter Wilks all the way through. She did all she could, but he died. Sometimes that's the way of it. They die on you, even after you've done everything a body possibly could."

She said it to make me feel better, but it made me feel worse, because I knew it wasn't true. A long-legged man patted me on the head, poor thing that I was.

"Rest assured, I'll take care of preparing Peter Wilks's body. It's the least I can do for such a one as he was."

The Widow Bartley shoed me inside. "Yes, Mary Jane, come and rest a while. Mr. Shackleford will prepare the burial, and make the funeral go as smooth as anyone could. Come in and drink some lemonade. You need some sugar in your veins, and some little cheer in your heart."

She gave me some, and I drank it, but afterwards she wouldn't let me pay. "No less than a Quaker should do for them who mourn," she told me.

"It must be nice to know you're a Quaker, or at least a some-thing. I don't know what I am anymore."

"Mary Jane, you don't have to be anything besides what you are, for there is more than enough goodness in you already," she told me.

Enough goodness to kill a man, I thought to myself.

The screen door banged open. "*Hullo!* It's good to see you both on this fine day!"

I turned around to see Eddie, carrying two big carpet-bags, coming through the screen door.

"My condolences, Mary Jane. I just heard that your uncle has passed away."

"That's right, Eddie, he died yesterday. I . . . I was with him when he went."

"May his memory be a blessing. Shall I walk you home?"

"I hope you will, Eddie."

Out on the porch, one of the men rushed to ask me, "Say there, Marjorie—no, umm . . . Miss Wilks! Do you know if all y'all's uncle made a will? An' d'y'know what might be in it? Not that it matters, at a time like this. But with me having been such a close friend and all . . ."

"No, he didn't leave a will, is what he told me, anyway."

We left them speculating as to whether Peter Wilks's six thousand dollars wasn't actually closer to seven, and how cheap the tannery might sell for, and other tender questions that natu-rally arise after the death of one's bosom friend.

—My Answer—

Once we were out of sight, Eddie took my hand, and I let him. It was the end of our time together, I knew, but I wanted us to enjoy these last few minutes.

A mocking-bird hopped from branch to branch above our heads, sharing a song.

Cha-chi-chi-chi-cha, cha-chi-chi-chi, cha-chi, cha-chi, cha-chi!

"That bird sings almost as good as you do, Eddie . . . though I doubt he has as many interesting things to sing about."

"I doubt it more, for he must have twice as many! Look at his dashing gray suit . . . surely his life is one fine party after the other."

"Look at you, Eddie, carrying only two bags today! Where have you put your inventory?"

"I lighten my load whenever I am in sight of new adventure!" He paused, looked into my eyes, and said, "I dare to hope that I will, this time, not be traveling alone."

"Yes, Eddie. During our time apart I have done a good deal of thinking."

"My own week has been one long *mitzvah*: all my wares I have given away, to those who endure affliction and bondage, as my people did before we were led out of Egypt . . . I am left with not a nickel to my name, but I am rich in freedom, compared to many."

"What is a *mitzvah*, Eddie?"

"Oh, how to explain? I suppose you might think of it as a good deed, but truly, it isn't charity. For a Jew, it's a responsibility."

I thought about my own week, how I had treated Sugar and

Candy, and I was ashamed of myself. "Eddie, you are a good person," I told him. "Far better than me."

"Hush, Mary Jane, it is not true. You would do the same, were you in my place."

How I wished I was what Eddie thought me to be, instead of what Sugar and Candy knew I was. *Is it too late for me to make it right?* I wondered to myself, then asked, "Eddie, can a *mitzvah* make up for having done someone wrong?"

"No," he said, shaking his head. "A *mitzvah* cannot erase the past, but it can be something, and something is always more than nothing."

"I see . . ."

We stopped under the sign for *La Douce Tannerie d'Wilks* and let go of our hands. Eddie pointed to the house where I'd been living for the past . . . two weeks? Ten weeks? I didn't know anymore. It seemed a lifetime had passed since we'd come from Fort Edwards.

"Mary Jane, my *chavrusa*, it is time that you must decide. Will you walk into that house, gather your things, and come with me? Or will we say *Goodbye* and part ways?"

"I believe we must part, Eddie. My uncle is gone now, but my sisters are still here, and they still need me very much . . . and I need them, too." I didn't realize how true it was until I said it out loud.

He paused, then took out his handkerchief and daubed his eyes. "I am disappointed, Mary Jane, but I will try to understand. Forgive me if I ask once more—are you certain?"

"Yes, Eddie. There . . . there are also other reasons that I don't know how to explain."

"Then you need not explain them. It is enough that you give me your answer. I am sad to think of being without you, but in time I will heal."

"I will miss you, Eddie, you should know that."

"What will happen to you now?" he asked me. "It would ease my mind to think of you happy and settled somewhere."

"I expect Peter Wilks's brothers will arrive soon, and me and the girls will be handed over to them."

"I see . . . best of luck, Mary Jane . . . In time, maybe we will meet again. We do not know how our destiny is written . . ."

"I would like that, Eddie. Let's hope so."

He took off his hat, and prepared to say a final *Goodbye*. I stopped him.

"No, wait—wait just a minute—I'll be right back, I promise." I ran inside and up the stairs, to my bedroom. When I came back down, I asked him to hold out his hand.

"This is for you, Eddie. I hope it serves you well." I pressed the *New Orleans Banking Company* ten-dollar bill into his hand.

"*Achh,* no! I cannot accept money from you, Mary Jane . . . our friendship is of far more value than—"

"It's not money, Eddie—not outside of New Orleans, any-way. It's just something I've been carrying around, not knowing what it's for. Now I know. It's for *you,* Eddie. It's to help you on your way. Please take it—who knows? It might bring you luck!"

"It already has, if it eases our parting. I will remember you, Mary Jane, and I will think only good things when I do." He walked backwards a few steps, placed his hand over his heart, and said, *"Shalom."*

The girls had run up beside me, wanting to say *Hello* to Eddie. I couldn't bear to tell them it was really *Farewell*. He shook their hands and patted their heads, then asked them:

"Hey, girls! Does anybody need an ark?"

"A what?"

"An *ark*! For animals, two-by-two."

"No . . ."

"Well, remember your friend Eddie, because if you ever *do* need an ark, I Noah fellow!"

I laughed in spite of myself, and it did me some good. He waved one last time, then turned and started back up the road we'd come on.

Away walked Eddie Applebaum, who was as good a friend as I ever had.

-Taking Care of My Own-

I watched Eddie walk away until he was out of sight, then turned back to the girls. Joanna was knelt down next to Cherry, pressing her ear to his hip while turning circles with his leg.

"How is your patient today, Doctor Joanna?" I asked her.

"He's fine, of course." She stood up. "I had an idea that maybe you could tell how a joint is working by turning it and listening at the same time. Pa always said that the hips go first, and it's a shame. Maybe if you knew early on you could do something for it."

"Cherry is a lucky dog to have you as his doctor, and I daresay he knows it, too." He was looking up at Joanna like she'd hung the moon just for him.

"Mary Jane, I know there's doctors for people, but are there doctors for animals, too?"

"I've never heard of one, Joanna. Everyone I've ever known doctors their own animals at home."

"But what about for when you've got a dog or a cat or a rabbit that's sick beyond what you know to do?"

"Maybe in the big cities they have that. They have every kind of job there."

I heard the piano playing from inside the house. Susan had gotten awful good on it, until by now she wanted to play only old songs written by dead people. Just then she was playing a song that sounded like it was written by somebody who knew he was going to die young, which those types did, more often than not.

I sat down on the bench next to her, and let her lean against me as she played. After she came to the end, I asked her, "How are you, Susan? I mean . . . how are you feeling about . . . what happened?"

It was hard to know what to say. I didn't want to pry, but I did want to let her know that I cared and would listen. I figured I'd open the door and let her decide if she wanted to walk through.

She laid her head on my shoulder. "I don't know," she told me. "I'm not afraid anymore; I feel much safer now that he's . . . gone. I just . . . I just feel so . . . *dirty.* No matter how many times I wash, I still feel like I can't get myself clean."

I didn't know what to do, but I wanted so badly to be a person who did. So I decided that I was.

"Susan, I can help you with that, but you have to trust me. Will you?" I asked her.

"I have always trusted you, Mary Jane. Since the first day I met you."

It's a hefty thing to have someone tell that to you. But on that day, it didn't feel like a burden—instead, it felt like a gift. A gift that I wanted to deserve.

I put my arm around her shoulder and gave it a quick squeeze. "Let me send Joanna and Cherry to the store to buy peppermint sticks—I'll be right back."

–Witch-Craft–

I took Susan by the hand and led her upstairs. On the way, we stopped in the empty bedroom where my three silk dresses were hung. I took down my favorite, the shot-silk, rosy-colored one, and carried it with us. We went into my room, and I closed the door.

I spoke clear and steady. "Our grandmother—who you never met—was a witch, as was her mother before her, and hers before, and so on, back to the beginning of time. Not the story-book kind of witches, but the real kind that can smell a thunderstorm from twenty miles off, and predict the harvest from the first sprout. Your ma and my ma both came down from these women, which means you and me and Joanna did also. That's how I know what to do, and somewhere inside, you do, too."

I took a deep breath and carried on. "Susan, sit down wherever feels best."

I took up my favorite dress, the one I had worked so hard on. I held it up to admire its shifting colors, pinkish-gold in the afternoon light. Then I tore the full length of it, from hem to waist. I did the same to the sleeves, and then to the bodice. I tore my beautiful dress into a pile of golden strips that I gathered together and laid in a shimmering pile.

I filled a basin with fresh rainwater from the cistern. I found my precious glass tube of rose oil and held it up to the window, enjoying the rainbow it created for the last time. Then I snapped the glass neck and let the oil drip out into the basin until it was all gone. I set the broken glass aside.

Susan watched me, horrified by what I was doing. "Mary Jane, your dress! Your rose oil! Those are for your wedding . . ."

"No, Susan. *This* is what they are for."

I picked up one of the cloth strips and placed it in the basin, pushing it under and swirling it around until it was soaked in rose-scented water. I pulled it out, squeezed it gently, and handed it to Susan.

"Wash yourself with this," I told her. "Wash yourself wherever you feel dirty."

She turned towards the wall and began to wash, her legs, her arms, her middle, herself—I don't know. It was private, and I didn't look. I wetted the strips one by one and handed them to her over her shoulder. We went on like this until every shred of my dress was gone.

There in my room, I sacrificed the most precious things I

had, trying to make her whole, trying to make her clean. And it did make her feel better . . . but it didn't make her clean.

Susan was already clean. She had always been clean, and she always would be. Just as you and me and every girl in the world is clean, no matter what happens to us.

"I feel stronger, Mary Jane," she told me.

"You know what? I do, too," I answered her.

I wish Peter Wilks had not done what he did. I wish it had been me that night, instead of her. I wish that me doing my best had been better. But those are three wishes that will not come true. I can never undo what happened to Susan, but I helped her set it down and begin to walk away. And I'm proud of that.

She moved some pillows to the floor and laid down on the carpet. The next I saw she was sleeping peacefully, warmed by a stray sunbeam from the late-afternoon sun.

–Getting Better–

I tiptoed out the door and sat down in the hallway. *I sure have come a long way without ever leaving Greenville,* I thought to myself.

I was proud of how I'd seen Susan through the darkness, ashamed of how I'd treated Sugar and Candy, and didn't know what to think about the death of Peter Wilks. Throughout it all, I'd done my best, and my best had turned out to be good . . . and terrible . . . and . . . I didn't know. More than anything, I'd wanted to be a *good* person. A good person doing the *right* thing.

Somehow, someway, I'll get the girls away from this place

where people are property, so it can't turn them, like it did me, I promised myself. *After I get them settled and happy, I'll go find someplace where I can finally be free and easy.*

Maybe I'll light out for the Western Territory, I considered. It was an exciting place I'd heard the trappers talk about, though I didn't know quite where it was. I did know that I couldn't go back to Fort Snelling, for a lot of reasons. I also couldn't bear the idea of going back to school to be civilized by Miss Whoever. I was already too much of a woman to be turned into a lady.

So there I was, all fired up thinking about the different things that I wanted to get away *from.* But life is funny, you know, because only a couple hours later, I met the person that I was always meant to get *to.*

He is the most beautiful young man in the world. He is wild and reckless and honest and kind and made of something tougher than nails and more flexible than rubber. He had hold of my heart from the first minute that I saw him.

Thank Heavens he was with the two biggest idiots that God ever created.

CHAPTER XXVII

-My Best Plan Yet-

"Mary Jane!" Joanna came bounding up the stairs with Cherry. "There's three men come to Greenville, just off a steamboat: one young and two old. The old ones say they're our—well, Susan and me's—uncles come to see Peter Wilks before he dies."

"Oh, Lord." I shook my head. "Here we go again."

"That's just it, Mary Jane. It's odd . . . I don't think that they really *can* be our uncles. They don't sound anything like Pa, or even Peter Wilks, for that matter."

"That is odd," I agreed.

"Then again, they did seem to already know a lot about us . . ."

"Did they recognize you? Did you talk to them, Joanna?"

"No, I was down at the river with Cherry. Near enough to hear it all, but out of sight."

"That's just as well. But something was . . . fishy . . . about it all?"

"Yes, but I can't put my finger on it . . ."

I looked her in the eye and asked, "Joanna, what do you feel in your *gut*? Are these men who they claim to be?"

She thought, then answered, "No." Then added, "I wouldn't put it past them to be only after Peter Wilks's gold."

"Joanna, I'm not too worried about that. Even if they do know that Peter Wilks had gold, they don't know where he hid it any more than we do."

"Of course we know where it's hid, Mary Jane! It's buried in the cellar."

"The *what*?" I was astonished, and that's putting it lightly.

"The hole in the cellar, the one that Peter Wilks kept going on about."

"*When* did he tell you that?"

"He told all of us, Mary Jane, you were there. *Inna oyle down th' ginnel*—he said it just the way Pa would have."

Of course! . . . Then I got an idea that turned into a brand-new plan.

"We'll have to keep one step ahead of them, then, whoever they are. Can you trust me, Joanna, to do what I must?"

"I have been, Mary Jane, all along."

Her and Susan both, I thought to myself, and took a deep breath. "All right, go in and wake your sister. Tell her your uncles are said to have come but don't tell her your suspicions just yet. It's too much to ask her to play a part just now, and some parts will need played."

"I will, Mary Jane, I'll do just what you said."

"Good girl. I'll go downstairs first and put some things in order. Oh, yes—tell Cherry to stay close to you, but out of sight for now. He'll be the ace up our sleeve: there if we need him, and a surprise if we do."

Joanna left, and I ran straight down to the cellar—*down th' ginnel,* as Peter Wilks would have said—and stomped all around listening for a hollow in the floor. It took me a bit, but I finally found the *oyle* off in one corner, where I grabbed a spade and started in digging. Not too far down I found his *big bag o' gold,* and it took me all my strength to haul it up.

I'd been weighing things by feel since Morfar showed me how, years ago. *Not five, and not seven—yup, nearer to six thousand dollars' worth—just as he'd claimed,* I reckoned.

Clink! Clinkety-clink-clink!

After you've had your hands around real gold coins, you don't forget the feel of it, nor the sound, neither. I was tempted to run off with the whole sack, right there and then. *No, not yet . . . too risky,* I decided.

I stuck both hands in and pulled out as much as I could hold, then knotted it into my two pockets, tight so it wouldn't jingle. It made my dress feel mighty heavy, but you couldn't see the bulges after I tied my apron on.

We'll slip away in the night, one of these nights—soon!—I'm sure I got more than enough to get the girls up to Fort Snelling, and me wherever I want from there! I congratulated myself on my new plan.

I plopped the sack with the rest of the money in it back into its hole. I kicked some loose dirt over it, to make it easy to find. Then I ran back upstairs to Peter Wilks's room, and found his body gone, meaning it was somewhere getting smoothed out for the funeral.

Paper . . . I need paper and ink. I searched the room, until I found his stationery drawer. I used my left hand to scribble out a note, messy and child-like, that I thought might pass for Peter Wilks's writing. It said:

New Testament of Mr. Peter Osbourne Wilks, proprietor
of Wilks Tannery, and resident of Greenville, Mississippi,
For my brothers Wilks.
WHAT TO DO IF I AM TAKEN BEFORE MY TIME
My Big House & half of the big bag of gold buried down
the ginnel to the girls my nieces George's girls Mary Jane,
Susan, and Joanna. & the ANIMALS them too, specially the big
brown dog that showed up a few years ago.
My Tannery & Lands & half of the big bag of gold down the
ginnel to my remaining living brothers.
I hereby verify it to be true even though I can't sign
my name too good because I'm sick but here's a mark,
I'm good for it.

I folded the paper into an envelope and wrote *Last Will and Testify for my Brothers* across the seal, then put it in the stationery drawer. I went into my room and put the gold pieces—four hundred and fifteen dollars' worth, once I counted it out—into a pillowcase and shoved it under my bed.

Tomorrow, all of Greenville would come to gawk at Peter Wilks's funeral, and me and the girls would be front and center. But after everybody'd finally gone home, we wouldn't be missed. That's when we'd pack up what-all money I had, and slip out before sun-rise.

When I went downstairs to find Susan and Joanna, I passed by Peter Wilks's body laid out in the parlor. Abner Shackelford was trying to stuff a blue tongue back into his head with a wooden spoon. I stopped and stared for a minute. Maybe I should have felt something, but I didn't. Not right then, anyway.

I heard people cheering outside, and came out to find Joanna and Susan looking up the road. A crowd of folks was skipping and dancing around the three strangers, heading straight for us, and hoping to see a big show. I decided we'd give them one.

"Joanna," I said to her, off to one side. "For now, no matter who these men are, we'll let them believe that *we* believe they're our uncles. It'll give me some time to size up how to handle them."

She nodded at me, and I knew she was on board.

—A Second Homecoming—

The crowd filled up the yard, everyone trying to get a place where they could see. Two men stepped forwards: one in a starchy black suit with a pious look on his face, the other flapping his arms and banging his fists in the air. It was quite an act, and you didn't have to be a genius to tell who was supposed to be Uncle Harvey, the preacher, from Uncle William, who can't talk or hear.

I took a side glance at Joanna, winked twice, then gave Uncle Preacher the biggest welcome-home-my-long-lost-uncle hug that I could manage, for everyone to see. Out of the corner of my eye I saw Joanna do the same to Uncle Won't-Talk, and the whole town cheered with joy over the sight.

Encouraged, I threw my hands up in jubilation, and kissed Uncle Preacher on his forehead. Then I thumped him on his back and hugged him again and again, until I'd gotten the whole crowd hugging and kissing and thumping and jubilating, too.

Somebody struck up a harmonica, and somebody else blew on a jug, and before I knew it, folks joined hands, bowed and curtseyed, and a square dance started up, spontaneous-like.

From my spot above the old man's shoulder, I scanned the yard. A young man carrying a mess of luggage caught my eye. He was about my height and about my weight and his blond hair was pulled back into a pony-tail . . . and his big shoulders and his blue eyes and his square jaw . . .

The about-my-height-blue-eyes-pony-tail boy was all alone at the dance, looking like the only person on Earth who didn't have a partner. All around him, folks were reeling and kicking up their heels, and getting more jovial with every twang of the harp. He looked down at his shoes, then up at the sky, then over at his shirt cuff where a button was missing.

And then he looked up at me, and our eyes locked together, and he smiled.

Ba-BOOM, Ba-BOOM, Ba-BOOM!

I felt it in my chest.

I let go of that old man and I jumped. I jumped off the porch with both hands held out. The about-my-height-blue-eyes-pony-tail boy dropped both suitcases and caught my hands in his. And weren't we suddenly in each other's arms, face to face?

He was as surprised as he'd ever been, I could tell. Then, a split second later, he smiled and looked as happy as he'd ever been—I could tell that, too.

We started to spin. Around and around we went, holding tight, like the two wings of a windmill bound together in the middle. We didn't stop until I was out of breath and my hair had come undone and my collar was torn and . . . and I wasn't myself because I was more than myself.

I didn't even know his name. I didn't know where he'd come from, and I didn't know where he was going. And I certainly didn't know whether he was a *good* man, or a . . .

All I knew was that my heart was pounding. It was pounding like Aunt Evelyn's did when she saw George, and like Ma's must've when she saw Pa.

Ba-BOOM, Ba-BOOM, Ba-BOOM!

It was pounding like mine did when I first saw that about-my-height-blue-eyes-pony-tail boy and we grabbed each other by the hands and spun together in a circle until we both fell down laughing.

-Introductions-

The Uncles high-tailed it inside to get a gander at their dead brother before the music even slowed down. The about-my-height-blue-eyes-pony-tail boy smiled at me one more time, then got up and followed behind them, looking none too eager to go. Half the town followed *him* in, looking eager enough to make up for it.

I got up and brushed the dust off. I glimpsed Cherry out past the barn keeping track of all the comings and goings. I looked for Susan and Joanna, and saw them on the porch, standing strong.

The next minute, we could hear the better part of Greenville inside sobbing and carrying on. Uncle Preacher must have been leading them in prayer, because a gaggle of women came out all solemn, to kiss us and lay a hand on our heads, and call us *dear little lambs*, and that sort of thing.

It was Mrs. Proctor and Mrs. Apthorp—or was it *Lothrop*?—and the rest who'd never shown any interest in us before that day. I caught sight of Widow Bartley standing off to the side, shaking her head over the whole display.

Then the men came outside singing:

Praise God, from whom all blessings flow;
Praise Him, all creatures here below . . .

Sort of, anyway . . . mostly they were just bellowing along with the melody. It sounded like wounded animals to me, but it did freshen up the women and make them feel bully again. Music is a good thing, on balance.

Uncle Preacher gave us a speech:

"Brothers and Sisters! *By Jove!* We've had a jolly bad time, my brother and I, but we're here now, I say! *Pip pip!* Our nieces three—*Mary Jane, Susan,* and *Joanna*—and us two—me, *Harvey,* and him, *William,* would be well chuffed if a few of the main principal friends of the family would take supper here. If my poor brother *Peter* could speak, I know who he would name, for they are names very dear to him, and mentioned often in his letters.

"To wit, as follows, vizz.: Rev. Mr. Hobson, and Deacon Lot Hovey, and Mr. Ben Rucker, and Abner Shackleford, and Levi Bell, and Doctor Robinson, and their wives, and the Widow Bartley, we'll all of us have a spot of tea. *Poppycock!* And again—*By Jove!*"

He had the names right, I'll give him that. And sure enough, they were all there—except for Levi Bell, who is the town lawyer, but that didn't bother me much. By then I knew to worry more when the lawyers do show up, than when they don't.

As for Uncle Preacher's English accent, he must have thought it'd done the trick, because he never felt the need to use it again. Uncle Won't-Talk, for his part, just kept smiling like a saphead and saying *Goo-goo—goo-goo-goo* all the time, like a baby.

Now, I've got a lot of problems, but being stupid isn't one of them. I knew full well those two men weren't the girls' uncles any more than Cherry was their big brother. What they were after wasn't hard to guess, for what is every scoundrel after, but money? Who they were, and how they already knew so much about us, is what I wanted to know.

And why was the about-my-height-blue-eyes-pony-tail boy hanging around the likes of them? Did that make him a scoundrel, too?

I didn't know the answers, but I was going to find out.

-Th' Oyle Down th' Ginnel-

I brought out the fake will I'd written not more than an hour ago, hoping to Heaven they'd all be fooled.

"Here!" I thrust the envelope into Uncle Preacher's hand. "This was our uncle Peter's special directions for when his brothers were come. Now I can rest my mind easy knowing I've done as he wished and got it to you."

I turned my eyes up innocent and trusting. Joanna came up and hugged Uncle Won't-Talk just to out-do me. Susan stood to the side looking sweeter naturally than we could by trying.

Uncle Preacher pulled out the letter and read it through, then wiped away a couple of fake tears. "Say, my dear girl—Where's the *ginnel*?" he asked me afterwards. As soon as I told him, he and Uncle Won't-Talk didn't walk—they *ran* straight down the cellar stairs.

I was sad to see the about-my-height-blue-eyes-pony-tail boy follow on their heels. I wanted to believe that he was somehow on our side. *I'll get Joanna to help me find out what he's up to,* I decided.

I took her aside, and asked, "Joanna, when we show them to

their rooms, can you take that pony-tail boy up to the attic and find out what you can? He's got an honest face, and might give out the real story."

"Sure I will, Mary Jane."

"Also, can you make sure Cherry stays here in the house, but out of sight?"

"Oh, he'll do anything I tell him to."

"Good. I don't trust these men and Cherry is our best protection, especially if he can roam free but secret."

I heard coins clinking down in the cellar and knew the Uncles had found the bag of gold I'd dug up, then buried back in.

By then the other half of Greenville had come inside to see what was happening, with Doctor Robinson right up front. I could tell by the look on his face that he was fixing to poke his nose in where it didn't belong.

We all gathered 'round as Uncle Preacher counted out the gold, then stacked it into two piles, and it took him *forever* to do it. Twice as long as it took the Rooster on his very first day. After what seemed like a year, I glanced at his piles to count the total, and wasn't it a full six thousand after all?

What about all that I took out earlier? Were they stupid enough to put money in just to get to the number some fool told them in town? Dealing with these two idiots was going to be easier than I thought.

Uncle Preacher puffed himself up for another speech:

"Friends all, my poor brother that lays yonder has done generous by these three poor little lambs that's left behind in the vale of sorrers fatherless and motherless . . ."

He wondered out loud what to do with their share of the money, then got the bright idea to ask Uncle Won't-Talk for his opinion: "If I know William—and I think I do—he—well, I'll jest ask him."

He flapped his hands towards Uncle Won't-Talk, who goo-gooed back at him. "I knowed it," Uncle Preacher announced, "I reckon this'll convince anybody the way we feels about it."

He swept the full six thousand back into the bag. "Here, Mary Jane, Susan, Joanner, take the money—take it all! It's the gift of him that lays yonder, cold but joyful."

I won't lie: I was dumbfounded by this turn of events. Not knowing what else to do, I jumped into his arms and gave him a big hug. Joanna did the same to Uncle Won't-Talk, poor little lambs as we were.

Uncle Preacher blubbered some under the sentiment, then told about how shocked they'd been to learn their brother was poorly, for he had written so often of the fine, robust health he enjoyed in Greenville amongst his dear friends that were gathered here together. At that, Doctor Robinson laughed right in his face.

Uncle Preacher just smiled and shoved out his paw for a handshake. "Is it my poor brother's dear good friend and physician? I—"

"Keep your hands off of me!" said the doctor. "You *talk* like an Englishman, do you? It's the worst imitation I ever heard. You, Peter Wilks's brother! You're a fraud, that's what you are!"

The Uncles went into a faint about how could anyone not believe they were the own bosom blood relatives of Peter Wilks, but the doctor wasn't having any of it. He turned to me and said, straight out:

"I was your uncle's friend, and I'm your friend, Mary Jane. I warn you as a friend to turn this pitiful rascal out—I beg you to do it. Will you?"

Damn you, Doctor Robinson! I wanted to say. The last thing I needed was a big old drama bringing everything to a halt. What I needed was for everything to keep going, and smoothly, too, as the sooner we got through this funeral, the sooner me and the girls could run off.

I knew I had to make a big gesture just then, something that would make the Uncles sure beyond a doubt that I had been taken in by their story.

I straightened up and said to Doctor Robinson: "*Here* is my answer!" Then I shoved the bag of gold back into Uncle Preacher's hands, and told him: "You and Uncle William, why, you *take* this six thousand dollars, all of it. Invest for me and my sisters any way you want to, and don't give us a receipt for it."

It wasn't much of a sacrifice. I still had two pockets full of gold, plus fifty-two dollars and twenty-eight cents in the jar upstairs.

The Uncles cried what looked like real tears, and I could tell they bought it hook, line, and sinker, but Doctor Robinson wasn't done lecturing me yet:

"All right; I wash my hands of the matter. But I warn you all that a time's coming when you're going to feel sick whenever you think of this day, Mary Jane."

"All right, Doctor," said Uncle Preacher, "we'll try and get 'em to send for you," which made everybody laugh, including me.

The doctor stormed out, sputtering. His pride was so hurt that I almost felt sorry for him, until I remembered how he had tried to cure Peter Wilks about as hard as I had.

–Friend or Foe?–

I took our guests upstairs and put Uncle Won't-Talk into Susan's old room. When I put Uncle Preacher in the room where my two dresses hung, I saw them and got the idea to sew the gold I'd taken from the bag into the hem of the yellow one.

If someone notices the money missing, they'll never think to look there, I thought to myself.

"Here, let me get these frocks and traps and such out of here," I said as I grabbed them by their hangers.

"Oh, no, now, now don't trouble yourself—we're family!" Uncle Preacher said. I smiled sweet as I could, and told him, "No, they'll be in your way, and I won't have that. I'll come 'round for them later."

I turned to Joanna: "Sister, dear," I said, sweet as pie, "will you take our young visitor up to the attic and show him where he can sleep?" She gave me a sly look as they went off, and I knew she'd be pumping him for information.

She came back down after not too long and told me quietly, "Well, his name is *Joe.*"

"*Joe,* huh? Hmm . . . Anything else?"

"Nothing, really. I think he's afraid of . . . umm, his traveling companions."

We need to make him feel safe, and then he'll tell us everything is what I was thinking.

"Joanna, listen. You and me, we're going to do something called friend-or-foe. It's what me and Morfar used to do when someone came into the Forks trying to sell stolen goods. The *foe*'s job is to dig at his story and get him sweating nervous . . . then the *friend* comes in and takes his side. By then he's so relieved to have a kind word tossed at him, he breaks open and tells you everything."

"I bet when he does, we'll see he's nothing like those Uncles," said Joanna. "Something about him makes me believe he's a good egg, down deep."

"That may be, but he's still got to prove it by telling us the truth." I went on: "You'll take supper with him in the kitchen, and work him over as the foe while I'm playing hostess in the dining room. After you've scared him good, I'll come in as the friend and he'll think I'm his rescue. Do you think you can do it, Joanna?"

"I can do it. I'll be as fiendish a foe as you've ever seen, Mary Jane. But I wish I knew who to take after . . . I haven't known very many *bad* people."

"Pretend you're given to good works," I said. "Those are some of the meanest people I've come across," I added, thinking of Pastor Martin and Pastor's Wife. Joanna nodded like she knew what I meant, but I was glad that she didn't.

I slunk into Uncle Preacher's room, but only had time to take my dresses down before I heard footsteps coming up the stairs. I went and stuffed them under my bed, then went downstairs to eat dinner in the dining room and make the Uncles feel like guests of honor. They talked their usual blather—or at least Uncle Preacher did; Uncle Won't-Talk just flapped his arms around like a trained seal.

For my part, I went on about how bad the biscuits were, and how mean the preserves was, and how ornery and tough the fried chicken was, just out of habit. I'd gotten so used to griping about every little thing Sugar did. The guests—they could tell the food was tip-top, and kept telling me so as if I was the one who'd actually made it.

I gave Joanna a good long time to be the *foe,* then I sailed in to do my part. And wasn't she carrying on just wonderful? My goodness, that girl is a natural. She had Joe up against the wall with his hand on the Bible—really it was just the dictionary— trying to bully the truth out of him.

"Well, then, I'll believe *some* of it; but I hope to gracious if I'll believe the rest," I heard her say as I walked in.

"What is it you won't *believe,* Joanna?" I said, sweet as anything. Joe was nervous as a treed possum, just the way we wanted him. He looked over at me like how a man on a sinking boat looks at a life-raft.

"It isn't right nor kind for you to talk so to him," I scolded Joanna, "and him a stranger and so far from his people. How would you like to be treated so?"

"That's always your way, Mary Jane—always sailing in to

help somebody before they're hurt. I haven't done anything to him. He's told some stretchers, and I said I wouldn't swallow it all. I guess he can stand a little thing like that, can't he?"

I stamped my foot. "I don't care whether it was little or whether it was big; he's here in our house and a stranger, and it wasn't good of you to say it. If you were in his place it would make you feel ashamed; and so you oughtn't to say a thing to another person that will make *them* feel ashamed."

"Why, Mary Jane, he said—"

"It doesn't make any difference what he *said*—that isn't the thing. The thing is for you to treat him *kind,* and not be saying things to make him remember he isn't in his own country and amongst his own folks."

"All right, then," said Joanna, playing her part perfectly, "*you* ask his pardon."

"I'm sorry, Joe. I'm so sorry we've not been the friends you've needed. I want so much for you to know that you can *trust* us, and that you can tell us *anything* that might weigh on your mind . . ."

He was just about to crack, by the looks of him standing there, wringing his hands and looking miserable. I stood and smiled kind at him, which wasn't hard. He was the most beautiful young man I'd ever seen, like I said. Yes, it was friend-or-foe, but it was also me wanting to get closer, and knowing the truth would be the best place to start.

Joe started to talk, but stopped himself before one whole word came out. Then he got an idea in his head, jumped, and ran upstairs, leaving us without so much as a *See-you-later.*

I turned to Joanna. "I guess you wrangled him pretty hard. Did *you* get anything out of him?"

"Not a thing, except for more lies, each one more foolish than the one before. He's sticking to their story as best he can and making up the difference with fibs whenever he comes to a thin place."

"Oh, no . . . I'd have thought . . ." I was disappointed and it probably showed on my face.

"He's not on *our* side, Mary Jane, and I'm sorry for it. I daresay he's hankering after that bag of gold just as much as the others are."

The girls went up to bed, and I was left behind, sitting in the dark kitchen and feeling as bad as I'd ever felt in my life. Joe was for sure on the side of the Uncles, and my heart broke a little because of it. No matter how wonderful he looked from the outside, Joe was a liar, and that hurt.

Of course, I didn't stop to consider all the different lies I had already told him.

–The Vigil–

I started out that night feeling low, and then I got lower.

It's tradition that someone in the family should sit up all night with the dead, on the night before the funeral. I figured it might as well be me, as I'd spent the most hours with him.

When I saw Peter Wilks's body all laid out and ready to go, I knew why that Abner Shackleford was the most popular man in town. Peter looked miles better dead than he ever did while alive. His face was painted with something that made him come off better-hearted than I knew he had been.

Then again, maybe Peter Wilks was good-hearted when he started out, like we all are in the beginning. Maybe if he could open those eyes, and I could look into them one more time, I'd find some kindness at the root of him, to remember him by.

Then I was sad, awful sad. I remembered the hairbrush next to the basin and the toenail clipper on the windowsill and his dead mother's bones, in the ground far away, and it was all so sad all over again.

I thought about the blue bottle with the white cap. I could feel its hard edges in my pocket. Maybe the medicine in it would have cured him. Maybe that dead man in front of me would still be breathing if I'd given it to him. The girls and me would still have had plenty of problems—and bad ones, too—but a man might be *alive* if I'd done different. That's a heavy thing.

I started to cry. Not bawling-like, but the tears dripped down, and I couldn't make them stop.

The Widow Bartley came in and sat down in the chair next to me. She pulled my head to the side onto her shoulder and said: "Death is an awful sad thing. Doesn't matter who it is, or what they did. You can't help feeling your own death when you see someone else's. You go ahead and grieve, Mary Jane, knowing you did everything for him that you possibly could."

I waited for a moment, while the truth built up in me like a stopped-up soda-pop. I didn't want to blow, but I had to. The guilt was just too much. I couldn't take one more minute of that good Quaker woman thinking me so much better than I was.

"But I *didn't* do all I possibly could, Widow Bartley." I took the little blue bottle out of my pocket and handed it to her. "I never gave him this."

She took it and saw that it was still full and unopened. She threw both arms around me and said, "Oh, my dear, you are innocent! This is nothing but colored water that I gave you. Peace of mind in a bottle, I thought it would be. You mustn't—*mustn't*—blame yourself for his passing."

She gave the bottle back to me and I felt relieved, until I didn't.

Later, during the darkest part of the night, the Widow Bartley got up and blew out all the candles but one. "You stay with him as you should, Mary Jane, but let your mind rest easy: it was God taking him home and not you sending him. I need to go back to the Store now, but I'll be back in time for the funeral." She kissed me on the forehead and left.

I sat on and waited for dawn. Once I thought I heard someone behind me, but when I looked, there was nobody there. I would have thought it a ghost, if I believed in ghosts, which I don't. It was only my sad thoughts, wandering around the room in circles, going nowhere.

The Widow Bartley'd been right: I wasn't a person who had killed. But I was a person who had decided not to help someone live. I held back what I thought might cure Peter Wilks, and I'll have to live with that. I still keep that blue bottle in my pocket and every time I touch it, I remember the sins of Peter Wilks, and my own that came after.

But I'd do it just the same all over again, I do know that. I couldn't see any other way then, and I can't see any other way now. I had a choice, and I made it.

I made the choice to keep my family safe.

CHAPTER XXVIII

–A Mitzvah–

The candle got dimmer as the dawn got brighter. After the sun was fully up, I went upstairs to stitch that four hundred and fifteen dollars of gold into the hem of my yellow dress. The weight of it felt good in my hands; it would be more than enough for what we needed. After I finished sewing, I shoved the dress under my bed and laid myself down next to the girls.

I couldn't sleep, no matter how I tried. I just laid there, staring at the wall. I tried naming off the queens of England . . . it usually works, but it didn't this time. My body was more than tired enough to sleep, it was my conscience that couldn't rest.

I'd done things in Greenville that I didn't feel good about, and not just to Peter Wilks. By then I knew myself to be a Mistress and not an Abolitionist—that's how Sugar and Candy saw me anyway, and what matters more than that? I'd become what I'd loathed more than anything, back when I was so sure how simple it all was. I'd given myself all kinds of excuses for it, but the truth was that I didn't have the courage to be anything more.

I remembered how Eddie had spent his last days in Greenville, doing *mitzvahs* for the people he was leaving behind. *Maybe that's how I should spend my last day,* I considered. It was too late for Peter Wilks to make amends, but maybe I could give something back to Sugar and Candy before we left them behind.

I got to the General Store to find the porch empty for a change. All of Greenville was at home getting gussied up for Peter Wilks's funeral. I opened the door and stuck my nose in. The Widow Bartley was sat behind the counter, having her morning coffee.

"*Hello*, Mary Jane. Are you feeling better? How are the girls holding up?"

"We're all right, I guess. But I've got some things to tell you, and some things to give you. Can we go into your back room and talk private?"

We went in and she closed the door good and shut, and locked it, too. I couldn't see much in the low light, but it seemed like the big pile of quilts was gone.

"What is it, then?" she asked me.

"Now that our uncles have come, the girls and I will be leaving soon, as I'm sure you expected." It wasn't exactly a lie, but it wasn't the whole truth, either. I was getting pretty good at finding the space in between.

"Mary Jane, I have my doubts about those two . . ."

"We'll be all right, don't you worry," I told her, but she didn't look convinced.

I handed her my yellow silk dress, all wadded up. "But before

I go, I wanted to give you this. Inside you'll find four hundred and fifteen dollars in gold coins that I stole from Peter Wilks after he died. I want it used to buy freedom for Sugar and Candy when the estate settles up. I trust you to do it. Will you?"

"Mary Jane, what are you doing? Who told you to do this?"

"No one. I just want to . . . to make things right. Peter Wilks believed their worth, together, added up to four hundred dollars, so this is surely enough to make them free."

The Widow Bartley sighed. "Oh, my dear, there's a lot you don't know. A judge can say *No,* I've seen it before. And even if they can buy their freedom, where are they to go? What are they to live on? A free life doesn't mean an easy one, especially after being someone's property."

"Can't they go up North, to the free states? That's what Eliza did with her boy Henry at the end of *Uncle Tom's Cab*—"

"Mary Jane, *Uncle Tom's Cabin* is a story that someone wrote about imaginary people. Sugar and Candy have their own story—a real one—and four hundred and fifteen dollars will not make you the hero of it. You need to understand that."

It's true that I wanted to quiet my conscience on the matter, but believe me when I say it wasn't only that. Planning a *mitzvah* had made me start hoping, too. Hoping that Sugar and Candy could get as far away from that tannery as they needed to. Hoping they could have their good times together out in the open, not just in secret and hiding. To splash and sing and snack on the best part of the roast every day or whenever, like a family does. By then I knew enough to know that such things are worth hoping for.

"Widow Bartley, even if I'm not a story-book hero, I'm here now. Answer me this: Would four hundred and fifteen dollars be enough to change the *plot* of Sugar and Candy's story?"

"Yes, dear, I believe it would."

"Then take it—it's Peter Wilks's money that they earned for him anyway—and do what you can. Will you?"

"Yes, Mary Jane. I promise I will." I gave over the dress and she folded it and put it on the shelf where the quilts had been. "You go on to the funeral now, and let me think about how to start."

While I walked, I wondered if the money would do any good, after all.

There, I've done my part, I told myself as I walked that dusty road for the umpteenth time. *Maybe there's some who would have done more, but I know many who would have done less. I did something, and something is always more than nothing.*

It might have counted as a real *mitzvah,* I don't know. Maybe I'll see Eddie again someday, and I can ask him. That sure would be nice.

-The Funeral-

On the road back from the General Store, I met Susan and Jo-anna walking towards me, with Cherry out in front, of course.

"Mary Jane, we came downstairs and didn't find you next to the body," said Susan. "We didn't know where you'd gone."

Joanna added: "I asked Cherry where you were and he ran to the gate and looked back at us to follow, then led us up this road." She knelt down and petted him. "And here she is, just like you said. Such a good boy!"

"The funeral is starting soon, it looks like," said Susan. "People are already inside eating sandwiches."

It was time to tell them. "Girls, there's nothing here for us—and so we're going to run away. I'll ask you to trust me for now, and not ask where, when, and how."

"But we'll go together?" Susan was concerned.

"Of course we will, girls."

"Of course we will, Susan," said Joanna, linking her arm through her sister's. "And Cherry's coming with us?"

"Yes, he's our best protection, as always," I said, and it was my turn to pet him. Darned if he didn't look serious like he understood.

We got back to the house just as Peter Wilks's funeral was gearing up full-force, and went to take our seats up front. Cherry tried to go in with us, glued to Joanna's leg as usual.

I told her what she already knew: "Joanna, he can't be at the funeral."

"I'll shut him down in the cellar," she said. "He'll be close enough to hear everything, and that'll settle him until it's over."

We sat down in the front row, next to Reverend Hobson, who was busy clearing his throat. When the piano started up, I saw real pain on Susan's face. The Reverend's wife was banging away on the keys, skreeky and colicky, but we all got up and sung anyway.

Rock of Ages, cleft for me,
let me hide myself in thee . . .

Then the Reverend began his sermon:

"Death. What is *death*? Why, it's the end. The end of every-thing. Think of all the little things that bring you joy. Being dead means you'll never do any of them ever again. Look at Peter Wilks, laying here dead. Whatever it was that brought him joy, he'll never do it again. He's deader than a doornail.

"Me, I'm a Reverend. I'm the head shepherd of you flock. All of you are going to die, some of you sooner than you think. And when your time comes, it's likely me who'll have to sit at your deathbed, watching the life drain out of you.

"'Reverend, I'm afraid!' you'll say to me. 'I don't want to die!' 'Well, you will,' I'll answer, 'and probably not too long from now.' 'Am I going to Heaven?' you'll ask me, because they always do. 'Hard to say,' I'll answer. 'But you'll find out soon.'"

Then we heard a dog bark. No, we heard a dog explode with barking. Everyone stopped to look at each other, but nobody said anything. The barking went on and on. All done and told, it was enough to shut the Reverend up for five minutes, which nobody felt too bad about, I'm willing to bet.

Joanna looked at me with her eyes wide as saucers. Over her shoulder I saw Abner Shackleford slip towards the exit. Then we heard him *stomp, stomp, stomp* down the cellar stairs.

There was more barking, then quiet, then footsteps up the stairs, and then Abner Shackleford gliding back into the room. *"He had a rat!"* he announced in a coarse whisper, loud enough for all to hear. Me and Joanna sat back and sighed; it was Cherry just being Cherry.

We followed the coffin to the graveyard, me and the girls

in black veils like the good little lambs we were. When we got to the grave, Uncle Preacher got up on his hind legs and said some rubbish about the dear departed while Uncle Won't-Talk flapped his arms around in the way we'd gotten used to seeing him do. Then the pallbearers let go the ropes and the coffin slid into a six-foot-deep hole, easy and square as if Peter Wilks had found his home at last.

I watched Joe through it all; there was a part of me that still hoped he'd give up the game, tell on the Uncles, and be our real friend. He didn't, though. He just followed behind the cheerfullest two bereaved brothers I'd ever seen, dragging his feet and looking sorry enough for all of them.

The girls slept that night in my bed with Cherry beside them on the floor, Joanna's hand draped over his ear. I kept my own ear pressed against the door, though I could barely keep my eyes open. The Uncles would surely sneak away under cover of darkness, I was certain, satisfied with six thousand dollars in gold. When they did, we'd take our chance and sneak off in the other direction.

Next to me sat our three bundles and a rope-leash for Cherry, all within arm's reach.

We were ready to run.

-Early Birds-

Just at dawn, I heard a rustling on the stairs, then the screen door slam, as our visitors left the house. The girls looked so peaceful curled up together, I figured I'd let them sleep a few more minutes while I went to round up provisions. Who knew how long it'd be before they slept safe and easy again?

I went outside, and on my way to the larder, I saw our three scoundrels coming back up the road. Joe looked just as sorry as he had the day before, but both Uncles were smiling like cats that caught the canary.

"My, oh, my, up and out of bed already, are you?" Uncle Preacher said, looking mighty pleased with himself. "We've just come from fixing the auction for tomorrow."

"An . . . an auction?"

"Why, of course! We'll sell off the house, the land, the tools—all of it!"

I should have expected it. The Uncles wouldn't be leaving until they had wrung every last penny out of Peter Wilks's estate.

"Yes Siree, getting up early always does pay off! While we were there, a 'ex-speculator,' he called himself, happened by the General Store, asking about the Wilks brothers. Before I could even shake his hand, he offered to buy my pro—err, *our* property off'n us, just like that."

I couldn't believe what I was hearing. "Did you . . . sell Sugar and Candy?"

"Oh, they have names, do they? You girls are too soft-hearted . . . but why, *Yes*, I sold 'em! See here: a hundred dollars in gold—real gold—he gave it to me on the spot, and promised me a hundred more upon delivery. Of course, I would have never accepted paper money from the likes of him. For all we know, he's nothing but a lying, cheating scoundrel looking to rob three poor girls during their darkest hour!"

I glanced over at Joe, who was looking more miserable with every passing word, which made me hopeful that he might bust in and tell on them, as now would be a pretty darn good time for it, but he didn't.

Sure enough, the "ex-speculator" came by after lunch and paid the Uncles another hundred dollars in gold. Just like that, Candy was sold up the river to Memphis, and Sugar was sold down the river to New Orleans. I don't want to tell you about how they tore that child from her mother, and how it took two men on either side to do it. Whatever you're imagining, it was worse than that. It was worse than what any Abolitionist ever wrote in a pamphlet, or will ever, for that matter.

When they were gone, I hung off the girls' necks and cried like never before, big heaving sobs until I couldn't breathe, but couldn't stop, either. I cried because the four hundred and fifteen dollars had come too late. I cried for all the different *Goodbyes* I'd had to say since I'd left home. I cried for all of my failed plans, and my fear that this next one might fail, too. I cried because I still missed being the girl I used to be.

I didn't stop crying until Reverend Hobson came through the gate and offered a hundred dollars for Susan's piano so his wife could keep skreeking and colicking on it from the comfort of home. When Uncle Preacher jumped for joy and yelled *Sold!* I saw a tear run down Susan's face.

I took her hand and squeezed it. "I'll find you another one, when we get where we're going," I whispered.

"When are we leaving here, Mary Jane, I need to know," she whispered back, like she couldn't take it anymore.

I couldn't see any more reason to wait on the Uncles. "To-night, girls, that's when we'll go. Just after dawn, so we'll have a little light. I promise. Tonight. No matter what."

Susan nodded. Joanna whistled for Cherry, and said she'd keep him close, and ready.

CHAPTER XXIX

–Thoughts Before Leaving–

I know I do an awful lot of crying in this story; it was kind of a crying time there for a bit. But I do have to tell you about one more time . . .

I was so tired that I fell asleep right away when we went to bed that night. It didn't last long, because I woke while it was still dark outside. After my eyes opened, they wouldn't stay shut.

I shook the girls gently and got them out of bed: "It's time, girls. You two take your bundles and tiptoe downstairs," I said, quiet as I could. "Let Cherry take you as far as the gate, and wait in the bushes with him. I'll be along soon." I figured I should get them out and away from the house before I went down to the kitchen and grabbed whatever food I could on the way out.

When I took up my bundle, it came to me that it was my last remaining dress that I was holding, the green one I'd made so long ago. The one that went with my hair just right, and brought out my eyes just so. Not so fancy as the others, but perfect to wear on . . . say, like a picnic . . . or fishing off a dock . . . or just to have a nice day out with someone special, someone like . . .

Plop-splash.

Dark splashes were showing up, one here, one there, in the silk that covered my lap. Quiet little tears fell steadily from my eyes, but not over our usual troubles. This time I was crying over Joe. Not because he was a liar, for by then it had come to me that I was a liar, too. No, I was sad over what wouldn't be, over something that I'd lost before I even got hold of it.

I *wanted* Joe. I wanted my own "young man," as Miss Frances would have put it. Not a civilized young man who'd buy me flowers and carry my parasol, but someone that I could sail up and down the Mississippi with. A young man who would get dirty with me and who I could finally come clean to. A voice deep inside of me wouldn't stop saying that Joe was that young man.

Of course, I would be all right without him—I was sure of that. I still had fifty-two dollars and twenty-eight cents, and it might not get us where we wanted to go, but it would get us somewhere. I'd already shown I could take care of my own self, and even take care of somebody else, if I had to. I could handle the future, whatever it brought. But from now on, I knew I'd always feel like something was missing.

I knew I didn't need Joe to be my hero, but I wanted him to be part of my plot.

–A Surprise Visitor–

So there I sat with my head in my hands, shedding tears, just before dawn. I hadn't noticed that my door was half-open, until I saw a hand reach in to open it all the way.

My heart dropped all the way into my shoes, thinking it one of the Uncles, but it bounced right back up again when I saw it was Joe.

Ba-BOOM, Ba-BOOM, Ba-BOOM!

He stood in the doorframe and said to me: "Miss Mary Jane, *you* can't a-bear to see people in trouble, and I can't, either—most always. Tell me about it."

"Oh, dear, dear, to think *we* aren't ever going to see each other anymore!" It just came blurting out of me.

Joe looked confused at that. I went to cover my tracks:

"Candy and Sugar, I meant . . . why, I don't know how I can ever be happy again, knowing . . . that mother and child . . . aren't ever going to see each other again . . ."

He reached out for my hand. "But they *will*—and inside of two weeks—and I *know* it!"

It was such good news, made even better as it came from him. My heart swelled full to pop, and went right on banging. There he was standing before me: the Joe that I wanted so badly. Whatever he told me from here on out would be the truth, I could feel it in my bones.

I threw my arms 'round his neck and asked him to tell it to me again, and again. I couldn't help it. When the truth breaks free, it sounds like music, and right then was starting the loveliest song I'd ever heard.

He blushed, then asked me, "Miss Mary Jane, is there any place out of town a little ways where you could go and stay three or four days?"

"Yes," I told him. I reckon I would have said *Yes* to anything he asked me right then.

"Mr. Lothrop's," I suggested. *Or is it Apthorp?* I thought to myself. "But why?"

"Never mind *why* yet. If I prove how I know that mother and daughter will see each other again inside of two weeks, will you go to Mr. Lothrop's and stay four days?"

Hell no! I'm not leaving your side, I wanted to say. Instead, I agreed:

"Four days! I'll stay a year!"

"All right," he said. "I don't want nothing more out of you than just your word—I druther have it than another man's kiss-the-Bible."

I busted out laughing at that, and didn't stop until my face reddened up, too.

Then he said, "If you don't mind it, I'll shut the door—and bolt it."

Ba-BOOM, Ba-BOOM, Ba-BOOM!

Then he sat down next to me, took a deep breath, and said:

"I got to tell the *truth,* and you want to brace up, Miss Mary, because it's a bad kind, and going to be hard to take, but there ain't no help for it."

And there it is: Truth. *A beautiful word from a beautiful mouth.*

"These uncles of yourn ain't no uncles at all; they're a couple of frauds—regular dead-beats."

Believe me when I say it took all my strength, body and soul, to act surprised by that. He went on: "There, now we're over the worst of it."

Then he opened up like a flower and told me every blame thing about himself. How he was from a town called St. Petersburg, how his pa wasn't at all a *good* man, and how the world had chucked him out on his own a few months ago.

I know where that is and I know all too well what that's like, I wanted to tell him.

He told me how much he loved floating down the Mississippi River. How he wouldn't stand to be civilized, and dreamed of setting out for adventure on the open roads, maybe to the *Territory.*

Me too! Me too! Me too! We were "made for each other," as Miss Frances would have put it.

Then he told me how it ate him up to have to lie to me, and that if he'd learned one thing at all, it was that he didn't want to be a *bad* man like those two Uncles. He told me how he'd fallen in with them against his better judgement, that they weren't Americans, or even Englishmen, and that Uncle Preacher was actually the King of France.

I spit when I heard that.

Then he reddened back up and said, bashful and awkward, how he hadn't liked to see me hugging and kissing on Uncle Preacher when they first showed up.

"That brute!" I burst out, mostly to show him that I hadn't liked it, either. "Come, don't waste a minute—" I jumped up and went for the door. "Not a *second*—we'll have those two tarred and feathered, and flung in the river!" Truth be told, I wanted to save him from those two scoundrels, and I thought that'd be the quickest way.

"Cert'nly," he agreed. "But do you mean *before* you go to Mr. Lothrop's, or—"

Oops. He must have a plan.

"Oh, what am I thinking about?" I sat down again. "Don't mind what I said—you won't, now, will you?" I took the chance to lay my hand on his, and he didn't nearly object. "I was so stirred up—now go on, you tell me what to do, and whatever you say, I'll do it." I was ready to hear his plan, and jump on board with it.

"Well," he said, "I got to travel with them a while longer, whether I want to or not—I druther not tell you why; and if you was to blow on them I'd be all right; but there'd be another person that you don't know about who'd be in big trouble. Well, we got to save him, hain't we? Well, then, we won't blow on them."

So he has a friend, or maybe even a brother, who needs him. Gosh, do I know how that feels.

"Miss Mary Jane, I'll tell you what we'll do, and you won't have to stay at Mr. Lothrop's long. How fur is it?" he asked me.

I didn't know, so I made something up: "A little short of four miles, back here." I pointed in a random direction.

A little white lie barely counts, I told myself.

"Well, that'll answer. Now you go along out there, and lay low till nine tonight, and then get home and put a candle in this window. If I don't turn up, wait till eleven, and *then* if I don't turn up it means I'm gone, and out of the way, and safe. Then you come out and get these beats jailed."

"Good," I said, "I'll do it."

Nine o'clock, I said to myself, *I'll see him at nine o'clock.* That's what I hoped for, anyway.

"And if I don't get away, but get took along with them, you must up and say I told you the whole thing, and you must stand by me all you can."

"Stand by you! Indeed I will. I won't let them touch a hair of your head!"

He took my hand again. "If I get away I sha'n't be here to prove these rapscallions ain't your uncles. If I was here, I could swear they was beats and bummers, but there's others can do that better—people that ain't going to be doubted as quick as I'd be. I'll tell you how to find them. Gimme a pencil and a piece of paper."

I found one and he scribbled.

"There—'Royal Nonesuch, Bricksville.' Put it away, and don't lose it. Send up to Bricksville and say they've got the men that played the Royal Nonesuch, and you'll have that entire town down here before you can hardly wink, Miss Mary. And they'll come a-biling, too."

I nodded, and he went on:

"Just let the auction go right along, and don't worry. Nobody don't have to pay for the things they buy till a whole day after, and the way we've fixed it the sale ain't going to count. Houses and land is just like with property—it warn't no sale, and the mother and daughter will be back before long. Why, your so-called uncles are in the worst kind of a fix, Miss Mary."

I agreed to his plan. "Well, I'll run down to breakfast now, and then I'll start straight for Mr. Lothrop's."

"That ain't the ticket—go before breakfast."

"Why?"

"What did you reckon I wanted you to go at all for, Miss Mary Jane?"

"Well, I never thought—and come to think, I don't know."

"Why, it's because there's no better book than what your face is. A body can read it off like coarse print. Do you reckon you can go and face your uncles, and never . . ."

I busted out laughing again.

"Yes, I'll go before breakfast," I told him after I caught my breath. "But leave my sisters here with them?"

"Yes; never mind about them. They might suspicion something if all of you was to go. I don't want you to see them, nor your sisters, nor nobody in this town; if a neighbor was to ask how is your uncles this morning your face would tell something. No, you go right along, Miss Mary Jane, and I'll tell Miss Susan to give your love to your uncles and say you've went away for a few hours to see a friend, and you'll be back tonight."

"But I won't have my love given to them—"

He agreed, smiling. "There's one more thing—that bag of money."

I shrugged: "Well, they've got that; and it makes me feel pretty silly to think how they got it."

"No, they hain't got it."

What?

"Who's got it?"

"I wish I knowed, but I don't. I had it, because I stole it from them; and I stole it to give to you."

I swooned when he said that. Then he said more.

"I know where I hid it, but I'm afraid it might not be there no more. I'm awful sorry, Miss Mary Jane, I done the best I could."

He did his best, and it didn't turn out like he'd hoped.

"I come nigh getting caught, and I had to shove it into the first place I come to—and it warn't a good place."

I couldn't bear to see him sorry. "Oh, stop blaming yourself—you couldn't help it; it wasn't your fault. Where did you hide it?"

He thought and hesitated. "I'd ruther not tell you, Miss Mary Jane, but I'll write it for you on a piece of paper, and you can read it along the road to Mr. Lothrop's, if you want to. Do you reckon that'll do?"

"Oh, yes." I handed him another piece of paper.

He scribbled something on it, folded it, and handed it over. When he looked at me, I saw that his eyes were watering, and knew that *Goodbye* was coming. Darned if my eyes didn't start to water, too, but not because I felt sad. Out of happiness, really. Because I'd found out the truth about him, and it was nothing but good.

I decided to say *Goodbye* first to spare him the pain. I thought of Margaret, and all she'd taught me, and remembered our parting.

I took Joe's hand and said to him: "*Goodbye.* I'm going to do everything just as you've told me; and if I don't ever see you again, I won't ever forget you and I'll think of you a many and a many a time, and . . . I'll pray for you, too!"

"I'll pray for you." It's what you grapple for when you need something beyond Goodbye.

And then he was gone.

I waited a good ten minutes, then shoved my bundle back under the bed, and stuffed the two folded papers into my pocket.

I was ready to run.

I ran down the stairs, out the door, and all the way to the gate, just as fast as my legs would carry me. I ran to find the girls and tell them everything.

–The River Calls–

"Joe told me the truth about everything! He's an honest—and *good*—young man, after all . . . ," I blurted out to Susan and Joanna, as soon as I got to them.

They were almost as happy about it as I was. Joanna told me how hard it had been to be the foe with him because she could tell that underneath he was good to the bone. Susan said she never thought he was anything *but* good because, after all, most people are. Cherry wagged his tail like he wasn't surprised, either.

I opened the papers Joe had written on and read them out to the girls. His spelling made me pretty sure he'd never spent much time in a schoolhouse. But there's a different kind of smart outside of the schoolhouse type, the kind you need when two impostor Uncles show up and try to take everything you have.

The first paper said only:

Royul Nunsuch, Bricksvil.

I explained to the girls: "That's the place where the Uncles were before they came here. Joe said they've been cheating folks all the way down the river and that if we send word to Bricksville, the whole town will come down boiling mad.

"Put that paper in your pocket for now," I told Joanna. "Hang on to it, and use it later if you have to."

I unfolded the second paper. It said:

I put it intha coffan.

"In the *coffin*?" Susan's eyes went wide. "Exactly what did he put in the coffin?"

"Peter Wilks's bag of gold with the full six thousand dollars in it!" I answered.

Joanna considered: "That was pretty smart, actually . . . most folks aren't about to go rummaging around a dead body, looking for something."

"Don't you see? Joe never meant to steal anything from us, and he wasn't about to let anybody else do it, either," I said, wearing the biggest smile I'd ever had.

I read the rest of the note privately to myself, as it had a part that I didn't want to share:

I was ther behind the door when you was setting up in vigal. You was a-crying an I was mighty sorree for you, Miss Mary Jane.

So, Joe was the ghost that I didn't believe in! I thought to myself.

"What's the rest of his plan, Mary Jane? Did he tell you?" Joanna broke me out of my thoughts.

"He told me some of it, but not all of it . . . but we trust him now, so we'll take the chance and do as he said—agreed?" They both nodded *Yes.*

"Good. He told me to go and stay away until about nine . . . then come back and put a candle in my window. I told him I'd go visit the Apthorps for the day, then come home and do it . . . or it might have been the *Lothrops* . . . I get them confused."

"You could be visiting Hannah. She's a Lothrop and about our age," suggested Joanna.

"No, that's the Apthorps," Susan put in. "I think, anyway."

"Well, I'm visiting one of them, if anybody asks. Now, you two go back to the house and act like you don't know any of what I just told you. And keep an eye on the Uncles, but don't get too close . . . keep Cherry with you."

"And you'll be back later . . . but where are you *really* going, Mary Jane?" Susan wanted to know.

"Hmm . . . I've got a mind to spend the day watching the river go by . . ." I said it on a whim, but it came out sounding sensible. When Joe was telling me about how he loved the Mississippi, I couldn't help but think of all the ways I love it, too. Maybe talking about what you love naturally makes you want to be by its side.

"Then *you* take Cherry with you, Mary Jane. He loves to swim more than anything, and that way, you won't be alone," said Joanna.

I looked to Susan, who nodded and said, "You take him, Mary Jane. I'm feeling fine and strong these days."

Joanna looped her arm through her sister's and gave it a

squeeze, and I was so proud of both of them I thought I would bust.

I whistled for Cherry and pointed him towards the river. "Go on, girls, back to the house before anyone misses you . . . and Joanna! Don't be too nice to Joe—remember, to him you're still the foe."

"I'll do it, but it won't be easy now that I know he is a good egg after all . . . ," Joanna answered, and Susan smiled.

Me and Cherry went down to the riverbank and I threw sticks for him, until I was tired of standing. Then I sat and watched the dragonflies dart and the waterbugs skate and the frogs hop from lily to lily, and he laid beside me. A pile of old broken boards and a length of rotten rope gave me the idea to build a raft, so I went ahead and spent most of the afternoon doing that. I'd never sailed on a raft before, but Joe had said floating down the river on a raft was the best way to feel free and easy and comfortable, and I wanted to see if he was right.

After I got my raft up and floating, I laid myself down on it and let the river take me however it wanted. The Mississippi was moving slow and so did we, with Cherry jumping off now and then to swim a few circles and cool off. Joe was dead right about how it is being on a raft, and I thought about how I'd tell him that, when I saw him again.

As the sun was setting, I shoved ashore and we started walking up-river, back to where we'd come from. The current had been slow-to-stopped all day, so it didn't take us too long to get there.

Just as we walked under the sign of *La Douce Tannerie d'Wilks*, it started in raining cats and dogs. Before we could get onto the porch a bolt of lightning went *Crack!* and split the whole sky in half. Cherry barked wildly, trying to figure out who'd done it and how to get at them. Me, on the other hand, all I could think about was getting my hands on a candle.

I did, then sat at my window and burned candle after candle, one after the other. Nine o'clock went by, then ten, then eleven, but I kept my post. I sat through the night, feeding a tiny flame with a gigantic hope, and sending a clear signal out to my beloved.

It didn't work, though. The sun came up at six, but Joe never came at all.

CHAPTER XXX

–Moving Fast–

I can't tell you every last detail of what happened next, not because I don't want to, but because I am a little fuzzy on it myself. I was distracted by my daydreams of a certain young man.

My heart still beat like crazy whenever I thought of Joe, and it wouldn't let me focus on much of anything else. I guess my memory of him was still so fresh, I could bring him near just by my thoughts. I don't know if that makes any sense to you, but it does to me.

In a nutshell, the whole world blew up and then came back together while I was on that raft floating down the Mississippi River. First, two fresh uncles showed up at *La Douce Tannerie d'Wilks* with the whole town on their heels. Then the whole crowd, plus all four uncles, barreled down to the graveyard and dug up Peter Wilks's body. They checked him all over for a tattoo that would tell the real uncles from the fakes. Of course, when they opened the coffin they discovered the bag of six thousand dollars in gold. Right then, a lightning storm hit, and our two fakes slipped away during the confusion, leaving the gold behind them.

It was a lot to take in, more so because all I cared about was *What happened to Joe?* The girls didn't know, though Susan said she thought she saw him slip off in the opposite direction, and Joanna said she hoped and prayed it meant he'd finally gotten away from those scoundrels once and for all. As for me, I wanted to cry when I heard Joe was well and truly gone, but I had to chin up and think of us and what we'd do next. Like I said, I found that daydreaming about him helped.

What else? The auction fell through, just like Joe said it would, but Lawyer Bell told us it could take as much as six months to clear everything up and return what-all was bought, and I naturally wondered if that included Sugar and Candy. When I asked him more about it, he told me there wasn't anything more to know.

-Two Good Men-

"I'm satisfied," said Lawyer Bell, handing back a set of papers. "These two men are your *bona-fide* uncles, girls, just as they've claimed."

"I could have told him that," Joanna whispered to me. "Uncle Reverend Harvey sounds just like Pa when he talks."

"And Uncle William's signs make *sense*," added Susan. It was her who'd picked up his language, flowing her hands slow and

tapping them sharp just like he did. I shook my head to think I'd been so taken with the sweet in Susan that I hadn't noticed her smart, like how when the moon is shining you can't properly appreciate the stars around it.

"And *my goodness* aren't they young?" I said to the girls. "I'd put Uncle Reverend Harvey at about thirty and Uncle William can't be older than seventeen!"

They were a fine-looking pair and fine-acting, too: level-headed, with respectful manners from the start. Me and the girls gave them our kindness, but we made them earn our trust. And they were kind to us—they even bought Cherry a big old knuckle bone. He obliged them and chewed it for a bit, then pushed the screen door open and went out adventuring, like he does every night. He never fails to be back by morning, though, when we find him dozing on the front steps.

Bit by bit, we opened up to Uncle Reverend Harvey and Uncle William and told them what-all we'd been through. I still let them think that Susan and Joanna are my sisters, though, and that I'm the oldest of us by a good long bit. Even if they don't believe it, I think they know it makes sense. Some lies are truer than the truth.

–Taking Our Leave–

"He's asking us where *we* want to go, now that Peter Wilks is dead," Susan translated what Uncle William had said with his hands.

"Tell him, we'll need to talk about it," I answered, and she did.

Our uncles needed to get back to England, as Uncle Reverend Harvey had a congregation to take care of. He was worried about the little baby who didn't thrive, and the old lady who might die without hearing her favorite Psalm.

I took the girls to the side, and told them, "I can't see myself back at Fort Snelling."

"We can't, either," said Joanna.

"She means . . . Mary Jane, we don't know our *morfar* or your ma but from their letters," said Susan, and I remembered when I'd said the same thing about Aunt Evelyn. "And our uncles say they're happy to have us live with them in Sheffield."

"I want to go to England!" said Joanna. "Uncle Reverend Harvey says there's an outdoors park in London where you can see a real live hippopotamus, and you can go to lectures where explorers tell all about the birds and turtles they found in South America."

"That does sound wonderful," I told her. "It's settled then." I put my arms around them. "We're off to the land of kings and queens!" It wasn't the Territory, but it'd still be quite the adventure, and I was mostly satisfied.

We all went up to the General Store, to see about five places on a steamboat to Dubuque, and another half-place for Cherry. From there we'd go by coach to Chicago, Uncle Reverend Harvey said, and from there on to Boston, where we'd set sail to Liverpool.

The Widow Bartley checked the schedule for us, and when we saw that the *Galenian* was due to stop in Greenville about three days hence, we were more than happy to wait. After I told our uncles about Mrs. Captain who had been so good to us, they said they wanted to meet her and thank her for themselves.

Uncle Reverend Harvey sent a telegram up to Fort Edwards, thinking it would do us all some good to stop for a week and see how Uncle George and Aunt Evelyn's graves had turned out. After she was done sending the message, I took Widow Bartley to the side and asked if Sugar and Candy had ever found each other or got freed or anything good came of it. I'd been asking her regularly, but she never had any news to share.

On that day, though, she looked at me hard. "Mary Jane, stop it. Honestly, the best thing you can do for them now is to forget that you ever knew them."

"But I *need* to know, Widow Bartley!"

"No, you *want* to know, and I'm telling you that their future is a far sight more important than your curiosity," she told me, and I dropped the subject.

I do still think on them now and then, and keep on hoping for the best. I can't help it.

-Laid to Rest-

On the morning we left, I split off early, promising the girls I'd be at the dock in good time to meet the boat. I wanted to visit Peter Wilks's grave before I left. I hadn't been to it yet, and it felt like the last door I should close on my way out of *La Douce Tannerie d'Wilks,* for my own sake, at least.

His tombstone was easy to find, as the dirt next to it was still loose and fresh. He'd been dug up once and buried twice since he died, and you won't find me surprised if somebody was to come and shovel him up all over again. No, Peter Wilks can't seem to rest easy in his grave, and maybe he shouldn't, given what-all he did when he was alive.

I, myself, haven't forgiven Peter Wilks, but I can say that I don't hate him anymore. He must have had it hard, having to leave home and start over in a new country from so young. Maybe when he was a boy, somewhere along the way, someone touched *him* in an awful, wrong manner and he hadn't had anyone to pull him away and keep him safe. It wouldn't excuse what he did, but it would explain it some.

Maybe that's just me taking the lazy way out, I don't know. I do know that it is easier to feel for the boy Peter Wilks was, than for the man I knew. And in the end, I think that amounts to something.

CHAPTER XXXI

-Smooth Sailing-

It wasn't Mrs. Captain standing next to the Rooster when he took our tickets, that much I knew. The face was familiar and unfamiliar all at the same time. I must have puzzled for five whole minutes before I recognized . . . it was the Racoon Man! Without his soot-black mask, he made a fine-looking normal-faced man that I couldn't pick out from any other.

He gave me the biggest smile I'd ever seen, then yelled out, "Come look who's here, my sweet!"

Of course he meant Mrs. Captain. When she came close enough to see it was me, she said, "Chickie! My dear, dear Chickie!—and Susan and Joanna! Our three good, smart, strong, capable girls!" There was a great deal of hugging all around, we were all so happy to be reunited.

"You've got a dog? You lucky!" The Rooster was playing

tug-of-war with Cherry, who loved him right away, enough, even, to let him win.

"Why, Rooster, look how you've grown!" said Susan, and he smiled in a way that made us all smile.

"I can tell you've been drinking your milk—good for you," added Joanna.

"Do you want me to show you what-all I engineered on Robert Fulton?" the Rooster asked, and the girls skipped off to the boiler room to ooh and ahh over whatever it might be.

Mrs. Captain stepped up to our uncles. "And who are these two fellows who brought you to me?" she was asking me, but looking at them.

"These are our uncles, Mrs. Captain," I said. "They've proved to be *good* men, and the girls love them very well." I said that part out of one side of my mouth, and not overly loud.

"Well, then I welcome you, all five, aboard the *Galenian*, and you should consider yourselves under the captain's special protection while you're on your way to . . . now, where in the world are you bound this time?"

"All the way up to Dubuque!" the Rooster chimed in, having taken our tickets. "That's clear as far north as she goes, Mr. Uncles. Won't we have a good time here on the *Galenian*, all together?"

"Oh, yes, we will!" Mrs. Captain answered for us. "Especially with my all-around-wonderful Rooster running her like the excellent boatman he's come to be! Why, there's none better on the river, I know it for a fact!"

The Rooster didn't puff up at the praise, but he smiled at her in a way that showed he'd gotten used to being appreciated, and couldn't love his mother hen back any more than he already did.

Our uncles looked up and down the decks and said what a fine boat we were on, and how they'd enjoy themselves watching the river for a bit. I think they wanted to give us some time alone with our friends, and I appreciated it.

Racoon Man showed our uncles to the place on the deck from where they could best enjoy the sights going by, and be up-wind from the pig-sty, to boot. After he came back, Mrs. Captain said, "Come then, Chickie, and let's the three of us catch up!"

"I reckon we've got plenty to tell, all around, and happy news, too," added the Racoon Man.

We climbed up to the top deck, and sat down together. Racoon Man told me how his lemonade invitation to Mrs. Captain was finally accepted, and turned into another invitation, and another, until they moved from outside the church to inside it, where they were married by a traveling minister who was happy to do it.

"And here I am, and I can hardly believe it!" The Racoon Man put his arm around Mrs. Captain. "Married to my own sweetie, outright *married*! Pretty good for a spuds-'n'-gravy man, don't you think?"

"I can't imagine anything better," I told them.

"And we're in the best shape ever. Between my Thomas's coal-connections and the Rooster's ticket-taking talents, the *Galenian* is making more-than-decent money, I don't mind saying," Mrs. Captain added to the conversation.

"And I must say, the Rooster looks happy and healthy as any kid anywhere who'd gotten a *good* start," I had to put in.

At that, I thought I saw the Racoon Man's eyes go a little watery. "We wouldn't trade him for anything in the world, would we, my sweet?" he asked Mrs. Captain, and you can probably imagine how she answered him.

Just then, the Rooster climbed up the ladder to us, with the girls following.

"There he is!" said Mrs. Captain. "Girls, I've got about five more years in me as a steamboat captain, and then I'll turn the *Galenian* over to my dear Rooster, and be proud to bursting to see what he does with it."

"Oh, you'll *see*," said the Rooster. "You'll see from right here on this deck because I am going to build you the nicest pilot-house that ever was! And every time we stop in Memphis you'll have a new map to study, and every time we put into New Orleans I'll come back with a crate of Florida lemons for my Racoon Man!"

He was dead serious, we could tell, but we all laughed anyway, just for the sheer delight of being together. Then the Rooster asked us if we wanted to hear him sing a tune, and we all said *Yes* right away. He stood himself up in front, cleared his throat, and sang out loud and proud while Racoon Man stomped to keep time:

Sing for my mammy, dance with my daddy,
Wait with my fam'ly for the boat to come in.
I shall have a fishy, on a little dishy,
We shall all have supper when the boat comes in!

We clapped and cheered and felt ourselves lucky to be in the company of such a smart, strong, capable boy.

-Just Rewards-

Didn't we have an overall good time while we were on the *Galenian*? Joanna spent her days on the lower deck mucking around with the horses and goats and chickens and what-have-you, with Cherry at her side.

Susan and I kept her company until we couldn't stand the smell anymore, then went to gaze at the riverbank for a while, or take instructions from the Rooster. After supper, you could always find Susan and Uncle William together, relaxing against two hay bales and chatting away with their hands.

When we docked in Memphis, Uncle Reverend Harvey sent us off to window-shop with Uncle William. We found out later that he'd gone to the jailhouse to sit and pray with whoever was wretched enough to have asked for it. When I asked him why he hadn't told us he was going to, he said that if you're truly given to good works, you spend your time doing them and not talking about them.

My thoughts were never far from Joe, but I wasn't pining or lovelorn or anything like that. Part of me still dreamed of us being together, I admit, but I decided I'd settle for knowing he's safe and whole and alive somewhere, after I heard about the tar and feathers.

One day, I struck a conversation up with a ma and pa that

were traveling up-river, just like us. The ma said they'd hurried down-river after they got word that the Nonesuch thieves had turned up at a farm near the Louisiana border. It was there they joined into the mob and got revenge for the five dollars they'd been cheated out of. I asked if there'd been a blue-eyes-pony-tail boy traveling with the two scoundrels, and was mighty relieved when they said *No*.

The whole family was still beaming over their trip to Pikesville, and told us how they'd rushed at the two criminals with torches, whooping and yelling, banging tin pans and blowing horns, like it was New Year's Day. The mother told how she, herself, had poured hot tar on their heads and how the blood ran when they ripped it off later. At this, the father gave a belly-laugh and slapped his thigh, while his children danced around him, excited for the day when they'd be grown up enough to do it, too.

They went on about how they'd rode them on a rail, then drug them to the gallows, and . . . I walked away before I could hear the end. Human beings *can* be awful cruel to one another. It was a dreadful thing just to hear about. I admit that I was sorry for those two poor pitiful rascals, like I couldn't ever feel any hardness against them any more in the world.

Maybe everyone deserves a little forgiveness for the bad things they've done. All I know is that on that day, the two Uncles got some from me.

-Better-Laid Plans-

One day while we were leaning over the rail counting lily pads, Susan said to me, "Mary Jane, I'm going to ask our uncles if we can't visit Nauvoo while we're at Fort Edwards. I know the Schmidts aren't likely to have stayed on, but . . ."

"You want to find the Schmidt Boy?" I asked her when she paused.

"You mean *Adolphus*, yes." She was all blushed up, but her eyes were shining. "There's something in my heart that won't let go of him . . ."

Joanna came and interrupted us:

"Is she asking about Nauvoo, Mary Jane? Because I want to go and say *Hello* to Margaret . . . and Cherry says he wants to meet Samson and Delilah—don't you, boy?" Of course, Cherry was wagging, *Yes, Yes, Yes!*

"I think that's a wonderful idea," I told them. "And I'm sure our uncles will oblige."

We all went back to what we were doing, pleased at the idea of getting to see our old friends again.

I knew the *Galenian* wouldn't stop at St. Petersburg on that run, but I still leaned over the rails as we passed by, wanting to get a good look at the place where Joe was from. The sun was just going down, and that last light of the day made the pretty little town look even prettier—with its flower gardens and new-painted fences.

It didn't look like somewhere Joe would want to stay for long, but I couldn't help but wonder if he was in there somewhere.

Then I couldn't help but think it was *now or never*, if I wanted to find out.

I pulled the girls aside, took a big breath, and told them, "Susan and Joanna . . . I have to go . . . to look for . . ." I tried to explain. "I know that he's not likely to be in St. Petersburg, but . . ."

"You want to find Joe?" Susan asked with a smile.

"We could always tell, Mary Jane," Joanna added.

"Yes, girls, there's something in my heart that won't let go of him," I said.

"Then you must go to him, and find out what that something is," Susan said, strong and clear.

I do love those two girls.

"I *will* go. I'll get off this boat and back down to St. Petersburg, one way or another."

"But what should we say when our uncles ask where you are?" Joanna wanted to know.

"Tell them that I'm grateful for all they've done for us, but that I've struck out on my own. Remind them that I'm nineteen years old—which they still believe is true—which would mean they can't legally *make* me go anywhere that I don't want to."

"I'm sure he'll be there, Mary Jane . . . but what if he's not?" Susan asked me as gently as she could.

"Wait out that week in Fort Edwards, and if I don't come back, promise me you'll go on without me. Get going where you want to go, and get doing what you want to do. We've learned it the hard way, girls: we have to reach out and grab the future we want, before the world pushes a different one onto us."

We hugged, all four of us, for a good long time. I can't deny that I shed a few tears to think of us leaving each other, but they came from the sweet kind of sad, mixed with happy.

I flew up the ladder, two rungs at a time. I was in a big hurry, for every minute that went by was sailing me further away from St. Petersburg. I found Mrs. Captain in the pilothouse cozy with a map, and the Racoon Man sat on the floor near her, with the Rooster teaching him knots.

"Mrs. Captain, I know this sounds crazy, but I need to get off the boat! . . . I've got a friend in St. Petersburg . . . maybe, that is . . . well, more than a friend—I *hope,* at least, but I don't . . ."

Before I could stutter any further, the Racoon Man burst out: "I say! It's the best thing in the world to have a special friend you can share a glass of lemonade with." He put his arm around Mrs. Captain. "Now, tell us *all about* this person, we want to know . . ."

Mrs. Captain sailed in to rescue me. "Why, there's no time for that, Thomas! I can see from her face that our Chickie's in love, and that's good enough for me."

The Rooster jumped to his feet: "Mary Jane, there's a place about three miles above where the shoal opens up; I'll be glad to row you to shore when we get there."

I tell you my eyes got a little wet at that. My heart had told me to go, my sisters were happy to let me, and my friends would see me on my way.

-A Parting of Ways-

I went to our place on the deck and dug out my bundle, which by now was only a copy of *A Child's History of England* and some odds and ends: a length of string, some tansey-flower tea, and a handful of walnuts. I left the string and medicine and nuts behind for the girls, stuffed into their bundles. They'd know how to make use of them, if it came to that.

Holding everything together was my green silk dress, the one I had started years ago at Fort Snelling. I untied it and shook it out; the mossy-green color was even finer than I remembered. Some dresses are a lot prettier in your mind than they end up in-person, but from the buttons on the collar to the embroidery on the hem, this one had turned out just how it was supposed to.

I knew I couldn't wear it to tramp along the river—we were more than four miles above St. Petersburg by then. Silk is delicate, and will tear if you pull it too often in the wrong way. My green dress was made to be a girl's thing, to do girl-things in.

Then again, I thought to myself, *silk is light and lively; it moves as you move, and falls close to your side. Every stitch on it was made with good, strong thread, and the oyster-shell buttons survived a whole ocean of battering waves. Maybe my dress is stronger than it looks.*

And anyway, I'm a girl—doesn't that make everything I do a girl-thing? Including tramping four miles south beside the Mississippi River.

I unbuttoned my old calico and let it fall to the floor. I saw it laying there and I didn't hate it. Ma had sewn it to be strong above all else, and over a few short months I had nursed, gardened, and honeyed in it, slept in it, ran in it, and not one hem of it had frayed. Sure, it was as gray as a dishrag and stiff as a fisherman's raincoat, but it had survived, and that's what mattered.

I moved the fifty-two dollars and twenty-eight cents, and the blue glass vial, out of the pocket of the calico and into the pocket of the silk. Then I slipped my green dress over my head and saw that what was once too big, now fit me perfectly.

I picked up my *A Child's History of England* and ran my finger up and down the spine. I thought of the many and a many queens in it, and how they'd also set out for destiny, mostly wearing silk. And what did they take with them when they went? I think it was a courageous heart, beating strong and hopeful for the future. I don't think it was a heavy book full of the past.

Folded into the pages was the note written to me by Joe. I pulled it out and buttoned it into my bodice, against my heart. I was ready to run, but it was different this time. For the first time in my life, I'd be running towards something, not away from it.

Then it was time for *Goodbye.* We gathered on the starboard-side, Mrs. Captain, the Rooster and the Racoon Man, Susan and Joanna—and Cherry, of course.

"*Fare-thee-well,* Mrs. Captain, you will always be my mother hen, and I love you," I told her, while the Rooster was untying the dinghy.

"Oh, my dear Chickie," she said, hugging me tight. "Your mother hen loves you right back, more than she can say . . ."

"Will you do me one last favor, then?"

"Why, anything for you girls!"

"Take this bundle." I handed her my favorite book, wrapped in sturdy calico. "Give it to the next girl you find all alone out here in this whole weary world. Tell her to use it however she wants, and to let go of it when she's ready."

"Oh, I will, I promise you, sure as anything. But I must say there'll never be another girl like you . . ."

"Yes, there will, Mrs. Captain. The world is full of girls like me. They may not know it, but I do. Tell them it's from *Mary Jane*, who wishes them all the luck they can carry."

I turned to Susan and Joanna. "Girls, you both have so much to look forward to . . . and you too, Cherry! Getting to go on a boat and sail across the ocean . . ." I bent down and he kissed me in that dog-way of his.

Susan took my hands in hers, then took Joanna's hand in her other hand, and said to us:

"Such is our parting, the three of us, who have come so far together."

I reached for Joanna as she reached for me.

"I do believe we'll be together again someday," said Joanna.

"Absolutely," I told them. "My heart won't let me believe anything else."

We kissed and hugged and said *I love you* to each other, just the way three sisters should, and I took my leave.

The last light of day was fading as the Rooster rowed me to shore.

"It will be full darkness by the time you get back to the *Galenian*," I told him. "I don't know how to thank you for being so brave."

"Oh, now, you don't owe me anything—I'm not afraid. I'm night watchman now, too, so it's no more than my job."

"Well, thank you anyway."

"You're more than welcome. Can I tell you a secret, Mary Jane?"

"Of course, dear Rooster."

"One of these times when we stop in Memphis, we're going to visit the courthouse, and Mrs. Captain and Racoon Man are going to *adopt* me, on paper and official. They say they want to be the ma and pa I should have had from the start. We just have to save up the money to pay the lawyers to arrange it, and we put a little aside each time I take the tickets, specially for that very thing."

"Why, that's wonderful!"

"Isn't it, though? We're going to be a real *family!*"

I had an idea, and a good one. "Rooster, you take this fifty-two dollars and twenty-eight cents I've been carrying around, not knowing what it's for. Please do have it. It's my chance for me to be part of how you three come together, and I want to take it."

"I'd like to, Chickie . . ."

"Then do!"

"I will, and I thank you for it—*we* thank you for it."

After we got to shore, I handed him everything that was left of all the money I'd ever had, and gladly, too.

He told me, "You know that if you ever need us, you can find us on the Mississippi River . . ."

"Somewhere in the thousand-mile stretch between Dubuque and New Orleans, to be precise!" I finished his sentence for him.

He pushed the dinghy back into the water, and made for the *Galenian*. Before he drifted too far down-stream I yelled out into the night:

"Thank you, Robert Fulton!"

"No, thank *you*, Robert Fulton!" the Rooster yelled back, knowing exactly what I meant.

CHAPTER XXXII

—A Tolerable Poor Boy—

I walked south along the river—could have been a mile, could have been two—until I was startled by a shout:

"Ho! Who's there?" It was a woman's voice. I spotted the glow of a lantern and saw the shadow of a house up ahead.

"Hullo! Hullo?" the voice repeated. "Come out and let me get a look at you, whoever you are."

She turned up the lantern, and from my hiding place in the woods, I got a look at her. She was awfully old—I'd say no less than thirty. She had a face like a turnip, and a body like a bigger turnip.

I knew I'd have to go make friends or she'd send somebody out to search with a gun. *But why would a girl be out by herself, this time of night?* is what I'd have to explain. Anybody would make a lone, lost girl stay put until morning; they'd think anything less a crime.

For the purpose at hand, I decided, *I won't be a girl at all.*

I pulled down my hair and stuffed it into a pony-tail. I yanked my skirt through to the back, then knotted it at my waist and *bam!* I had trousers. I walked a bit to try them out—it was a good job, I thought. Nobody would know me, even in the day-time, hardly.

I stepped into the clearing, walked up to her, and shook her hand.

"Come in," she said, holding her door open, and when I did, she looked me all over with her little turnip eyes, and asked: "What might your name be?"

"Silas Williams."

"Where 'bouts do you live? In this neighborhood?"

"No'm. In St. Petersburg. I've walked all the way here from Rock Island and I'm all tired out."

"Hungry, too, I reckon. I'll find you something."

"No'm, I ain't hungry. I was so hungry I had to stop two miles above here, it's what makes me out so late."

"It's still a ways to St. Petersburg. You better stay here to-night."

"No," I said, "I'll rest a while, I reckon, and go on. I ain't afeared of the dark."

"Nonsense. I won't let you go by yourself. My husband will be in by-and-by—maybe in an hour and a half—then I'll send him along with you."

Now I'm in a fix, I thought to myself. I settled down into a chair. She went to jabbering about her relations up-river—the kind of rot you care about when you're ancient as thirty years old, I guess. I folded my hands politely and leaned forwards. I saw a spool of thread and a needle beside me, and I picked it up and began to fidget.

She got herself so riled up about her brother-in-law and his miscreant ways that I figured she'd forgot all about her husband and his gun. I took my chance and shifted around, getting ready to leave.

"I do thank you for your hospitality, Ma'am. I ain't supposing you get many visitors out this way . . ."

"Hmm . . . you know there was a blue-eyes-pony-tail boy, about your height, that came through not too long ago. Say . . . you're not his brother, are you?"

Ba-BOOM, Ba-BOOM, Ba-BOOM!

Joe! Joe was here! I wanted to jump with joy, and my face probably showed it.

"And what did you say your name was, young man?"

"Joe! . . . no, I mean . . . Silas! . . . Silas Williams."

Oops! I got so uneasy I couldn't stand it. I went to threading the needle I was holding using only my left hand—like I said, it's a nervous habit. When I caught myself, I put it down, hoping she hadn't noticed. I think she did, because she took on a mean tone and said real sharp:

"You do a *boy* tolerable poor, you know. You might've fooled some up North, but you can't fool me."

"Umm . . . but I *ain't* a-fooling!"

"Come now, no boy could do that trick to thread a needle . . ."

"I *swear* I ain't, Ma'am . . ."

"Then prove it."

And that's when things got strange. She wanted me to do some tests, like catch a lump of lead and show her how I'd kill a rat.

I wouldn't, I wanted to say, *I've got a dog for that.*

Then she tricked me with the name-thing again . . . *Silas, Siberius, whatever . . .* trying to back me into a corner.

It was no use. I stood up and told her:

"You know what? You're right, Ma'am. I *am* a girl." I un-knotted my skirts and shook down my hair. "And I've still got some distance ahead of me. So thank you for the conversation and I'll say *Good night.*"

"Ha! I knew as much! What are you doing, all by yourself? Probably chasing after some boy." She shook her head like that was the worst thing in the world a girl could do.

"With all due respect, Ma'am, you wouldn't understand even if I told you. So kindly point me towards St. Petersburg, and I'll take my leave and not bother you any longer."

"It's that way." She pointed, but not very kindly. "Be off and good riddance to you. Girls who chase boys come to a bad end and everyone knows it. But I expect you haven't seen much of the world, and will just have to learn the hard way . . ."

She might have said more, but I didn't hear her. I was too busy walking away.

–Into the Fog–

What I walked into was solid white and still.

A fog had come up, thick as pea soup. You see that some-times at the end of a long hot day, after the cool night air settles in. I walked on, knowing I'd get to the river sooner or later, for where else could that wet air be coming from?

I couldn't see my own hand in front of my face, and I know because I tried. My eyes weren't good for much, so I perked up my ears. There was sound all around me, strange and unfamiliar, but not anything I could make out as rushing water. Not a thing looks nor sounds natural in a fog.

When I did find the Mississippi, it wasn't with my eyes *or* ears—it was with my feet—namely, when they both got wet. I stumbled in deep, too—I could feel the water around my knees, but warmed from the day's sun and so pleasant.

I sat down on the riverbank and took off my shoes. I thought I'd let them dry a little and wait for the sun to peek back up. I was good and tired, having been up all night being interrogated by a turnip. *I'll just take a little cat-nap,* I said to myself.

When I woke up the fog was gone, the sky was blue, and the birds were singing. I squinted up at the sun until it was blocked out altogether by two huge brown eyes. They stared down at me, blinking and wondering who I was.

Stood over me was a horse that I'd never seen before, carrying a man that I *had* seen before, but not lately.

-Two Travelers-

"Peter Pond?"

I couldn't believe it, but I couldn't *not* believe it, either. We never did know what he did in the summer, or where-all he got to while doing it.

"And . . . and who's this you're riding?" I asked him. "Why, isn't he a . . . good . . . strong one!" I said it to be hopeful, though Peter Pond's new horse was far from hearty.

"*Le recontrer . . .* I got him for a song, practically stole him . . . but I was in ze bad spot—mid-nowhere, foot-sore, without a horse . . ."

I looked the animal up and down, from his sway-back to his broken horseshoes. He was in for a hard winter, a warm-blood like that, trekking through the frozen boundary waters.

I didn't ask Peter Pond what had happened to Gusty, and he didn't ask me where I'd been, or where I was going. Maybe neither of us wanted to know the answers.

"Awww, *Marie Jeanne,* you've grown up." He said it as if it was something to be sad about.

I tried to cheer him up by answering: "No, I'm not! I'm no taller than when you saw me last."

"*Non, non*—not in size—in spirit. You have grown . . . *older* somehow."

Five years in five months, I wanted to say, but I could see from his eyes that my last joke hadn't taken. So I told him the truth instead:

"*Oui,* Peter Pond, I believe I am older somehow. The world does that to you."

He patted his new horse on the flank. "*Je sais, Marie Jeanne.* Don't I know it . . ." We stood for a moment without talking.

There in the quiet, and for the first time ever, I wondered what Peter Pond's story was. The story of his life, that is: growing up, growing big, and getting old. It came to me then that all the people I'd met since leaving home—even the ones that came into my life for only a day or two—every one of them had their own story. A story that I couldn't tell you, even if I tried. A story big enough to fill a book.

Knowing that has stuck with me. My life has been different since I figured it out.

We didn't tell our stories to each other, Peter Pond and me. In fact, we didn't say another word. We walked together a little ways, then tipped our hats and parted. We did what two travelers do, when they share the same road, but not the destination.

CHAPTER XXXIII

-Evangeline-

When I walked into St. Petersburg, it was silent and empty as a tomb. I followed Main Street to what seemed like downtown, then stopped and looked around.

"Are you the new girl?" came a voice from behind me.

I guessed that I fit the bill. "I am," I hollered back.

"Come on over and we'll make friends!" She motioned me towards her.

This is good luck, I thought to myself. If anybody could help me find Joe, it'd be a girl my age.

When I got closer, she smiled and even did a curtsey. Darned if she didn't look like a character from a story-book, in her white ruffled dress with blue flowers all around.

"I am pleased to meet you. My name is Evangeline." She opened the front gate, then closed it with me inside and shook my hand in a friendly way.

"Hmm . . . Evangeline . . ." I searched my memory.

"Yes, *E-van-ge-line*," she said, and opened a pretty little book with the word *Longfellow* stamped down the spine. "Listen to this—" She began to read aloud:

> "*. . . and Evangeline, kneeling beside him,*
> *Kissed his dying lips, and laid his head on her bosom.*' "

"Isn't that just the most romantic thing you've ever heard?"

"Oh, yes." I wanted to be agreeable. "It's just that . . . well, I can't ever recall hearing of any Queen Evangeline."

"Is that *bad*?" Evangeline asked me. She seemed to be reconsidering her opinion of her own name.

"Oh, no," I said, "it's just that every girl I ever knew had a queen's name. One year at school we had two Marys and two Catherines at the same time. Even Ma, who is Ida, was named after an ancient queen of the *hjemmeland*, says Morfar. I've had this idea that every girl goes back to some queen or other . . . *Evangeline*, though . . . it's odd . . ."

"Well . . . ," she blurted out, "what about Rebecca? Because that's my middle name."

"Oh, *Rebecca*, now, that's really something! Yes, Rebecca is a very fine name to have, as she was wife to Isaac and mother to Jacob who was the father of Israel."

Evangeline put her arm through mine, and seemed happy again. "And what should I call *you*, my dear?"

"Me? I'm *Mary Jane*, and I'm named after two queens . . .

Say, where is everybody? This is a good-sized town for nobody in it."

"They're all at church, of course, it's Sunday! There's a Social on today, but I woke up with a headache and begged off. Now tell me all about you, Miss Mary Jane—you said you had a ma and a *mor-father* or something like that? Did you move here with them?"

"Yes . . ."

"Which is to be your house, then? I do hope it will be *in town*," she asked me.

". . . It will be *real* close to here. Probably right around the corner, on Main Street."

"Oh, isn't that fine?" Evangeline jumped up and down, clapping her hands. "We can walk to school together! But listen, a girl named Amy Lawrence will want to be friends with you, but you must *promise* that I will always be your first-best friend and she can only be your second."

She made a fist, stuck out her pinky-finger, and waited for mine. I felt sick inside, having already told lies to a girl who'd been nothing but kind to me from the first minute I knew her.

"What's wrong?" Evangeline looked at my sad face. "Won't you promise?"

I hung my head. "I would, Evangeline, but . . ."

"But what? You don't *want* to?"

"I do, but—it's just not *honest,* and I can't pretend it is," I said miserably.

Evangeline burst into tears. "Oh, you can tell! Of course you can—a true heart can always tell. I'm sorry I lied to you, Mary Jane. I don't know why I did."

I stepped forwards and put my arms around her, she looked so unhappy.

"E-ee-e-vann-geh-line," she hiccupped, "is not my name! I'm only *Becky*."

"Now, now . . . *Becky* is a fine name, remember Queen Rebecca? You know, I like Becky *much* better than Evangeline, when I compare."

"Oh, Mary Jane, *you* will always be my first-best friend even if I don't deserve to be yours! I read the name *Evangeline* in my book and thought it so fine, but it was wrong to lie to you, and I am sorry."

I took a deep breath. "Becky, I'm sorry, too, awful sorry. I'm not sure how to tell you this, but I've lied to you as well."

"Are you not *Mary Jane*, then? Oh, it does not matter at all, just tell me your true name and we will be even," she said.

"No, it's that . . . well, I'm not the new girl you're waiting for. I'm not going to live around the corner. In fact, just yesterday I ran off from my family to come to St. Petersburg."

"You did?" Her eyes were wide. "What for?"

I took a deep breath and told her: "I'm looking for a *boy*. A certain boy. That I met once. That my heart won't let me forget."

At that Becky almost fainted. "How *romantic*! I know all the families in town. You must tell me who he is, and I will help you."

"His first name is Joe, and he comes from St. Petersburg. That's really all I know."

"Joe *Harper*?" Becky was thrilled. "Why, that's wonderful! His sister, Suzy, is my third—no fourth—best friend," she said, counting me in, I guessed. "I know exactly where they live . . . and also, Joe Harper is the bosom friend of *my* Tom!"

"Another thing, Becky, Joe doesn't know I was coming to St. Petersburg. In fact, nobody but you knows I'm here."

"Of course! He will have to find you—no, he must *rescue* you—that would be best." Becky looked like she was doing sums in her head until she jumped up and said, "I know! McDougal's cave!"

–McDougal's Cave–

Becky had quite a plan: "You will be hopelessly lost inside the caverns, and I will go find Joe and tell him that a beautiful red-headed lady—"

"Auburn. My hair is *auburn*," I couldn't help but put in.

"Yes, well, that there's a lady lost in McDougal's cave pining after her true love . . . he will mount a search, then find you, then bring you back . . . and the whole town will turn out and we can have a party at my house, and Alice will make a sponge cake."

It sounded like quite a circus, but I didn't have a better idea. It did seem perfect for Joe and me to come back together out-of-doors with dirt underneath our feet.

"Quickly, let's get you into the cave before church lets out and anyone sees you," she said, heading inside. She came back carrying a basket with some candles and matches in it.

"You have good shoes, that will be a blessing," she said. "For we will have to walk the five miles south." She sat down and traded her Sunday shoes for her weekday ones, and tied the laces with double knots.

We walked out of town and up to what Becky called Lover's Leap. I had pictured a steep cliff, but it couldn't have towered more than six feet above the riverbank. From there, we still had a ways to go, she told me, and said she'd sing to make the miles go by faster. The song wasn't my style—more like Susan's—but I could tell that Becky liked it awful well, so I hummed along after I got the gist.

Soon shall we meet again,
Meet never to sever.
Then shall love freely flow,
Round us both forever . . .

Quite a few verses went by before we finally came to a hole in the rocks that looked to be no more than a foxes' den. Becky set down the goods she'd been carrying and slithered in quite handily. She told me to light one of the candles and hand it to her, so I did. Then she said: "Now you come in."

I hesitated, and she saw me do it, and told me: "Don't you worry, Mary Jane, I know this cave inside and out, every inch of it."

I dove in as best I could. I'm naturally broader than Becky by quite a bit, so I had to turn my head, hunch up one shoulder, and stretch the other one down. I squeezed my way through, ending up in a heap on the floor.

It was dead dark except for the dim glow of Becky's candle, but things brightened up considerably after my eyes got used to what light there was.

Becky took my hand and led me along the passageways, deep into the cave. We twisted and turned corners until she pointed down at a bubbling spring with glassy crystals all up and down the walls, like a fairy-land you'd visit in your dreams. Above our heads, *Becky + Tom* was etched into the rock. I looked sidewise at Becky, and she blushed up red, which explained everything.

Just after, the cave opened out, big as a parlor, and somebody—or some-*bodies*—had made the room quite cozy. The ground was covered with waxed linen, and there was a pile of sheepskins in the corner. Curiously, there was a stack of papers, bound together and tied with a ribbon, carefully set away from any wetness.

She lit a second candle and handed it to me, and that seemed to make things bright as day. "Becky, it's wonderful," I told her. "How did you find this place?"

"Why, it's always been here—since before the Tamaroa Indians got run off, even. All the kids come here for a lark now and then, though they don't often come in this far."

"I guess *somebody* comes this far . . . ," I teased her.

"Yes, well, sometimes I do come here with Tom," she admitted, "and one time we *did* play a kissing game, but . . ." There was something about the way she said it that made me wonder if it was only *one time,* but I said nothing, as it was none of my business.

"Mostly I come here to read and study those pages." She pointed to the pile in the corner.

"What are they?" I asked her.

"It's my first-favorite book: *Anatomy: Descriptive and Surgical,* by someone called Henry Gray. You can look through it as much as you like, and if you find something interesting, I can teach it to you. Never mind the ripped-out sheets, they're the ones I stole from a teacher, before Papa bought me my own copy as a present."

As she handed it to me, it fell open at the bookmark, to a chapter called "Female Organs of Generation." It had pictures of . . . what also looked like caves.

"And now you must wait here until I find Joe Harper and tell him how I met a heart-sick girl headed for McDougal's cave. I'll make sure he picks up that you're the Mary Jane he's been pining for, and point him in the right direction. All you have to do is sit here and wait, and then be completely overcome when he shows up."

She kissed me before she left, but turned back to ask if I needed anything.

"Truth be told, I'd rather like to have a pencil on me," I said.

"Oh, that's easy. There's two over there, where I keep my book," she told me, and was gone.

Soon, I'd see Joe again! The idea made me happy, but also nervous. I didn't have a needle and thread to one-hand over it, so I decided to take a look through Becky's book instead. I couldn't get interested, as it didn't have much of a plot, and trying just made me sleepier and sleepier. I laid down on a sheepskin and drifted off, expecting happy dreams.

A few hours later, I woke to someone gently shaking me.

"Joe?" I said, looking up, my eyes blurry and my thinking confused.

"No, dear, it's just me." It was Becky, looking sadder than all the sad things in the world. "I hate to tell you this, Mary Jane, but Joe's not in St. Petersburg anymore."

-The Real Thing-

Becky was fixed to cry over it all.

"After I left you, I went straight to Joe's house, like I said I would. Mrs. Harper said he'd went off with his gang to play pirates on Jackson Island two days ago and didn't come home on the ferry. Then his sister Suzy took me outside to talk privately, and she told me, that he told her, that he was going for good and not ever coming back. I'm so, so sorry, Mary Jane."

She was sad, but I was mostly confused.

"Becky, who exactly is *Mrs. Harper*?"

"Why, his mother, of course."

"But Joe doesn't have a mother, Becky."

"Well, yes he does, Mary Jane! Everyone has a mother."

"Not Joe. He never knew his mother—and his pa was somebody he'd of been better off not knowing, from what he's told me."

"But all the boys and girls live with their mothers and fathers, that's just what you *do* in St. Petersburg."

"Joe has people who love him. He talked about a widow . . . Douglas? . . . who had taken him in, and taught him to read and write . . ."

She cut me off: "Mary Jane, tell me what Joe looks like."

419

"About my height, broad shoulders, blue eyes, pony-tail . . ."

"Wait! You can't mean *Huck*? *Huckleberry Finn*?"

It sounded exactly like the kind of happy-go-lucky name folks might give to a boy like Joe. "I certainly *hope* so . . . ," I answered, "if there's a chance he's here . . ."

"Oh, how exciting! We all *love* Huck, even though I can't say I would ever want to live as he does."

"Where might he be?" I asked her, eager as anything.

"Somewhere in St. Petersburg . . . I saw him just yesterday. He didn't look very happy, probably because he was wearing a shirt collar . . . he chafes, I'm sure you know."

"I can well imagine, Becky."

"*Ahh* . . . It's true love that's driving you, Mary Jane, I could see it from the first." She was so happy for me. "I'll go tell him you're here—but it won't be the same . . . he's not a *rescuing-you* type of boy, he's more of a *partners-in-crime* kind of boy."

I hugged her because she was exactly right. "Becky, I'm grateful to you for all you've done, but I think these last few steps towards Joe—*umm, Huck?*—are ones that I have to take for myself."

"I understand. Let me walk you to the house where he stays, and there I'll leave you to your fate. But promise you'll tell me all about what happens . . . I've got a feeling it will be *such* a romantic story . . ."

"I want to, Becky, I promise."

We crawled out of McDougal's cave just as the sun was setting for the night. Becky led me into town, and we bid *Farewell* to each other in the back yard of a prim white house, underneath a second-floor window with a rope hanging out of it.

–Easy Climbing–

It was a rope made out of a twisted bedsheet, knotted every few feet for easy climbing out of the window—or into it.

Far above, an endless web of twinkling stars were nearly out-shone by the fullest moon I'd ever seen.

When you've got a moon like that you should use it for something.

I unbuttoned my collar and pulled out Joe's note, the one I'd carried so far. I took Becky's pencil out from my pocket, and on the back of the paper, I wrote this:

Dear Joe (I guess I'll always call you <u>Joe</u>, if you let me),

It's Mary Jane. I'm came here by way of the river to find you. I've thought of you many, many-a million-times.

Remember when you told me the truth? I've come to St. Petersburg to return the favor because I'm done lying to the people that I care about. Here it is in a nutshell:

Those aren't my sisters,

I'm not nearly nineteen,

I'm still a long way from being sorry that Peter Wilks is dead.

I'm going to light out for the Territory because they'll civilize me otherwise, and I can't stand it. Do you want to come with? Bring your friend if you want, the one hiding that I never saw.

My pockets might be empty but my heart isn't. I've got two cousins up North, three good friends on the Galenian, and a dog that can kill a rat. If you want to put a light in your window, I'll be outside waiting for you. I'm watching out for your candle just like you watched for mine down in Greenville that night.

I've traveled more than a thousand miles since the ice broke up. I came all this way for something and I think it was you.

Yours truly,
Mary Jane

I folded the paper, and put it back where it had been, next to my heart. I climbed up the rope that was hanging from the window. It was one long mess of overhand knots—I would have used a timber hitch—but it worked as well as it needed to.

When I got to the windowsill, I slipped the folded paper through the gap. I thought I heard a rustling inside as I slid back down to the ground.

I found a soft spot in the grass, and sat down to wait.

CHAPTER THE LAST

—A Dream Nursed in Darkness—

Crauwk-croak! Crauwk-croak! Crauwk-croak!

It's past midnight: I can feel it in my bones. Yesterday has run out, and Today is already full—pressed to its seams with something like hope. The hope of a warm rain fixing to fall, of one unlit candle, and of a whole Company of bullfrogs croaking up at Heaven as if their hearts would break. All of us sitting in the darkness and waiting for an answer.

I looked backwards and forwards on my life and saw how far I'd come, and how far I still wanted to go. I'd looked outside myself and found adventure. I'd looked inside myself and found courage.

I looked down at my hands that had nursed and gardened and honeyed, and counted and prayed and maybe killed. Then I looked up and saw his light come on.

THE END

A Note on the Text

Mark Twain (also known as Samuel Clemens, born 1835) first published *Adventures of Huckleberry Finn* in 1885. His protagonist, *Huck,* was based on a childhood friend from the 1840s. The protagonist of this book, *Mary Jane,* also appears within *Adventures of Huckleberry Finn,* as do *Susan* and *Joanna,* both sets of *uncles, Widow Bartley, Dr. Robinson, Peter Wilks* (deceased), and many others; their dialogue is included, in part or in full, just as Twain wrote it. The characters in this book that do not appear in Twain's original have their roots in real people that lived in America during the early 1800s.

Morfar could have been one of the eight Norwegian laborers transported to Canada in 1814 to clear land at the northern tip of Lake Winnipeg under a three-year contract of indentured servitude. Such laborers often saved for years in order to bring family; *Ma* is an example of a daughter who traveled across the ocean in the hope of joining her father.

By 1846, there were more than one hundred fur-trading posts in the Minnesota Territory, each with its own cohort of trappers, clerks, and voyageurs. *Peter Pond* (born 1740) was a Connecticut-born trapper, voyageur, trader, and explorer who came to the Northwest Territory in 1765 and never left. The fur-trapping and fur-trading areas of Minnesota first belonged to the Ojibwe (also known as the Chippewa) to the north and the Eastern-Dakota Sioux to the south. The *Ojibwe girl* whom Mary Jane meets near Red Lake originated from the stories of Nodinens (born circa 1840), an Ojibwe woman who described her childhood on Mille Lacs Lake to Frances Densmore in 1918. *Father Potatoes* is meant to represent Nicolas-Marie-Joseph Frémiot (born 1818), one of the many churchmen of the time intent on eradicating Ojibwe culture. In 1849, Frémiot established a residential school as part of the Indian Mission near Fort William, Ontario. It remained in operation until 1970.

During the 1840s, the Mighty Mississippi served as home to hundreds of steamboat captains; each one specialized in a specific portion of the river's two-thousand-mile length. *Mrs. Captain* originated from George Byron Merrick (born 1841), who worked his way up from cabin boy to steamboat pilot, then contributed his memoirs to the *Saturday Evening Post* of Burlington, Iowa. As steamboat traffic grew, businesses sprang up beside the Mississippi River in order to sell goods and supplies to passing ships and their passengers. *Racoon Man* is based upon Thomas James Mulgrew (born 1867), who supplied coal from the Hansen & Lincoln Company from 1885 to 1893.

Many of the people in the Northwestern Territory had not come to it by choice. *The Rooster* could easily have been one of the 150,000 orphaned children forcibly relocated from New

York City to Iowa and elsewhere in the Midwest, as a source of child labor for farms and businesses. *Pa* could have been any one of the seven thousand American soldiers sent west in 1846 to protect almost two million square miles of territory, most of whom were posted at Army forts along the Mississippi River.

Women were outnumbered by men by a factor of ten across the frontier during the early 1800s, often living in harsh circumstances. *Aunt Evelyn* was drawn from the diary of Sarah Welch Hill (born 1803), a farm woman who struggled to survive with her two children in Durham County, Ontario, after her husband died in 1854. *Miss Frances Ramsay Simpson* (born 1812) was an Englishwoman who left London for the Forks in 1830; her diary describes an onerous journey during which she strives to preserve her feminine modesty in a challenging new world.

Antebellum religion included a strange mix of fanaticism and bigotry; end-of-days predictions were common, as was violence against minority groups. The *Schmidt family* was patterned after the family of Amanda Barnes Smith (born 1809), a Mormon woman who narrowly escaped the 1838 Haun's Mill massacre with her daughters after her husband and son were murdered by the anti-Mormon mob. She followed Joseph Smith to Illinois, and after surviving the 1846 Battle of Nauvoo, she followed Brigham Young to Utah in 1850.

Twain made it clear in his original that Peter Wilks enslaved a group of people to work at his tannery, but did not mention any of them by name. Julia Brown (born 1852) was one of the four million people enslaved in the United States during the mid-1800s; she recounted her childhood in Georgia to the

Federal Writers' Project in 1936. Her descriptions of traveling speculators, visiting doctors, needing a pass for travel, and the forced separation of her family formed a foundation for *Sugar* and *Candy*. I also relied upon the memoirs of Peter Bruner (born 1845), in which he described the Kentucky tannery where he was enslaved as a child, including his experience of being thrown into a tanning vat and nearly drowned by the man who enslaved him.

Antebellum society was notable for a large proportion of transient roles: trappers, traders, missionaries, soldiers, boatmen, and pioneers who did not stay in one place very long. Perhaps the most mobile of Americans were the peddlers who traveled town to town to supply frontier families with odd items of necessity and luxury. *Eddie Applebaum* is patterned after Edward Rosewater (born 1841), a Jewish boy who immigrated to the United States with his family in 1854 and struck out on his own soon after. Once he picked up telegraph skills, he accompanied Union forces, and was responsible for the transmission of Lincoln's Emancipation Proclamation in 1863.

Most of the scenes depicted in this book are grounded in real places, events, and phenomena of the nineteenth century. *The Forks* (established 1738) played an important role in the fur trade, and is open for visitation near the city of Winnipeg. Descriptions of life at a trading post were informed by the records of nearby Brandon House (established 1793), including the 1815 fire that destroyed it, and the rebuilding efforts that followed. Nineteenth-century exchange values for beaver pelts and other types of fur were obtained from the Minnesota History Center in St. Paul.

By 1823, four overland trails were in use to haul furs south and supplies north between Manitoba and the American Fur Company headquarters in St. Paul. At their peak, the trails moved more than six hundred tons of freight every year, carried by two-wheeled carts pulled by horses, oxen, and dogs. Red Lake, the place where *Mary Jane* encounters an *Ojibwe girl,* has been home to the Anishinaabe peoples since the 1600s; today it is the site of the Red Lake Indian Reservation, organized under the Red Lake Band of Chippewa.

Between 1805 and 1825, the US Army built five large forts along the Mississippi River in order to help occupy territory acquired by the Louisiana Purchase of 1803. This string of forts supervised seven hundred miles of the nation's main waterway, from northernmost Fort Snelling (established 1822) to the Jefferson Barracks (established 1825), located near St. Louis, Missouri. Fort Edwards (established 1814), located twenty miles south of Nauvoo, Illinois, was abandoned by the military in 1824, to be taken over by the American Fur Company.

More than one thousand steamboats were in operation on the Mississippi River during the first half of the nineteenth century; each one mentioned in this book, from the record-setting *Smelter* to the notoriously pokey *Uncle Toby,* was active during the 1840s. The luxury sternwheeler *Minnesota Belle* is described accurately down to her lunch menu; the Missouri Riverboat *Saluda,* which *Mrs. Captain* describes as unsafe, exploded on April 9, 1852, due to an overfed boiler, killing more than one hundred people.

The lead-hauling *Galenian* sailed as far north as Dubuque

and spent her winters on the Ohio River; her layout is patterned after that of the *City of Hawkinsville,* a sunken steamboat protected within the Florida Underwater Archaeological Preserve. The description of the *Galenian*'s steam engine, including her boiler, is based on Robert Fulton's (born 1765) notes for his 1811 patent. The timetable and ticket prices of Mississippi River travel were calculated using mile-marker maps and historical documents provided by the US Army Corps of Engineers.

The purpose of religion in Early America was not limited to spirituality; it also served to inject diversion, variety, and drama into daily life. The description of the camp meeting that *Pastor Martin* alludes to was informed by William Cooper Howell's (born 1807) account of the first meeting that he attended near Springfield, Ohio, at the age of thirteen. The Coach Whip Band furnished music for numerous camp meetings held in the Dubuque area during the 1800s, and did indeed include the dance tune "Prairie Queen" as part of their repertoire.

Anticipation of an apocalypse was an almost universal feature of Protestant doctrine during the early 1800s, and no group took its preparation more seriously than the Millerites. In 1844, more than fifty thousand followers of William Miller (born 1782) discarded everything they owned in preparation for their imminent ascension to heaven on October 22, the day that Miller had calculated from a biblical timeline and was ever-after to be known as "The Great Disappointment." A small number of faithful continued to follow Miller, and in 1863, they founded the Seventh-Day Adventist Church, which has grown to more than twenty million followers worldwide.

The deforestation bemoaned by the *old-feller* reflects the voracious logging of the 1840s that emptied the North Woods of its massive Hemlock pines, such that today, it is nearly impossible to find a pine tree older than one hundred years within the state of Wisconsin. The sawmills of the time, powered by the newly invented steam engine, worked around the clock trying to keep up with the insatiable demand for lumber to build the burgeoning cities of St. Louis, Memphis, and New Orleans. Horrible accidents were not uncommon as logs were forced against jammed saw blades, and were often followed by explosive sawdust fires.

Prior to the United States' adoption of the Gold Standard in 1873, paper money on the frontier was provincial; that is, its value was confined to the region under the influence of the bank of issue. This was especially problematic for travelers, as there was no surefire way to preserve the value of liquid assets while on the move, leading many to favor trade in more universally coveted objects such as furs, weapons, and precious metals. Smaller banks were also subject to sudden collapse, as the value of their currency tanked against that of the larger, guaranteed banks on the East Coast. The massive banking collapses of 1837 through 1845 triggered crises within countless frontier families; one widespread solution was for male children to leave home and make their way into the US Army, which doubled in size between 1835 and 1848 as a result of these new recruits.

The illness suffered by *Father Potatoes, Mary Jane, Aunt Evelyn*, and *Peter Wilks* featured symptoms in keeping with typhoid fever, a common ailment on the frontier, which, if left untreated, proves fatal in one out of four cases; it is largely transmitted through the handling of food, and carriers may be both healthy and unaware. The Ojibwe used decoctions of dogbane for sedation, five-finger root to stop bleeding, horsemint to salve a burn, mayapple to soothe the bowels, mugwort to stop diarrhea, and wild pea to disinfect a wound. The tansey plant was considered a medicine of last resort, used to trigger seizures in the hopes of disrupting a cycle of fever.

Though sparsely represented, the legal system exerted absolute power over certain aspects of life on the frontier. Because the laws of the eighteenth and early nineteenth centuries viewed children as economic assets based on the household labor they could provide, guardianship was assigned by judges according to laws of inheritance. Prior to the 1860s, the mother's line had no rights to family children if any member of the father's line could be located and proved to be nonindigent.

Sanctioned state militia perpetrated most of the violence against the Mormon communities on the frontier. Missouri Governor Liburn Boggs's 1838 executive order raised four hundred soldiers under the following commission: "The Mormons must be treated as enemies, and must be exterminated or driven from the state." After fleeing with his followers to Nauvoo, Illinois, founder and prophet Joseph Smith was murdered in his jail cell while awaiting trial in 1844, a crime in which local law enforcement was clearly complicit.

Tarring and feathering was an accepted form of extrajudicial punishment in early America; the practice persisted well into the nineteenth century on the frontier. The description found in this book was drawn from the *London Advertiser*'s 1774 account of the tarring and feathering of English customs agent John Malcom (born 1723) in the days leading up to the Boston Tea Party.

Monetary values assigned to the bodies and potential labor of enslaved people were based on data obtained from the 1830–1860 New Orleans Notarial Archives. It is true that corpses of enslaved persons, including children, were sold for the purpose of medical dissection. The description of enslaved people in shackles being driven by their captors was based on the eyewitness account of Ethan Andrews (born 1787), who watched as the slave-trading firm of Franklin & Armfield assembled approximately three hundred enslaved men, women, and children in preparation for a forced march from Alexandria, Virginia, to Natchez, Mississippi, in 1834.

Aside from a handful of brave actors, the Abolition movement in the Northwest Territory was more about objecting to moral depravity than working toward equality. The book *Uncle Tom's Cabin*, a melodrama of white saviorhood, was instrumental in propagating this attitude: published in 1852, it quickly became the bestselling book of the nineteenth century, second only to the Bible.

Before the first transcontinental telegraph message could be sent in 1861, a continuous line of galvanized wire had to be strung across the entire three-thousand-mile length of America. In addition, every twenty miles along the way, the wire required power from a battery. Every two months, each battery required maintenance, which included siphoning the toxic waste product zinc sulphate out of the barrel housing the zinc and copper electrodes. This unpleasant and dangerous job was described in detail by telegrapher George A. "Lightning" Ellsworth (born 1843) in his memoir.

The more benign tasks described in this book, from harvesting honey to tying mariners' knots to preparing the dead for burial, are depicted as accurately as historical documents allowed.

I wish to explain about some, perhaps unfamiliar, speech patterns found in the dialogue. *Father Schmidt*'s speech carries a Downeast Maine accent and *Peter Wilks* exhibits a northern Yorkshire dialect: Whitby parish, to be precise. *Mary Jane* has the great good fortune to employ the rural Midwestern dialect shared by the author. I only mention this lest the reader suppose that all these characters were trying to talk alike and not succeeding.

To close, I'll note that all the animals in this story have their origins in various pets that I have owned or known. *That-cat* reflects a tabby named Tiger who lived in the stuffing of my grandfather's couch. *Mr. Hare-ington* recalls a rabbit named Mr. Bun-bun, who bit me once, and nobody else ever. As for the horses, *Gusty* was the name of the gentle quarter horse upon whom I first learned to ride; *Samson* reflects Wrigley, the gentle Clydesdale upon which my son first learned to ride; and *Delilah* reflects Penny, who spent her days bossing Wrigley around the pasture. *Cherry* allowed me to resurrect a magnificent Chesapeake Bay retriever named Buck, who was loved beyond measure by his family, and could indeed kill a rat.

Suggested Reading

Berry, Daina Ramey. (2017). *The Price for Their Pound of Flesh: The Value of the Enslaved, from Womb to Grave, in the Building of a Nation.* Beacon Press.

Carter, Kathryn, Ed. (2002). *The Small Details of Life: 20 Diaries by Women in Canada, 1830–1996.* University of Toronto Press.

Densmore, Frances (1929). *Chippewa Customs. Bureau of American Ethnology Bulletin.* 86:1–204 (see especially chapter 42).

Diner, Hasia R. (2015). *Roads Taken: The Great Jewish Migrations to the New World and the Peddlers Who Forged the Way.* Yale University Press.

Federal Writers' Project (1936–1938). *Slave Narrative Project* (see especially vol. 4, Georgia, part 1: Brown, Julia, pp. 141–153, and vol. 7, Kentucky, Bogie-Woods [with combined interviews of others]: Bruner, Peter, pp. 88–90).

Gates, Charles M., Ed. (1933). *Five fur traders of the Northwest: being the narrative of Peter Pond and the diaries of John Macdonell, Archibald N. McLeod, Hugh Faries, and Thomas Connor.* Minnesota Historical Society Press (as reprinted in 1965 with corrections).

Goodman, Nancy and Goodman, Robert (2003). *Paddlewheels on the Upper Mississippi 1823–1854.* University of Minnesota Press.

Jones, Evan (1966). *Citadel in the Wilderness: The Story of Fort Snelling and the Old Northwest Frontier.* Coward-McCann, Inc.

The Mark Twain Papers (2003). *The Works of Mark Twain, Volume 8: Adventures of Huckleberry Finn, Including Working Notes and Revisions.* University of California Press.

Mason, Mary Ann (1996). *From Father's Property to Children's Rights: The History of Child Custody in the United States.* Columbia University Press.

Merrick, George Byron (1909). *Old Times on the Upper Mississippi: The Recollections of a Steamboat Pilot from 1854 to 1863.* A. H. Clark Company.

Newell, Clayton R. (2014). *The Regular Army Before the Civil War 1845–1860.* United States Army Center of Military History Publication 75-1.

Tullidge, Edward W. (1877). *The Women of Mormondom.* Tullidge & Crandall (see especially chapter XV).

Acknowledgments

The difference between a file on your computer and a book on the shelf is a great deal of work done by people who are not the author. *Adventures of Mary Jane* would never have happened without Beverly Horowitz, who trusted in me as I wrote, revised, rewrote, and re-revised. She never faltered in her belief that we would get where we were going, even when I couldn't say where that was. Barbara Kingsolver graciously helped me start this book, and cheered me across the finish line. I owe a great debt to Laura Bonner, Rebecca Gudelis, and Erin Malone for smoothing the way. Tina Bennett and Adrian LeBlanc continue to be generous in their guidance, and Svetlana Katz has become the compass by which I find my way toward the story I want to tell.

One of the great tragedies of writing is that one cannot truly be both an author and a reader of the same book. Clint Conrad, Andy Ebly, Connie Luhmann, and Heather Schmidt were constant sources of support and encouragement throughout this process. I am grateful to Carol Langner, Erica Morrow, Andy

Rivkin, Elvira Schmidt, and Jennifer VanBuren for reading early portions of this book. I am particularly indebted to the young adult readers who helped me shape the tempo of the action, namely Charles Conrad and Norah Ohly: your feedback has made all the difference.

I wish to thank the many scholars whose work I relied upon while educating myself about nineteenth-century America; I list them here, separated by theme. If you want to know more about Mary Jane's world, their work is the place to start. Politics and society in early America: Bradley J. Birzer, Richard J. Ellis, Daniel Feller, David S. Heidler, Kristin O'Brassill-Kulfan, and David S. Reynolds; Ojibwe culture and Native American history: John P. Bowes, Michelle Defoe, Barbara A. Mann, Jeffrey Ostler, Dawn Peterson, and Mary Lethert Wingerd; the institution of slavery in America: Richard Bell, Yvonne Chireau, Eric Herschthal, Martha S. Jones, Stephanie E. Jones-Rogers, Joshua A. Lynn, Philip D. Morgan, Daina Ramey Berry, and Calvin Schermer-horn; women's experience of the American frontier: Melanie Kirkpatrick and Sarah M. S. Pearsall; child custody in early America: Janet Graham, Edward Gray, and Mary Ann Mason; Jewish peddlers on the American frontier: Hasia R. Diner, Jonathan D. Sarna, Benjamin Shapell, Dan Shore, and Shari Rabin; Mormon history: Richard L. Bushman, Benjamin E. Park, and Thomas Richards, Jr.; religious fervor in early America: Chris Babits, Christopher J. Blythe, Matthew W. Dougherty, Adam Morris, Emily Ogden, Jack N. Rakove, and Eric C. Smith; the fur trade in Canada and Minnesota: Harry W. Duckworth, Stacy

Nation-Knapper, and Robert C. Wheeler; banks and money of the 1800s: Stephen W. Campbell, Joshua R. Greenberg, Paul Kahan, and Sharon Ann Murphy; frontier medicine: David Dary, Frances Densmore, and Victoria Johnson.

I want to particularly mention Robert L. Reece and his series of Not Today stories (NotTodayStories.com), which helped me contextualize the slave narratives of the Federal Writers' Project, and Daniel N. Gullotta's podcast *The Age of Jackson,* which introduced me to many of the scholars mentioned previously.

Vanessa Veselka's article "The Lack of Female Road Narratives and Why It Matters," which appeared in Volume One of *The American Reader* (2012), was pivotal in the development of the plot for this book. Huck Finn's story has been reimagined into modern times by many talented authors: my favorite example is *Finn* by Matthew Olshan, who provided me with valuable encouragement along the way. I credit Jean Genet's *Miracle of the Rose* (1946) for the phrase that marks the final chapter of this book: "[We] must dream a long time in order to act with grandeur, and dreaming is nursed in darkness."

I am grateful to the park rangers who welcomed me to the campgrounds I frequented while I was charting Mary Jane's path, including Rock Creek State Park, Iowa; Nauvoo State Park, Illinois; Lake Chicot State Park, Arkansas; Natchez State Park, Mississippi; and St. Bernard State Park, Louisiana; I am grateful to Bill Hagopian for always being up for coming along. I thank the captains and crews of the *Betsey Northrup* and the *Jonathan Padelford,* who took me out onto the Mississippi River, and who let me board early to examine the wheel and imagine the boiler, and slowed her down so I could take a thousand or so photos of Pig's Eye Island. I will forever be grateful for the time I spent aboard the 175-foot stern-wheeler *General John Newton* (est. 1899), aka Minnesota Centennial Showboat, watching her final seasons in 2015 and 2016. God bless the person who starts her up again.

A big *Thank you* to the folks at the Minnesota Historical Society and Historic Fort Snelling who answered my endless questions and let me stay past closing time, at the Sawmill Museum of Clinton, Iowa, for firing up the old ripsaw, at the University of Guelph Honey Bee Research Centre for preserving such sweetness, and at the Schlesinger Library at Harvard University for introducing me to the letters, diaries, love notes, and copybooks of dozens of nineteenth-century young women. We should all be grateful to the National Park Service, the US Forest Service, and the Departments of Natural Resources that preserve and maintain the outdoor open spaces where we may walk and watch and dream, including Gooseberry Falls, Jay Cooke, and Frontenac State Parks, as well as Voyageurs National Park, the Boundary Waters Canoe Area Wilderness, the Superior National Forest, and the Mississippi River Trail.

My final, and fondest, *Thank you* is to our protagonist, Miss Mary Jane, for she and I have grown closer than I ever imagined we could. We have been constant companions these many months, and I will miss her more than I can say, though letting her go was always the point.

Dear Mary Jane: You have shared all your secrets with me,

and coming to know you has been one of the greatest joys of my life. Take a deep breath now, and go. Go out into the world and live your story. Make friends where you can and enemies where you must, and take one last piece of advice with you: Always keep to the river, Mary Jane, carry needle and thread, and remember that your author loves you.

About the Author

HOPE JAHREN is a teacher, scientist, and booklover living in Oslo, Norway. Recognized by *Time* in 2016 as one of the 100 most influential people in the world, Jahren is the recipient of three Fulbright Awards and was named one of the "Brilliant 10" by *Popular Science* magazine in 2005. She is the author of two works of nonfiction: *The Story of More* and *Lab Girl,* winner of the National Book Critics Circle Award for Autobiography. *Adventures of Mary Jane* is her first work of fiction.

hopejahrensurecanwrite.com
@hopejahren